SEE JANE RUN!

A Jane Yeats Mystery

SEE JANE RUN!

A Jane Yeats Mystery

BY LIZ BRADY

Second
Story
Press

Library and Archives Canada Cataloguing in Publication

Brady, Elizabeth
See Jane run! / Liz Brady.

(A Jane Yeats mystery)
ISBN 1-896764-91-6

I. Title. II. Series: Brady, Elizabeth
Jane Yeats mystery.

PS8553.R24S43 2004   C813'.54   C2004-905270-5

Edited by Doris Cowan
Copyedited by Alison Reid
Cover photo © Getty Images
Cover design by Laura McCurdy
Text design by P. Rutter

Printed in Canada on 100% post-consumer recycled paper

*Second Story Press gratefully acknowledges the support of the Ontario Arts
Council and the Canada Council for the Arts for our publishing program.
We acknowledge the financial support of the Government of Canada through
the Book Publishing Industry Development Program, and the Government
of Ontario through the Ontario Media Development Corporation's
Ontario Book Initiative.*

Canada Council   Conseil des Arts
for the Arts   du Canada

ONTARIO ARTS COUNCIL
CONSEIL DES ARTS DE L'ONTARIO

Published by
Second Story Press
720 Bathurst Street, Suite 301
Toronto, ON
M5S 2R4
www.secondstorypress.on.ca

This book is for my father, James Anderson Brady (1919-2003), in memory of what might have been ...

I missed his funeral,
Those quiet walkers
And sideways talkers
Shoaling out of his lane
To the respectable
Purring of the hearse ...
They move in equal pace
With the habitual
Slow consolation
Of a dawdling engine,
The line lifted, hand
Over fist, cold sunshine
On the water, the land
Banked under fog: that morning
I was taken in his boat,
The screw purling, turning
Indolent fathoms white,
I tasted freedom with him.
To get out early, haul
Steadily off the bottom,
Dispraise the catch, and smile
As you find a rhythm
Working you, slow mile by mile,
Into your proper haunt
Somewhere, well out, beyond ...

Dawn-sniffing revenant,
Plodder through midnight rain,
Question me again.

— Seamus Heaney
from "Casualty"

ACKNOWLEDGEMENTS

I AM SO GRATEFUL TO DORIS COWAN, my editor, for her expertise, encouragement, and entertaining remarks; to Alison Reid, for a superb job of copy editing and for making valuable suggestions; to Second Story Press — especially Margie Wolfe, Laura McCurdy and Corina Eberle — for their many efforts on my behalf. To the Ontario Arts Council, Writers' Reserve program, I extend my appreciation for a grant that enabled me to finish this book.

For keeping my pantry well-stocked with their laughter and support, I am deeply indebted to Patti Brady, Teresa Galati, Leona Gom, Lena Iannaci, Michelle Lawrie, Lucy Robinson, and Landsay Tom.

Also, my love and gratitude to Annie Hoover, dear friend of many years (notwithstanding her professional inclination to practice therapy), for advising me on subjects germane to this novel. Any mistakes are my own. I still see through a glass, darkly!

I'd tell of that great queen
Who stood amid a silence by the thorn
Until two lovers came out of the air
With bodies made out of soft fire. The one,
About whose face birds wagged their fiery wings,
Said, 'Aengus and his sweetheart give their thanks
To Maeve and to Maeve's household, owing all
In owing them the bride-bed that gives peace.'
Then Maeve: 'O Aengus, Master of all lovers,
A thousand years ago you held high talk
With the first kings of many-pillared Cruachan.
O when will you grow weary?'
　　　They had vanished,
But out of the dark air over her head there came
A murmur of soft words and meeting lips.

— W. B. Yeats,
"The Old Age of Queen Maeve"

PROLOGUE

SHORT WILLIE WAS SWEEPING his cell. In this skit, he was always Fred. The broom got to be Ginger. He bowed to his lady. "Shall we dance?"

They waltzed across the small floor, while Willie, his cobalt eyes expressionless, crooned in her ear:

> The way you flashed your cunt
> The way you tried to flee
> The memory of the hunt
> Oh, no, they can't take that away from me
> The way I creamed my jeans
> The way you screamed off-key
> The way you haunt my dreams
> No, no, they can't take that away from me.

Prison is only a cage if the bird forgets what it feels like to fly. Willie proved that every time he soared into one of his fantasies. It was all about focus, what you concentrated on. He tugged the broom closer to his chest, glided it past the stainless steel toilet bolted to the wall and across the concrete, humming a dead monotone into the bristles:

> We may never, never meet again
> On the bloody road to love
> But I'll always, always keep

The memory of ...
The way I held my knife
The way we shagged till three
The way I snatched your life
No, no, they can't take that away from me.
No, they can't take that away from me.

Willie knew what the dickheads were up to, transferring him here. He didn't belong here and they knew it. In the Special Handling Unit, the super-max slammer for the elite, Willie had got respect. SHU was a gladiator school for killers so violent they got their own penitentiary, way out in Sainte-Anne-des-Plaines, a desolate armpit on the outskirts of Montreal, but it gave its inmates real distinction. Millhaven, this place, was a kiddie joint by comparison.

Willie thought of his peers: the "Beast of British Columbia," Clifford Olson (serial child killer: eleven hits); New Brunswick's Allan Légère, the "Monster of the Miramichi" (ambidextrous: three women, one elderly priest); William Fyfe (five women and counting ...); Michael Wayne McCray (five women and counting ...). Bit of a pissing match, though, with all that competition, but there was always some kind of diversion popping up to break the boredom — a hostage taking, a riot, a rape, an attempted escape, a suicide, only one successful murder while Willie was there, but people kept trying.

In SHU he'd been segregated and safe from the freaks (Willie included the guards) who'd prey on anything with a pulse. His only company in the square cell was the camera in the upper corner whose beady little eye tracked his every twitch. Some of the inmates went all paranoid because of the cameras. Not Willie. They could watch him if they wanted. He liked the attention. He got out only one hour a day to exercise alone. Even his meals were delivered to his cell on a tray pushed through a narrow slit in the door. He was excluded from crap jobs like cleaning floors and doing meals on wheels. Couldn't go to the common room for a game of cards. Nobody visited him. He refused to meet with the prison chaplain. He experienced less fellowship than a Trappist monk. SHU thought denial of privileges was a hardship — Willie didn't give a rat's ass. His need to socialize was non-existent: his real audience was on the outside. Other needs he took care of himself.

So when they sent him over here he knew it was a setup. Here, twice a day he got put into general population. The authorities had deliberately put his ass on the line to ensure that he wouldn't survive long enough to watch his pubic hairs turn gray. His transfer warrant, signed by the deputy commissioner himself, noted that William Shortt "had participated in constructive activities and demonstrated increasing capacity to interact with others." Had this capacity ever been put to the test, Willie would have made short work of the "others" at the end of a long blade. He'd told the psychologist about his genuine loathing for contact with other inmates, yet the asshole had rated him "pro-social." But the shrink was the one who designed the correctional treatment plans, so he had a vested interest in claiming success, thereby proving they all worked harder than Jesus on the incorrigibles.

For sure, his transfer was a frame. Sooner or later he'd get stabbed up. That was okay, given how he'd taught himself to live one day at a time to the max. Ginger the Broom was only one of his props. Prison had not stifled his creativity.

Maximum security also carried the burden of rehabilitation, a project Willie was not committed to. He no more thought that monsters like himself were capable of self-improvement than he believed Jesus was hot on saving him. But going along with the programs was part of the gig, another way to while away your time. Willie enrolled in them all: drug and alcohol abuse, anger management, problem solving and redirectional goal setting.

But it seriously pissed him off that he got no respect. It was a bit of joke when you considered the trash doing their time in this particular joint. If you judge a man by his body count, Short Willie figured he should be the godfather of woman-hunters. So many violent rapes he'd forgotten half of them. Plus the five kills he'd copped to. For that, he got shunned and reviled. They treated him like a perv with AIDS.

On the outside, he'd been a celebrity. Probably got more headlines in his prime than Mike Tyson. But fans are fickle. After he got sent down, the spotlight — still focused on Paul Bernardo and Karla Homolka — had shifted to fresh monsters. Just this February the cops finally arrested a suspect in Vancouver's Downtown Eastside hooker murders. Robert "Willie" Pickton, of Piggy Palace fame, had been charged with fifteen murders so far. By the time they got through digging up his body farm, Pickton would have dozens of wasted broads to his credit, and Willie Shortt would be looking like Mr. Nice Guy. He'd be demoted to the minor leagues.

Short Willie chuckled. Always keep your best card up your sleeve. Soon he'd be playing his ace. Yesterday he'd phoned his lawyer and asked for a meeting. Told the fat slug to plan for a big press conference afterward. What Willie had to say was so shocking his ratings would soar right off the top of the charts. They'd really be paying attention then. That's what he'd always craved way more even than raping and slashing: attention. All eyes on Willie.

The guard came and opened his iron-grille door. Willie headed for the cafeteria, grabbed a tray and joined the line, keeping a wary eye out for any shit that might go down around him. Pity you couldn't watch your own back, except on a surveillance camera. Even then, the momentary time lapse between what you saw and what was happening would give your assailant the edge.

A tray crashed on the far side of the room. A crowd quickly circled the downed man. Somebody shouted, "It's Fats Oliver. He's pitched a heart attack."

Willie was pissed off that everyone's attention got diverted to the victim. Now he'd have to wait for his corned-beef hash.

The attack didn't come from behind. He instinctively turned to face the guy tapping him on the shoulder. The knife slipped between Willie's ribs and into his heart as smoothly as navigating soft butter.

Two words burbled from his mouth before he hit ground. "I lied."

Nobody seemed to be listening.

Oh yes, they just took that away from him.

CHAPTER 1

EARLY ONE JUNE MORNING five weeks later summer struck like a steam hammer. For three months it beat the bejesus out of us. The city fathers declared heat emergencies and smog alerts, warning people to find relief indoors, embrace their air conditioners, drink lots of water. The garbage collectors heeded their bosses by declaring a strike that persisted until green plastic mountains grew on street corners. City parks were converted to dump sites. Only the rats were smiling.

Catholics felt obliged to add huge dollops of guilt to the stew. The Pope was scheduled to visit for World Youth week. The faithful shuddered at the thought of the Infallible nostrils quivering to the stench of simmering megatons of festering meat scraps infused with discarded diapers. No one could be blamed for failing to forecast that the poop from thousands of devout bums would flood from the Porta-Potties into adjoining businesses. The insurance companies did not interpret this messy mishap as an act of God.

Under the sweltering sun rap music blared from the open windows of muscle cars. Seagulls screamed an unholy accompaniment as they scavenged abandoned pizza slices. Above the ubiquitous humming of air conditioners rose an awful buzzing as millions of sated maggots metamorphosed into blowflies.

Clouds held dust instead of rain. Grass yellowed to straw, dry tree leaves fell to dry ground, flowers grew dejected and no breeze blew. The city took on the character of a ghost town when the midday sun was working its worst. Those who had shelter retreated into it. Homeless people abandoned the streets for ravines and parks. Nights weren't much cooler because the humidity persisted. Sex slumped in the popularity polls. Only the criminally minded maintained their nocturnal activity levels. Pinheaded bigots torched a synagogue and murdered a Hassidic Jew, father of six. Gang members shot other gang members for violating their moral code. Hypervexed husbands and lovers still managed to exterminate their exes and offspring. Yet more felons found the energy to rape, rob and rook. Crooked CEOs and accountants cooked the books, whole libraries of them.

Toronto the Good was rapidly shaking off its halo, its degeneration presided over by the worst municipal government in two decades and a mayor so stupid that he'd be an embarrassment to a flock of turkeys. Maybe I've become jaded. Proximity to the mean streets has changed my way of seeing. Losing your virginity is like that.

I will always remember those months as the Great Inferno. Especially because they turned into my own personal blast furnace ...

It began as a simple project. A built-in bookcase to house the spawn of books proliferating faster than dust bunnies. With neurotic precision, I'd measured the wall, designed the unit to house everything from paperbacks to oversize reference works and compiled a materials list. Even incorporated some display cases to accommodate the beyond-tasteful objets d'art I'd collect when I won the lottery. Just a simple saw-sand-screw job. What I hadn't prepared for was what the jigsaw would break open: my latest worst memory was blasted instantaneously into overdrive.

Last year I donated the tips of four fingers on my left hand to a homicidal maniac equipped with a darkroom guillotine. A crafty surgeon spent six hours reconnecting the severed bits to their stumps. For all his finesse, my restored hand resembled an artifact from Dr. Frankenstein's apprenticeship. The sensation in them was iffy, they tingled when they should have slumbered and my grip was way under par. Still, it was much better than the alternative. What bothered me most were the flashbacks, sudden as summer lightning, triggered unexpectedly one day, more predictably another — like when I try to perform any operation that involves a blade. Chopping vegetables for an innocent stir-fry can rocket me back to the moments preceding the deadly *whoosh* of the slicing arm. Some nights these fright videos bolt me into sweat-heavy consciousness. Some days they paralyze me in midstride. Usually I can drink them back into abeyance.

Planks all marked up, I reached for the first board, aligned the cut mark with the blade, secured it with my repaired hand and turned on the saw. The tool kicked into action, pitching me straight into a panic attack. I collapsed to the floor and watched the saw boogie away in antic aimlessness beside me. My back pressed to the wall, heart thumping and chest as tight as cheap panty hose, I yanked the cord from the outlet. Forced myself to Zen-breathe.

Relaxing in the path of a speeding bullet is a challenge. A bigger one is putting yourself in the way of a second bullet. I recalled my mother's words from once upon a time. "So you fell offa your bike and broke your arm. Coulda been worse. Bikes don't grow on trees, but your arm's healed, eh? So hop back on the goddamn thing and remember to steer better next time."

I rose to my feet, steadied myself and plugged in the cord. Before the saw could vault back into freaky life, I turned to my mantra in the face of evil. Chanting *fuck fear ... ommm ... fuck fear ... ommm* restored my courage. In a spirit of Amazonian mastery, I gripped the tool, flicked the red On button, then watched in horror as my body repeated its slapstick pratfall.

Maybe the sound was unnerving me. I cranked up the radio to full volume, with no regard for the neighbors on either side of my row house. The venerable Nina to the south was all but deaf. And call it payback time for the jerk tenant to the north, sixty years younger than Nina, whose ears had also gone the way of Eric Clapton's — and for the same reason. "The Tracks of My Tears" drowned out the jigsaw. I was back in business. Forty sawdusty minutes later, several stacks of pine planks stood as aromatic witness to the triumph of Motown over mind.

My admiration for my own capacity to conquer fear by cunning, and without resorting to the enabling hand of alcohol, had tweaked my thirst. I headed for the fridge, where a shelf of Smithwick's awaited my eager clutch. The phone interrupted my reward for outstanding bravery.

"Jane?" *Male voice, familiar.*

"Who else? My dog's so smart he refuses to answer the phone."

"It's Sam." *Sam Brewer, retired crime reporter, good friend.*

"What's up, buddy?"

"Um ... are you alone?"

"No, I'm cuddled up next to Russell Crowe. Why?"

"Because I need to tell you something that ... um ... might upset you."

I rapidly scanned my crisis checklist: my mom, my dog and my best friend had been okay a few hours ago. "So spit it out, mate."

"The cops have called a press conference for tomorrow morning. To announce the autopsy results on Ruth Rosenberg."

I froze. "This should interest me?" For six years I'd made a career of avoiding any and all media coverage connected to Pete's murder. Anyone even vaguely close to me knew that.

"Hear me, Jane. William Shortt was *not* responsible for Rosenberg's death. Already some people are wondering if maybe he lied about the other murders he confessed to — including those of Laura and Pete. I thought you needed to know that before it hits the press."

Sam's words tocked around my skull, lunatic as errant ping-pong balls. For six years the only certainty separating me from the occupants of padded cells was the knowledge that the bastard who stole my lover's life and foreclosed mine was pissing away the remainder of his twisted days behind bars, and mere weeks ago I'd heard the welcome news that a fellow inmate had expedited him to that particular blast furnace in hell reserved for the souls of the eternally damned.

I screamed into the phone. "Thanks for the favor, Sam. You fucking thought I needed to know that? I need to know that like I need to know my mother's died."

"Jane, I'm coming over."

He hung up before I could tell him to get stuffed.

I made my way straight to the refrigerator, unloaded six cans of Smithwick's and set them on the coffee table. Set B. B. King to wailing and strumming, live at the Apollo. Cranked up the volume. A Rothmans between my lips, I popped the first can and began to lubricate my way through an unwanted trip down memory lane.

He was in the wrong place at the wrong time.

Alternative scenarios to avoidable disasters career through our brains relentless as the melody of a dreadful pop song. *Had I but known ... If only ...* In the years since Pete's murder my gray matter had rehearsed them all. Over and over and over again. Pete would still be alive, our shared lives still be on track ... *If* he'd left our apartment an hour sooner, he'd have arrived at Laura's before the killer did. Knowing another man was there,

Shortt surely would have postponed Laura's appointment with her maker. *If* Pete had arrived just sixty minutes later, he'd have happened on the scene from hell, her tortured body splayed and displayed in a manner that no human eyes should ever have to bear witness to. Eventually, though, Pete would have recovered and our lives could have resumed.

"He was in the wrong place at the wrong time." Those were the words of one of the two cops who'd arrived at my door to break the news shortly after their bodies were discovered. I guess Detective Sergeant Roy Urquhart figured they offered some kind of explanation where none was possible. The other cop, Detective Hunter, just offered his sympathy, looked as if he meant it and kindly hovered in the background.

Urquhart went on: "Our initial assessment of the crime scene is pointing to the same guy who's killed three other women this summer. Laura Payne was his intended target. It looks like Peter may have broken into her apartment when she didn't answer the door. He may have heard something violent going down or have had reason to believe that she might be in danger. Whatever. Your boyfriend got himself in the way of a man ruthless enough to kill a witness with no more conscience than he'd swat a fly. If it's any consolation, Ms. Yeats, there are indications that Peter didn't go down without putting up a damn good fight."

If it's any consolation ... Consolation? I'd just been told the love of my life had been slaughtered and somebody's talking *con-so-la-tion?* There could be no consolation. Not then, not even now, six years down that desolate road. Not ever. With more persistence than I'd previously applied to any task, I had banished all memories of that first night without him and avoided all references to his murder. Refusing to follow the case in the media, to discuss it with Etta or friends, I'd wrapped myself in a mantle of ignorance. Everyone soon learned that even to approach the subject was to step on a land mine. During the trial, which raised another media blizzard, I lost myself on a small island off the coast of Cuba. Only one fact was of any consequence: Pete was gone.

Within three weeks of Pete's funeral, William Shortt confessed to all five murders while undergoing psychiatric assessment for his capacity to stand trial. He had pleaded guilty and been sentenced to life imprisonment with no possibility of parole. Even had I been together enough to avenge Pete's death, the opportunity never presented itself.

Today I learned that the bastard who destroyed our lives was still out there uncaught and unpunished. And I hadn't even finished celebrating William Shortt's death.

Someone knocked at the door just as my crushed beer can hit the wall and B. B. King launched full tilt into "Since I Met You, Baby." In no mood to face the guy who wanted to read my water meter, sell me a miraculous new energy-efficient shower head or convert me to the Church of Whosever Latter-Day Saints, I cracked another beer. Unfortunately, my blinds and screen window were open.

Sam's face materialized amid a fan of hollyhock leaves. Oh, yeah, Sam said he was coming over. Whatever. His voice easily penetrated the screen. "If you don't open the door, my foot will be obliged to."

"Door's open, Sam."

Sam always makes me feel well dressed, notwithstanding the Goodwill rags and tatty jeans that comprise my normal attire. Today was no exception. A halo of messy curls circled his Blue Jays cap, peak pointed unfashionably forward. Faded black T-shirt from a long-cherished Grateful Dead tour, unevenly cut off jeans and sandals so worn that they might have been handed down through a line of succession that began with Jesus. Under any other circumstances I would have been happy to see his silly face.

He sat opposite me, glancing at the discarded beer can resting against the wall. "Hard to find good help these days, eh, Jane?" I did penance for my housekeeping transgressions by turning down the volume on my CD player.

Not wanting to make him any more uncomfortable than he already appeared, I still couldn't come up with a witty riposte. Taking in the four Smithwick's lined up in front of me, he helped himself to one. Probably a charitable gesture: one less for me to drown in.

"I want to apologize for breaking the news on the phone, Jane. That was stupid of me. I should have known to come over."

I lit a cigarette and snorkeled the smoke deep into my lungs. "Yeah, well, in this case the medium is not the message, Sam. The message is the same bad news no matter how it arrives."

Sam Brewer and I were acquainted for a couple of years through our newspaper work before the deaths of our respective mates struck at roughly the same time. Dawn, to whom he'd been happily married since their university graduation, had succumbed to breast cancer a few weeks before Pete died. Suddenly we found ourselves close friends. Friday nights after work we drew together as naturally as filings to a magnet, boozing away in a grungy bar favored by none of our colleagues, usually in companionable silence, each of us numb and dumb with grief. We were comfortable with each other as with no one else, implicitly understanding the need for an escape from making conversation, from listening as if one cared while our decent colleagues rattled on about mortgage payments, new cars or Junior's hockey performance, from networking to advance our careers. With the loss of the one dearest to us, we felt our lives had slipped the leash of conviviality and community. Those Friday-night vigils Sam and I observed marked a welcome reprieve from loneliness and solitary drinking.

As self-absorbed as I was today, I couldn't pretend that Sam didn't fathom my pain.

"Jane, all those months while I just had to stand back and watch Dawn die, the only thing that came even close to her pain was my rage at not being able to do a fucking thing about it. All I could do was be there. I couldn't fix it, I couldn't slow it down, I didn't even have the power to alleviate her pain the way the nurses could. If all that torture she endured — the surgery, the chemo, the radiation — couldn't do a goddamn thing to save her, what could I do? Just be there. And that wasn't enough. I had such a rage in me that I was afraid I'd tear into tiny pieces the first person who looked at me the wrong way."

Sam tilted a long swill of beer down his throat. He tried to meet my eyes, but I kept them fixed on a Theo Dimson poster. "You see, when Dawn passed away I wanted someone I could grab by the throat, curse forward and backward through seven generations, then kill as slowly and painfully as she had died. I desperately needed some son of a bitch I could exhaust all that rage on."

I looked straight at him then. "That's why people invented God. So we always had someone to blame — someone so safely out of reach that we were saved from murdering him. But why are you telling me this now, Sam? I had someone to blame, remember? I just found out I don't."

The shrill ringing of the phone punctuated my blasphemy. We listened to the message as my answering machine kicked in. "Hi, Jane. It's Terry Richardson from the *Star.* I'm hoping to set up an interview to discuss your reaction to the Rosenberg autopsy results. You can reach me on my cell at 416-731-8998 ... Oh yeah, I'm sorry for your loss and for how this news must be opening up old wounds."

My current beer can I tossed in the direction of the phone. After it dinged off the wall onto a quarry tile, Sam made his point with brutal clarity. "If my wife's killer had been a person and not a disease, I'd have found a way to get to him before the cops or the courts did."

"Let me get this straight, Sam. You're doing one of two things. Either you're telling me it's good that I no longer know for sure who killed Laura and Pete, and you're encouraging me to hunt him down and kill him. Or you're discouraging me from even thinking about it. Which is it?"

He drained his beer and helped us both to another. "I'm not sure. I guess I'm just trying to understand your frame of mind at the moment."

"I can't help you out much on that score because I don't want to understand it myself. I'm planning to obliterate my frame of mind with booze."

"And after that?" was all he asked. Sam met his current wife, Louise, when his first wife was dying in Princess Margaret Hospital. Louise showed up every day to attend to another patient — her younger sister. Within the same week, both were devastated and bonded by grief. Their tentative friendship eventually deepened into love. When the incredible notion struck him that there was, perhaps, renewed life beyond such devastation, Sam's beer consumption plummeted. I've always appreciated his unwillingness to elect himself an evangelist for sobriety.

"And after that?" he repeated.

"I don't know."

"I won't get in the way of your plan to get hammered. In your place, I'd sure as hell do the same." He fidgeted with his beer can, his thumb fretting the smooth surface in search of a peelable label. "We've come to know each other pretty well,

Jane. I know this has hit you hard. So I'd put some serious money on you doing something extreme. I just want to be sure that if you hurt anybody, it'll be the piece of crap who deserves it and not yourself."

He did know me well. The thought of violent revenge had occurred to me about two seconds after I heard that Pete's killer might still be roaming the streets, free to eat, drink, screw, sleep, make merry and more mayhem. The man who confessed to his murder, I'd never had a chance to hurt: Shortt had never been out of police custody.

"If I was going to go after Pete's killer, first I'd have to know who it was, Sam. Are the cops going to reopen their investigation?"

"I've already talked to a couple of my old contacts in the force. Now that I'm retired, they seem willing to tell me more than they did in the old days, when I might have rushed into print with disclosures from 'unidentified sources.'" He paused. "Guess they figure the sting's been taken out of my tail."

After his remarriage, Sam had quit the paper. Guilt-ridden by the knowledge that he'd spent more time with Dawn dying than with Dawn healthy, he swore that he wouldn't make the same mistake again. He soon discovered that what worked for his second marriage was working against his lust for crime writing. The publication of a well-received book on an investigation I'd been at the center of (but refused to write up) had temporarily alleviated his hunger to cover a story. Obviously he was at loose ends again.

"This morning Ernie told me that they are planning on reopening only one investigation — into Ruth Rosenberg's murder. Apparently the brass have decided they don't have the resources to open up the whole can of worms. Nor do they want to be seen admitting that the entire initial investigation might have been seriously flawed."

"But doesn't that amount to their having decided that Shortt *did* kill the other four?"

"That's probably their line of reasoning — or at least their fervent hope."

"But why cop to four murders you did commit and then credit yourself with one that belongs to somebody else?"

"Maybe to enhance your notoriety. Shortt loved the lime-light — so much that more than one psychologist has suggested that's what motivated him from the start, even more than a lunatic sex-and-violence drive." Sam watched me closely while I opened the last beer. "You know, you're doing something way out of character."

I braked my grin just short of a sneer. "What's that, Sam, drinking too much?" I realized that I had slurred my question in a manner characteristic of W. C. Fields sailing three sheets to the wind. I was quickly getting drunk. Good, things were going according to plan. Sam, bless him, ignored my shoddy enunciation.

"Apart from the homicide team that worked the case, I probably knew more about it than anybody. Yet you never once asked me a single question — not about the investigation, Shortt, his sentencing or my thoughts on the subject. For six years I expected you to break out of that mood, and you didn't. Suddenly I've just fielded three questions. What's that about? I mean, can we agree that you've just decided to pull your head out of the sand and take a hard look at the circumstances surrounding Pete's death?"

"Yeah, we can agree to that much."

"Then let me begin at the beginning of today's breaking news." Sam summarized the situation as proficiently as an accomplished lecturer obliged to pack *Ulysses* into a single class. "A year ago, Ruth Rosenberg's family started pressing for an exhumation of her body. Her brother, Dr. Jonathan Rosenberg, was convinced that enough doubt persisted about whether Shortt was indeed her killer to warrant a second look. Jonathan's reputation as a heavy-hitting fundraiser for the Tories added real clout to his request. When the attorney general agreed to permit the exhumation, an independent forensic specialist at the University of Toronto was asked to conduct the autopsy.

"An examination of semen recovered from the victim's pubic hair — overlooked in the first autopsy conducted by the Institute of Forensic Science and in any case probably too small a trace to have been detected by then-current technology — has just been proved not to match Shortt's DNA. This doesn't exonerate him: Rosenberg might have had sex with another man prior to her murder. Her fiancé immediately consented to a police request for a saliva sample, and it wasn't his semen either. Because there's no reason to doubt her monogamy, the DNA finding appears strongly indicative of belonging to her rapist-killer. But without a match, it remains inconclusive. Shortt could have used a condom.

"A second finding points to a major discrepancy between Shortt's confession and the manner in which she was killed. He claimed to have strangled Rosenberg with his hands using a great deal of force. However, her hyoid bone —"

"Sam, remind me about dem bones."

"Sure: the hyoid's the one supporting the tongue and tongue muscles. Anyway, it wasn't fractured and there were no fractures or signs of trauma to her cervical vertebrae. Finding the hyoid uninjured doesn't exclude manual strangulation, but there were no fingertip bruises and indentations. There were ligature marks on her throat."

"So Shortt lied about the manner of killing, or forgot how he killed her — or falsely confessed to the crime. What's your best guess about it all, Sam?"

Again the phone interrupted our conversation. This time it

was a crime reporter from the *Globe and Mail,* with a repeat of the *Star's* request, more genteelly worded. I shrugged. "Guess it's true, Sam — you can run but you can't hide."

"In hindsight, my best guess is that William Shortt took credit for *five* murders he never committed."

"So where do I begin?"

Sam jumped from his chair as hastily as I'd responded. "Let me go to my car. I brought along something I didn't bring into the house because I wasn't sure you'd be interested in looking at it."

He returned with a $20 parking ticket and a slim file folder. "This will get you started. It contains printouts of all the articles I wrote on the case. Let me know after you've read them if you really want to pursue this thing. Then we can pull together all the print coverage, my notes and interview tapes ..."

"Thanks, Sam." I hugged him.

"You do that so you can watch me blush. Just one more thing, before I leave you with that. They say working the crime beat hardens you up. I covered the Bernardo trial and know it's not true. And watching you recover from your last gig totally invalidated the idea. This case couldn't be any more up close and personal. So don't open that file unless you are very, very sure that you can deal with the contents."

I promised. I lied.

CHAPTER 2

ON THE FIRST ANNIVERSARY of Pete's death I honored a promise to my mother and made an appointment with a therapist. Etta does not frighten easily. But my prolonged near-catatonic retreat into a space where even she couldn't reach me terrified her. So for three months I endured weekly fifty-minute sessions with Dr. Anna Hoffman, a sweet middle-aged Middle European woman whose only failing was to have overdosed on Freud. She had to do all the work. Freudians find such role reversals stressful. When I decided to terminate our relationship, the dear lady looked relieved.

Then and now, most of Dr. Hoffman's suggestions struck me as sound. My rage at Pete's death was consuming my life, dominating my waking and sleeping. Perhaps I felt guilty or somehow responsible for not saving him. By perpetuating the collateral harm the killer caused me I was extending his power. Etc.

She lost me the day she suggested that I consider the redemptive power of love. Love, I snapped back at her, was not in the cards. Love was not a folly I'd commit ever again. Old, established loves would abide. For Mom, for my best friend, Silver, and a very few cherished others. But even these had taken on a tentative aspect. Before Pete's death, I'd never given more than a glancing thought to my mother's age — my shortsightedness abetted, of course, by her camouflage as a youthful tart. Now, when I scour average-life-span charts in the newspapers, or when the Queen celebrates another birthday, I automatically subtract Etta's age and mull over the difference. I do not attend Silver's birthday parties, famous throughout the art community. And I ignore the white hairs sprouting around Max's snout.

The only passing years I observe are my own, and those I hasten along with liberal applications of beer and nicotine.

Etta likes to quote Marlene Dietrich's notion of broken-heart therapy: "The best way to get over someone is to get under someone else." One drunken night I slept with a stranger. On more sober occasions, casually with two fine people (but never at the same time). It didn't work. In my experience, sexual shenanigans only deepen your loneliness when you're not sharing them with the one you love. I stopped indulging in lite sex.

The only person who knew and loved Pete as much as I did was his mother. And she was lucky enough to die when he was still young, strong — and alive.

Did I mention that my prescription for obliterating the hard facts of Pete's death included booze and denial? They had the unfortunate side effect of raiding the happy side of my memory bank. Recently I've had trouble recalling Pete's face without prompting from the photographs of us I'd buried in a drawer the day he'd been interred. My favorite I had tucked into his coffin. *Vaya con Dios,* my darling.

The damage to my psyche would not mend. But my lost-and-found fingers could. While I was healing from my latest battle wounds, I went into hibernation to finish writing *Malign Neglect,* my exposé of police malpractices and incompetence in the case of a serial killer. My agent, a woman so aggressive you'd swear she packs more testosterone than a Russian discus thrower, sold the book well before I delivered the first draft of the manuscript. My advance was startling.

The exercise of writing it all out was cathartic. During the climax of the real drama, I stood face-to-face with a serial killer, confronting him in a scene of murder *interruptus*. But somehow I had distanced myself from the woman I was then. Writing the book did nothing to erase the horror of his deeds, but I took great comfort in putting a human face to his victims. Women the media could not refrain from referring to as "drug-addicted prostitutes" — as though their addiction coupled with job description somehow mitigated his crimes and excused the shabby way the police had conducted their much-belated investigations. When a cop friend, Ernie Sivcoski, disingenuously complained about the bad rap I'd given the force, I suggested that he tell his buddies to regard *Malign Neglect* as a self-help manual. Maybe my book nudged a few readers toward a more sympathetic take on sex workers. Fat chance it could prompt the boys in power to change the punitive laws that complicate and further endanger their lives.

After six months of editing, proofing, design and printing, the book materialized and assumed the status of a commodity. Suddenly I was a hot property. The mere hint of impending celebrity drove me further into seclusion. I have only one life, and I prefer to keep it private.

On a very few occasions I caved in to pressure from my publicist and did a reading and signing, but I refused a book tour. My publisher, knowing that stress drives me to drink and surliness unbecoming a Canadian, relented. When some rave reviews appeared in top American newspapers, my publisher invested its resources in promotion and distribution. For a few weeks, my agent peppered me with sales triumphs — international rights, foreign-language rights, a book-club selection, a made-for-TV movie ... it was horrible.

Although I'd done everything I could to inject into my book the vestigial scholarly bacteria still infecting my intelligence, my subject remained sensational. Truth be told, it would not have been much less successful had I fired off an instant book to feed the Jerry Springer crowd. Take a serial-killer plot and add the writer's firsthand involvement in tracking down the perp and you have a best-seller recipe.

Instant celebrity and a serious income. Both would be fleeting. Still, it was all too much to cope with. Leaving Max in the care of Silver, I fled back to Cuba. There I was recognized only as a woman who enjoyed a daiquiri, danced well and aced her dive test.

For a full fifteen minutes after Sam's departure I sat and stared at the file folder he'd left on my coffee table. Then I did the stupidest thing I've ever packed into a folly-ridden life.

Compulsion. Without a thought about the wisdom of what I was about to do, I opened Sam's file. It was slim. So are letter bombs. My friend had saved his articles in two formats, text-only and PDF. I extracted the two PDFs.

The banner headline of Sam's first article screamed, "Police investigating double homicide." Immediately below were two photographs, set side by side. Of Pete. Of Laura.

It was one of my favorite photos of Pete, one I'd taken when we were camping the previous summer in Killarney Provincial Park. Here it had been cropped to a head-and-shoulders shot of a tanned, handsome, carefree young man grinning as if he'd just won the lottery. That's exactly what I'd said to him as I viewed his goofy grin through the lens.

"I have, love, I have," he said, laughing. "I won you."

And I remembered what Photoshop had cropped: Pete's body. A swimmer's physique, broad shouldered and stout chested, tapering to a slim waist, taut butt and powerful long legs. As I sat today on the living-room floor, flesh memories crowded my consciousness until I could feel him against me. First pressing, urgent, his lust matching mine. The memory so intense that he was inside me. Always Pete was inside me as no other lover ever, before or since. Then his body was soft, yielding, protectively snuggling his length against the back of me as we fell asleep, sated as sinners, innocent as infants.

I shuddered myself back into reality and examined Laura's face for the first time. It was a good, strong face, framed by short-cropped, wavy black hair: a face attractive without being airbrush-beautiful, it was open, expectant, curious. The expression made me think that her photo might also have been taken by a lover. Laura was ready to step out of the frame and into another adventure. She reminded me of a young Sigourney Weaver.

I popped open another Smithwick's. *Age shall not weary them, nor the years condemn ...*

"FUCK, FUCK, DOUBLE AND TRIPLE FUCK," I screamed into the tight dead air of my shrinking house. "Better they should grow weary, even condemned: that's the goddamn price we pay for getting to live beyond thirty. And who wouldn't choose to pay it? But before some of us even get to vote, some homicidal SOB comes along and forecloses on every option — but YOU GET TO DIE YOUNG."

Something in my genetic programming must have short-circuited. Or maybe it's that somewhere along the rocky road I lost the talent for recovery. When kind folks console me with "Ah, but you've got your good memories," I just don't get it. It's the good and precious memories that draw blood, that have sucked the life out of me since Pete's death. Memories are only and ever this much: heart-wrenching daily memos of what once was fine and beautiful in a life now bereft of what drenched with sweet wonder the very drawing of breath.

Rallying what resources I could, diminished though they were by semi-inebriation, I focused on the text of Sam's article.

TORONTO — Toronto police are investigating the 36th and 37th homicides of the year after two people were found slain in an apartment in Toronto's east end Thursday night.

Police spokesperson Landsay Tom said that police were responding to a missing person report when they discovered the two bodies. A woman, identified as Laura Payne, 28, the occupant of the apartment, and a man, identified as Peter Findley, 29, were pronounced dead at the scene.

The bodies were sent to the Centre for Forensic Sciences where full forensic autopsies will be performed.

Tom said that officers have yet to determine either the motive for the crime or the identity of the killer.

Although he refused to disclose how Payne and Findley were murdered, speculation is growing that the serial killer responsible for the deaths earlier this year of Linda Bailey, Ruth Rosenberg and Sandra Priest may be the perpetrator.

Tom urged that the media refrain from speculation about this possibility until further evidence is forthcoming.

Relatives of the deceased could not be contacted by phone. "Family members don't want to speak with the media at the present time," Tom said.

It is known that Laura Payne, a clinical psychologist, was the only child of Dr. Rodney Payne, a University of Toronto philosophy professor. Peter Findley, award-winning independent documentary filmmaker, was the partner of well-known crime writer Jane Yeats, with whom he resided.

Anyone with information about this incident is asked to contact Detective Sergeant Carl Dewey of the Major Crime Unit at (416) 678-3429.

The second article was shorter, but more brutal:

Police chief cautions against speculations about double homicide
TORONTO — Amid rumors that a serial killer may have struck again, Toronto police are continuing their investigation into a double murder last Thursday. Preliminary autopsy reports have revealed that Laura Payne had been strangled and Peter Findley bludgeoned to death.

Police Chief Raymond Underhill sought to reassure Torontonians that their city is safe, releasing a statement yesterday that called the five murders an "aberration."

"The city's homicide rate remains very low and serial killers are very uncommon. While there is evidence suggesting a link between the killings of Linda Bailey, Ruth Rosenberg and Sandra Priest, we still have no evidence whatsoever linking this double murder to the same perpetrator," said Chief Underhill.

"We are working as hard as we can at the present time and remain confident that arrests will be made in these cases."

Bludgeoned to death. I couldn't take this. My chest tightened until my breathing was reduced to quick, shallow gasps. I couldn't stay in this house another minute. This house, which I had worked so hard to convert into a sanctuary, had been compromised, polluted by the intrusion of these particulars. My house was a toxic waste dump.

Grabbing my wallet and cigarettes, I stumbled out the door. Whatever it took, I needed to obliterate the picture my tormented brain kept flashing across my sight line: Pete's sweet face smashed and broken — along with my sanity.

CHAPTER 3

WET, BLOODIED AND SHIVERING, I came to consciousness. A manic percussionist was beating on the walls of my skull. I seemed to be lying facedown on a concrete bed. Only one eye would open. The other was crusted shut. I made another concerted effort to get my chin off the pavement. My right hand, the one with the normal fingers, managed to check out the recalcitrant eye and came away bloody.

Someone must have followed me from the bar and attacked me in a dark laneway. I could just make out the blurred outline of a garbage pail. I touched it. It was real.

What bar? And why had I ventured down a laneway? I had to get home. As I pushed myself to my knees, a black wave flung me back into oblivion ...

I recovered consciousness. Now I was lying on a *real* bed. The walls of the room were a hue of lime not found on the color wheel that includes hospital green. And the nurse hulking at the end of the bed looked meaner than Nurse Ratchet of *One Flew Over the Cuckoo's Nest*. Only someone wanting to drive a rich, elderly aunt into a terminal stroke would hire her.

I pushed the words past my furred tongue and cracked lips. "I want to report a murder. Last night."

This got the attention of She-Who-Is-Not Florence Nightingale. "Who was murdered?"

"I was."

My surly caregiver snapped, "I've seen that fucking movie.

D.O.A.,1949. Shitty 1988 remake with Dennis Quaid and Meg Ryan. So don't think I'm about to tell you that you drank a luminous toxic matter that will kill you within two weeks." She paused. "You probably don't have that long."

My best friend loomed even larger than her normal six-foot three-hundred-pound frame. As if her personality isn't enough of an imposition already.

Time to rally my thespian resources before she killed me on the spot. "Hi, Silver. I was just about to make some breakfast. Care to join me?" I chirped.

"I ate breakfast nine hours ago. Care to tell *me* what happened?"

I tried to rally my surviving gray cells. Nine hours ago: must be mid-afternoon or so. A jagged sliver of hundred-proof agony pierced my skull — along with the realization that telling the truth would be the line of least painful resistance. "Um ... I don't remember. But I think I got mugged."

"In your own backyard? By someone who left your wallet and money behind? I don't think so."

"You don't have to shout. I'm the victim here."

She brought her face so close to mine that it shattered into pixels. Or maybe I had a concussion.

"I don't have to shout, eh? Well, fasten your seat belt, lady. I'm just beginning and the volume is going to increase. This morning I'm driving my contented body home from a very successful date and I think, *Hey, why don't I swing by Jane's place for coffee?* So I pull up to the front of the house, then freak because before I get out of the car I can see that your door's partly open. Max is barking like he's discovered a body — which he has. I find you collapsed, unconscious and bleeding outside your back door, which is wide open. After checking to make sure that nothing was broken — apart from your brain — I carried you upstairs. You've been sleeping it off ever since."

"Thanks, Silver. It's lucky you came by."

What she volleyed back at my delicate eardrums I'd call a howl. "What's *lucky* is you didn't wake up in the drunk tank. What's *lucky* is it's not winter because I'd be at the morgue identifying your pathetic remains."

Max was at my side, in his subdued mode. When I reached over to pat his head I noticed a bruise the size of a September zucchini running down the side of my arm. "Ah ... I remember. When I got home Max needed to pee, so I let him out the back door."

"That must be when you decided to camp out on the concrete."

I worked strenuously to recollect what had seduced me into this mishap. "Hey, I just popped into the Dundalk for a pint. I was feeling a bit down. Guess the last thing I needed was another beer — or six or seven." The Dundalk, a rowdy sports bar but fifteen giant steps from my door, I normally avoid unless I want to catch a Jays' game on the monster screen. "I headed home when the wrestling came on."

Silver obliged me with the summary and wrap-up. "Let's look on the bright side. To the best of your ability to remember, you didn't get into a barroom brawl, you didn't hit on some innocent man — or woman — stupid enough to think you were good for a sodden quickie. No collateral damage, then, unless we take into account your battered body, your reputation and your self-esteem. None of which you've given a shit about since Pete died."

She was speeding along on a train that called for instant derailing. "Silver, I'm parched. Could you get me something to drink?"

"Sure. Juice, water or a Coke?"

"A beer would do the trick, thanks."

To my surprise, she headed for the kitchen. I heard the

fridge door open, followed by the sound of one can popping, then two, three, etc. Cold beer gurgled into the sink. Cans got crushed underfoot on the quarry tiles. Silver returned with a huge Slurpee cup of tap water on the rocks.

"I am in no mood for comedy. Play the clown with me and I'll finish off what you already started."

Had history allowed Joseph Brant to partner with Silver, the Mohawk Nation would now be governing this country. Not a bad thing.

She seated herself on the side of the bed. "Drink up while I take us on a quick stroll along the dark side of the street. Listen up. As your friend, as a mere *spectator* to your decline, I have to tell you the past six years have not been a pretty sight. I've watched you making every effort to slowly kill yourself. And you rejected my help. No one can accuse me of killing you softly with kindness, but somehow you managed to fast-talk your way out of every conversation I tried to initiate."

"So why didn't you bail on the friendship?"

Her nostrils twitched before settling into a hostile flare. "The stench of self-pity is clogging this room. Why didn't I abandon you? Like Pete did — right? Now hear this: *Pete had no choice.* I did."

"Thank you for hanging in."

"What I'm looking for here is absolution, not gratitude. I've never felt guiltier in my life. I should be able to rescue you. I know you're heading down a path so well worn it could be the friggin' Martyrs' Shrine. The only variation is in the boring details of how you get there: liver gives up, heart cramps, brain strokes out, whatever ... you croak."

"Call me a drunken slut, but never call me *boring.*"

A fierce determination scrawled across her countenance.

Her silence gave me a moment to reflect. As an Indian, Silver has witnessed so many useless deaths among her people, whatever the weapon — RCMP bullets, booze, drugs, gasoline or glue fumes. And it all came down to one thing: they lost the will to live or got it stolen from them. As a card-carrying member of the gay community, Silver has witnessed the passing of many friends to AIDS.

When she spoke, I knew we were on the same page. "Looking at you, I'm seeing a woman who actually has a *choice* about whether she gets to live or die. So here's the cosmic question: *What's it gonna be? Are you fucking going to live or die?* Because, my friend, I'm not spending another wooden nickel watching you self-destruct."

I couldn't lie to her, not any more. But I didn't know the answer.

"You having no religion and not a single conviction that might restore you to sanity, I'm going to suggest that you invoke the only two things I've ever seen propel your sorry ass off a bar stool."

In her left hand she clutched Sam Brewer's news articles I'd been reading last night. "Since you've finally decided to take a trip down memory lane, why don't you get creative? You can investigate those murders and you can write about them. And you can do both way more effectively when you're sober."

She plunked down on the floor, from which vantage point she continued to drill her clear eyes into my blurred focus. "So what's it gonna be, Jane? I'm not leaving here without a declaration you'd stake Etta's life on."

I took time to frame my reply. Investigate. Write. My friend was correct. That was my only remaining option. *Why had Pete died? How had I so failed him that I'd refused to pursue that question?* All along I'd taken the easy way out and blamed God. But even at the zenith of my rage, I'd never really believed that God, with whom I've failed to maintain even the most tenuous of relationships, had murdered Laura, along with Pete, hapless witness to her desecration. Not that God's failure to intervene when innocents suffer could be deemed an exceptional circumstance.

William Shortt's confession had seemed to answer the *who* of those murders. The *why* I had consigned to Pete's being "in the wrong place at the wrong time," an answer no less insufficient today than it was the moment I'd first heard it. Instead of pursuing the truth and maybe laying one demon to rest, I'd plugged my brain into a series of investigations and books situated at a safe remove from my shattered world.

Silver was at my side to remind me that the clock had run down on prevarication. "My friend, this is not *Who Wants to Be a Millionaire?* This is your life. So what's it gonna be?"

"Investigate, for sure. I can't commit to the writing bit, not now."

What gave those words titanic force were the sacrilegious ones I'd left unspoken: I will investigate until I hunt down Pete's real killer. Then I will quickly pass "write" and go straight to *kill the bastard.*

A startling thought. I realized I meant it. If I found him, I would kill him.

CHAPTER 4

WHEN I WALKED INTO SWEET DREAMS I found my mother at the bar, hunched over a morning paper. Her short body was swathed in a long dress as nasty as the one Loretta Lynn is sporting on the album cover of *Coal Miner's Daughter.* In fact, the bibbed, frilly concoction is *precisely* that nasty: whenever Etta wants a new frock she simply hands her seamstress a photo of one of her country music legends. Thank God she hasn't yet taken a shine to Willie Nelson.

She barely lifted her head to acknowledge my arrival. Her strategy was familiar to me: Jane's gotta be in some big mental mess, so leave her alone about it and eventually she'll get to what's grieving her.

"What's up, Ma?"

"I'm thinking that maybe it's a good thing if the government keeps forcing the universities to raise tuition fees so high they'll put us back to the time when only rich brats could afford an education."

As well as having an honorary Ph.D. in country-music history, Etta is a bar-stool philosopher. "So what's the good part?"

"Take your Supreme Court of Canada here," she said, jabbing the front page. "Now, them folks all gotta be so damned educated they never had time for nothing but studying before they hit thirty, right? But from what they been saying lately, I reckon too much education does peculiar things to a human's brain."

When her accent takes on that fighting Irish note I don't argue. Interruptions, especially dissenting opinions, are verboten.

"Beats me why farmers is still buying fertilizer when all they need to do is take a truck to Ottawa or wherever these wigs meet and just shovel up the crap. Listen to this: 'A four-judge majority of the Supreme Court of Canada ruled yesterday that although there is an undeniable distinction between country singing and nude dancing, the difference is so slight that a Quebec bar should be permitted to trade in its jukebox and sawdust floors for naked women and a stage. Personal value judgments should play no part in such matters, the majority added — including whether one finds nude dancing more or less deplorable than cowboy singing.'

"Now that's the very kind of highfalutin nonsense that's causing this country to fall apart. Like it takes a couple of frigging degrees to clue you in to there being a monstrous difference between cowboy singing and nude dancing. Not to mention the fact that to call what Shania Twain or Faith Hill or Trisha Yearwood or the Dixie Chicks or Patsy Cline or Maybelle Carter do 'cowboy singing' should send them back to the dictionary. Calling both of them 'deplorable' — that only goes to show how education ruins you for the simple pleasures of life."

"I can't argue you with you there, Mom."

"Course you can't. You only got one degree. Trust me, before I read the words I knew where this was going. Straight to anti-sex."

Etta's not one for conspiracy theories, but she never fails to sniff out a right-wing, born-again agenda simmering away on the back burner. She snorted in some Cameo smog and resumed: "'Three dissenting judges insisted that moral judgments are very much part of the equation. "Whereas erotic entertainment seeks to sexually arouse the audience by the stripping and suggestive behavior engaged in by the performers, country-and-western shows seek to entertain by providing a showcase for the special talents of singers, musicians or dancers," Judge Foucault argued.' My dear, nothing in my experience has ever suggested that sexual arousal is anything but a good thing — 'cept, of course, when we're talking child molesters and other perverts, which ain't the case here."

"So ... the difference between country music and stripping is one of degree, not kind." Every Socrates needs his straight man, I figure.

She shook her head, slightly shifting her wig du jour. "Maybe even your one degree was a mistake, girl. I object to them taking the sexy out of country." Redirecting her eyelids, drooping as much from mascara as from the passage of time, to the offensive article, she shrieked, "And here's where it gets racist. 'Irish pubs usually offer Irish melodies, but may have to be transformed next season into a different ambiance offering karaoke,' Judge Irigaray said."

"Mom, I think the judge is suggesting that business owners have to keep up with market trends. You know, they survive by following in the tracks of the money."

"You should have dropped outta school right after they taught you how to type, Jane. I don't have to know the meaning of *ambiance* to know that you don't yank out your roots just to lure into your bar a bunch of hosers who gotta sing along to Tom Jones to get their peckers up."

I looked around the four cavernous walls, took in a quick visual swallow of Etta's shrine to Nashville. "Etta, you wrote the book on ambiance."

"This is your lucky day, dear. I'll take that as a compliment." Into a guitar-shaped souvenir ashtray, she snuffed out her carmine-smeared Cameo. "I heard about your bad news — about the autopsy and all. You're looking better than I expected."

My skin quivered to the keen scrutiny of her eyes. "Yeah, yeah. I'm fine. Don't worry about me."

"'Don't worry,' she says. Half an hour you've been in here without pulling a draft or lighting up a smoke. Not to mention that mother of a bruise on your arm."

I went behind the bar and mixed myself a cranberry-and-orange-juice cocktail. "I took the pledge. *Sláinte*," I toasted her. "The bruise I got renovating."

"Yeah, and I'm always walking into doorknobs."

"At your height, this must come as no surprise, Ma."

"Now I know you got something up your sleeve. Some cockeyed scheme to set things right."

"Some things can never be set right." Time to switch gears if I wanted to keep my mother in the dark about my plans for exacting an eye for an eye. "Remember when I was a kid, how Granny used to tell me bedtime stories?"

Her eyes sparkled. "How could I forget, girl? She raised me on the same stories."

I have few memories of my grandparents. Etta's father and Seamus's mother died years before I was born. When I was young, Seamus's father was still alive, but Etta wouldn't let him in the house. Early in her marriage she'd once made the mistake of inviting him for dinner. Three months later he left — also at her invitation — having drunk his way through her food money and brought home women Etta says were the kind decent philanderers shielded their families from.

My maternal grandmother, Brigid, lived with us until her death the year I went off to university. Of her my memories were all good.

"Granny O'Connell would sit by the side of the bed, stare at the wallpaper for a few moments as if she were reading from the *Tain Bo,* then straight off the top of her head launch into some marvelous tale of goddesses who turned from hags into beauties after receiving a king's kiss, or of great bloody battles in which powerful combatants shape-shifted into animals, or of women tall and fierce as men who ran faster than horses and charged with swords and battleaxes and fell upon their enemies screaming like banshees ..."

On a misty morning I can still conjure the clash of swords, the frenzy of warfare, the ghostly apparitions stalking the ramparts ...

Etta patted my hand. "Thanks for reminding me, dear. You know, if them old myths are anything to go by, Irish women had it real good — before the Christians spread over the country like ticks on a dog and screwed it all up. Girls got educated, women could inherit property and keep it even after they was stupid enough to get married. They had a big say in their clan's military and political goings-on. When they got raped, there was laws to help them out. Same for divorce." She cackled, "They could also in dabble in polyandry whenever it struck their fancy — but what kind of a benefit is that?"

Again she reached for the pack of Cameos, her acrylic fingernails securing it a good inch in front of her fingertips. "I wouldn't have minded living back then, you know. Women were real impressive. Rulers and warriors. They kicked ass. Queen Scathach of Skye taught our great hero Cuchulainn everything he knew. Aoife, his son's mother, was also a warrior. But the greatest of all was Queen Maeve of Cruachan, daughter of the high king of Ireland."

Reminiscing was something Mom and I rarely did. Our recent family tree was wired with explosives. But the old stories were always bonding.

Etta sucked in a huge drag of her peppermint coffin nail and grinned. "You've heard the old line: 'Balls,' said the queen, 'if I had them I'd be king.' Well, Maeve had big balls — Ailill the Asshole, her husband, only got to be king by marrying her.

My favourite story of all the ones your grandmother told me was
'The Cattle Raid of Cooley.'"

"Go for it, Mom." I remembered the tale, but Etta's
retelling was a trip, mixing venerable text and tacky vernacular.
She it was, and not the ancients, who dubbed Ailill "The
Asshole."

"This legendary battle began in bed. Ailill and Maeve,
king and queen of Connaught, lay between the sheets in their
chamber at the fort in Cruachan. Mistaking himself for the cock
of the walk after doing the dirty with his wife, Ailill reminded
her how much better off she was since marrying him. 'Hold on
now, you, I was fine enough and wealthy enough before I ever
saw the face of you! If anything, you are a kept man,' she retorted haughtily.

"There ensued a pissing match between them two about
whose fortune was the greatest. To settle the issue they ran outside the fort and had their possessions piled up side by side. On
two hills of Cruachan there rose two mountains. Next they
assembled all their animals. The king and queen fumed at each
other across the tumult of beasts. The contest was decided when
the Asshole dragged in his white-horned bull, for which Maeve
had no match. Technically, this would make him the ruler of
their household.

"Never one to settle for being bested by a man, she decided
to borrow the Brown Bull of Cuailnge, the finest in Ireland and
the pride of Ulster. If its owner would deliver it himself, she
promised him many rich rewards — including 'my own friendly thighs on top of that.'

"When they refused her offer, she up and rallied her army
and invaded Ulster to steal the beast. They got to scrapping,
with Cuchulainn leading the red knights against Maeve and her
blokes. Both armies suffered such great losses the valley was
almost filled with their bodies, and nobody knows what the hell

finally happened. Some say Maeve did get the bull, but when it was penned with Ailill's bull, the two beasts killed each other. Now that his white-horned baby was dead, Maeve got to rule the roost again. Buddy bailed, of course. Others say the Brown Bull gored apart the White Bull and sometime later Maeve hired a hit man to bump off the Asshole."

What's not to like about genealogy?

She shook her head. "But it's not like any of that counts for much in the lives of Irish women. Since then it's been a down-hill slide. My marriage to your father, may he rest in pieces, is a perfect example of how far we've sunk from them glorious heights."

She butted out her cigarette with a ferocity fueled by out-rages beyond recall, then slipped into gloom astride bitter memories.

I nudged her arm. "Hey, Ma, you wouldn't be offended if I said you remind me of Maeve."

She grinned and fiddled with a lock of platinum hair. "Thank you, dear. Maeve was the one who taunted her husband, 'I have never had one man without another waiting by the bed.' A girl looking to spice up her sex life couldn't have a better role model."

Nor, I mused to myself, could a girl looking to be a warrior queen.

"But even Maeve came to a bad end. She got killed by a lump of hard cheese fired out of a slingshot."

I said nothing. Etta was scrutinizing my face. "You know, Jane, I can see that you're changing in ways I don't approve of. Like you're becoming a good listener. Now that's un-Irish. We disapprove of people who don't speak until they're spoken to. Mark my words, they're not to be trusted."

"Maybe I'm tired of competing with you for air space, Etta."

"Sure and it's more likely you're hiding some nasty new intention under that flat rock you call a brain."

I clammed up. The last thing I wanted was for Etta to suspect my real intentions.

CHAPTER 5

JANE, WARRIOR QUEEN. It had a good ring to it.

I was three days into boot camp. Every morning I exercised so rigorously that my body made short work of the organic produce I packed into it. My kidneys were even more efficient at processing the water I was drinking in place of beer. My liver must have been doing cartwheels. Temperance made it easier to limit myself to ten cigarettes a day, twenty less than my habitual intake. Keeping my body and mind busy was essential to staying with the program.

Representations of Queen Maeve place a squirrel and a bird on her shoulder to symbolize her animal attributes. I've never detected any symbols of her promiscuity, unless you count the Victoria's Secret robe. Always at hand are her shield and sword.

My emblematic animals are already in place: Max, a wallful of mice and enough squirrels in the yard to keep a Dutch tulip breeder in Armanis.

Her shield and sword: *time to do some virtual shopping for the weaponry.* No matter how well I prepared myself for my fantasized encounter with Pete's killer, an Amazonian physique and a keen mind wouldn't cut the mustard. If I'd been carrying a gun the night last year when I chased down that murderous lunatic, people wouldn't still be wincing when they look at my left hand.

I booted up my iBook and did a brisk walk through the electronic mall, popping in and out of targeted sites, bargain hunting on eBay, pausing over coffee in a chat room for gun freaks, scanning posts on a couple of boards. Ninety minutes later, I was about to depart cyberspace armed with all the information I needed to make my purchase in the real world when someone knocked at the door with the force of Gareth demanding entrance to the Castle Perilous.

I do have friends ... first Sam, now Ernie at my door with that concerned expression.

Few people would ever mistake Ernie Sivcoski for a homicide detective. Maybe an elite athlete, maybe some hunk enshrined in a Hugo Boss ad. Humbling as it is to admit, our brief gig as lovers owed much to his body and how he draped it. Whatever attracted him to me, poster girl for the fuck-fashion movement, I've never guessed.

Today he was sporting an expression as thoughtfully assembled as his gear. I couldn't read it. Dangerous as a concealed weapon — no, it *is* a concealed weapon — diplomacy always sucks in spades.

Call me stupid, a woman who never learns from past mistakes: I let him in. He hugged me, but carefully, in a gesture I could easily read: he knew I'd heard about the autopsy results and figured I had to be in a fragile state. Little did he guess I felt as fragile as fossilized furry mammoth scat.

Max sped in from the backyard and snarled at Ernie.

"I've known this dog since he was a pup, Jane. Why the hell does he still go all rabid when he sees me?"

"It's a territorial thing. He doesn't like most men, especially ones I've slept with."

"That must keep him busy."

Ernie turned his head to watch Max slink into the kitchen. Something caught his eye. Shit. Why had I set my computer to sleep only after twenty minutes had passed? Ernie's solicitude evaporated the moment he set eyes on the screen, currently displaying a Web page splashed with handgun graphics courtesy of SIGARMS, Inc.

"Best you have a seat, my friend. You're looking a little agitated."

He settled his toned butt on my sofa. "I came here thinking you'd be a basket case. But it looks like you're turning into Buffy the Vampire Slayer."

I raised my Evian bottle in salute. No point whatsoever in shitting Ernie. He hadn't risen through the ranks without establishing a track record that would make Chief Inspector Maigret envious. "Congratulations, Lord Detective of Deduction. Can I get you a drink?"

He glanced at my bottle. "Funny I didn't hear about the beer strike. Yes to a coffee, though. Fill me in here. What's with the mail-order gun page?"

"A writer is always researching."

"Don't shit me, Jane. What the hell do you hope to accomplish that a first-class homicide team didn't?"

"Find out who really killed Pete," I proclaimed from the kitchen.

"That means you're assuming William Shortt didn't. How do you propose to accomplish that task?"

"I thought I'd start by going over the case files on William Shortt's rapes and *alleged* murders to see if the evidence was actually pointing in some other direction."

"Which files you think I'll let you see." His expression was not encouraging.

"There you go again, Ernie the Magnificent Mind Reader. Why else did you come here but to console me? It's not like I invited you over."

It seemed wise not to remind him how much he owed me. How *very* much — and that's not even counting the sex. Given that the Toronto Police Services had paid me a $100,000 reward

for services recently rendered, if not fingers severed, Ernie probably considered that debt paid in full.

He lit up a Rothmans, raised an eyebrow when I refused
one. Seated downwind of him, I prayed for a bracing waft of
secondhand toxins. He smoked it almost to the filter before
speaking. For once I chose not to break a pregnant silence.

"I did not come here expecting to be blackmailed. I am not
a librarian, and those files normally don't circulate. If I told you
why I'm running the risk of lending them to you, we'd both
blush." Ernie crossed, uncrossed and recrossed his legs. "If I had
the kind of heart that breaks, you would have left mine in
pieces. If I had the intelligence and the attention span of a fruit
fly, I *never* would have shared with you anything even vaguely
related to my work."

Again he took to rearranging his lovely thighs. "But you
kinda got under my skin and you've stayed there — like a fucking tick."

"Ernie, that's gotta be the sweetest thing any man ever said
to me." Sad as it is to admit, his twisted tribute came close.

He sipped from his mug. "The only thing even vaguely
domestic you do well is brew a good cup of coffee. You are light-
years away from being the kind of woman I'm normally attracted to. And even though I know I didn't exactly fit your defini-
tion of a partner, if you hadn't met Pete, well ..."

"Ernie, if it's any consolation, after I met Pete even
Michelangelo's *David* was out of the running."

His eyes locked mine. "Yeah, well, in my life you don't run
across a lot of love stories. Maybe it's the job. Maybe it's because
most of us just lose faith in happy endings. You and Pete —
now that should have been a happy ending. Some son of a bitch
queered it. You seem convinced we nailed the wrong son of a
bitch. I'm not so sure, but your suspicion seems to be getting
you healthy and sober. So who am I to get in the way of the

program?"

I haven't hugged Ernie since last we made love. That was so long ago that dinosaurs were pooping where Alberta oil sands now rule. He held me like a long-lost sister. We broke apart only when Max bit into Ernie's shoe.

Ernie pulled back. "Obviously I've overstayed your dog's welcome. I'll be here tomorrow morning at eight-thirty sharp with more than a plain brown envelope. If anyone ever finds out that you've seen the files, I'll sell you down the river to save my career."

"Ernie, I solemnly swear on Etta's best pair of cowboy boots." Madonna and Bruce Springsteen own several pairs of ornately tooled boots made by a renowned local bootmeister who also crafts footwear for She Who Birthed Me.

Ernie knows my mother. So he also knows where oaths connected to her fit into my scheme of things. He nodded. The deal was sealed.

I was ecstatic. No time to waste before the next step. As soon as Ernie's car turned the corner, I fired up my Sportster and raced off for Hank's bike shop to equip myself with a new hog. Hank is the mechanic who maintained my first Fat Boy, taught me how to customize it and sold me the Sportster I've been riding for two years. Recently Hank got bitten by the entrepreneurial bug and expanded his repair business to house a salesroom. It was crammed with classics he'd lovingly rebuilt and some new seducers.

Stepping into Hank's sanctuary transported me to Harley heaven.

For there at the Pearly Gates stood the ultimate road warrior, hot off the line, way hotter than Saint Peter and gleaming brighter than his halo. Until this moment I'd glimpsed this celestial machine only in a photograph in the "Wheels" section of the Saturday *Post.* I approached, heart thudding and body parts afire. Tenderly I stroked his silver flank.

The V-Rod. Water cooled, fastest power cruiser on any market. Road tests rate its performance as surpassing even its beauty. The American designers collaborated with the Porsche guys to produce a V-twin 1130 cc fuel-injected engine that pulls to 150 km/h in second gear, blazes to 220 three gears later. Finally, the gods have devised a Harley with the technology to match its ballsy carapace.

"Want to take it for a spin?" Hank was grinning at my transparent joy. He must trust me more than his own mother. There can't be more than six of these babies in the country.

Five minutes later, my lock on the grips the only thing preventing the wind from sucking me into its vortex, I screamed my proposal to just under three hundred kilos of awesome power yoked to heavy-metal glam. "Marry me and you'll never regret it."

His dowry I've already described. With a few extras tossed in, the bride price was $30,000 — before taxes. I was so far gone I decided to pony it up — in cash.

On one condition. Hank has "affiliations" with some clubs whose membership doesn't include any Old Boys who graduated from Upper Canada College. I might be asking him for a special favor.

"Hank, here's the deal. I want this bike. If I buy it from you, you've got to be looking at a fat commission."

He glanced at the Sportster I rode in on. I love the way that man can smoke a cigarette down to the filter and talk without disturbing the ash. "Hey, I'll knock off a few grand for the trade-in. Almost as much as you paid me for it in the first place. I know you take real good care of your machines."

"That's not enough, Hank."

"So how do I sweeten the deal?" He was looking anxious.

His begrimed fingers crushed the can of Blue he'd sucked dry after extinguishing his cigarette butt with a twist of his tooled cowboy boot.

I put on a face sweeter than Shirley Temple's on the Good Ship Lollipop. "You throw in a handgun."

Hank, the epitome of cool under pressure, jumped back. "I throw in a fucking what?"

"You heard me, man. And not just any old gun. I'm wanting a SIG Sauer P239. I'll settle for the Nitron finish, but the two-tone number would match my boots." My turnaround on the topic of guns would make Charlton Heston proud enough to adopt me.

He shook his head while his right index finger picked away at the rose tattoo on his left forearm. "Only a broad would give a shit what it looks like. I suppose you want the short trigger and the night sights, too?"

I should worry about the short-trigger version when we're talking illegally acquired handguns. "Just the night sights, Hank."

I broke the silence. "Thirty grand, c-a-s-h."

"Yeah, well, I'll have to make a couple of phone calls, eh? But I think I can come up with something. But I ain't handing it over to you myself. I promised my girlfriend I wouldn't do nothin' to get me tossed back in the joint. So I'll be hooking you up with Walter. He's an Angel, right? Nomads chapter. Wears a patch marked 'Filthy Few.'"

My biker vocab is good enough to handle the translation. That patch means Walter has killed for the club.

I stifled my apprehension. "Yeah, yeah, so Wally won't be wearing a gardenia in his lapel."

"You chose a good gun, Jane. Trustworthy, real accurate. Small, light, real easy to conceal — but it gives you serious firepower. I'll phone you in a coupla hours, after I talk to the guy.

Don't give him no money. Gun's on me. Walter owes me."

He continued to pick shyly at his rose, which was long stemmed. "Way I look at it, woman like you goes shopping for a gun, she's gotta have a fuckin' good reason."

I offered him my hand. "You got that right, Hank. And thanks for asking me no questions."

"You told me no lies. So let's trade bikes, eh?"

I felt no regret as I handed over my Sportster into Hank's foster care. "It's a nice bike, but I never felt as powerful riding it as I did astride Fat Boy."

"That's 'cause you weren't," confirmed my guru. "You're looking at the difference between a poodle and a pit bull, right?" He patted the seat of my V-Rod after having filled its tank. When his muscles twitched, the petals of the rose fluttered. "Actually this mother is more like a cross between a race-horse and a rottweiler. Trust me, you'll feel more than powerful. This bitch could take out a concrete wall and keep on boogying, eh?"

I wrote Hank a check and saddled up for glory.

Shop till you've got the goods to drop somebody. Whether I would ever really fire the damn thing at a human being was a question I put on the back burner.

Just past the witching hour, "Filthy Few" Walter and I connected in the back room of a bar you can access only from the rear, and only after you've been frisked and certified by a stand-in for Popeye's buddy, Bluto.

My date could have served as the template for a stereotyped biker, except for the button-down collar lurking underneath the regulation leather jacket. Something about his face warned me I shouldn't go inquiring into his sartorial quirks.

In short, Walter was not the kind of guy you'd take home to Mom, even if her name was Etta. But I wasn't looking for a long-term gig. And he wasn't into prolonging our dalliance. He reached into his jacket to extract a black holster. "This holster clips onto the back of your belt, FBI-style. Thought you might want some heat you can carry discreet."

From its smooth leather envelope he pulled something that looked just like its JPEG incarnation on the SIG Sauer Web site. From another jacket pocket he produced a Baggie stuffed with bullets. Good thing: I'd forgotten to order them.

"Hey, lady, way I see it, every broad should carry a gun."

Yeah, Walter, with guys like you littering the streets, not a bad idea. I did not say this out loud.

Calling on a similar exchange from *L.A. Law*, I cradled the gun in my hand as if I was reminding myself of familiar contours I'd only temporarily misplaced, maybe the curve of an ex-lover's butt.

Holding the gun triggered a memory. Not exactly a *madeleine* moment compliments of Proust, but helpful nonetheless. When I was a kid, Seamus — my father — took me on a few educational field trips. One was to an Irish bar in Hamilton where we snacked on pigs' feet while I learned to shoot darts. Another was to a rural garbage dump where Seamus taught me how to shoot rats. Even though I wasn't the son he'd wanted, my father saw me as his sole surviving hope for raising the family profile within the IRA, much dimmed by his precipitate flight from Dublin the day following an "incident."

I descend from a long line of violent people embedded in a violent culture. I sniffed the barrel. Gun oil, but no telltale powder smell.

"Hey," retorted Walter, "that's a brand-new rod. A virgin. Never been fired. No registration, being as it fell offa the back of a truck." He sounded offended but offered me a beer and passed his cigarette pack my way. Graciously, I declined both.

Once you got past the criminal record, wardrobe, beer gut

and fractured vocabulary — not to mention whatever liberal prejudices were weighing you down, Walter was kind of cute.

Something I needed even more than bullets was nagging at me. "Walter, I've been shitting you, man. I can't handle this gun any better than I can a pair of chopsticks. Will you help me out with some training?"

He beamed a smile wide enough to escape the facial hair. His hirsute paw clamped down so hard on my left hand that for a moment I was worried its reattached tips might shake loose.

"Honey, you're on for Saturday. You let me ride you to our private shooting range on that V-Rod and you got a deal."

To shoot, or not to shoot? A little target practice can't hurt anyone.

CHAPTER 6

I WAS STRIDING ALONG the hallway of a low-rent apartment building devoid of distinguishing features. It could have been any such building, anywhere in the world. Walls so grimy it was impossible to tell their original color, worn carpet stained to dirt hue, just one functioning light bulb, doors as understated as the lid of a pauper's casket. Silence behind them so profound the occupants might all be dead.

Apparently I knew where I was going. Reaching the last door on the left, I slid my key into the lock. When I turned the handle, the door refused me entry. As I stepped back to check my keys, the handle jumped to frantic life from within. It swiveled from side to side to no effect, then someone on the other side yanked it until the door threatened to burst its frame.

I watched, mesmerized, passive as a couch potato. Something was very wrong on the far side. I continued to watch as the heavy-metal soundtrack kicked in, the *zzzzzzzz-brrrrrrr* of a huge drill bit slowly channeling through the lock. Someone was mightily determined to get out. To get at me.

Max's querulous whining wakened me. Pushing a strand of wet hair from my face I sat upright, sucking air into my tight chest. Hypervigilant at 3:17 a.m., according to my Swatch's luminous dial. *If I lapse back into sleep, will my assailant's face be revealed as the door crashes to the floor?* Best not to give the nocturnal, menacing part of my brain a chance to introduce us.

Enough already. With that dead certainty nightmares

bestow on the off-guard mind, I knew my would-be assailant was male and that he was intent on killing me. He was no stranger. In diverse cunning disguises he has stalked my sleep since childhood. However he shape-shifts, I identify him by his deadliest weapon: it takes only his fatal approach to paralyze me. Strong and belligerent when awake, asleep I freeze in my tracks, hapless victim of a homicidal lunatic. Roadkill. I grew myself up to be the opposite of a victim. His capacity to reduce me to a little girl drenching the sheets with sweat and pee shames me.

What most puts me off about Freud is his prurience. Not the silly penis-envy thing. The first Harley I felt thrumming between my thighs banished that. Dream interpretations that encourage me to regard the deadly drill bit as wish fulfillment are fanciful rubbish. Even if it was a *huge* drill bit.

No, Siggie, this nightmare was about dread. Fear of freezing when most I need to be galvanized into self-protection. My putative assailant had been locked *inside* my apartment: the danger lurked within me. After years of hiding, the ancient fear stalker had returned to mock the Warrior Queen, even as she was bringing her body to a degree of fitness it hadn't known since I was a young track star. Dragging every single protesting muscle and sinew into the service of battle — only to be rendered less threatening than a quadriplegic.

Normally I don't like to think positively, to regard whatever shit goes down as a learning experience. Rose-tinted lenses skew your perception of reality. But tonight I brushed aside my reluctance to play Pollyanna and gave even this nightmare an optimistic cast. My body would be ready to take down Pete's destroyer. The gun would help too. It was my brain that was the problem. What if it failed to beep all the right neurons into action? My desire for revenge was pure, and growing stronger. Fear was the only thing that could disable me — it was the only point of entry. And fear could render me as vulnerable as a new-born.

So how could I bully my mind into casting off fear as surely as my body was sloughing off years of neglect and out-right punishment? Now, giving up the Rothmans and the Smithwick's testified to a generous whack of hitherto inaccessible willpower. But could I bulletproof my mind? That I didn't know.

If you cave in, you won't get to write the final chapter.

Who said that? I looked around the bedroom. Nobody here but me and Max. My dog is smart, but a total numskull with language. Where had the words come from? Don't shrinks call such unsolicited voice mails "auditory hallucinations"? For sure, I was cracking up.

The voice spoke again and I recognized it. It was my love. It was Pete. *If you cave in, you won't get to write the final chapter.*

The dead never really go away. They speak to us all the time. Whether we hear them boils down to whether we're listening.

The dead speak most eloquently from the autopsy table. Pete was warning me. *About the paralysis, love — get over it. Or you'll be dead, too.* Nobody could be a better authority than Pete on what this maniac I had set my targets on was capable of doing.

My throat screamed for a cool cascade of beer, my lungs for a nicotine scorch. *What the hell am I supposed to do, Pete? I don't want to turn my back, run away, cower out of sight for the rest of my shabby life — but what if I put myself in the hands of the self-same god who let you die?*

Just when you most need Casper the Friendly Ghost, he bails on you.

My brain was buzzing too fast for falling asleep to be an option. I got out of bed, gave my dog a reassuring hug and stumbled downstairs to brew up some coffee. Spun a Big Mama Thornton CD and sped to the cut called "Nightmare." Three-hundred-pound blues lady wailing alongside a funky tinkle of piano:

> Nightmare, last night I had a nightmare
> I woke up screaming 'cause I was dreaming
> Lord, my man was gone ...
> I feel so blue, my dream came true
> Lord, my man is gone ...

Call me a control freak. Pete got it right about the one thing that could propel me beyond fear of freezing. Better even than Smithwick's had, better than the Continental Dark slipping down my throat, his message soothed me.

What had he said? *Getting to write the final chapter.* I was *living* the book of my life. No fucking way any freak on the planet was going to script my death.

Chekhov said, "Don't introduce a gun into a story unless you plan to use it." I did.

I returned to bed just as the eastern sky was lightening.

Good night, Pete, wherever you are.

CHAPTER 7

MY HEART WILL GO ON.
Celine Dion woke me. Her husband may regard such awakenings as a good thing. I blame it on CBC's need to ratchet up the Canadian content. I'd set the radio alarm just two hours earlier, knowing my need to sleep would overwhelm my internal alarm. Grumpily I reached over to my night table and punched the Off button. Celine's heart mercifully expired.

Before filling the kettle, I let Max out the back door. I used to perform that ritual in reverse order, but age seems to be having a cruel effect on my dog's bladder. He gushed a bucket against the rear fence, then tiptoed through the imaginary tulips, where he deposited several two-drop calling cards. I'm learning from my dog how to keep something vital in reserve.

While Max rooted happily in his bowl of Science Diet, I downed two cups of French Roast, three waffles drenched in maple syrup and five rashers of bacon. Cholesterol City, I know, but surely my body deserves some compensation for the beer-and-nicotine drought. The next hour I divided up between free weights and my exercise bike. I keep them in the basement so visitors won't suspect my dirty fitness secret. Letting go of a dissolute image, years in the crafting, is not easy work.

Ernie arrived just as I was drying my hair, having dressed first. Normally I perform those rituals in reverse order. But Ernie and I have a history — the kind of history that prompts me to greet his visits fully clothed so as to avoid any misunderstanding about my current expectations or desires.

This morning was all about business. After removing a heavy carton from the trunk of his unmarked car, Ernie moved briskly to my door. Max's hostility matched my pleasure at the sight of him setting down the carton.

Ernie accepted my offer of coffee, and we exchanged brief pleasantries. I complimented him on his designer gear, which he knows I hate. He congratulated me for having a good-hair day, to which he knows I am indifferent. Over such hypocrisy our eye contact broke. We were both staring at the carton sitting on the floor between us.

"I like my job, Jane. And I'm really enjoying my promotion. So I don't want it all to end here." His eyes laser-pointed at the carton. "You've got this shit on loan for twenty-four hours. I'll be back same time tomorrow morning to retrieve it. What you do with it in the meantime is your business."

He lifted the lid. "There's thousands of pages in here. Obviously you can't go over them between now and tomorrow morning. So I need you to swear that you'll destroy any copies you make as soon as you've read them. As for giving up where you got these files, should anybody push you to divulge — well, I won't insult you by asking you to repeat the assurance you gave me yesterday."

I nodded from the honest wee corner of my black heart.

"You'll have to trust me that what's in there is the important stuff, Jane. I'd have had to hire a van to deliver *all* the case materials on the rapes and murders. That move would not have escaped even the dumbest constable's notice. Anyway, your beautiful chestnut hair would have turned gray in the time it would take you to sift through all those docs. So I've narrowed it down to six thick binders. The black one contains the investigative summaries for Short Willie's rapes. The four blue ones are all the critical docs related to his first three murders. The stuff for the ... umm ... double homicide I put in a red binder."

He didn't have to tell me why. Red to alert me. Red is for Stop. In the red binder he'd gathered everything relevant to the final murders: Laura and Pete.

"Red is for *proceed with caution,* Jane." He stood up. "Don't overestimate your strength or your new sobriety. What's in there traumatized seasoned homicide cops and crime reporters. Maybe it even freaked out other freaks. Maybe that's why Short Willie is six feet under. Don't even think about going there unless you know you'll be able to come out on the far side with your sanity still intact."

"I hear you." *But I'm not listening.*

Ernie headed for the door, then turned back. "I'm not a cultured guy, Jane. So when some people say a book or a painting or a piece of music changed their lives, I don't know what the hell they're talking about. But I *do* know that everyone who came close to these cases got twisted out of shape."

Max unaccountably restrained himself as we bade good-bye.

I had a lot to do in a short time. My first priority was getting the case materials photocopied. The carton was crammed nearly to its lid. In spite of its horrific contents, no stench of the necropolis filled the room as I removed the binders and set them on the floor. Unopened they appeared innocent as a diligent student lawyer's term notes.

The black binder holding the investigative reports on the rapes I could hold back and study later today. Short Willie had left no doubt in anyone's mind that he was the predator responsible for brutally assaulting at least twelve women. In addition to his confession, the prosecution had hard physical evidence — including DNA and reliable witness statements — to nail him to the wall.

What I wanted from the black binder was information

about the crime scenes, Willie's MO and an impression of his preferred victims. From them I hoped to become familiar with the defining quirks that established him as the author of these horrible crimes. Then, when I turned to the subsequent chapters in his career, after his alleged self-promotion to serial killer, I'd have developed a nose for whether he'd written them, too. *Keep working the literary-detection metaphors,* I told myself, eager to grasp any device that might help distance me from emotions that, if triggered, surely would hobble my capacity for clear thinking.

I ran across the street to catch my neighbor before he left for work. Yang Ling owns a QwikCopy franchise on College Street, in the heart of university territory. The very night a few months ago he'd moved his young family into the row house across from mine, the pipes burst and flooded his basement. I'd come to his assistance and negotiated the best deal I could from my emergency plumber. Once a week since then his daughter knocks at my door and shyly hands me a plate of Chinese sweets.

When I explained my immediate need to copy thousands of pages of highly confidential information, Yang suggested I put my documents in the trunk of his car and ride with him to the shop. Shortly after he opened the door at nine sharp, the huge space filled with anxiety-ridden students.

"Final term papers and exam time," explained Yang. "Most of them are copying notes from students who actually attended class or they're printing out essays they've bought on-line." He led me into his office at the back and gestured to a machine against the rear wall. "That's a high-speed copier with an automatic feeder. Just pile your documents into the tray here and press this button."

I thanked him, then screwed up my nerve to pose an urgent request. "Yang, one of these binders I can't even open. It ... um ... contains things I'm not quite ready to look at. When I'm done copying the four blue binders, could you feed the contents of the red one into the machine for me?"

He looked puzzled but agreed. "Why don't you take a break when you're finished and wander around the campus for a while, then go for lunch? There's a good Indian restaurant four doors west of here. I'll finish up the job while you're eating."

Everything went according to plan, except that when I returned, stuffed with pakoras, tandoori chicken, veg curry, rice and burfi, Yang was retching into a wastepaper bin. "I'm sorry," he apologized. "But those photographs ..."

I felt as if I'd stolen his virginity without giving him a nanosecond of pleasure in return. Chalk up one more normal person to the traumatized list. What so horrified Yang must have been the crime scene and autopsy photos. Of Laura. Of Pete.

Yang had no personal attachment to the victims. I remembered Ernie's warning that I not overestimate my own capacity for dealing with this paper chamber of horrors. *At what cost was I prepared to dismiss it?*

Yang had returned all the case materials to their original binders and packed them and my photocopies into two cartons. I called a cab, after having had to insist on paying my neighbor. His reluctance got overwhelmed by my need to expiate my guilt, however inadequately, for having exposed him to sights most of us go to our graves without viewing. Except at the movies or on TV, where all the corpses get to walk away after the final scene.

CHAPTER 8

I PHONED ERNIE AND ARRANGED to return the binders to his home that evening. Then I took Max for a long run through Trinity-Bellwoods Park a few blocks south of my house. I jogged up and down the deep bowl at the centre of that huge green space until my brain slipped into white-out, the blank slate I needed it to be when I began my study of the rape files.

Max seemed indifferent to my confession that I was leaving him with Silver for a few days while I went away. "Think of all the burgers she'll slip you," I reminded him. Silver is an excellent caregiver, but one day I discovered that she'd been filling his water bowl with Coke. "Works for me," she'd said with a shrug in the face of my objection.

Before plunging into the investigative summaries of Short Willie's sexual assaults, I prepped myself with a battery of protective fictions. *Assume the mindset of a historian, detached and aloof. Your interest in these documents is purely objective. Keep your feelings remote and compartmentalized. Identify with neither predator nor victim.* My mantra was beginning to sound like a job description for the kind of god who, having observed the little sparrow fall, redirects his unperturbed attention to a catastrophic earthquake.

For the next four hours I worked through the black binder, taking careful point-form notes. Whenever some horrific detail threatened to nudge me into empathy for a victim, I pretended she was just a character in a grim psychological thriller, the fictional creation of some writer's overheated imagination. My ruse worked, for the time being.

Driven by whatever demonic force motivates a man to stalk, trap, subdue, torture and otherwise violate a woman, Willie had manifested great cunning but scant imagination. His MO boiled down to repetition with no significant variation — until he grew more fevered near the end. Over time, his savage lust must have built up a tolerance for rapes that began to pale into garden variety, inadequate to sate his bent cravings. In the performance of the final three assaults, he escalated the violence factor and embroidered his handiwork with one horrific new wrinkle.

In late summer 1996 after the arrest of William Shortt, a series of rapes taking place between June 1995 and August of the following year in Toronto ceased. Known as the Lone Raper, a nickname given him by a cheesy journalist for his habit of wearing a mask during the commission of his crimes, he'd embarked on a reign of fear that left the tabloids screeching, "Who is that masked man?" The question was answered when Shortt later confessed to the sexual assault of twelve women during this fourteen-month period.

That summer was even hotter than this one. It was the longest and most oppressive heat wave in the city since Toronto began keeping weather records back in the middle of the nineteenth century. The smog umbrella suspended over our fair city trapped car-exhaust fumes and efficiently recycled them through our lungs. People situated on extreme ends of the age spectrum — infants and the elderly — suffered the worst. Some poorer folks, not buffered by climate-controlled environments, died. People left the doors and windows open, hoping vainly for a current of cool air. Lush green plants, severed from rain forests and transplanted to urban gardens, thrived — along with the Lone Raper.

Driven by the simple need to get a night's sleep, women living alone exchanged the safety of locked ground-floor windows for a cooling draft of air. For a dozen of them, that decision ensured a lifetime plagued by recurring nightmares that no shrink, tranquilizer or sleeping pill ever could erase.

All twelve women rented small ground-floor apartments in low-rise, slightly down-at-the-heels buildings. Not what you'd call "low-rent" dwellings: no such accommodation remains in this city, unless you call a park bench or a shelter "home" — and even those come at a cost. Every year a hundred thousand new residents gravitate to the Big Smog. The existing housing stock has not grown to meet their influx, nor have municipal politicians made the problem a priority.

Without the luxury of central air conditioning, the occupants of these buildings are left to choose between tossing about all night on sweat-soaked beds or leaving themselves open to predation. The Lone Raper caught his victims unawares as they entered their apartments. His point of entry and exit was always the open window. If it was screened, his knife made quick work of that flimsy obstacle. He invariably attacked them from behind and quickly subdued them by holding to their throats the scalpel he later used to remove his trophies.

His first crime set the basic pattern for the following eleven. On June 3, 1995, twenty-year-old Helen Gardner was raped in her ground-floor apartment on Jarvis Street. A 911 call from an anonymous male alerted emergency services to the victim's whereabouts. She was found on her bed, naked, hog-tied with rope and gagged with duct tape. Her assailant had fled the crime scene with what was to become his trademark souvenir: his victim's left nipple, which he'd excised with near-surgical exactitude. The wound was dressed with a crude bandage improvised from one cup severed from Gardner's bra, tightly secured by four crisscrossed strips of duct tape. Before leaving, he virtually sterilized his operating theatre.

His final three crimes repeated this pattern with one variation: Willie made an addition to his collection — his victim's
clitoris. This act of genital mutilation he performed with as
much precision as he excised the left nipple. He was no slasher.

Gardner later described her assailant as a white male of
average height and build. He had been wearing jeans, white
sneakers, blue surgical scrubs, cap and mask, latex gloves and
shoe covers. His weapon was a scalpel. She remembered his eyes
as ice blue and expressionless, his voice a dead monotone, almost
uninflected as it menaced, coaxed and cajoled.

The third rape had sent up a red flag to the investigators:
serial rapist. They promptly enlisted the services of a seasoned
profiler. Virginia Hardy observed that the perpetrator's choice of
trophies might be signifying an attempt to desexualize each victim — to compensate for his own sexual inadequacy by making
her "less a woman." Her insight was strengthened by the fact
that the assailant never exposed his penis. Instead he penetrated
his victims, vaginally and rectally, with whatever "found" object
was at hand in the apartment. He usually improvised with
something he took from the kitchen — a long-necked wine or
condiment bottle, a wooden spoon, barbecue tongs, a turkey
baster, a bone-handled knife sharpener. Once he settled on a bud
vase, which broke in the victim's rectum.

After his arrest, Shortt told police interrogators that schoolyard bullies had taunted him with the nickname "Short Willie."
It stuck. Although a medical examination revealed that he was
endowed with a penis of average proportions, Shortt never
shook the crippling conviction that he was hung no more gen-
erously than a gerbil.

Also of particular interest to the profiler were his surgical
garb and the fact that he went out of his way to ensure than his
victims didn't die from their wounds. The tight bandaging and

his phone alerts indicated a desire that they not bleed to death prior to their subsequent prompt discovery. Given the number of needless risks he took, it seemed evident that he was in this for the ego-boost that such degrading crimes bestow on bent psyches. His MO had been carefully contrived. It gave his crimes a unique "signature," marking him as the author of each and every rape. It further established him as a "writer" far more clever than his peers. The operating-room gear served to disguise enough distinguishing facial features to assure his anonymity. His post-op aseptic procedures removed or contaminated any trace evidence.

The profiler was careful to qualify another of her observations. The surgeon persona pointed to a man eager to elevate his social status — his work with the scalpel was neat but not the mark of a professional. It was also a significant contributing factor to his success in escaping detection. But he could have accomplished the same end simply by blindfolding his victims, all of whom had been subdued from behind before glimpsing him. Instead he went to considerable trouble to ensure that they witnessed his performance. Were spectators to their own violation.

Shortt crafted his crimes as theatre. A highly organized director, he enacted each scene as part of a ritualistic sequence, calmly orchestrating every step in precise accordance with whatever lunatic script governed his vision. Before leaving the stage, he cleaned up with a mania for neat and tidy that is the dream of every roommate, the nightmare of every forensics team.

I took a break to walk Max again. We both needed a walk on the wild side.

While he romped and dispensed pee as if it was holy water, I thought about time and timing. Short Willie had carefully timed his attacks to coincide with the victim's return to her residence from work or school. Obviously he stalked his victims long enough to learn about their schedules and lifestyles. To calculate precisely the time it would take him to enter their apartments, disguise himself and prepare to catch them unawares as they entered the door. They would have been tired after a day's work, leached of any residual energy by the torrid heat and intent on throwing off their damp clothes, enjoying a cool shower and a cold beverage.

Another, albeit unintentional, aspect of Willie's timing abetted his escaping detection: serendipitous history. When he committed his last rape, the Metro Toronto Police Service was just beginning to study the recommendations of a groundbreaking review into the Paul Bernardo investigations. Bernardo, a sadistic serial rapist and killer, had eluded capture entirely due to police error — "systemic failure," in the language of the report (a euphemism for an official cock-up of gargantuan dimensions). Mr. Justice Archie Campbell's recommendations became a blueprint for restructuring the conduct of future serial sexual assault investigations. But it would be another five years before the all the major recommendations were implemented ... and a revision of the species before human error could be eliminated.

History favored Willie a second time. Driven by concern that public awareness of a serial rapist could quickly burgeon into panic, the police made a decision that would knock one more huge dent in their public image. They chose not to warn women in the neighborhood or to take any other steps to protect them.

In her report on a different sexual-assault investigation, another judge made short work of the force's justification that warning potential victims would render them "hysterical" and jeopardize the investigation. One brave victim sued the Board of Commissioners of Police. Madam Justice Jean MacFarland accepted "Jane Doe's" allegation that she and other women had been used as "bait." MacFarland found that the police investigation was irresponsible and grossly negligent: the police had failed utterly in their duty to protect women. Her recommendations to the Toronto Police Services numbered fifty-seven. Again, they came too late to smarten up the sexual assault squad investigating Willie's crimes.

The investigators into Willie's assaults tried hard, and taking into consideration the handicaps under which they laboured, the worst they could be accused of is inefficiency. There was no dedicated system of case management, and no specialized sexual-assault team. The RCMP ViCLAS case linkage system came into being the year following Shortt's conviction. Despite their best efforts, they trailed uselessly in the wake of a very smart rapist.

The cops followed standard protocol. They interviewed the first officer at every scene. And the victim, when and if she'd recovered sufficient emotional stability after medical treatment to speak of her experience. There were never any other witnesses, reliable or otherwise. Nobody saw him lurking, loitering or climbing in or out a window, so nobody could view a lineup of likely suspects or known offenders. Even so, police rounded up and interviewed all high-risk residents within a wide radius of the crime scenes, none of whose MOs manifested even the vaguest resemblance to the perp's. Most had alibis; the others were ruled out for one compelling reason or another.

They examined, photographed, sketched and processed the crime scenes. Of himself, the rapist left behind nothing — no trace evidence, no body fluids, no fingerprints. The crime lab meticulously analyzed the rope and the duct tape Willie had used to truss and gag his victims. Nothing so tricky as embedded calico-cat hairs materialized to put a cunning detective in mind of a feline-loving wanker enshrined in a nonexistent data bank. Reality so often disappoints a TV viewer's expectations.

So many assaults at least provided them ample opportunities for developing a victim profile. Criminologists live in hope that something in a victim's social, medical and mental-health history might point to why she was targeted and maybe help them establish the manner and circumstances of her assault. When they luck out, the victim profile focuses an investigation.

A veteran criminologist made a thorough study of all available information on the women: race, age, height, weight, family, friends, acquaintances, education, employment, residence and neighborhood. Included in his reckoning was background information about their history and lifestyle: overall personal habits, hobbies, criminal and medical histories.

Here, too, Willie disappointed the experts. The victim composite was no more helpful than the rapist's description as a white male, twenty to fifty years old, of average height and build with blue eyes and a boring voice. All his victims were white, or close enough to it they wouldn't be perceived otherwise. Most fell within the twenty-to-forty age range — although one victim, a diabetic, was old enough to have suffered a near-fatal heart attack during her violation. Like him, their physical appearance could only be generalized as average. Some tall, some short, most in between. Some fat, some thin, most in between. Some blond-haired, some black, most brown. Blue, hazel, brown or black-eyed — he wasn't picky.

The victims' relationships with family, friends and acquaintances spanned the normal range from functional to moderately dysfunctional. Some were college/university students, others were employed in a variety of jobs from hair stylist to lab technician. One was unemployed, a woman on disability benefits, confined by multiple sclerosis to a wheelchair (from which Willie had thoughtfully removed her to work his worst). Nothing exceptional in their lifestyles. No criminal records (excepting two convictions, one for possession of marijuana, the other for inciting to riot during an anti-poverty demo).

Their sole exceptionality was having fallen prey to a sadist.

Liberal psychology has it that few sane men could ever perpetrate the kind of assaults to which William Shortt freely confessed. The record shows that ruthless interrogation was not needed. The interviews were conducted by the book. As the audiotape began to roll, Willie jumped up to the mike and claimed bragging rights. He recounted his crimes detail by abominable detail, pausing only infrequently to consult his mental photo album. Other aides-mémoire he led the cops to when they searched his house.

He directed them to a large ceramic cookie jar in the shape of a clown's head atop his refrigerator. In it they found his collection: a dozen nipples and three clitorises, in varying stages of desiccation. Innocuous as dehydrated chickpeas and sun-dried tomatoes — until the poor cops realized precisely what was rattling around in the jar.

I whistled for Max to return to my side, chuckling as he delayed his response long enough to terrorize another squirrel. How I envy my mutt his curiosity that extends beyond nothing he can't handle, his leashed-in daring, the blind trust he extends to me. His innocence of cookie jars gone wrong.

CHAPTER 9

MY PARTNER AND I RETURNED to find Silver ensconced on my sofa, centered in the concavity her body has impressed into the middle cushion over the years, empress of all she surveyed. She was sucking back a Coke as she read from the rape file. Setting it down on the coffee table as if it was a clump of used toilet tissue from which she badly wanted to distance herself, she looked up at me and my dog. Her eyes came equipped with night sights.

"Normal people read stuff from the best-seller list. If this collection of short stories fell into the hands of a normal person, I'd be sending her off to a shrink. You are already crazy, Jane Yeats, so I'm sending you off to Manitoulin."

Max bounded over to Silver, braked just short of her knees and fawned. This unseemly display left me wishing I'd trained him to express more than his bladder and bowels outdoors.

"What makes you think I need a holiday?"

She reached into her backpack for another Coke. "Who said anything about a holiday? Manitoulin is where you get to go instead of the rehab clinic I should have booked you into last week."

"So give me the brochure."

"No problem. Isolated cabin owned by a friend of mine. Miles away from any beer store or nicotine dispenser. Close to another friend of mine who will ensure that you don't relapse. Wildflowers, trees, rocks and water. Canoe. Just the place to plow your way through your gory reading list — *without falling off the wagon.*"

Why argue? Silver had scored some major points, not the least of them being my strong urge to hit on the Dundalk Tavern for a pint or five of hopsy oblivion. Anyways, I always lose when we duel. That's why she and Etta have forged a life-long bond. "So give me a map and the keys."

She reached into the front pocket of her backpack. "Here's the map. No keys because the cabin doesn't have a lock. Toronto it ain't." She tossed me another bit of paper. "Here's the ferry schedule. Now's their busiest time of year, so I've booked you for the 1:30 p.m. departure Monday from Tobermory. You should leave here no later than seven in the morning."

She crushed her pop can between fingers strong enough to poke holes in concrete, levitated her bulk from the sofa with the grace of a fawn and bored those night sights into my retinas. "So be there for the ferry. I'll come around to pick up Max Sunday night at nine."

When she left I got right back to Short Willie's rapes. There were leads. Thousands of leads. Many got lost in the ensuing avalanche of paperwork. Those that were followed up on led to women with genuine axes to grind against violent partners who proved to be innocent of little save having committed the par-ticular rapes under investigation, disgruntled ex-girlfriends and wives with faux axes but real grievances, cranks and dead-ends. And the usual loony-tunes sobbed buckets of remorse over crimes they only wished they'd committed.

Willie's victims had only two features in common: they were accessible and they lived alone.

A miscalculation around the last fact should have terminat-ed Short Willie's rape spree. In our times, to live alone is not to be unpartnered. His final victim, Sharon Melrose, had a boyfriend who kept the key to her apartment tucked into the pocket of his jeans. On August 24, following a night's revelry at a nearby sports bar, Bill Sanderson and his buddies staggered off after the Blue Jays' victory in high hopes of getting laid. Sanderson let himself into Sharon's apartment just as Willie was depositing his trophies into a Baggie. This unscripted intrusion left Willie with no option but sudden flight. He was obliged to forgo his post-op Molly Maid routine. While the boyfriend froze in his tracks at the bloody spectacle of his partner taped and trussed across her bed, Willie made a hasty exit through the bedroom window.

He frantically tore off the surgical gear outside Sharon Melrose's window. In his haste to discard his costume, maybe Willie forgot that his mask was smeared with damning DNA.

All day I'd been putting off phoning Etta. She'd demand an explanation for my vacating the city for a few days. More for my protection than hers, I wanted to avoid alarming her. Already she'd twigged to the fact that I was rooting around the circumstances of Pete's murder. If she further guessed my investigation might involve studying the grim details surrounding his death, she'd nail my feet to the floor.

Mom was so caught up in her latest project that the news of my trip barely registered. "I guess you seen in the paper that the Roy Rogers–Dale Evans museum is up for sale, eh?"

"Uh, no, I missed it. Must have been too busy packing and all. You're not thinking of buying it, are you?"

She snorted. "It's in the friggin' Mohave Desert. But I'll tell you what I am going to buy — Trigger and Bullet."

Please, God, tell me it's not Alzheimer's. "Mom, don't let anybody scam you. Trigger and Bullet died years before Roy and Dale got elevated to the Big Ranch."

"Ya think I don't know that? Point is, Roy had them stuffed

and mounted. Trigger and Bullet was on exhibit in the muse-um. I got a contact in California who's going to put in a bid for me. He told me they might try and sell them separate, but I fig-ure no way anybody's gonna go that sacrilegious. I mean, that would be as bad as sending two orphans off to different foster homes."

"Well ... good luck. Should you get lucky, have you thought about where you might put them?"

She paused to flick her Bic and suck a Cameo. "Yep. I even drew a little sketch. On the wall to the right of the stage — I'm going get my carpenter to build a ... what do ya call that thing around the Nativity scene?"

Yegawds. "A crèche?"

"That's it."

I told her I'd be back by Sunday.

"Happy trails, dear."

As I was gingerly hanging up the phone, Silver stopped by with her van to pick up Max, his food supply and favorite bone.

"Have a productive stay. You'll like it up there. Just make sure you don't drive yourself over the edge with all your sum-mer beach reading." She pulled me into a generous hug.

"Silver, aren't you just the slightest bit nervous about being on TV tomorrow night?" My friend had been selected to receive a National Aboriginal Achievement Award. Silver is one of the finest artists in this country. Any recognition that comes her way is so well deserved.

"Nope."

"What are you going to wear?" I'd seldom seen her in any-thing but a paint-smeared T-shirt and oversize denim overalls.

She grinned. "Remember that dress Halle Berry wore to the Academy Awards a while back? I got a local designer to do a knock-off for me."

"You'll be arrested for indecent exposure." Curled up, Halle Berry could fit into one cup of Silver's bra.

"That's the plan."

Max ran ahead of her to the door.

"Stay sober, eh?"

CHAPTER 10

THE FIVE BINDERS FIT NICELY into Harley's Beetle Bags.
I dressed for my trip with no less fussy a sense of ritual than a
gay priest preparing to celebrate Easter Mass. The Levi's, Aran
sweater salvaged from the Goodwill and hockey socks were mere
primer for my leather chaps, biker jacket (with "action back for
ease of movement," promised the catalog), boots and Road King
Classic gloves (featuring an "ergonomic thumb for added mobil-
ity and gel-padded palm for anti-vibration"). I tucked up my
long curls into a helmet way more threatening than anything
Queen Maeve ever could have fantasized.

The bill for this armor might have bought me a fetching
designer cocktail dress, heels and gold earrings from Holt
Renfrew. But the *femme* look is about exposure, décolletage and
attention getting. My Harley-Davidson MotorClothes guaran-
tee protection and anonymity.

My mother tells me my bike and its matching apparel gen-
der-bend me in ways she finds decidedly unalluring. That's the
point, of course: fully geared up astride six-hundred-plus
pounds and 115 horses of long, low and raked machine, I'm a
formidable dragster. My bike is a carapace, even my head pok-
ing out of it shielded and aggressive. Stripped of anybody's perception of Jane Yeats as a woman, as a creature vulnerable to
attack ... as prey.

Out of the city, I cruised along highways and country roads,
my feet way forward on the pegs, boots in the breeze. As Harley

gobbled up the miles between home and destination, my normally hyperactive brain meandered on about the venerable history of my wheels. The original Harleys were designed to replace the horse on the vast and rugged American terrain once ruled by John Wayne. Resilient enough for farmhands, those old darlings could be repaired by a blacksmith. My surrogate beast is more cyborg than horse. God forbid anything should happen to her — it would take a neurosurgeon to repair the damage.

I christened her Maeve.

We roared north for four hours until we reached Tobermory at the tip of the Bruce Peninsula. Maeve started out with a full tank, so I had to stop only once en route to top up the premium. The two-hour ferry ride on *Chi-Cheemaun* landed us at South Baymouth on Manitoulin's south shore by 4:00 p.m. Another hour and I was dismounting, back stiff and bone weary, at my destination.

The weathered log cabin that awaited me, nestled in old-growth pines and cedars, fit so unobtrusively into its environment that it might have sprouted there as naturally as the ferns and wildflowers that twined up to its edges. I let myself into a huge room dominated by a ceiling-high stone fireplace. Behind it lay a small kitchen, bedroom and loo. The cabin was simple without being Spartan, a perfect space for retreat.

Peaceful as it was, I did not expect to find repose here. I unpacked my saddlebags. The murder files had left only enough room for a few clothes. If I wanted to eat, I'd have to head out for groceries.

As I set the files on a long harvest table, I noticed an envelope addressed to me propped up against a vase bursting with wildflowers. Inside was a note from Silver's friend Martin Chee Chee, offering a few instructions about where to find essential stuff and inviting me to help myself to whatever food remained in his cupboards and fridge. On inspection, the kitchen appeared to have been recently stocked. Grateful that I could postpone my shopping, I decided to make my way down the steep embankment leading to the lake.

The sun was still warm on my skin. Noting with delight a canoe pulled well out of the water and tethered by a long rope to the base of a small birch, I strolled along the rocky shoreline, greedily inhaling clean air and a humusy fragrance of leaves, moss, bark and newly unfurled ferns. Only lapping waves, birdsong and the occasional exuberantly leaping fish punctuated the silence. For the first time in years I'd be able to watch the sun rise and set, lose myself in a night sky pierced by stars unobscured by city lights. Dared I hope for the northern lights? Was it the right time of year? Perhaps Mother Nature would tranquilize me so well that tonight I would fall into a deep restorative sleep. I'd need it after looking into the nightmare files.

My feet were cramped from ten hours' imprisonment in my boots. I liberated them, pulled off my socks and rolled up my jeans. The water near the shore was warmer than I'd anticipated.

What the hell. My hair and skin were grimy with road dust. So off came all my clothes. Slipping and stumbling over algae-glazed stones, I ran a few yards into the water before diving beneath the surface. Mother of God. It was so cold that I came up gasping. I swam with strong, hard strokes well into the lake, then turned and swam parallel to the shoreline. Carefree as a sea otter — sans insulating fat. Before hypothermia could make any serious inroads, I returned to the beach, grabbed my clothes and beat a hasty path up to the cabin. A huge blazing fire would be just the thing.

I made my naked way straight to the pile of kindling and stacked logs beside the fireplace. As I reached for a box of matches on the mantel, a voice from nearby said, "Um ... excuse me."

Grabbing the longest log I could get my hands on, I swung round to do battle. A tiny crone rose from the sofa, eyes aglitter with mischief.

She grinned. "My name is Shirley Scarecrow. Silver told me you were coming today. I came to say hello and make sure you have everything you need."

Nothing in Shirley's demeanor alluded to my nudity. *Why should I introduce the subject?* "I'm Jane." When she extended her hand, I crossed the floor to grasp it. That's when she began to laugh — so hard that her diminutive body shook her back onto the sofa. Her glee was contagious. We were both still in stitches as I finished tugging on my jeans and sweater.

When she returned from the kitchen with a pot of tea I had an impressive fire going. Although I'd come up here for the solitude, I soon found myself happily abandoning myself to Shirley's company. She told me some wonderful stories about the history of the island. Her Ojibwa ancestors were from the Wikwemikong Reserve on the eastern end of Manitoulin. In 1836 a treaty had promised Native people the island as a refuge. Less than thirty years later, the government wanted more land for white settlement. A second treaty was offered: in exchange for ceding their lands to the government, each family head would receive one hundred acres.

"They had no manners, my people," Shirley said with a chuckle. "They didn't want to give up their ancestral lands in exchange for a few cottage lots, so they refused to sign the treaty. Today ours is the only unceded reserve in Canada. Three hundred square miles and not many more people living there than get stuffed into a high-rise apartment building in Toronto. The rez is a real mix of traditional and modern. You can buy everything from beadwork to submarine sandwiches. If you don't visit Wikwemikong this trip, Jane, you should come back in August for our powwow."

"Thank you. I'd like that," I said, gratefully sipping the hot tea.

"I can see you're tired." She rose from the sofa, not a trace of arthritis apparent in her fluid movements. "Silver said you were planning on doing a lot of studying while you're here. So I won't be interrupting your work. Kagawong, the village a couple of miles down the road, has got most everything you'll need — gas station, grocery store, some shops, a post office, marina, even a library and art gallery. LCBO's right next to the church, but I think Silver put your name on their shit list."

She extended her arm due east. "If you want to visit me, I'm along the bay there, behind that clump of birches just before the big outcropping. Easiest way to get to my place is by canoe. And the fishing's real good around here. Jumbo perch, bass, whitefish, pike, chinook, near every kind of trout. If you feel like trying your luck, I'll take you out in my boat. We could have a good fry-up one night."

"How are you getting home?"

"Along the trail. There's still enough fire left in the sun to keep me from tripping over the tree roots."

I stood outside to watch her straight back disappear into the forest.

CHAPTER 11

I WOKE UP AT SUNRISE AND TREATED myself to morning coffee on the mammoth granite rock guarding the shoreline. Through a cloudless sky the sun worked its slow ascent over sapphire water that refracted its rays into gently undulating spikes of fire. Over old hardwood forest dense with maple, basswood, birch and ash, its floor carpeted with trilliums, lilies of the valley, violets, jacks-in-the-pulpit, and more species of fern than I have fingers. Over the thick green moss climbing the rising rock faces. Over me. A gentle benison unknown to me in the Big Smoke.

Intent on breakfast, an osprey hovered, then dove toward the surface of the lake. Just before hitting the water, he swung his legs forward and bent his wings back, then plunged feetfirst into the water. Grasping a fish in his talons, he soared away.

Throwing off my oversize T-shirt, I hopped into the water. When it met my chin, I began to swim. And so I continued until my arms sagged with fatigue.

Back on shore, I collected some flat stones and skipped them across the water. For a few moments I revisited childhood, counting every bounce, challenging myself with each toss to get the next one to skip longer and farther. As I gripped the last stone my eye caught something embedded in it. A tiny intact fish skeleton. I put it in my pocket. Today it will serve as a paperweight, perhaps as an amulet when I need solid grounding.

Prior to his confession, both sides of the criminal justice system were vying to stake their claim on Willie's brain. The Crown needed to establish his fitness to stand trial. Defense attorney B. B. Claiborne was surely hoping his client would turn out to be a victim of childhood sexual abuse, a sufferer from a fried gene or grievous head injury that had scrambled his moral programming, a schizophrenic who refused to take his meds, or the spawn of a remote mother and alcoholic father. In other words, a tragically misunderstood nobody driven to commit the unspeakable by forces utterly beyond his control.

Willie, already a celebrity, got sent to Penetanguishene for a thirty-day psychiatric assessment. He read the transfer as an invitation to further enhance his profile. This he accomplished in spades by elaborating on his original confession to twelve rapes. He had, he proudly admitted, also murdered five people. The assessment team found him polite, cooperative — and fit to stand trial.

I began with the newspaper clippings detailing the first three murders.

> May 29, 1996 — Police are investigating the death of Linda Bailey, 31, who was found early this morning in her apartment close to College and Bathurst. The building superintendent called police to the scene after receiving complaints from residents about a bad smell.
>
> Police said only that the victim had been strangled. No other details were forthcoming.
>
> Bailey moved to Toronto from Liverpool ten years ago to join her brother, who was studying engineering at the University of Toronto. She worked for the past six years as executive assistant at the Ontario Association of Physiotherapists.

Executive Director Frances Ridpath said that Linda Bailey was a valued employee who will be sorely missed by her friends and colleagues. Bailey, who leaves no children, recently separated from her husband.

Eileen O'Donnell, who lives nearby, said that Bailey's neighbors were shocked by her murder. "Palmerston is a special street in a historic neighborhood. One does not expect such appalling things to happen here. Personally speaking, I am very troubled by the conversion of some lovely old homes into rental units. This can bring riffraff into the community."

The victim's parents are traveling to Toronto from their home in Liverpool. Her brother, Julian, currently employed by Waterfront Systems, was unavailable for comment.

June 22, 1996 — Police are investigating the death of Ruth Rosenberg, 25, who was found last night in her Kensington Market apartment. A close friend of the deceased, Janet Davies, went to her apartment for a planned dinner date. When Rosenberg failed to answer the door, her friend entered the unlocked apartment and discovered the body. She immediately alerted 911.

Police said only that the victim had been strangled. No other details were forthcoming.

Rosenberg was a third-year student at the Ontario College of Art and Design. Faculty member Gunter Frobel said that Ruth Rosenberg was the most promising student he'd ever taught. Rosenberg's photographs were featured in the annual exhibition of student work held this May. One of her photographs drew considerable controversy at the time for its gritty depiction of a sexual encounter in a laneway. Toronto's Dark/Pixel Gallery had scheduled a show for late summer of photographs shot in Rosenberg's Kensington Market neighborhood. A documentary exploring lesbian erotic domination, directed and produced by Rosenberg and Davies, won an award in this year's Hot Docs festival.

The victim is survived by her parents, Mark Rosenberg and Caitlin Shanahan, of Saltspring Island, and by her brother, Jonathan, a plastic surgeon living in Toronto. Her family was unavailable for comment.

Fellow students are planning a candlelight vigil to be held at the College on Friday evening.

Police are continuing their investigation into the murder of Linda Bailey, found strangled in her apartment on May 29. "It's simply impossible to draw any links between these two unfortunate deaths at this point in time," commented Gail Trillin, media relations contact for the department.

July 17, 1996 — Police are investigating the death of Sandra Priest, 28, who was found late this morning in her West End apartment after she failed to show up for work.

Police said only that the victim had been strangled. No other details were forthcoming.

Priest worked as a nurse at Toronto's Hospital for Sick Children. Last year she was a key witness in the trial of Joyce Bates, convicted in the deaths of three infants in the hospital's intensive care unit. Priest's testimony was critical to the Crown's case against the defendant, and she was credited with the apprehension of a "mercy killer" who might well have gone on to commit further murders.

"Sandra was a most able nurse and a very brave woman," said Sophie Clark, who attended nursing school with the victim and worked with her at the hospital. "As soon as she sensed that something was terribly wrong on the ward, she came forward with her suspicions. Given the climate at the time, she knew she could have been putting her own career on the line."

Earlier this year the victim's parents, Dennis and Martha Barker, were killed in a tragic car accident when returning to Oakville from their Muskoka cottage. Priest had no siblings.

Priest's death marks the third in what may be a series of recent strangulations in the Toronto area. Police are continuing their investigations into the murders of Linda Bailey, 31, found strangled in her apartment on May 29, and Ruth Rosenberg, 25, discovered in similar circumstances on June 22. Criminologists generally agree that three murders point to a serial killer. "We are investigating the possibility of a serial killer, of course, " remarked Gail Trillin, media relations contact for the department. "But so far we have no firm evidence to indicate that this is a likelihood."

Trillin did offer the following advice: "Nonetheless, we are strongly advising all women in the city, especially those living alone, against opening their doors to strangers. None of the victims' residences showed any signs of forced entry. So we believe that the killer probably talked his way into their apartments. Do not, under any circumstances, invite a stranger — however persuasive he may be, into your home. We are also recommending that women living alone keep their windows locked night and day — in spite of the heat."

I studied the murder books for each case. Not to put too fine a critical point on the police conduct, my inner scholar quickly picked up the subtext: "The Complete Idiot's Guide to Screwing Up a Murder Investigation." Investigators had summarily genuflected at each station of the procedural cross. Could it be that the police had been demoralized and distracted by the current round of allegations of corruption against the force? All three investigations would have been surefire candidates for an independent inquiry, had not Short Willie confessed.

Basic crime scene protocol was adhered to — in minimalist fashion. The first officer at the scene was interviewed. The primary crime scene, the bedroom where each body was located, had been examined to identify potential evidence. Ditto the other rooms of the apartment. Only a rudimentary check of the area where the suspect had entered and left the building was made: the area was too large and police resources were limited. Photographs were taken of the overall scene and of any seeming evidence. A crime-scene technician sketched the layout and positions of the victim and evidence. The physical evidence had been identified, evaluated and collected for analysis at the crime lab.

Within the first twenty-four hours police had talked to possible witnesses, canvassing the occupants of each residence. Nobody had seen or heard anything untoward to alert them to a murder taking place within their building. Most kept to themselves and knew the other occupants' names only from their mailboxes.

Forensic testing of the scant evidence yielded not a thing to rival the astounding findings that routinely get zinged at *CSI* fans.

The three murder books were thinner than I'd expected. Normally every action the police take relative to an investigation generates a report: interviews, follow-ups, evidence. Ernie told me he'd culled from the files everything that seemed inconsequential. I'd have to check up on what he'd weeded out when I got back to Toronto.

My brain felt as clogged as a Trivial Pursuit champ's. Today's study had accomplished one good thing: finally I had a sense of how to make my investigation workable. Today it didn't seem to matter a big damn that I lacked the resources of the police, whether they chose to reopen one or all three of these cases. The fourth case — contained in the red-alert binder I would postpone looking into until tomorrow — was the one I'd focus on.

Assuming that Pete simply had been in the wrong place at the wrong time, Laura stood out as more than collateral damage. To figure out who might have killed her, I needed to find out a lot more about her life — family, friends, colleagues ... and lovers. And there I could have an edge. People who might not have fully disclosed what they knew about her to the police might be more inclined to confide in me. I was linked to Pete who was linked to Laura.

Laura's father, Dr. Rodney Payne, could be a good contact. I had a blurred memory of having met him at the police station following the discovery of the bodies. Like me, he had probably been in such an advanced state of shock that nothing much was being picked up on his radar. I do remember his near-hysterical insistence that the police do everything in their power to ensure that the media be kept at bay.

And Laura was a clinical psychologist. I'd look into her colleagues at the time.

All that would bring Pete back into the frame. En route, it might bring his relationship with Laura into a more detailed view. *Was I ready for that?*

We'd last been together twelve hours before he died. My plans for breakfast in bed went the way of the dodo bird when Pete said he'd happily settle for a breast in place of a grapefruit. The activity that ensued called for an athlete's high-carb intake, but we managed to complete the course with not a trace of nutrients or supplements in our systems.

Whenever we made love, we romped and frolicked with childlike innocence accompanied by very grown up expertise. That last morning of our togetherness, I expressed my amazement that our desire had survived the long haul. Pete grinned. "Love, woman — that's the engine."

I sang him a few bars of "You Make Me Feel like a Natural Woman" before showering and racing off to interview the ex-wife of a judge convicted for murdering his trophy girlfriend. I was researching a book on Hizzoner's injudicious proclivities.

Shortly after seven I arrived home with a takeout carton laden with sushi and four bottles of Japanese beer, determined to file the ex-wife's bilious recollections for attention another day. I discovered a hastily scrawled note from Pete taped to the hall mirror: "Jane: Called out on URGENT [underscored three times] business. Home ASAP. Aftertaste of grapefruit lingered all day. Looking forward to same breakfast menu tomorrow — or a late-night snack! You are my reason for being. Love you, Pete."

From the outset of our relationship, we'd naturally fallen into a practice of never inquiring into the other's whereabouts. What we shared of the time we spent apart was offered up on a strictly volunteer basis. The trust between us was that complete.

Two hours later I ran to the door to greet him, figuring he'd forgotten his keys in his haste to hare off wherever. One glance at the faces of the two detectives told me more than I've ever needed to know about anything, including the existence of God.

Pete's murder shattered my trust in most everything. *If I discovered that his life had a shadow side, could I go there?* Yes, I could. I knew that nothing in Pete's life, known or unknown, would ever change how I felt about him or how much I loved him. I trusted him even after death did us part. *But could I trust myself?* My capacity to absorb shock has always been an important tool in my survival kit. But the moment Urquhart broke the news, survival dropped a couple of places lower on my list of priorities. All my capacities tanked.

But now the equation had altered. Knowing Pete's killer was out there laughing at me had brought my will to live back with a surge of rage that went right to my head. Someone said that revenge is a dish best eaten cold. Today my platter was white-hot. My lust for revenge would carry me through long enough to exterminate Pete's killer.

I ran deep into the woods, tripping over ancient tree roots and swatting aside irksome branches. Soon I found myself sobbing a line from a Gordie Lightfoot song. "When the green, dark forest was too silent to be real. Too silent to be real ... "

On that island everything about me was dense with renewal. I was embraced by burgeoning green. Nature's reward to Canadians for enduring Siberian-brutal winters. And I came there to study death.

Would this quest of mine be worth the emotional expense? What would be its outcome? Could I stop now, even if I wanted to? I had reached a point of obsession, and I couldn't think beyond it to a space where peace of mind might prevail.

And when I found the murdering scumbag? Was I really capable of taking a life? In a voice as resolute as Moses', I declaimed to the trees. "A malignant life form is different. You do not hesitate to expunge it." My mission landed me on Old Testament terrain. An eye for an eye. A life for a life. One worthless killer losing his life to pay for the stolen lives of at least two innocents. You could almost say the bastard would be getting a bargain.

What if I found him in the company of someone he loves? Should I wipe out that person as well, just to even things up? *Not a problem:* it is impossible to believe that a creature utterly devoid of compassion could even begin to fathom love for another.

"Vengeance is mine!" I shouted to the silent lake. Could that be so wrong? Where was the Lord that horrible night? Had no vigilant guardian angel been assigned to the watch? Guess they were too busy taking care of other business to protect my love. But now there was an avenging angel. Me.

That unholy day I renewed my vow to solve Pete's murder — and Laura's. I imagined feeling the gun in my hands, felt the kick as I fired it. My brain was spinning faster than a dervish. I realized I was going to do it. As for what happened after that, I really didn't care.

CHAPTER 12

SHIRLEY WAS SITTING ON THE PORCH STEP when I staggered on limp legs back to the cabin.

"Something I never understood." The twinkle of her eyes told me she understood all too well. "When the university people write about our legends, they say the creatures in them are just symbols ... metaphors for our deepest fears and longings. Because we had no science, we didn't understand about nature. We tried to control the world by calling on the supernatural."

"Makes sense to me, Shirley."

She laughed, her vocal cords a musical instrument. "Maybe that's what I'm doing when I paint.

"I don't know what our friend Silver told you about me," she continued, her eyes scanning the lake. "But I left the reserve for the big city when I was just a kid. It was on the streets of Toronto that I met the evil spirits. Booze and drugs and hunger aren't metaphors. Up here I can find the four directions with my eyes closed. Up here it's easy to remember where you come from, how you fit in. Down there I lost track of all that. I almost died.

"Down there I step into bear traps."

She slapped my knee. "In time I found my way back home. I guess the only real teaching I brought back with me was that the Windigo lives inside of you, if you let yourself grow weak enough for him to make a home there."

"Tell me about the Windigo." It seemed I'd been granted

the loan of another grandmother to fill my needy ears with ancestral legends.

"In the old days our people sometimes starved in the wintertime. If someone became so hungry that he broke tribal custom and ate the flesh of another person, the spirit of the Windigo inhabited him. The Windigo rides the winter wind and howls like no human. Some say his heart is made of ice. He stalks the forests searching for lost hunters. He eats them when darkness falls.

"When he finds a host, the same thing happens to him: his heart turns to ice. He can't feel human emotions. He becomes violent and no longer fit to be with healthy folks. He endangers the whole community."

We moved into the cabin while I brewed a pot of tea. Shirley glanced over at the old harvest table that was serving as my desk. "I looked at the papers you'd spread across the table there. I guess it was the photographs of those young women's bodies that put me in mind of the Windigo. That killer you're hunting, Jane: don't get too close to him. The shape-shifter knows many paths to your spirit — even dreaming of him or hearing him pass by opens up a door. No one is ever the same after encountering the Windigo. He plays with your vision."

Ernie had warned me that everyone connected with the murders attributed to Short Willie got twisted out of shape.

"There are four realms of human existence on the medicine wheel. They should be kept in balance. But I'm thinking of those two you especially need to remember. The North is your physical self, the Warrior. The South is your spirit, the Healer. Looking at you now, I get the feeling that your Warrior has battled your Healer to the ground."

"But surely it takes a warrior to defeat the Windigo." *How could I have imagined I was going to kill anybody?*

"One Ojibwa story tells us that a medicine man named Big

Goose killed the Windigo by turning into Missahba the giant. But he only did it with the help of Manitou. Others believed that the only way to kill the Windigo was to burn the body of its host into ashes."

"Thank you. Silver doesn't tell me stories like that. In fact, Silver doesn't talk much at all — except when she's angry with me. She says if she needed to chatter, she'd either be a writer or the Mohawk Nation's answer to Oprah Winfrey."

Shirley chuckled. "Silver knows the stories of our people. If you look real close, you'll see them dancing in the background of her paintings. But she's a new generation. She mixes tradition with what she sees in the city. Everything I paint is built around the circle. The Sacred Hoop, the symbol of Mother Earth. It's how I honor the importance of grandparents, the family, mother and child. It's a safe circle I've chosen. Our friend Silver is one brave woman. Her work takes us into the darkness beyond that circle of kindness and comfort. She's brave like you're brave. So now I've got two friends to worry about."

She left me with a small book of Native legends for children. I settled in beside the dying fire and read them aloud. Her exquisite illustrations brought each tale to exuberant life. *Would I ever grow into the strength to let such redemptive light back into my heart?* I knew true lightness of being as a child when I wandered alone into the woods on summer days, clambered down the banks of a small river, lay on my belly, fists propping up my chin and watching, time suspended, as a corps of water spiders skittered across the sun-dappled surface, delicate dancers against a scrim of marsh marigolds.

Just when I thought I'd lost it forever, lightness returned to my world in the form of Pete ... then it fled, tugging in its wake my man and all our luminous possibilities.

Oo–AH–ho. oo–AH–ho. oo–AH–ho.

When the loon cries, the whole lake is attentive.

Oo–AH–ho. oo–AH–ho. oo–AH–ho.

His nocturnal lament unpleats the surface of the water, planes over the rocky shore, rises to lose itself somewhere deep in a clutch of evergreen.

My head tilts moonward, an involuntary keening escapes my throat, mingles with the bird's mourning. I rededicate myself to driving out the Windigo.

Oo–AH–ho. oo–AH–ho. oo–AH–ho.

Over this vast and broody wilderness, a darkness deeper than any personal sorrow prevails.

CHAPTER 13

I DECIDED TO REVIEW ALL THE DOCUMENTS in the red binder and to analyze them in the manner I hoped the homicide investigators followed. Scrunching my eyes almost shut, I assembled the crime scene and autopsy photos into a pile, which I turned facedown, knowing that if I looked at them first, I would be able to go no further.

I studied the crime-scene diagrams, read the autopsy, forensic and toxicology reports, and the police reports. There were no witness statements.

The investigative summary told me very little I hadn't already gleaned from Sam's articles. I skimmed through it.

VICTIMS	Laura Payne, female white, 28 years old
	Peter Findley, male white, 29 years old
DATE	August 30, 1996
LOCATION	364 Logan Drive, 2nd floor apartment of house (victim's residence)
HISTORY	The victims' bodies were discovered in Payne's bedroom after the police acted on a missing person report filed by her father, Dr. Rodney Payne. The autopsies revealed that Payne had died of manual strangulation and that Findley had died of massive trauma to the head.

Next I checked out the newspaper articles, which proved what I had suspected when I first read Sam's two terse and discreet contributions. My friend must have been protecting me. Given that he is the best crime reporter in the city and that his sources outrival his colleagues', Sam would have been privy to all the information the police were willing to leak — that much, and more.

Other reporters did not forgo specifics. All mentioned how brutal the crime was. *What the hell were the lead investigators thinking when they released these details?* No one knew better than they the importance of preserving confidentiality in ongoing cases.

One paper reported that the police chief had informed the public that a $10,000 reward was being offered for any information leading to the killer. "This particular crime is one of the most brutal I have seen in my career." Other reporters wrote fanciful fictions about victim impact based on no input at all from me or from Laura's father, who had apparently also remained unavailable. I wanted to talk to him.

The bodies had been sent to the Centre for Forensic Sciences for full forensic autopsies.

AUTOPSY: LAURA PAYNE

28 years old

5' 2"

120 pounds

Found dead on the floor of her bedroom on August 30, 1996.

The number, severity, locations and orientation of these injuries are indicative of death as a result of manual strangulation.

The results boiled down to this. There was no bruising to her vaginal and rectal areas that would be consistent with vaginal and anal rape. No semen was found in either area. It was clear she lived for several minutes after the attack.

The next report I read in detail. It began with the simple facts.

AUTOPSY: PETER FINDLEY

29 years old

6' 2"

175 pounds

Found dead on the floor of Laura Payne's bedroom on August 30, 1996.

The number, severity, locations and orientation of these injuries are indicative of multiple impacts received as a result of beating. Cause of death was blunt-force trauma.

It went on to itemize each injury. I flinched at every one of them, recalling how gently we had caressed each other, remembering the tender regard for flesh and bone that love engenders.

Brutal crimes defy understanding by ordinary people whose knowledge of violence derives from their experience of accidents or TV viewing.

Again I had placed myself within range of unspeakable acts. But this time it was deeply personal. And yet again my puzzlement at how any human being could commit such deeds, then get on with the business of everyday life, utterly bewilders me.

The basic crime reconstruction strongly indicated that Laura was dead — or so close to expiring as to no longer matter — when Pete entered her apartment. The killer probably had other designs on her body, but Pete's intrusion led him to grab whatever blunt weapon was at hand and turn it on Pete. Given that Pete was a strong and very fit man, my guess was that the killer had enough time to conceal himself, perhaps behind the door, when Pete knocked and knocked.

Damage to Pete's hands and arms indicated that he did not go gentle into that horrible night, but with one hell of a battle.

Having read that much and survived by putting my brain on automatic pilot, I reached for the dreaded crime-scene and autopsy photos. Fully expecting that they would drive me into total insanity, I was surprised to discover that their impact was minimal: these two people looked nothing like they had in life. I pretended these mauled incarnations were stills from a schlock horror movie.

Laura's once-pretty face had been brutalized into a lurid death mask. Her face and neck were congested and dark red, her eyes bulging. Her neck bore deep bruises and abrasions, indicating that her killer had used more force than was necessary.

Pete's face and head were so crushed and bloodied by the blows he'd received that he was unrecognizable in the crime-scene photos. Even in pictures taken after he was cleaned up following the autopsy, I never could have identified him had it not been for that telltale birthmark just above his butt, to the left.

Before walking away from my task, I needed to mentally summarize, compare and contrast the broad strokes of my review. I took a few deep breaths, sat down on the cabin steps and gazed across the lake, Shirley-style. Maybe its depths held the answer.

Recalling the abundantly detailed case materials compiled for Short Willie's serial rapes, particularly evidence about his MO and the autopsy results, I was startled by the paucity of both these critical investigative leads for the murders to which he confessed.

The autopsy results were so unremarkable that they might have been prepared from a rape-strangulation-murder template. The forensics were unhelpful. Nothing to aid in identifying the killer: no fingerprints, no DNA, and trace evidence that would narrow down the suspect list to fewer than 90 percent of the residents of Toronto. Except for the newly processed DNA trace that reopened the Ruth Rosenberg file.

Most disappointing was the sketchy MO. Only broad similarities existed between the killings of the four women. All the victims were white, all were close together in age. But their physical descriptions had nothing remarkable in common, and their dwellings were located in different areas of the city. None had reported being stalked, and none appeared to have disgruntled partners or ex-boyfriends. The first three had been raped, both vaginally and rectally, but only a trace of semen, then too small to nail, had been found.

Linda Bailey, Sandra Priest and Laura had been manually strangled with roughly the same degree of force. Ruth Rosenberg died of ligature strangulation. All had been found on their beds (except for Laura, who was found on the floor of her bedroom), naked, bound with items of their own (electrical cords, the drawstring from a pair of sweat pants, long shoelaces, panty hose, a shredded bedsheet), with a sock stuck in their mouths to silence them.

It was assumed that their killer had used some kind of weapon to frighten them into compliance; their bodies were, however, free of any signs of mutilation – apart from what his hands and penis substitutes had wreaked. Laura had been strangled in a similar fashion but not sexually assaulted. Investigators assumed that Pete's arrival at the apartment interrupted the killer before he could complete his "pattern."

Pattern — what pattern? Based on everything I had examined in the four murder binders, the evidence for discerning a particularly distinctive pattern, one that might set these crimes apart from many of their kind, was truly underwhelming. If there were any links between the twelve serial rapes and the murders, none had been recorded.

And what I most wanted — evidence suggesting that

Laura's murder either was or was not the work of the man (assuming that they all came down to one serial killer) who committed the first three murders — simply did not materialize from these sketchy accounts.

There was no physical evidence to connect Short Willie to the strangling murders, nor were there any eyewitnesses. The entire case against him seemed to be based on his confession.

I knew that Willie's statement in that confession was voluminous and lavishly detailed. Given the near absence of details in the murder binders, I had no way of evaluating the accuracy of Willie's claims against the known facts. Information about the circumstances of the crimes could have been available to him, though, and from several sources. My prime candidate was leaks from within the police force. Details might have been divulged to him, intentionally or inadvertently, by officers under great pressure to wrap up the investigation. It was also possible that someone in prison, perhaps an inmate incarcerated on an unrelated offense, had coached Short Willie on the details.

I was beginning to see why Jonathan Rosenberg, brother of the second victim, had pressed so hard for an independent autopsy. Presumably he had even more reasons for believing William Shortt to be innocent of Ruth's murder.

Throughout my review of the evidence, I had made no notes. Every word, every photo and drawing was permanently etched into my brain.

I needed a drink as never before. I needed a head transplant. The former was not at hand, and the latter not covered by my medical insurance.

Heart aching, head spinning with gruesome details, instinctively I made my way to the water. Drowning is, I guess, as good a way as any to commit suicide. Virginia Woolf weighted down the pockets of her cardigan and walked into the River

Ouse. "Suicide while the balance of her mind was disturbed" was the verdict.

Why do we have such difficulty accepting that someone might choose to end her life while in an absolutely *rational* state of mind?

It was the kind of night so achingly perfect that you could imagine romantic honeymooners paddling their way into a cherished lifelong memory.

At the water's edge I removed my sandals and stripped off my clothes. My mind was perfectly balanced, poised dead center at the fulcrum, one scale freighted with hot rage, the other with a cold desire for revenge — in exact measure. I entered the water and began stroking a fierce crawl. I would swim my body into exhaustion, my head into a tabula rasa. Then fall into a deep restorative sleep. For I had work to do.

I needed to stay alive long enough to kill the man who had despoiled those two young bodies. When I tracked him down I would show him the most horrific of the crime-scene photos — just to ensure that when he arrived in hell he'd know why. In Technicolor.

CHAPTER 14

MY WOODLAND "ESCAPE" WAS OVER. From isolated cabin to leafy privileged enclave within twenty-four hours.

When I'm driving Maeve, especially through congested city streets, normally I totally focus on gridlock. Today my brain was spinning in nervous anticipation of meeting Dr. Jonathan Rosenberg. This would mark the first time I'd had contact with a family member of one of Short Willie's alleged victims. Except for Laura's father, whose presence at the police station I had barely registered when Silver took me in to identify Pete.

I was heading north in the city toward the Forest Hill district, home to many of the city's wealthiest people and to two of its oldest, toniest private schools. As I cruised along a winding, leaf-canopied street with elegant mansions set well back on huge, landscaped lots, I felt as if I'd entered a little Eden.

I pitied the residents — none of whom were anywhere to be seen. Forest Hill seems deprived, lacking everything that gives Little Italy its distinctiveness: noise, garbage-strewn crowded sidewalks, public urinals masquerading as laneways, traffic congestion and exhaust fumes, grapevines, not to mention our generous complement of wildlife (including nutcases, druggies and their dealers, club-goers and rats). And nary a bingo parlor in sight.

I chased my bigoted thoughts away. Death erases all distinctions, including those of class. Rosenberg lost his sister and

I lost my lover. This puts us on the same emotional playing field. How, I wondered, had Ruth's murder fractured his life?

Wishing Maeve's muffler were less deafening, I turned into a curved driveway leading to the front of a three-story gray stone mansion large enough to accommodate all the inhabitants of my block. The grounds of the oversize lot were so flawlessly maintained that they must have required the services of a full-time gardener. As I stood gaping at an exotic tree in full blossom, the front door was opened by a man who didn't look one bit like Jeeves.

His strained face relaxed a bit when I removed my helmet. "You wouldn't believe how much I want a V-Rod!" he exclaimed. His eyes grazed my bike like a lover's.

"Trust me, I would."

As he extended his hand to greet me, I noticed that his fingers were longer than his five-foot-eight height hinted. He was a thinly built man in his mid-thirties. A deep tan contrasted with prematurely gray hair.

This was the man who had so mistrusted the results of the investigation into Ruth Rosenberg's murder that he had successfully argued for an independent autopsy on his sister's remains. Some very potent reasons must have fueled his willingness, and that of his family members, to endure the trauma of having her body exhumed.

"Thank you for agreeing to see me," I said, as he led me to a sunroom overlooking the back garden. "Believe me when I say that I am well situated to understand how upsetting my request must have been."

"Actually, Jane, it's an odd kind of relief to be in the company of someone who must know *exactly* what I, and my family, have been through since Ruth's murder."

I shook my head. "We haven't walked identical paths, though, Jonathan. You took the brave route of pursuing what seemed to you to be an injustice. Until very recently, I devoted myself to drinking away the experience — and obsessively writing books about crimes that happened to *other* people."

He had the good taste not to stare at my unique fingers, so I took a pass on mentioning how they'd acquired their distinction.

"Then we're not so unalike. The word *obsessive* tells it all. After Ruth died I plunged myself into eighteen-hour workdays. That was my route to not standing up to the pain." He smiled ruefully. "Burying oneself in work is very easy to do in my profession. Cosmetic surgery has become a complement to a good wardrobe."

I squirmed in my chair, needing to draw his attention away from my incipient crows' feet and back to my agenda. "When did you decide to request the exhumation?"

His expression didn't register the distress he must have felt. "Almost two years ago my wife, Sylvia, threatened to leave me if I didn't curtail my schedule and devote a reasonable amount of time to family life. Because I wanted to save my marriage, I knew I had to find a way to sort through some of the questions that had been haunting me. Until they were addressed, I couldn't just 'move on,' as the Pollyannas say."

A photograph on the opposite wall momentarily distracted me. Forefronting a rubble-strewn street, a chicken and a dog face off. I think it's a Jeff Wall.

"A short while ago I felt inclined to stick a large cork in the mouth of anyone who mouthed 'time to move on' messages. How did you do it?"

"I decided to study the investigation with a view to seeing if I really did have substantial grounds for doubting that Ruth's killer had been identified."

"Knowing that Shortt was serving a life sentence was all that kept me from losing it, Jonathan. When I heard the news about the autopsy results, my sanity went on vacation for a few days."

He smiled gently. "I hope you're not beating yourself up over that. Here's how I went about passing myself off as compos mentis. I was fortunate enough to be able to cut my appointments and surgery almost by half. I did all my research related to the murders from my office. Had Sylvia realized what I was doing, I think she would have doubted my sanity. Ironically, it was my pursuit of the truth that saved me from a major crack-up. Once I'd embarked on the project, I began to understand why it is, for example, that bereaved parents found organizations to combat drunk driving. It gives a focus to one's anguish."

He looked at me as if seeking confirmation.

"And your success in forcing the autopsy has resulted in my own project to conduct a private investigation into my fiancé's murder. I'm just in the early stages, but it's already seized all my attention. It would be really helpful if you could tell me what reasons led you to doubt the case against Shortt."

He began to enumerate the reasons on the tips of those elegant fingers. "There wasn't a single eyewitness to place Shortt even near any of the four crime scenes. There wasn't a crumb of physical evidence connecting him to the murders. Although he had no alibi for any of the times in question, that would be true of many people who live alone. But the real clincher was his so-called confession."

"I've examined most of the case materials, but I haven't yet seen the transcript of his confession. How did you get your hands on it?"

He paused to take a sip of his tea. "At the time, I didn't really know if it was in the public domain — but I didn't care to discover that it might not be. Nor did I want to alert anyone to my interest in it. So I'm afraid I exerted some pressure on a fellow Tory who shall remain nameless. He gave me a clandestine copy." He shrugged. "To be honest, I felt no guilt about doing that."

I smiled. "Nor should you. Those case materials I just mentioned arrived in my hands via a similarly unorthodox route."

"If you like, I can give you the transcript. It's served its purpose for me."

"Thanks. I very much want it. After all, it seems that Shortt's confession provided the *only* reason the policed closed the files on the murders."

"Good, I'll give it to you before you leave. For the moment, I'll just summarize my main issues with it. As I read through it — it's very long — I began to get a sense of Shortt as a blowhard who was probably enjoying all the attention he was stirring up. He talks his way through each of the murders almost as though he's memorized the details, kind of like an actor speaking his lines."

He hesitated. "It struck me as a performance by a braggart who would have taken credit for masterminding the Holocaust if another evil little inadequate hadn't beaten him to it."

"And at that point he must already have known that he would be spending the rest of his life in prison for the rapes alone. So he had nothing further to lose by confessing to the murders," I commented.

He slapped his knee. "That's right. In fact, by adding the distinction of being a serial killer to his serial rapist tag, he had much to *gain* if his motive was to further enhance his notoriety. And perhaps he mistakenly thought that he might even profit from his crimes by selling his story."

I set down my teacup with the reverence its provenance demanded. "Did the main details he provided about each crime — what the victims were wearing, the layout of their apartments, how he killed them ... whatever — seem to jibe with the facts and the autopsy findings?"

"That, too, seemed peculiar. I've always heard that serial killers relish reliving their crimes, especially the ones who take away trophies. So you'd expect him to provide a very detailed account of the murders, above all the manner in which he murdered his victims. But concrete details are very thin on the ground in that confession, as you'll discover. And he said he strangled Ruth with his hands when, in fact, she died from ligature strangulation. Whatever correct details he did provide — presumably enough of them to convince the police that he was their man, could have originated from a number of sources. By then, most of it was public knowledge, anyway."

I nodded. "As an ex-crime reporter, I was astonished to read a few of the more lurid newspaper accounts written *prior* to his arrest. The information they divulged certainly got released without the approval of the police chief. But an officer close to the investigation could have inadvertently leaked it. They were all under a lot of pressure."

Jonathan was shaking. "I'm so relieved my part in having the case reopened is over. The whole process exhausted me. Odd, isn't it? — the final straw was a consequence of my success. Having to read the new autopsy results was ... was ..." He began to sob. Until that moment I hadn't realized what a very tight leash he'd had on his feelings.

I swiftly seated myself beside him and held my hand on his arm until he composed himself. "I am so sorry. My questions did this to you. I'll leave right away, Jonathan."

I rose to go.

He looked up through his tears. "No, Ruth's killer did this to me. And I am fully aware that you haven't even asked the question most important to you. So please go ahead."

"Do you think that the same man who killed Ruth also killed Pete and Laura?"

He wasted not a second on reflection. "No, I don't. Obviously that's something you'll want to determine for yourself, but the murder of Pete and Laura didn't match up. I believe one individual *did* kill Ruth and the other two women. I recall a few critical dissimilarities in the MOs, and between the first three victim profiles and the final two. I'm sure you'll find more anomalies. And keep in mind that the investigation into their murders was short-lived and incomplete. Soon after their murders Shortt confessed."

He excused himself to fetch the transcript of the confession. Handing it to me, he fixed me with his eyes. "Be very kind to yourself, Jane. You are about to enter the Chamber of Horrors."

CHAPTER 15

DURING THE COURSE OF MY BEDRAGGLED LIFE, I've spent far more time reading than socializing. Usually I find my work-related reading as interesting as what I devour for pleasure and edification. The transcript of Short Willie's murder confession now stood out as the prime exception.

At the very least, the speaker of these words was a serial rapist. My reason for subjecting myself to the ordeal of reading his twisted tale was compelling. Was Jonathan Rosenberg correct in his assessment of the confession as a fiction concocted by a celebrity-hungry braggart, or were the police right? Had Shortt really murdered the other four people?

When I had read through to the end of the hundred-plus pages, I knew that I'd put my money on Rosenberg's best guess. Short Willie was a pathological fabulist. He told so many lies that if he said it was hot, you'd reach for a sweater; if he said it was Tuesday, you'd check the calendar.

Although he had spoken with his lawyer, B. B. Claiborne, he requested that Claiborne not be present during his interrogation. He had refused a polygraph exam. Could this be because they are so accurate?

I saw little reason to regret that his confession hadn't been captured on videotape. His body language merely would have added another dimension to his lack of credibility. And I was grateful I didn't have to endure his virtual physical presence as well as his braggadocio.

It was clear from the transcript that he had not been unduly pressured during his interrogation. No trickery, no threats, no lying about evidence the police never had. Indeed, he needed no prompting. Pity that Willie missed the opportunity to broaden his audience, I thought, recalling the American guy who confessed to murder while he was on-line talking to his support group for problem drinkers.

Anomalies and unanswered questions abounded — none of which were raised at the trial, of course, for the simple reason that he stood trial only for the rapes. Without breaking a sweat, any skilled defense lawyer could have persuaded a jury that Willie's confession was unreliable.

Of those facts in his narrative that did not fit the crime scenes, one riveted my attention. It occurred near the end, when he finally got around to describing how he killed Laura and Pete. Perhaps at this juncture in his marathon guilt fest, he was too exhausted to recall the details accurately. But this was a whopper. He said that he first attacked Pete and then Laura. In fact, the physical evidence had established that Laura was strangled *before* Pete was bludgeoned. It seemed highly unlikely that Pete had even been present prior to the murderer's attack on Laura.

Added to this major chronological error was a significant omission. He made no mention of using gloves. A light switch on Laura's hall wall bore a bloody glove pattern.

Whoever reviewed and approved this transcript, other than the police, must have given it only cursory attention.

My exercise in harrowing reading strengthened my belief that I was on the right track. Correction: I wasn't on the *wrong* track.

As I set the document aside, the now-familiar quandary resurfaced: *to shoot, or not to shoot.*

I was definitely motoring down the road toward my goal:

confrontation of the monster who had killed my lover. And I was picking up speed. Part of me felt like a passenger; another part of me was doing the driving. As far as I could gauge, I calmly intended to kill that person, whoever he was. But now that it had begun to look as if I might actually find him, I had divided into two people. One Jane Yeats was coldly and methodically proceeding toward the moment when she would execute her lover's killer. The other Jane Yeats was standing by, nervous, appalled and derisive — *What? You're going to do what? Get real.*

CHAPTER 16

BY WAY OF CONGRATULATING Silver and Max for surviving my absence, I treated them to dinner on the back patio of a restaurant that tolerates my dog.

Picking up on my noir mood, my friend regaled me with stories about the sensation her wisp of a dress had created the night she received her National Aboriginal Achievement Award. "So much of my anatomy was hanging out, the TV crew didn't know where to focus," she said, chortling.

Once she had satisfied herself that I spent my time up north sober, Silver avoided interrogating me about my research. Instead we talked about the beauty of the land and of Shirley. "Maybe we'll go up there together sometime soon," said Silver.

Her suggestion surprised me. Silver leaves Toronto even less often than I — and we have never vacationed together. Sensing my hesitation, she pressed me to commit to a date. I promised to think about it.

She gave me a suspicious look. "Why won't you say yes or no? You sound like you're not sure you'll be alive come September."

I didn't know what to tell her.

I fell into bed hoping to sleep around the clock. Alas, this was not to be. On the other hand, how many people get to say that they live in a neighborhood where everyone wakes up at the same moment?

At 4:00 a.m. I was shocked into consciousness by an explosion that radiated shock waves so intense that my house took on the character of a giant vibrator. Max leaped up, farted and raced for shelter in the basement.

As I tugged on a pair of shorts and a T-shirt, I ran through the possibilities. Ruling out a gunshot (too loud, unless the neighborhood gangbangers had landed a rocket launcher) and an earthquake (no fault lines in the vicinity), I settled on an explosion. Paranoid as I had become, I knew my house wasn't the target (not close enough). By the time the sirens started wailing nearby, I was out the door. Looking north to College Street, I could see the flashing red lights of emergency vehicles converging. Leaking gas pipe? Arson? Bomb?

Just around the corner, police were already scouring the interior of Fellini's, an upscale restaurant owned by a downscale rat who got shot last summer by another local mobster while he was in the kitchen. Eleven months later, the shooter remained at large. Although several neighbors had made sightings, none had come forward to police with their news. Little Italy is a small village within a huge city. See no evil — *omertà*.

Maybe the shooter had returned to inflict more damage on his enemy.

Other cops were busy stringing yellow barrier tape in a huge semicircle that enclosed both the immediate site and the broader area littered with glass, bits of concrete, iron and wood. The entire glass front of the restaurant had been blown out. The windows in adjoining buildings and directly across the street had been shattered. The letters on the marquee of the Royal Cinema had fallen to the sidewalk. But the blast hadn't penetrated the interior of Fellini's. Everything looked intact, ready for customers brave enough to chow down in a war zone. The bomb must have been small and placed outside the restaurant.

The gathering crowd was abuzz with speculation. My

self-consciousness at having failed to put on a bra in my haste to check out the action quickly disappeared when I caught sight of several neighbors in their pajamas. An elderly gent in his bathrobe approached the scene on his walker. I was momentarily distracted by a much younger man clad only in telltale briefs. I did muster the decency to look away when I noticed him showing equivalent interest in my T-shirt. Times like this a girl can't get too uppity about the male gaze.

Pete: Because you're mine, I walk the line.

Holding court in front of the used bookstore was my favorite bartender from the Dundalk Tavern. "Hey, Benny, what's the scoop?"

"Cops should interview me, eh?" He quickly added, "Not that I'd tell them nothin', of course. But Marco, the asshole who owns this hot-dog stand, got beat up twice last week. The way I see it, he's lucky it wasn't him got blown away."

"What's Marco done this time? I heard he got shot last summer because he was bonking the shooter's wife."

Somebody behind me laughed. "You got shitty sources, lady. One of them priests was bonking the shooter's wife — still is, for all we know. Marco got shot for the same reason his place got bombed. You don't go borrowing big-time from the wrong people and then forget to pay them back."

God forbid the folks at Visa should adopt such a heavy approach to debt collection.

Benny pointed across to the linen-draped tables. "Fuck, how cheap can them wineglasses be?" All were sitting still intact on the tables.

"Meg Ryan ate here last week, you know," piped up another local resident.

"Yeah," replied Benny, "don't be too impressed. So did I."

When word spread that no one had been hurt, many in the crowd quickly lost interest and began heading home. Already the newly risen sun was packing serious heat as I ambled south, grateful yet again that I'd moved to an interesting part of the city.

I brewed myself some strong coffee. Max slowly made his way up the basement stairs, tail tightly tucked between his craven legs. I gave his bowed head a few reassuring pats.

"I never hired you as a bodyguard, fleabag." His tatty tail resumed its normal position as he chowed down on Science Diet.

" ... Police are already regarding the blast as suspicious, although it is too early to rule out accident as the cause of the explosion," announced CBC Radio. Good thing the cops don't leap to conclusions as swiftly as my neighbors. We'd all be in jail.

I sipped my coffee. That bang-up signaled an appropriate start to this particular day.

Nearing the end of our marathon shoot-out at a members-only range hidden in the bush fifty miles north of the city, "Filthy Few" Walter thumped me between the shoulders. "You got a natural app-tit-tood."

My novice success can't have been due to the fact that the bespoke targets were uniformed cops and members of a rival biker gang. "Walter, you should have been a teacher."

He shrugged. "I gotta tell ya, girl, there's a whack more money in what I do."

Yeah, but there promises to be a whack more satisfaction in what I plan to do with this gun, I thought.

When I suggested that he take the driver's seat for our ride back to the city, Walter all but cried for joy. As we merged into the heavy stream of traffic heading south on the Don Valley Parkway, he wove in and out with the finesse of a champion. "Yeee-haa!" he screamed into the wind. "This motherfucker rocks!"

On impulse I invited him for a beer at Sweet Dreams. All the while we were there, Etta busied herself pretending she was busy. As my companion slurped down the suds, I looked with longing at his chill-beaded can of Blue. It grew larger and larger until it occupied my entire field of vision. It became iconic, an Andy Warhol can of beer magnified and multiplied across a huge canvas.

Oblivious to my suffering, Walter confided that he was looking for a new contract. "So as to pay for my own V-Rod." He patted his Filthy Few patch. A contract by any other name . . .

I promised to file his name in my mental Rolodex. "But don't expect me to call anytime soon, Walter. The lesson you gave me today was all about me getting in the face of a large rat I fully intend to take out all by myself."

Walter high-fived me. "Girl, you rock."

When I said good-bye, Etta yanked me to her sequined bosom in an uncharacteristic hug. "He's not your type, dear," she hissed.

CHAPTER 17

THE FOLLOWING MORNING THE BEDSIDE PHONE wakened me. I must have forgotten to mute it before I stumbled into bed after 2:00 a.m. I stretched to answer it without sitting up.

"Is that Jane Yeats?" a surly voice inquired to a background of bar noise.

"Barely. What the hell time is it?"

"You need to talk to me." My caller's deep snort put me in mind of postnasal drip.

I kept my voice in check. "Is that an invitation or a threat?"

"Just a fact, lady. You been asking around about Short Willie, right? You're the dead guy's girlfriend. You need to talk to me." There was that snort again.

I was wide awake. "Whoever you are, how in hell would you know I've been asking around about anything but the weather?"

"Maybe I made up that part, eh? Maybe I ain't your usual hoser. Maybe I read the newspapers and put one and one together."

"So, of all the people who read newspapers, why are you the one I need to talk to?"

"Because I was a friend of his. We was in the joint together when he got killed. I know stuff nobody else does."

My inner Lois Lane smelled a rat. "So why would you want to tell me? And who is your friend?"

"You're a crime writer. Maybe I figured out you got an interest in finding out some stuff. Maybe you could do something with my information — something that would make me a happy man. I got a big grudge to settle, but if I try to nail the asshole myself I'll get killed." Snort. Maybe he had an allergy.

What made me think this guy wouldn't lose as much sleep over my death as I'd already lost because of his call? "You may be right about my needing to talk to you. But just so I don't waste my time tracing down a crank call, maybe you could tell me your name — and your friend's name."

"Christopher Anderson. Promise to hook up with me and I'll tell you my friend's name."

Praise the Lord. His name rang a bell. One of the inmates called to testify at the coroner's inquest into Short Willie's murder. Of course, he could be lying. But I wasn't about to risk breaking contact with him at this juncture. I could probably locate a photo of him, at least get a good description before meeting him. Would he go for meeting me someplace public, where I could discreetly exit if he didn't fit the look?

"I'd like to talk to you as soon as possible, Christopher. Tonight I was planning on going to a country bar for a Johnny Cash tribute. Would it be okay if we met there? I'll go early to get us a couple of good seats and we'd have time to talk before the show."

His voice leaped from surly to jubilant. "Would it be okay? Johnny fucking-Folsom-Prison-and-fucking-San-Quentin Cash? He's my hero."

"So meet me at Sweet Dreams on the Danforth at, say, seven. It's just east of Broadview."

"I know where it is. Bunch of ex-cons hang out there. Joint's owned by a great old broad." Snort.

Who was I to disagree? "Yeah. When you walk in, just ask the bartender or the great old broad to point me out, Christopher."

I hung up the phone. Time to refuel, then poke around for the visual skinny on Mr. Anderson. In sixty minutes flat, I'd showered, briskly walked Max and headed sans canine companion two blocks north to Canicatti's for their cholesterol-laden $3.95 breakfast special. When I returned home, I phoned Sam Brewer. After expressing considerable discomfort about why I was interested in Anderson's appearance, he relented. "White male of the species, dredged from the shallow end of the gene pool, about five-six, hundred and eighty pounds, dark hair, balding, face shaped like a wedge of pie, most distinguishing characteristic is the missing right ear — easy to spot because the remaining one is so prominent it parts his greasy locks. Wouldn't look out of place in your average lineup of weasels."

My need for a photograph evaporated.

Maeve ate up the pavement between my house and Sweet Dreams so greedily that she had me yearning for a big road trip. For years I've dreamed of tracing the coastal roads from Dawson to San Diego. Maybe I'll make the cruise this year — if I live long enough.

I parked at the rear of the brick fortress that houses my mother's governing obsession and entered through the back door. Etta was sitting at the bar with her stool swiveled to face her domain. Of course she'd dressed for the occasion. To honor the Man in Black, she was kitted out from wig to toe in the funeral color. Only during bad-hair hours does she wear a wig. Her bottle-blond locks cascade well past her bony shoulder blades in wanton abandon (a habit they picked up from their roots). But I guess even her locks couldn't make the color transition fast enough. From the neck up she looked like Connie Francis in her "My Happiness" period. (Did Connie have any other period?) From the neck down, Etta was a Mark Rothko study in ebony.

As I approached, she eyed me less enthusiastically. "Every time I see you, you look more like one of them Dykes on Bikes."

I had laid on the leather S/M a bit lavishly. Hey, I was hooking up with an ex-con. No way I wanted to pass for a Barbie.

"What can I say, Ma? You look like a woman who'd pitch June Carter into a jealous hissy fit." I stashed my helmet behind the bar and gave my curly mane a finger-combing.

Etta sucked hard on a Cameo. "Yeah, well, she'd have good reason to get jealous. If my hormones ever fail me, which —" she tapped wood with five black acrylic nails as long as the ends of her pointy-toed boots "— I got no reason to suspect they ever will, all I gotta do is think of that awesome baritone rumbling, 'Hello, I'm Johnny Cash.' Guaranteed to send me into meltdown every time. I mean, on stage that man would grab you by the short and curlies from the first note, and he didn't let go till the last."

"Pubic hair aside, what have you got lined up for tonight?"

"No less than the Legend deserves. I got a few local bands doing some covers, and a Johnny Cash impersonator so good he should be in Nashville. And I rehearsed all of them to death 'cause I wanted it chronological and classy."

"Are you planning on any Carter Family stuff?"

Etta's vigorous nod was not strong enough to disturb a lacquered hair. "Of course. How could I leave out Johnny's mother-in-law? Do you know, Mother Maybelle Carter led the singing on the title track of the Nitty Gritty Dirt Band's *Will the Circle Be Unbroken* album in 1971? She was sixty-two years old at the time. Is that not cool? Anyways, I got a drag queen who does a real convincing June Carter."

Some things cannot be contained. "Tell me she's going to sing 'A Boy Named Sue.'"

Etta stubbed out her cigarette with undue ferocity. "If I thought you was being a smartass, girl, I'd have Kobo toss you out the same door you come in."

I pressed my Nashville-reverence button. Kobo, my mother's bouncer, trained as a sumo wrestler. His career got interrupted when he was sent down for assault. Maybe he only sat on the victim.

Just as Etta was launching into her historical lecture on the 1956 Sun recording session that had Elvis Presley, Carl Perkins, Jerry Lee Lewis and Johnny Cash in the same studio, a creature who'd slouched in through the swinging doors caught my eye. Might have been the one ear.

I stood up. "Etta, my date's here. Hope the show goes well." I slipped away before she could spot Christopher. Not that she's ever lobbied on behalf of doctors and lawyers as candidates for my affection, but convicted felons stretch even her limits.

Christopher Anderson's jacket, shirt and jeans gave denim a stretch the manufacturer had never intended. His head was from a panel of comic-book artwork. I led him to my reserved table close to the stage, the rear wall of which was studded with enlargements of Johnny Cash cover art from Etta's LP collection, circling an even bigger-than-life-size cardboard cutout of the Man in Black.

I glanced at my Swatch, reliably glowing like an artifact from Homer Simpson's workplace. We had an hour before the show got under way.

CHAPTER 18

NAMES CAN DO FUNNY THINGS to your brain. God help me, I was sitting across from the One-Eared Beast and thinking "Christopher Robin." May he be as much Winnie as Pooh.

I ordered him a pitcher of Blue. He somehow presented as a power drinker whose tastes did not run to imported. The waiter knew to serve me a mug of alcohol-free, for appearance's sake. My newfound sobriety wouldn't impress Christopher, who was busy rolling a cigarette. It had been a while since I'd seen that skill practised on anything but a joint, let alone with such finesse.

He surveyed the landscape through a cobra's eyes. "Way cool."

Guy must have been raised in a barn. Mindful of the clock, I said, "Christopher, if it's okay with you I'd like for us to cut to the chase so we can sit back and relax when the show starts."

He offered me one of the two smokes he'd rolled. A gentleman. "No problem, but call me Ferret, eh? Christopher is for choir boys, which I ain't."

Graciously I refused his nicotine. "No, but thanks anyway, Ferret. Doctor made me quit because of the asthma attacks." I got past the nickname without a sputter, it being so apt. Reminded myself not to relax for a New York minute, though: ferrets are such dangerous little critters. "I want to hear what you think I need to know."

"I ain't much for telling stories or long jokes — otherwise

I'd do better when the cops haul me in, ha-ha. So fire some questions at me."

Questions are what I do. If I phrase them right, answers become my ammo. "Let me pass this one by you: given that Short Willie had to be near the top of Canada's most reviled list — inside and outside of the joint — why did he get transferred from SHU to Millhaven? Millhaven's got a rep for inmate murders."

Ferret drew so hard on his fag that his mouth configured itself into a semblance of a different orifice. "That one's a no-brainer. Somebody wanted him dead."

"But there's a whole process in place for transferring an inmate from super-max to max. Willie hadn't exactly been a model prisoner in the SHU." I sipped from under the shallow foam of my faux beer.

Ferret swilled Labatt's approximation of the real thing. "Makes you wonder what was going down, don't it? Ha-ha."

"So we take it for granted that there was a hidden agenda behind his getting moved to Millhaven. Any idea who might have been behind his transfer?"

Ferret cut from the chase to the kill, nailing me with his squinting-into-the-desert-sun eyes. "The murder. I seen it go down." Snort.

"At the coroner's inquest, you testified that you hadn't seen a thing, that you were too busy watching the scene around the heart-attack victim."

Narrow eyes raked my leather gear. "You might look tough, but you gotta be a virgin when it comes to life on the inside. Rat on another inmate and you sign your own death sentence. Guaranteed."

He was about to stub out his cigarette into one of Etta's ash-trays, a black-plastic repro of an upturned ten-gallon hat, when he changed his mind, pocketed the butt after extinguishing it between his fingertips and filed the souvenir ashtray in the same folder.

"What happened in the cafeteria, Ferret?"

He shrugged. "It all happened real fast. Everybody's looking toward the commotion goin' down around Fats Oliver who's crashed to the floor, eh? Short Willie takes one stab in the chest from the guy behind him in line. How it went down was, Buddy taps Willie on the shoulder, Willie turns around to see who's knocking, Buddy stiffs him faster than you can say 'oh, fuck.'"

Ferret betrayed no signs of post-traumatic stress disorder. Maybe he was just good at hiding his feelings.

"Did Willie manage to say anything before he croaked?"

Ferret was impressed. "Funny you should ask. Nobody at the inquiry did." He rubbed his missing ear. "Come to think of it ... yeah. He said, 'I lied.' It came out kind of watery-like, on accounta the blood and all." Double snort.

I scrolled down my memory bank. "Apparently the weapon went missing as fast as it sank into wee Willie's heart. But the stab wound gave up a good description of the knife. The forensics expert said it was about five inches long, one inch wide. Double-edged. Sharp, smooth, non-serrated cutting edges. Sturdy, not a thin blade like a kitchen knife. All in all, definitely not cafeteria-issue cutlery."

"And it weren't no sharpened toothbrush or some spoon that got ground down in the machine shop, neither. Came from the outside, for sure."

Already I was getting tired of feeding questions he ate up faster than Max attacked a burger and without volunteering more than a single morsel in return. Guess he likes to dance. "How do weapons get inside?"

Ferret was enjoying his professorial role. *Who could blame the man for savoring such a rare performance?* He exhausted his beer stock straight from the pitcher and wiped his mouth on his sleeve. "Wouldn't hurt none if you got me another one of them," he hinted. "Booze helps me talk." Snort.

Already I had guessed that something more potent than Blue was propelling his mouth. Whatever. I signaled our server for another pitcher.

"Weapons get inside same ways as drugs and booze and smokes. Lots of ways. When I was in Millhaven, they came in every day through the garbage system. You got your secure areas, then you got your not-so-secure areas where visitors drop off gifts when the guards is looking the other way."

Ferret hit a first by offering me a goodie with no prompting. "Them smuggled weapons maybe find their way to an inmate who'll do a favor in exchange for some drugs."

At the risk of being called a virgin again, I said, "But there's still got to be a big risk involved for the hit man, Ferret. Isn't the joint swarming with surveillance cameras, especially in high-traffic, high-risk zones like the cafeteria?"

When Ferret raised the pitcher to his thin lips, he wasn't stalling for time to consult his mental notes. The grin that shaped those lips into a response surpassed sardonic.

"Hey, inmates get found murdered on ranges where only one inmate at a time is released from his cell. Guess you could say them particular cells opened up all by themselves. And then you got your punch clocks at the end of each range for the guards to punch in so the bosses can check to make sure the guards are inspecting the ranges regular."

A further pause while he revisited the pitcher. "Another buddy of mine got done in when the punch clocks wasn't working for some other mysterious reason. We all figured the guards trashed them, eh. Same for the panic buttons in our cells. They're supposed to ring in the guards' room. But they get disconnected when it's convenient, also by magic. Sometimes guards forget to patrol the range."

As I nodded, he bolted to his feet. "Gotta piss."

Back in his chair, two quarts lighter, he continued. "The situation weren't no different when Willie bit it. And the same old shit went down when his death got investigated. Nobody official ever gets found responsible for what they done wrong — takin' responsibility, I have to tell you, is the kinda crap us inmates get shoved down our throats in all them rehab programs."

I worked hard at concealing my shock. I'm a child of the late sixties. The generation before mine traded in religion for civil rights — for everybody, no matter how tenuous one's claim on them.

Swatch blinked me a warning that we were moving into countdown for Etta's show, give or take the usual fifteen-minute delay.

"You saw the weapon, Ferret. You had to see who was using it."

"Why didn't you ask me straight up? Lifer name of Gary Kemp killed Short Willie. Fucker was right ahead of me in line, eh? He done it. Then he yanks the knife outta the perverted prick's chest and it gets passed on down the line till it evaporates. Hey, I was second man on the relay team. Meantime, Kemp's disappeared into the crowd around Fats."

"Bring me up to speed on this cowboy movie. Kemp is the hired gun. He makes some kind of a deal to kill our boy Willie in exchange for some kind of reward. The hit is scheduled for a time when the cameras are down or get shut down and the planned diversion takes place. Fats Oliver fakes a heart attack. Didn't that look suspicious?"

He shook his head. "No way. Old pecker weighed in at three hundred and he had diabetes and angina. He was always popping them nitro pills. Sure, he was playing possum, but at the inquest it came out that even the prison doctor assumed his heart attack was legit. And it coulda bin. Fats croaked before the inquest. However you figure it, it's still gonna look like the killer was just waiting for the right opportunity to pop up."

Show time, wrap time. I suspected that Ferret's really big card was still tucked up his faded blue sleeve. Probably he was holding it back until he decided whether I could be trusted with the truly dangerous disclosure. Or he might have been setting the stage to hit on me for money.

"Okay, we've covered means, motive, opportunity and perp. Is that everything I need to know?"

He grinned through crooked teeth begging for a bleach job — the few that hadn't gone the way of his ear. "I already gave you enough for a good story."

"For sure, Ferret, for sure and you're looking at a grateful woman. Maybe I've even got enough info to press for a new inquiry into Willie's death."

Wrong bait.

"From what I hear, a writer don't have to reveal his sources. Right?"

No time to cloud the waters by scaring off my informant with a cautionary note about the litigious perils attendant on running afoul of disclosure rules.

I was fast running out of patience. "Whatever you tell me and whoever leans on me to give up where it came from, whatever means they use ... trust me: it won't be the first time. You want to know about having the screws put to you? A few years back I did a book on corruption in the higher ranks of the Toronto police force. I didn't get to scoop that major poop without help from some people who stood to lose a whole lot by talking to me. I never shopped them, man— not even when I stood to lose more than four fingertips. I'm an investigative crime writer. Whether you make it big in my trade totally depends on your snitches. Rat out on just one of them and you're looking for another career — or worse. Same reason you lied at the coroner's inquest, right?"

It was difficult to gauge how well I was doing. Ferret had taken to rubbing his missing ear so vigorously that it occurred to me he might have lost it to friction.

I soldiered on with my presentation. "And I've never had to pay a cent for any information that came my way. Maybe 90 percent of people tip you off because they've got it in for whomever they're tattling on. The other 10 percent blab because they are genuinely outraged by the scumbag they've stumbled on. Either way, I respect their right to remain in the shadows. I blow the whistle, I've got laws to protect my butt."

Mendacity occupies a prominent slot in my conversational tool kit.

All the while I was delivering my rant Ferret was studying my face. As if for confirmation of something he'd intuited there, his eyes switched to my fingers. "Hey, don't get me wrong. I ain't asking for money. Maybe you guessed already that injustice don't particularly offend me — me being a repeat offender, ha-ha."

There ensued a brief pause while we savored his pun.

Ferret lapsed into the ethical branch of criminal philosophy. "Even God's gotta get with the program and agree that Willie's murder was a case of *real* justice gettin' done — something the court never done. Lifers got nothing more to lose in the system, eh? They get a free murder or two. Hey, I sat in that goddamn courtroom. Everybody, even the judge, was thinking the same thing, just nobody said it out loud: *the twisted bastard deserved way worse than he got.*"

He began rolling another smoke. "Dude — I mean, girl — what a fuckin' farce. All that trouble and expense to get justice for some son of a bitch who raped more broads than the two of us got fingers and toes, who also confessed to killing four other broads ..."

Ferret lunged for an effect that hit the mark: "*Plus your man.* I mean, shit, give me a break. When Willie croaked, name one human being on the planet who gave a mouse fart."

He clenched the beer pitcher so hard between his hairy paws that I was waiting for the crunch. "I got such a hate-on for the motherfucker I figure set up the whole hit, you wouldn't believe it."

Ferret stared across the table, the black pinpricks at the core of those blue marbles lasering into my soul. "Level with me, Jane — you ever hate anybody so much you laid awake at night imagining all the gross ways you could make him pay for what he done to you? Like, if his heart was on fire, you wouldn't piss down his throat?"

That was a no-brainer. Much as the truth should have shamed me, I didn't trouble to hide it. "Yes. The bastard who killed Pete."

"What about the butcher who sliced off them fingers of yours?"

"Nope. They're only appendages. Spare parts. Pete was my life. So who set up the hit?"

Ferret observed two seconds of silence before coughing out a name thick as a lump of phlegm. "Jerry Stone. He's a guard. Also head of their union."

Bingo.

A technician began checking out the lights and sound system. Etta's performers were about to rock.

Ferret stared deep enough into his beer pitcher that he might have been searching for the meaning of life. "Motherfucker Stone bum-fucked me my first night on the range. I still got the piles to prove it."

Ferret's admission came out somewhere between a whisper

and a hiss. From the neck up he'd turned deep purple. His mouth opened to say more, but the words never made it past his lips.

"Rape is rape, man, no matter who's doing it to whom." I could think of nothing more to offer by way of condolence, but my observation was sincere.

His eyes ventured brief contact with mine. The admission had reduced him to a shattered little boy.

After assuring myself that Ferret had mined his entire vein of information, I ordered him a third pitcher by way of thanks — hoping the bartender had the wits to water it down even more. We sat back as Mom's tribute to the Man in Black unfolded.

Etta's impersonator took to the stage. Under more forgiving lights he could have passed for the original. Marvelous voice, too. When he launched into "I Walk the Line" — not exactly my mother's theme song — I glimpsed her dancing with one of her regulars. When he launched into "Folsom Prison Blues," Ferret confided, "Johnny mighta wrote more murder songs than anybody, but he never actually killed nobody."

Number-Two Fan delivered this fact in a tone smacking of disappointment in his hero. "He did get busted seven or eight times for drugs. And once he got jailed just for picking flowers at two in the morning. The only time he spent in the pen was when he was performing there. Still, ya gotta hand it to him, the man knows where guys like me is coming from."

Step into the spotlight, Christopher Anderson. Etta now had a serious challenger for her country-music-historian title.

The drag queen did sing "A Boy Named Sue." The audience broke up. Ferret laughed so hard I got the illusion his missing ear was wriggling along in delight.

When the show ended, my date seemed reluctant to leave. His confidence had dropped another deep notch. "Uh, I had a real good time tonight. Don't suppose I could see you again, eh?" Frigid blue eyes thawed and puddled on the lino.

I stood up and extended my hand. Gripped his sweaty paw in a John Wayne lock. "Ferret, you've been straight with me and I appreciate that — big time. So big I'm going to be totally straight with you." I tossed in a nervous giggle. "Thing is, man, I'm not straight. I stopped sleeping with men after Pete." My turn to snort.

He got to twitching on the spot. "Fuck, them hooters had me fooled. I took you for a *real* broad." He paused to muster a penis-saving comeback. "No big problem. I'm a married man, right?" He rescanned the territory between my neck and waist. "But you should do the world of men a favor and think twice about who ya sleep with."

Like I said, the guy was a gentleman.

One more detail. When Etta's Johnny Cash clone hit the line, "I shot a man in Reno just to watch him die," Ferret went ape-shit with hooting and clapping his approval.

I could relate. When I find Pete's killer, I'll be tempted to do the same.

CHAPTER 19

I SCORED LAST NIGHT'S DATE with Ferret an eight out of ten on the information-gathering scale. By handing over more than one serious lead, he'd brought me several steps closer to finding Pete's killer.

The odds of verifying his information were slim. Small chance that I, armed with few resources beyond rage, could penetrate the thick blanket of deceit and concealment that had smothered the coroner's inquiry into Short Willie's death. The more promising approach was for me to devise the surest route to investigating the life and times of Jerry Stone.

Under pressure of the massive psychic fallout that showers down on every victim of sexual violation, Ferret had fingered Gary Kemp, a lifer, as Short Willie's killer, and Stone as the guard who bribed him to do the dirty. That catapulted my investigation two jumps up the chain of command.

But how to nail the next link? Who paid off or blackmailed Stone? And why? Or maybe Stone had Willie offed for purely personal reasons.

My brain went into lockdown. When thinker's block strikes, I know better than to push against the bars. I spent the rest of the week diverting my mind from anything related to my stalled investigation. The tangle of weeds in my front and back yards suffered such a makeover that they surfaced as a garden. Colonies of dust bunnies found a new home in the vacuum-cleaner bag. A mutiny of spiders were rendered homeless. Flat surfaces concealed by dust reintroduced themselves. Dirty laundry turned clean. The fridge sprouted fresh dairy, fruit and veggies. Even the basement submitted to a makeover.

The morning I'd set aside for coaxing the toilet back into flushing got assigned a new priority on my to-do list when I picked up the paper. The news hadn't made the front page, but it shot to the forefront of my attention: "Head of guards' union killed in Millhaven riot."

From nine short paragraphs I learned that Jerry Stone had suffered multiple and fatal stab wounds at the hands of unknown assailants. During a two-day lockdown ordered after weapons had been found in an unspecified number of cells, inmates sabotaged the new electronically monitored cell locks. Immediately on escaping, they swarmed Stone tighter than a media scrum. Although a CCCR camera videotaped the scene, it was impossible to tell precisely who did what. To whom they did the nasty was not an issue: when the scrum broke up, Stone's pin-cushion body was bleeding pints onto the concrete. Police were investigating his death, and prison officials said an inquiry was expected.

Whatever his sins, Jerry Stone had paid up in spades. He came swiftly to a gory and solitary end in a place as devoid of compassion as Hitler's ovens.

My slumbering gray cells kicked into high gear. What were his sins? From everything I'd learned about Stone, his popularity among the inmates was low enough to make him a favored target. Was it his rep as a brutal bully that got him elected head of the correctional officers' union? If you take by way of example the thug who heads up the Toronto police union, the answer was clear. Was his addiction to buggery a clue to his demise? That one I'd never know the answer to, which put me in the company of the rare few who also cared and would never know. The promised inquiry would be no more enlightening than Short Willie's had been.

If I'd left any sin of housekeeping omission unattended, I might have given in to despair. On the face of it, Stone's slaughter looked like a major setback to my investigation. Time to quickly pass discouragement and regroup my forces.

I put a positive spin on the situation. Stone never would have agreed to talk with me anyway — unless I'd had some concrete and nasty bribe to offer. All I did have only amounted to the dubious word of Ferret, an unreliable narrator to rival Bill Clinton on the subject of what constitutes a sex act. Ferret's already-questionable veracity had been further tainted by his mania to avenge his rape. Stone would have had zilch to gain by subjecting himself to my questions.

I compiled a mental checklist of the possible motives underlying Stone's murder — the first of which didn't even qualify as a motive:

1. Stone's murder was the result of a random act of violence. The inmates' pent-up rage found a convenient outlet during the riot. He was not a target. He was roadkill en route to a mindless vengeance trip.

2. Stone was the target of an inside hit and the riot merely a happy accident for someone who wanted him dead. The problem with this conjecture was that a horde of inmates had it in for him, many of them with good reason. Narrowing the candidates down to a shortlist was a Herculean task that promised to dead-end.

Stone was the victim of a planned hit that originated from the outside and had been waiting for the right occasion. Given Ferret's not-unsubstantiated reflections on prison mishaps, the riot itself could have been deliberately triggered. Once again, the motives circling this option could be legion.

Only one of my conjectures intrigued me: if Ferret told it true, Stone could have been silenced because he was directly linked to the man who arranged the hit on Short Willie. Whether Stone's murder got chalked up to chance or design, it served the same purpose: the final link had been broken.

Attached to this third possibility was a worrisome corollary: the proximity of Stone's croaking to my conversation with Ferret. *Was that coincidence or were those two events connected?* Surely Ferret wouldn't have troubled to hook up with me — not to mention have revealed his painful reason for hating Stone — if he had the juice to off the guard himself. I dismissed it as coincidence.

I closed my eyes and leaned back while my inner coach advised me to invest my energy in other directions.

Into the stillness one question kept blinking a beacon. *Why was Short Willie terminated?*

Last words are rarely significant. Those of us who don't gasp our last in silence probably say something no more telling than *get me the bedpan.* If we're Canadian, *if it's not any trouble, pass me the bedpan, please.*

"I lied." Short Willie had managed to croak out two words before he got swept to glory. "I lied."

Now, Willie had built a career on lying about almost everything — on several occasions, including even his name. *Had there been a particular lie or lies he needed to recant with his final gasp?*

DNA findings had obliged Willie to cop to the rapes. Not a shred of evidence of any nature had pressured him to confess to the murders. He *volunteered* information that would have remained buried at least long enough for him to extend his killing spree by several more victims.

Ruth Rosenberg's autopsy had established that Willie

probably hadn't murdered her. Was that what he had lied about? It seemed that he'd taken credit for at least one murder he didn't commit. But why recant? He was clever enough to have staged eleven rapes without leaving a single clue to his identity or a trace of evidence. Could he have been stupid enough to think if he recanted he might get his sentence reduced, even at this late stage? That seemed far-fetched. And how could he have proved that he didn't kill Rosenberg, when he'd gone out of his way to establish the very opposite in his confession? Did he think the police would reopen their investigation into five murders they'd happily closed the files on, solely on his unreliable word?

Had Shortt not obliged them with a confession, the police would still be looking for the killer — and pressed to resolve the case no later than yesterday. They had no proof of any link between him and the victims, no witnesses who could place him and any of the victims together on the night they were killed, and not a shred of material evidence.

During a press conference far more self-congratulatory than circumstances warranted, the police assured the press that Shortt had provided them with information on each murder that only the killer could know. A community whose fears were tipping over into full-scale panic had been calmed by the knowledge that the killer had been apprehended and caged. The pressure-cooker investigation was terminated: the cops had erected a shield against political and media bullets.

Because he never stood trial for the murders, the Crown hadn't been obliged to prepare a fail-safe case against him. After all, there could be no reasonable doubt, not even in the mind of the most skeptical juror. *Or could there be?* Everyone had taken Willie at his word — after he'd provided enough details to persuade homicide investigators that he was the killer. Prior to his confession, how well had they conducted the investigation?

Following his confession, how thoroughly had they wrapped up the case? These were not rhetorical questions. But the cops held their press conference, then the media persuaded the public that Willie was guilty, the mayor stopped leaning on the chief of police to make an arrest, and the chief let up on the homicide squad. The city breathed a collective sigh of relief — and the murders stopped.

Everyone was happy — including Willie. Why rain on their parade?

That Willie had sadistically raped twelve women, there could be no reasonable doubt. Science had confirmed his confession. But Rosenberg's autopsy raised doubt about at least one of his murders. Four others could follow. Willie hadn't so much been wrongfully alleged to have killed Ruth Rosenberg as he had wrongfully confessed. Why would he confess to something he hadn't done? In for a penny, in for a pound. Could the opposite be true? If he hadn't murdered Rosenberg, perhaps he hadn't murdered anyone.

"I lied." Why would anyone in his right mind falsely confess to five killings? Had Willie been in his right mind? Who might know the most about the shadow zone in Willie's truth scale?

My gray cells were skating the thin ice of psychology. Not my domain. There are people who incriminate themselves from a desire to be famous. Was that what had propelled Willie into the confessional in the first place? And if so, why would he have been running back to it to deconfess?

After consulting my notes, I picked up the phone and punched in the number of Willie's prison shrink.

CHAPTER 20

"I'M SORRY, MADAM, Dr. David Stern is no longer in the employ of the Correctional Service of Canada."

My voice assumed a geriatric quaver. "Oh, dear, I'm David's Aunt Lottie from Victoria. I'm just visiting Toronto for a few days with my friend Mabel and I was so hoping I could talk to my nephew, maybe have tea with him. He's my favorite nephew. Well, he's my only nephew although my other sister Ethel has four lovely girls."

The Millhaven receptionist wanted me off the line. "Don't tell anyone where you got this information, but Dr. Stern left us to go into private practice in Toronto."

I pushed a few unbreakables off my desk and held the receiver to the floor as they hit. "Oh my goodness, I can't seem to find a phone book in my room here. I'm staying at a nice little bed and breakfast my friend Lucy back home recommended. It's very nicely appointed, although the breakfasts do leave a little bit to be desired ... you wouldn't have his phone number handy, would you?"

A voice grown weary with my autobiography gave me Stern's office number.

She'd hung up before I could say bless you, dear.

The next voice brought to me courtesy of Ma Bell was male. I'm thinking that John Irvin, the sweet gay administrative aide on *NYPD Blue*, has enhanced the appeal of phone answering as a non-trad job for men. Turned out I had the shrink himself on the line. He sure didn't sound light in his loafers.

He parried my request for a meeting to discuss William Shortt, whom he'd counseled in Millhaven, with a question. "Are you the Jane Yeats who wrote *Malign Neglect?*"

Uh-oh. Mendacity was not an option: all my books have jacket photos. In my experience, many people are loath to talk to true-crime writers, especially people who've been part of the justice system. "Yes."

"We can meet tomorrow — for lunch, if that works for you. I've got a rare two-hour break between appointments, thanks to a cancellation. My office is on Harbord. Where are you?"

"I live almost around the corner."

"Then why don't we meet at Bar Italia? Is twelve-thirty okay?"

The following morning I had an appointment to get my hair cut. Much as I've grown attached to the shoulder-length curly chestnut locks that echo depictions of Queen Maeve, most everything else about me these days is feeling like a lean, no-frills machine. After instructing the stylist to seriously layer my mane and reduce it by three inches, I closed my eyes and lost myself in the Blue Rodeo CD belting out of the corner speakers. I've given up trying to converse with people in the appearance-service industry, who always predicate their chatter on the mistaken assumption that I'm a normal fashionista.

When I returned home I stared at myself in the hall mirror long enough to realize that the improvement from the neck up was screeching dismay at everything below. So I exchanged my Harley T-shirt and black jeans for a pale yellow cotton sweater and blue jeans. Went so far as to replace my biker boots with a newish pair of sneakers. Inebriated by my lapse into quasi-femininity, I poked some silver earrings through holes partly sealed over from disuse. Good thing there wasn't a tube of lipstick in the house. I might have run totally amok.

Realizing that I hadn't asked David how I might recognize him, I arrived five minutes early to ensure that he could spot me when he walked in. Executed in stainless steel and chill tones, Bar Italia is a sterile postmodern recreation of an autopsy room. A woman whose natural elegance blitzed my pretenses to real womanhood seated me at a booth midway down the oblong room. A moment later, a server so thin her bony frame screamed "food-free diet" materialized at my table, raising a tweezed-to-near-extinction eyebrow in interrogation. "Pint of Smithwick's, right?"

This was embarrassing, training the neighborhood bars to my new sobriety. "No, large cranberry and orange juice, please." She recovered from dumbstruck and scurried away.

In her tracks arrived a man who was a close match for Pierce Brosnan, except for the monk's fringe of blond hair. As he extended his hand, I made a failed attempt to stand up. The table was bolted to the floor too close to my seat. Pleated at mid-torso, I grasped his hand, matching his firmness with over-compensation.

He shrugged off his suede jacket and ordered a half carafe of red wine, after checking out my drinks preference. Hard to tell for sure, but he looked a bit taken aback when I told him I wasn't drinking. *How could he tell that I was riding a shaky wagon?* The way some shrinks can insinuate their way, unbidden, into your secret life is but one of many reasons I avoid them.

Our anorexic server lingered a bit while she transferred his wine from carafe to glass. She even paused to wait for him to take a trial sip and see if it was to his liking. Hey, this was house wine. Evidently her hormones were about to propel her into an impromptu table dance. She looked unhappy when he smiled and pronounced it fine. Maybe he intuited that any less positive a response would have her scouring the shelves for bottle of

Château Mouton Rothschild to slip into the house carafe.

I could think of not one damn comment to break the ice, my hormones also being in an agitated state. Since Pete's death, this is a rare and generally unwelcome reaction. *Because you're mine, I walk the line.*

Dr. Stern reached into a worn leather briefcase and extracted a copy of *Malign Neglect*. "If I'm behaving like a fan, that's entirely due to the fact that I am. This is a terrific book. My career has brought me into contact with a swarm of rapists and killers. Your book puts a human face on their victims. I was very moved. Would you autograph it for me?"

No one ever taught me how to deal with praise. For once, I chose not to respond with some silly self-deprecating remark. "Thank you very much."

My hand shook as I inscribed the book. I resisted a sudden impulse to include my phone number. That's for horny girls who scrawl on washroom walls.

"Most honest scribes caution readers that it's a mistake to meet their favorite writers. We usually disappoint their expectations."

He smiled before sipping his wine. "Are you in the habit of issuing that alert?"

"I don't have to, simply because I avoid making public appearances. Occasionally I caved in to pressure from my publisher and did a reading or an interview, but the consequences were such that the publicist quickly decided my assets were best appreciated on the printed page."

We both laughed. "You're not comfortable in the spotlight? Most people would kill their grandmothers for the opportunity."

"Writing has at least one thing in common with masturbation. They're both solitary vices. Book promotion demands temperamental traits on the far side of the attention-seeking spectrum. A few writers can move from seclusion into performance without a hiccup once their books are written — and I admire that. But I can think of no worse hell than a book tour. Besides, celebrity is un-Canadian. We've got bylaws against it."

I had exhausted my juice supply. Our server passed with a Creemore in a frosted Pilsener glass. I almost ambushed her.

"Then how wise I was to jump at the chance to meet you." He glanced down at our menus. "Shall we order?" We were both able to do so without consulting them. He chose the pork tenderloin and avocado on panino. I settled on the seafood pasta.

"Now I've confessed my motivation in agreeing to meet with you, it's your turn. Your book gives me the sense that psychologists and psychiatrists don't figure very high in your esteem — to put it mildly. So why pick on me?"

"I can see that my disdain isn't ruffling any of your feathers, so I'm guessing that you're good at what you do. My knowledge of shrinks has been mostly limited to those who flit in and out of the justice system — as dueling banjos in the courtroom or as the experts who sign on the dotted line that gets dangerous offenders paroled for an encore performance."

Without taking his eyes from mine, he chomped from his sandwich and chewed contentedly. "I could mount an argument, but my heart wouldn't be in it."

"Is that why you left correctional services?"

He nodded. "A big part of it. When I entered the field, I really did believe in rehabilitation. To a young idealist fresh out of school, rehab programs seemed a much more attractive concept than retribution. But my caseload in both institutions I worked for was heavily weighted with inmates who'd survived committing the unspeakable without a trace of remorse — not to mention any intention of changing their ways. They were in counseling because they were mandated to be, because it was a way to break the boredom and gain Brownie points with the parole board, or because they wanted an audience for their self-indulgent whingeing."

"Private practice has to be more gratifying."

"You've heard the joke about 'How many psychiatrists does it take to change a light bulb?'"

"Five. One to hold the ladder and four to convince the light bulb it wants to change."

"My clients come to me because they sincerely want to modify behaviors that aren't working for them or the people they care about. So, yes, all I have to do now is hold the ladder."

Our chocolate mousse cake arrived. "Had we enjoyed our meals?" the server inquired in David's direction only.

"Very much, thank you," he said. "But my companion surpasses even your chef's splendid offerings." His eyes were twinkling. "Jane, you've been more than polite in not pursuing your agenda. So hit me with your questions about William Shortt."

I'd almost forgotten my agenda. Must have been the food. "I want your naked take on him. In order to help me understand why he did his crimes."

Much as I liked this man, I couldn't bring myself to tell him the reason for my obsessive interest. If he caught a whiff of my intention to avenge Pete's death, he'd reach for his cell phone and alert the white-jacketed guys with the butterfly nets.

"My best answer is going to disappoint you. William Shortt raped all those women, then launched into a killing spree because he saw no reason not to. It made him feel good. He was a pathetically inadequate man whose entire identity was constructed on those rapes and murders: they made him a somebody."

"T. S. Eliot said that 'it is better, in a paradoxical way, to do evil than to do nothing: at least we exist.'" David sipped his coffee. "In the case of serial rapists and murderers, Eliot was right.

Doing evil not only confirms their existence, it has the added bonus of making nobodies into celebrities — with the collusion of the media."

He shook his head. "These guys have groupies, you know. A quick Web search locates tons of sites devoted to everything from celebrating their kills, titillating the surfer with graphic details of their MOs, compiling victim lists as if they were baseball stats, flogging collectibles like Charles Manson T-shirts, Richard Speck comic books and serial-killer trading cards. There's even a subgenre of pop music devoted to their exploits — songs by the Talking Heads, the Police, Guns 'n' Roses. Soon e-Bay will be auctioning off relics on behalf of their families."

I like a man who can give good rant.

"John Wayne Gacy's clown paintings are hotter than an Emily Carr." I recalled another of Canada's homicidal hype-artists: "Clifford Olson worked the media for years. In addition to the murders he was known to have committed, he claimed intimate knowledge of dozens of unsolved murders. And that was a good ruse. He conned a newspaper editor into eighteen months of fruitless meetings, somehow got the prison warden to sign an agreement allowing him to make a dozen videotapes by promising to disclose new information about the cold cases. He actually registered copyright on the videos and came up with a title for them worthy of a Ph.D. candidate: 'Motivational Sexual Homicide Patterns of Serial Child Killer Clifford Robert Olson.'"

David grimaced. "William Shortt fits that mold. The man craved attention even more than a junkie his next fix. He was beyond rehab, beyond redemption — certainly in this world. Even in that hellhole we call Millhaven, he was happy as a lark reliving his crimes."

I had to ask. "Did he relive his fantasies by talking to you about them?"

"No, those re-enactments he confined to his cell, to his

imagination. He worked very hard at controlling our sessions. He just lapsed into silence whenever I tried to draw him in that direction — although he was happy to take full credit for his atrocities. Gave his self-esteem a major boost."

He paused. "Not that anything he might have told me could have incriminated him any further than his own confession."

"David, I've read the transcripts of those confessions, and I know there's audiotape to back them up. Nothing indicates that he was pressured to confess to the murders — he bloody well volunteered. And the details he provided of what transpired at the crime scenes, those he couldn't have faked. The cops must have held back on some critical information only the perp could have known."

"Yes, and his memory was phenomenal, almost mimetic. His IQ wouldn't have challenged a chicken's under the best of circumstances, but his memory for detail was exceptional. He'd remember from one session to another precisely what I'd been wearing, and he could recite damn close to verbatim comments I'd made weeks earlier. Of course, the details of his crimes would remain fresh in his mind simply because he rehearsed them so often. He didn't need porn mags."

I screwed up every thespian resource I owned for the one question I couldn't leave without posing. "Did he ever talk about the night he killed Laura Payne?"

"No, and that was a significant occasion. That night marked his last kills — and the first time he took a male victim."

I couldn't check the tears.

David reached across the table for my hand, the one with the peculiar fingertips. "It's okay, Jane, let them flow. I know that Peter Findley was your lover. And I am so very sorry for your loss."

Through those goddamn tears I managed to choke out a tremulous "thank you." My desperate need to grasp something that might propel me at least one baby step forward enabled me to blurt, "Just one more question, David: the final session you had with Shortt before his murder — can you recall anything that set it apart from the others?"

His quick response suggested that nothing had diminished his memory of those encounters with the monster. "Yes. It was different in two regards. It was clear from the previous session that he'd slipped into a major depression. But that afternoon he seemed strangely wired, almost high — although I don't think he was buzzed on anything. He hated drugs so much that he even refused Prozac. Nor did I think he was bipolar. It was as though he was anticipating something spectacular was due to happen."

David sipped the last of his cappuccino. "And he asked me a question, which was unusual. Usually he was attentive only to his own ramblings. Prior to that day, he'd made it very clear what he thought of my expertise. He asked me a variation of that old puzzler about how people can know when a liar is telling the truth."

David glanced at his watch. "I'm sorry, but I have to get back to the office for my next appointment." From his back pocket he swiftly dealt two cards, a gold American Express for our server and a business card for me. Before handing it over he scribbled in his home phone number. "Please call me anytime if you think there's anything else I can help you with. You seem to be intent on working up your own profile of Shortt. If you want to pass by me any notion you develop about him ... whatever. Anything I can do to help. Your loss is stupendous."

"I appreciate that so much. And the time you've taken today." When we shook hands, my grip was less forbidding than our initial hand-to-hand contact.

"And please don't hesitate to contact me for *any* reason." He blushed. "This lunch has proven to be an exception to your rule: meeting Jane Yeats fell far short of a disappointment for this reader."

He walked away before I could return the blush. That would be the one that was suffusing my face — and a few sites farther south.

On the short walk home I recited my mantra. *Because you're mine ...*

In moments of great loneliness, exacerbated by beer, I'd taken a few lovers since Pete died. Two were fine people, prime candidates for a long-term gig. Shortly after lust tipped over into intimacy, I'd bailed. In my grieving mind, it was possible to be unfaithful to a dead man. But lately, my investigation into his murder was bringing Pete back to me in Technicolor and in the present tense. My desire to avenge him forced me to rule out any distractions en route to the finale.

Still, Dr. David Stern could be a great friend. But did my heart have room to accommodate him now, when all intimacies could be so swiftly erased?

CHAPTER 21

SHORTLY AFTER NINE THAT NIGHT I'd just settled into watching the second installment of *Rebus*. This episode was based on *Dead Souls,* a novel I had devoured while the ink was still wet. Just as Ian Rankin's dour detective inspector was toppling into another binge, the bloody phone rang.

"What?" I snapped, bypassing "hello."

"Oops. I was worried I might catch you at a bad time. I can call back tomorrow morning."

My cast of nice male callers is fewer than the usual suspects in a home video. This makes short work of narrowing them down. The velvet voice confirmed my ready identification.

"Oh, shit — I mean, gosh — I'm sorry, David. It's just a TV show."

"Ha. I can smell another Rankin junkie from blocks away. Hey, I always tape *Rebus.*"

I flung my phone phobia on the trash heap. "Then why don't you talk and then let me borrow tonight's tape by way of recompense?"

He chuckled. "At the risk of sounding like a total geek, why don't you come over for dinner one night — after which I'll screen my Rankin collection."

"It's a deal, if I can supply the microwave popcorn. But please let me take a rain check until I've completed my current project."

"Great. I'm calling tonight because something occurred to

me while I was mulling over our conversation, when I had a break between appointments with one client who's worried about her attachment to her ailing cat and another whose wife just discovered he's into cross-dressing."

"After Millhaven, that sounds like comic relief."

"It is, but it's very unfunny to them, of course. Anyway, you asked me if I'd remarked on anything that set my final session with Shortt apart from the others. There was one detail I'd forgotten. As he was leaving the room, he turned and blurted, 'I'm gonna phone my lawyer.' At the time I thought he was threatening to blow the whistle on me for some imagined professional transgression. But just this afternoon it occurred to me that maybe contacting his lawyer was part of some plan he'd devised to enliven his life ... such as finding a novel way to regain the media attention he'd lost. That would account for his otherwise inexplicable rebound from clinical depression."

This was intriguing. "So my next step should be to contact his defense lawyer. From what I know of B.B. Claiborne, that could cost me a thousand loonies a minute."

"I doubt it. Man's got an ego that could inflate the Hindenburg. He'll dive at the chance to talk to a true-crime writer who's likely to get him even more press."

"Ironic, isn't it, David? Sounds like he and Shortt have that much in common: an insatiable craving for attention."

"None of us are quite as far removed as we like to believe from what we most abhor."

Was my lust for revenge so obvious that it had Dr. David suspecting that only a bullet separated me from a hired assassin? Nah.

Before signing off, I thanked him and we reaffirmed our commitment to a Rebus fest. Should I make it through this dark night of my soul, that promised date just might flicker as the light at the end of my tunnel.

The entry in the *Canadian Who's Who* for B.B. Claiborne, QC, senior partner at Claiborne and Associates, read like a template of success for aspiring criminal defense lawyers. A member of the Ontario bar for forty years, he had served on the editorial boards of every important legal journal in the country, written enough articles to clog a law student's arteries, taught criminal law at the University of Toronto and Osgoode Hall Law School and lectured at the Bar Admission Course in Criminal Law. No stranger to the media, he had authored an elegant exercise in hagiography, *Claiborne: My Career in Crime,* hosted a TV series on famous murder trials, is a frequently consulted expert on several radio and TV programs and pulls down fat fees on the lecture circuit.

In the courtroom, he deployed a theatrical style reminiscent of F. Lee Bailey and Johnnie Cochran. His high-profile clients included the likes of wife murderers, serial killers and mass murderers — men whose own mothers long ago gave up defending them. Without exception, he obtains sentences far more lenient than his clients deserve. In one notorious case, he secured the exoneration of a justly convicted multiple child killer by working every loophole known to the system (and a few unknown until he evoked them). Witnesses for the prosecution often got subjected to cross-examinations that left them humiliated, discredited and diminished. B.B.'s talent for seducing jurors into seeing things his way is so refined that by the time he ends his summation, they can't distinguish truth from spin.

All this he justifies by invoking the *presumption* of innocence, a marvelous gift that Mother Justice bestows equally on the blameless and the guilty. That he often tips the scales of justice in favor of the guilty is all part of the system, the price we pay for struggling to be fair. He can't be faulted for exploiting its weaknesses. Guys like B.B. keep our adversarial system on its toes — and some of us in need of meds for high blood pressure.

Who's Who does not document his fondness for alcohol, reputed to have fueled his brilliant opening arguments, cross-examinations and summations. Nor is his lechery recorded, except in the psyches of the women he's hit on.

"I assume I owe the honor of this visit to your desire to write me up."

The message I left with the receptionist at B.B. Claiborne's office had resulted in a return call from the Big Man himself and an invitation to his Rosedale starter home.

Perversity in the impending face of flagrant wealth displays again made me dress down for the occasion. Perhaps his low ranking of writers on the Great Scale of Being prompted him to do the same. It was evident, though, from our respective garb that we shared radically divergent notions of "casual" dress. Yet his Movado watch, cashmere turtleneck, earth-tone coordinated pleated cords and Gucci loafers failed to snuff out the unpleasant odor emanating from his pores. And someone forgot to tell him that wigs have no place on a man's head outside a British courtroom.

Under dim lights, he could have passed for one of his clients, post-makeover for a courtroom appearance. Over the course of his career, some of their dirt had rubbed off and accumulated under the skin. I recovered my professional aplomb by reminding myself that this dude probably got closer to the truth behind Short Willie's many masks than anyone on the planet.

"Yes, Mr. Claiborne. I went to the editor of *Toronto Life* with a proposal for an article detailing your representation of William Shortt. She commissioned me to deliver a feature story."

He paused to suck on his cigar through fat fingers while an

apparently mute Della Street set a silver tray on the Louis-what-ever table separating us. Because he didn't trouble to introduce us, or thank her, I was left wondering whether she was his wife or servant. Probably the distinction was negligible. Hadn't the poor woman clued in to the fact that the route to garnering his attention lay in committing a crime so gross you earned a Hannibal Lector badge?

He tilted a generous gush of Laphroaig into a cut-glass vessel thick enough to restore Helen Keller to vision. "Drop the Mister. Call me B.B."

Now Bee-Bee sounds to me awfully like one of those ladies of both sexes who advertise their erotic services in the back pages of disreputable magazines, but who was I to demur?

"Are you sure I can't enliven your coffee?"

Without pausing to hear my response, he topped up my Spode cup. "And every good story needs a hook, Miss Yeats. You pitched your proposal by linking it to renewed public interest in the Shortt case ... provoked, no doubt, by the results of the digging-up of one of his alleged victims?"

His rhetorical question led me directly into the subject at my hand. "*Alleged* victims? Was there ever any doubt in your mind that he killed those five people?"

He waved his cigar in a dismissive gesture. "My dear, guilty or innocent — five victims, four, three, two, one or none —with any miscreant it's all the same to me. Except, of course, when it comes to how I *design* my defense. Keep in mind that I'm defending my client, not the crime."

As if to confirm his fellowship with other artists, his eyes briefly flitted to a decent bronze casting of Degas's *Little Dancer.* "Building a defense is pure architecture, my dear. Pure archi-tecture. Better, of course, if one begins construction on a secure foundation set on uncontaminated soil, as it were. In the absence of such optimal conditions, knowing beforehand that you are erecting your case on uncertain ground serves to stimulate the imagination. Clarence Darrow once said, 'Inside every lawyer is the wreck of a poet.'"

"And H. L. Mencken famously said of Darrow, 'A bolt from heaven will fetch him in the end,'" I parried. "It must strain even a poet's rhetorical resources to put a positive spin on rape." My riposte was greeted by a reptilian smile.

Cigar funk was clogging my view. *What would Queen Maeve say under the circumstances?* I desperately needed a bull of similar quality.

"Forgive me if I'm mistaken, but I take it from what you've just said that you were never in any doubt about Shortt's guilt?"

His smoking turd had self-extinguished. "There wasn't a shred of doubt in my mind that as a rapist the man was without peer in his field. That's precisely what attracted me to him."

While he flailed about trying to relight his stogie, I transferred my laced coffee to a nearby vase. Now was not the time to renew my drinking: alcohol would swiftly erase what few inhibitions kept me from punching this asshole in his privileged paunch.

"Of course the DNA evidence left not a shred of doubt in anyone else's mind about his career as a rapist. But the murders — haven't a few people who got close to the case, including Dr. Jonathan Rosenberg, expressed their doubts about his taking credit for them?"

"A confession is a confession is a confession. While my client was resident in a psychiatric facility, where he confessed, I negotiated with the Crown to obtain the best deal for my client conceivable under those unhappy circumstances."

"That masterful plea bargain meant Shortt never stood trial for the very murders to which he'd confessed."

"His confession left me very little wiggle room — the best I could manage was to persuade the Crown to modify a few of the circumstances of his inevitable confinement." He lavishly refreshed his glass. "The reason my client never stood trial for the murders was that the Crown simply had insufficient evidence to ensure a conviction."

I used the small window his pause provided to revise my interview strategy. B.B.'s ego responded to flattery with more flatulence, smoke and mirrors. When Ailill really pissed off Maeve, she volleyed with a jab to his nuts.

"Something's stuck in my craw, here, B.B. If Shortt's confession was bogus, then the real killer — or killers — is still out there, unpunished and adding further victims to his biography. Didn't that tweak your conscience?"

"For an alleged professional in your field, I'm shocked and appalled at how readily you confuse my job description with that of a homicide detective. Whether or not my client's confession was legitimate, the mere fact of it gave me that tiny bit of leeway with the Crown on his sentencing for the rapes. The fact that the police didn't have enough hard evidence for the Crown to develop an effective prosecutorial strategy was entirely *their* fault. Call it a classic 'rush to judgment' case. It was their job to amass sufficient evidence to lay charges and secure a conviction. If any real doubt remained in their minds about who actually perpetrated those murders, they should have continued the investigation and secured enough evidence for a first-degree-murder conviction. Instead, in their overzealousness to convict him, they leaped at his confession and failed to pursue any other theory or leads."

This man is an original. Hope they broke the mold. "Why didn't the cops press on with the investigation? They already had Shortt safely behind bars and had more than enough solid evidence to make an airtight case on the rapes and send him away for life."

"The reasons are abundantly clear to anyone who takes the

time to study the history of wrongful convictions in this country. Their most powerful motivator in the instance of the serial murders attributed to Shortt, wrongly or not, was political pressure."

"Did Shortt ever give you any concrete reason for believing that he was innocent of the murders?"

He sucked on his cigar as if it was an aspirator. "To answer that, my dear, would be to betray client privilege, notwithstanding his untimely demise. I've since reflected, though, that even a novice profiler could have pointed the police investigation in a different direction."

I had to keep unclenching my fingers from the pugilistic fist they persisted in forming. It's unladylike to punch an old man in the face, and definitely not recommended as the best way to terminate an interview.

"I understand that he intended to phone you the very day he was killed."

My mentor splashed himself another four fat fingers of single malt. "I see you've made short work of your coffee. Why don't we forget the coffee this round?"

As he extended the bottle across the table I placed my mangled hand over my cup. "No, thanks, I'm driving."

"Yes, and a splendid charger it is you rode in on. We should call you Jane d'Arc."

"Yes, my Harley is less of a gas-guzzler than that Bentley in your driveway. I'm assuming the Rolls must be in for servicing."

After paying his own witticism the tribute of an avuncular chuckle (the uncle who's about to molest you), he resumed. "To answer your question: I did not speak with William on the day of his demise. If you're wondering what message of significant import might have motivated him to call me, you should understand that he regarded me as his agent. He probably had another idea he wanted me to pitch to a publisher or a film company. Alas, we'll never know what fresh creative concept he took to his grave."

Not surprising Willie might have so regarded B.B., whose tireless self-promotion and lust for the spotlight rivaled his own.

"You haven't once cautioned me that anything you've said is off the record. Aren't you concerned about how some of your remarks might go down with my readers?"

"I'm an institution in this country, Miss Yeats. An in-sti-tu-tion who graciously bears the burden of numerous honorary degrees, not to mention the Order of Canada. I am our country's most celebrated defense lawyer — and justly so, I might add. People enjoy my flair, my joie de vivre. It's a scarce commodity in a nation devoted to bland. And I'm nearing the end of 'a long and distinguished career,' to quote many of your colleagues. The bottom line will remain the number of acquittals I've racked up." His theatrical inflections served to insert quotation marks around the laudatory press citations to which he'd alluded.

"Irrespective of your defendants' guilt."

"No, no, no, my dear, *dis*respective of their guilt. Guilt is like marriage vows: it gets in the way of one's pursuing the wealth of diversions life offers the adventurous spirit. In any case, my moral beliefs should never interfere with the course of justice."

"And the truth — where does that fit into your passion for seeing justice done?"

Another avuncular smile. "Truth — you speak the word like a Platonist, as if it somehow dropped into legal discourse already capitalized. Truth is a mere commodity."

I rose before he could signal his wish for my departure. "B.B., I have to thank you for this meeting. Talking with you has had an effect I hadn't anticipated: it's reminded me of why I write."

He dismissed my words as no more irksome than a fruit fly

buzzing about his bulbous nose. "Were I a less astute observer of human behavior, I might be tempted to interpret your words as a compliment. I do hope law school never tempted you, Ms. Yeats. Your ... um ... talents clearly would find a more congenial home in the priesthood than the courtroom."

"And yours, sir, equally at home on stage or in the gutter."

My stomach was threatening to reveal its contents to an unsuspecting audience. I fled for the door as B.B. Claiborne struggled to levitate his corpulent frame from its brocade nest.

"I don't much care for you, Ms. Yeats — "

"Shit, and that's a major drag. Just as I was beginning to feel all the signs of falling in love again." Retch.

" — notwithstanding your rough edges, I've found it a rare delight to be in the company of such a candid woman. So I'm going to toss you a dog biscuit. Between me and you, dear, Shortt was as innocent of murder as I am of hubris."

You gotta hand it to the upscale dirtball. He had a real gift for irony.

Puffing from the exertion of hoisting his great blob of a body, he said, "If he did murder anyone, it certainly wasn't your lover. As you pursue your folly — please don't think for a moment that I believed a writer of your reputation for targeting the big guns in the justice system intends to write a laudatory piece on me — think 'copycat.'"

I settled for a plea bargain with my stomach. Max would give up a burger for the fart that catapulted me across the threshold.

My meeting with Canada's most celebrated defense lawyer had been less informative than I'd hoped. I hadn't really expected him to discuss anything privileged that might breach his client's confidentiality, but with Shortt dispatched to glory, his privacy was no longer an issue. What I could readily comprehend was why Claiborne would want his own cockroach of a conscience to remain undisturbed under its flat rock.

At least it hammered the final coffin nail into Willie's confession.

CHAPTER 22

HOWEVER OFTEN THE COURSE OF NATURE gets perverted, the spectacle of parents wasted by grief at their child's death never loses its sting. All would happily have bargained away their own lives in exchange. An old colleague of mine whispered at her son's wake, "The only good to come out of my Colin's death is that it's made the prospect of my own so much easier to contemplate."

Some parents survive by burying themselves in work, some by devoting themselves to a project related to the cause of their child's death, others by slipping into drink and denial. All are diminished beyond measure.

For his sake, I was hoping that Dr. Rodney Payne had managed his grief over the past six years better than I.

Steeling myself for meeting Laura's father, I walked north on Spadina toward Willcocks Street. The humidity had lifted just enough to make this a pleasant exercise. The downtown university campus has changed so much since my undergrad days that it's scarcely recognizable, but just entering the environs never fails to press my nostalgia button. Sometimes I regret not having done graduate work and secured myself a professorship. My instincts have always tended to action over contemplation, though.

Truth be told, the University of Toronto Faculty Club, where I'd agreed to meet Dr. Payne for lunch, is the primary reason an academic career sometimes beckons. I strongly disapprove of exclusive private clubs, mainly because I've never been invited to join one. Yet I could sit within these walls all day, reading and hoisting the occasional pint — interrupted, of course, by lecturing, marking papers, writing articles and attending committee meetings. There's a downside to every job.

He was waiting for me outside the entrance to the Wedgwood Blue Room. Normally I prefer the more casual atmosphere of the Pub, but this room's nineteenth-century elegance seemed a perfect backdrop for the courtly gentleman who warmly greeted me. He was wearing a pale green short-sleeved shirt and fawn corduroys.

"Ms. Yeats, I'm so very pleased to meet you." As he stooped from a great and lean height to take my hand, a shock of thick white hair fell over his forehead.

I returned his firm handshake. "As I am to meet you, Professor Payne. Please call me Jane."

"Then you must agree to call me Rodney."

Shortly after we were seated at a table by the windows, he invited me to choose a bottle of wine. "Rodney," I confessed, "I've drunk so little wine since graduating this university that I wouldn't know where to begin."

He chuckled. "That's either very remiss of you to neglect your palate or very restrained. I can safely assume, then, that you're a Stoic rather than an Epicure?"

I looked him in the eye. "Recently Reformed Drunk would be the accurate description. Since hearing that the degenerate who killed my fiancé — and your daughter, Laura — is still free, I've quit drinking entirely."

If it's possible to clear one's throat with discretion, my lunch companion managed it. "Ah ... just so. To be honest, since that very same moment I've chosen a course far less commendable than yours: I have resolutely taken to having more tipples than are wise for a man of my age."

My own confession prompted him to drop his formality a notch. "Actually I've gotten quite drunk on a few occasions." His hands shook as he studied the wine menu. "I've always been a moderate social drinker, but I never anticipated that this horrible nightmare would be given new life."

"I'm sorry to have plunged us so quickly into the subject."

"Don't apologize, Jane. I suspect that for both of us there is no other subject that so commands our attention. Even my tried-and-true consolations in difficult times — reading a few pages of Marcus Aurelius or George Eliot, listening to Bach — no longer work."

What wisdom could I offer a distinguished professor? "Do you know what's worked for me in the past? Researching and writing a book. I know that your bibliography is twice the length of that wine list. Might starting a new book help you now?"

He looked across at me over the top of his reading glasses. "You must be a mind reader. Just two evenings ago, instead of pouring a third whiskey, I jotted down some ideas. Although my field is moral philosophy, I've never given much prolonged thought to the subject of violence — certainly not of the variety we're witnessing these days. Did you see, for example, the story in this morning's *Star?* 'A short life of endless turmoil,' it was titled."

"Yes. The case of the parents who left their dismembered daughter's body parts in green garbage bags in two city parks. The father justified murdering her by saying that she'd been an obstinate and temperamental child. She was five years old."

He banged his fist on the table. "My response to reading that story was very selfish, I'm afraid. As a scholar, I've always tried to read dispassionately. But all I could think was that a father taking his daughter's life is unimaginable to me, a pacifist in my mother's womb. Yet I would kill whoever murdered my Laura. I should be ashamed of myself."

"No, Rodney, you should take great comfort in knowing that your love for her takes precedence over your scholarly training."

"Thank you. That seismic shift in my thinking provoked me to consider writing about violence from a perspective mediated by personal experience. You see, I've always worked toward developing a kind of moral calculus — a set of axioms that provide a code of just conduct any of us might invoke when we're tempted to violence … a framework to steer us into nonviolent alternatives. That has been my life's work. Since Laura's murder, I've been contemplating the conditions under which one might justifiably choose to act violently."

Should I feel good about this unexpected validation of my own homicidal impulses from a learned man whose personal rap sheet probably extended no further than killing houseflies?

The white tablecloths, the white napkins persisted in putting me in mind of purity. But our topic drew me back to purity defiled. "I was, though, impressed by the police investigation that led to the arrest of that little girl's parents."

He studied a pallid watercolor on the far wall. "In sharp contrast to their investigation into the murders of our loved ones."

"Do you plan to examine notions of 'just conduct' when the justice system fails to deliver justice? Is an individual who suffers from some unpunished crime ever justified in seeking personal vengeance?"

"Ah, today the state separates justice from punishment and retribution. The courts regard sentencing as remedial, not punitive."

"And look where that has led us. I'm more inclined to an Old Testament take. 'An eye for an eye.'"

"And look where that's led us, Jane."

Perhaps his inner lecturer returned him to an earlier thread in our dialogue. Or perhaps it was the silence with which I met his remark.

"Jane, you referred to your own writing as having rescued you 'in the past.' What's working for you in the present?"

"I guess it's no coincidence that we've embarked on similar subjects. As you may have guessed, I'm devoting most of my waking hours to crime and retribution."

"What makes me suspect that our approaches may diverge?"

"Perhaps you've read my books?" We both laughed.

He shook his head. "I'm ashamed to confess that my reading is confined to a very narrow circle of scholars. My wife always used to joke that I'd found an infallible recipe for ennui. I am, though, aware of what you've written — even old farts surf the Web. You've won a number of distinguished awards, for which I congratulate you."

Praise never fails to gobsmack me. "Let's just say that my approach is more active than contemplative."

His thick white brows contracted into one impressive caterpillar as he frowned. "Action rarely fails to be more dangerous than contemplation, my dear. While no one could better understand your motivation than I, you must be very careful."

Deprived of his only child, this gentle man had not forgotten how to be fatherly.

"Caution is not my middle name, but I won't take any unnecessary risks." I lied in the interest of moving the conversation backward. To six years ago. "Do I have your permission to ask some questions about your daughter? There are some things I very much need to know, but I'll understand your reluctance to go there."

"Talking about Laura keeps her memory alive. My friends get very concerned when I mention her name — understandably,

I guess. In today's parlance, I should have 'moved on.' I'm especially willing to do anything I can to help you find out who killed your loved one and mine. As I remarked earlier, I'm afraid the police haven't done a very good job of it."

He placed his utensils on his empty plate and settled back in his chair.

"Rodney, would you describe your relationship with Laura?"

"We'd always been close, but my wife's death drew us even closer. Irene died from a rare cancer when Laura was just fifteen. We'd both loved her very much. She and Laura had the usual mother–teenage daughter spats, of course, but nothing beyond the norm. And I was lucky enough to have found in Irene my better half. When she was gone, Laura and I fell into taking care of each other. Because we enjoyed many of the same things, that wasn't so onerous — once the initial shock of grief had diminished."

He leaned forward. "A few years later, when Laura was studying to become a clinical psychologist, we used to debate topics of mutual interest over dinner. The deviant side of human nature fascinated her as much as the moral side intrigues me. Once she was in practice, her thoroughly pragmatic approach certainly overshadowed my theoretical perspective."

His right hand circled the air, as if to summon her voice. "She would say, 'Abstract thought doesn't cut it for me, Dad.' She had to find concrete ways to help her clients put themselves together again."

His expression, hitherto quite serene, collapsed into pain. "I'll always wonder if the failure of her project led to her murder."

My ears pricked up. "Do you have any *specific* failure in mind?"

"Indeed I do," he replied in the determined voice of a much

younger man. "Laura came to me about two weeks before she died. Even in my company she never transgressed client privilege, but that particular evening she confided that one of her clients had broken down during a therapy session and confessed to a number of crimes for which he'd never been found out. She must have felt that he presented a clear danger to himself or to others, but she was very conflicted about how to proceed."

His eyes looked keenly focused on a distant lectern. "The father in me won out over the ethicist: I advised her to go straight to the police. For some reason — and it must have been very compelling — she was reluctant to do so. She said she'd confer with her colleague, Hazel Duncan, before making a decision."

"And did she contact the police?"

"Not to my knowledge. The next time we spoke, she told me that after talking to Hazel, she'd decided to talk to your Peter about her dilemma. Peter's presence in her apartment that horrible night certainly suggests that she went ahead with her resolve."

So Pete had not been the target. He *had* been in the wrong place at the wrong time. If only the gentle, enveloping Wedgwood blue with its classical white figures could suck me into its promise of tranquil sky. Pete was a good and compassionate man. Was that the only reason he had responded to Laura's request for a meeting? Or could he have harbored another, less benevolent, motive?

"Pete never told me much about his friendship with Laura. Had they been close for a long time?"

"Oh yes," answered Dr. Payne. "I should qualify that: close, but not in frequent contact. You see, they met as undergraduates, in a fourth-year seminar they both felt was a waste of time. Apparently they took to skipping the occasional seminar in favor of meeting in the coffee shop. After graduating they lost touch for a few years. Then they chanced to meet at a conference. From then on, they made a point of getting together once or twice a year. More than that I do not know — except that Laura held your partner in very high regard. She once told me that Peter Findley had more integrity than anyone she'd ever known. And a wicked sense of humor."

The strawberries in Devon cream were so delicious that they might have come from the garden I'm always scheming to plant. Pete's integrity and sense of humor I could testify to. *But his fidelity?* I scrambled for a delicate way of posing my question. "Was Laura involved with anyone at the time of her death?" Might that one slip by the professor's keen radar?

"Oh yes, my dear. You needn't worry on that account. My daughter was a devout lesbian."

Good on him: the disclosure of his daughter's sexual identity hadn't disturbed a crumb of his composure. Not for the first time did I thank Sappho for blessings received.

"Did you see Laura again, that is, *after* the conversation during which she expressed concern about her client?"

"No. And it's very silly of me, I guess, to regret that I didn't. After all, there's no reason to suppose that it would have been that grand summary meeting we all wish we'd enjoyed after we've lost someone dear. But I would give anything to have had just another garden-variety meeting of the sort we always loved."

How precisely his sentiment echoed one of my deeper regrets.

"I was, though, expecting a phone call from Laura confirming our plans to meet for lunch. When she didn't call, I phoned her office. She'd always been a woman of her word, you see. Hazel Duncan told me that Laura hadn't shown up for work that morning. Nor had she notified the office that she wouldn't be in that day. Hazel hadn't been able to reach her at home either.

Hazel is not an alarmist, and she was very upset."

"Laura and Hazel were friends?" I asked.

"Yes, they were more than colleagues. And Hazel knew that Laura had good reason to be distressed about one of her clients. In any case, that's when I decided to phone the police and report my daughter missing. At the time, I was embarrassed by my overreaction. To catch their attention, I trotted out my position at the university, for which bit of credential flashing I remain ashamed. The parent of a prostitute should be taken no less seriously, of course. I did have the grace to feel embarrassed. Looking back, I guess that's as good an example of irony as anyone might think of."

"How did the police respond to your call?"

"Their response marked the only efficient aspect of the brief investigation that ensued. Apparently an officer who happened to be close to Laura's apartment responded by heading directly to her place. Discovering the door to be unlocked, he entered." Rodney paused to stare out the window. "The rest you know."

"Do you know the name of the responding officer?"

"No, I was never told."

"You've said enough to make me conclude that your estimation of their subsequent investigation is as low as mine."

His eyes returned to meet mine. "Shortly after Laura's body and Peter's were discovered, two detectives appeared at my home to inform me that my daughter had been murdered. They were not unkind. After all, there can be no gentle way of breaking that sort of news to a parent. But I did rather expect to see them again. One can only assume that William Shortt's confession shortly thereafter obviated any further need for them to speak to family members of the deceased."

I had exhausted my list of questions. "Thanks very much for talking with me. It can't have been easy. And thanks for this delicious lunch, from a woman who often neglects to eat."

He signed the bill and passed it back to the server. "Jane, you've done a very thorough job of interviewing me. Now I've got a firmer grasp on the reasons underlying your success as a researcher. But is there anything I can do for you personally?"

I smiled. "Yes, Rodney, there is. Two things, actually. You can ask Hazel Duncan to be as forthcoming as possible with me. And you can agree to meet with me again on a strictly social basis. You see, I've very much enjoyed your company, painful as our discussion has been."

"I'd be flattered." He scribbled his phone number and e-mail address on a scrap of paper retrieved from his shirt pocket.

We walked the short block to Spadina together. As I turned back to glimpse his stooped frame waiting for traffic to slacken, I impulsively called out his name. "Professor, I've forgotten one thing." I ran over and hugged him. Sudden tears sprang to his eyes and mine.

"Do take ever such good care, Ms. Yeats."

CHAPTER 23

HE DARTED FROM THE BOTTOM of the tank straight for a small group of cherry-nosed fish schooling near the surface, rapidly dispersing them. You see it everywhere: boyz defending their territory.

"She's aptly named, isn't she? *Pelvicachromis pulcher.* It means 'beautiful-colored belly.' They're commonly known as Kribs."

I turned to face the source of my edification. Standing at the entrance to the waiting room was an attractive woman with a wry smile on her face. In her early forties, I guessed, although her trim body could pass for twenty.

I returned my attention to the beautifully planted aquarium. "Because that fish is aggressive, I took it for a male."

"Look more closely and you'll see why she's being so defensive."

Within a radius of about five inches, a cloud of maybe one hundred tiny striped fish moved in short bursts, comical foragers that picked and nipped at the gravel, rocks, driftwood and plants. One strayed too far from the mother ship. Ma Krib gulped it down, making sushi of her own baby.

"Oops! And progressive parents disapprove of spanking their kids."

"Keep watching."

Having returned to the center of her busy fold, the mother spat her offspring back amid its sibs.

"Tending to the needs of an entire village would seem work

enough for one woman. Why don't you remove those cherry-nosed bastards that are making her life even more stressful?"

"Those little bastards are Rummy-Nose Tetras. I put them in the tank to act as dither fish. Kribs are shy fish that prefer to hang out near the bottom of the tank, often hiding among the rocks and caves, making it difficult to watch them. But the dither fish are more venturesome. When the Kribs see them roaming about the tank, they get a signal that it's safe to come out. They're gentle fish, no threat to the Kribs. But they do sharpen the mother Krib's protective instincts — and they distract her from eating her own fry."

"But would she actually kill another fish who did pose a threat?"

"Swiftly and without mercy. That's the simple economy of nature. In fact, every time she spawns I have to remove the male. She turns on him as soon as he's done fertilizing her eggs."

"Your aquarium is teeming with metaphors."

Three minutes into a fish lecture and I'd neglected to introduce myself to the lecturer. Hand extended, I moved toward Hazel Duncan. "Sorry about that. I'm Jane Yeats."

"If I hadn't already guessed that and had mistaken you for a new client, I might be wondering why you seem to obsess around aggression."

I stiffened. "I'm hoping that was a joke, because I am *not* presenting myself as a candidate for therapy. I am here to ask you a few questions about your late colleague, Laura Payne." Shit, once again I'd witlessly invoked my talent for getting things off on the wrong foot.

The lady must have been inoculated against hostility. "And I've made space in my appointment book to accommodate your visit, so let's invest the remainder of our interview in pursuing how I can help you."

She warmed up a degree as she led me into her office. Like

the waiting room, this one was designed to induce relaxation. Soft color scheme, subdued lighting, non-challenging artwork, comfortable seating. Duncan herself appeared to have taken the blueprint for her professional appearance from the decor. Recently refurbished, stylish layered haircut, subtle makeup that brightened her fair skin. Flowered silk blouse and beige linen pants. Silver earrings and a bracelet that looked Mexican. Sexy green pointy-toed boots, as likely to grow bunions as to attract attention.

Our shift from waiting room to inner sanctum triggered a shift in her conversational mode. There she had been forthcoming on the subject of tropical fish, but here she seemed inclined to silence. Gently smiling like a blissed-out Buddha, waiting for me to take the initiative. I know that trick. I've been to a shrink.

Time for a gentle nudge in the right direction. "Professor Payne spoke with you shortly after I met with him. I hope he encouraged you to talk freely with me."

"I'm prepared to talk as freely as client privilege allows, Ms. Yeats."

"I hope it extends to giving me any information that might advance my investigation."

Into the silence that followed my words I interjected, "My investigation into the murder of my fiancé — and your colleague. I think it's fair to say that many minds, including yours, might find a measure of peace knowing that their killer was finally brought to justice."

"Of course you're right. And for the record, Laura was much more than a colleague. She was a dear friend. I'm intensely interested in seeing her killer called to account."

Oh, I doubt that, I thought. I totally doubt that you share my obsession with seeing the bastard brought down. It seemed best to leave my sentiment unvoiced.

"Was Laura good at her job?"

"More than good — she was superb. She radiated an aura of vulnerability that encouraged clients to confide in her. And she went about helping them deal with their issues in a very pragmatic way."

"We're agreed upon the agenda: we would both like her killer brought to justice. Maybe it will help kick things off if I tell you that I'm looking for any connection that might exist between Laura's caseload and her killer. Perhaps some clues to the identity of the perp are lurking in her files. Professor Payne told me that she had spoken to him regarding her concern about a specific client. A man she said had admitted during a therapy session to having committed a number of crimes for which he'd never been discovered. It was her feeling that this man presented a clear danger to himself, maybe to others. She didn't know how to deal with this information. Professor Payne thought it likely that Laura had discussed her concern with you."

Duncan's reply alerted me to the fact that I should be posing outright questions, not ending my verbal paragraphs with a statement.

"I think you'll get a better grasp of the landscape if I describe the general nature of our work at the clinic. Trauma Management Group was founded to offer counseling services to individuals and their families in the aftermath of a crisis. Referrals to us are made through a whole range of community partners, including police, fire and ambulance, victim crisis workers, clergy and employers."

A growing suspicion that I was watching the construction of smoke and mirrors prompted me to remark, "That scans like page one of a PowerPoint presentation. Could you maybe limit your Magical Mystery Tour to my reason for being here?"

Her composure suffered readjustment. "If you have the patience to hear me out, you'll understand why this background preamble is so important."

I stared back at her with a semblance of patient listening convincing enough to rival Mona Lisa's.

"Privilege is particularly important to our clients because it upholds the right of psychotherapists to maintain their confidence. Numerous surveys about what police officers want from a counseling program have confirmed strict confidentiality to be at the very top of their list — closely followed by their preference for the professional's having no connection with the police department. The latter we've already secured. The former we must be constantly vigilant about maintaining."

Okay. She'd thrown up an alert about what she wasn't prepared to divulge. Or maybe she was letting me know that her professional code of ethics might be driving her to be more circumspect than she'd like. I assumed that her pause seemed targeted at narrowing down the very broad field of clients from anyone who'd experienced a high-stress situation in the course of their work ... to cops. And without being explicit about her strategy. Surely her references to "police officers" and the "police department" hadn't been slips of the tongue.

"What issues do — for example — police officers present with?"

Her smile held more than a hint of complicity. "Law enforcement ranks right up at the top of stressful jobs. Officers continually confront the effects of murders, violent assaults, accidents and serious personal injury. This exposure impacts not only the individual officers but also their families. What we're asked to deal with has come to be known as 'police trauma syndrome.'"

Forgive me, Miss Manners, for I have snapped. "These days your profession has built an industry around creating a syndrome to fit every conceivable human behavior. What distinguishes police trauma syndrome from the thousands of others?"

My rude attempt to push her into speaking less like a text-book failed. "Current definitions of post-traumatic stress disorder don't take into account the situations in which a person may be *repeatedly* exposed to catastrophic trauma. Law enforcement officers suffer such events routinely."

"You want to me ask you what the symptoms of this PTS are. I'm asking."

She should have told me to piss off. But think how many clients such a directive would drive out of her lucrative practice.

"The symptoms can develop over time or acutely after a single catastrophic event. They're most clearly manifested in the statistics: high divorce rates, suicide, domestic violence, heart attacks and stroke, cancer, depression, alcoholism."

"So give me a symptom that separates cops suffering this syndrome from the rest of us."

If Duncan felt tempted to create another trauma victim on the spot by slapping me upside the head, she gave no indication. "Then I won't attempt to impress you with statistics. Perhaps if I underscore one symptom ... suicide springs to mind. If you need your 'promising lead' to be alive, I may have to disappoint you."

Could Pete's killer be dead? In any case, I still needed the details.

"In the interest of cutting to the chase here, let me suggest a hypothesis: the client Laura was so concerned about killed himself. Maybe that so upset her she needed to consult you — and speak to Pete — because she felt guilty about not spotting the warning signs. Maybe she was privy to *why* he committed suicide."

Silence.

I exploded. "Listen up, Madam Shrink. My lover got dead. So did your friend. While I'm ripping apart my life and my sanity trying to get to the bottom of why two fine people are rotting in their graves, you are busy doing a really good imitation of a talking Psych 101 textbook."

My fist bruised itself on the surface of her cherry desk, punctuating my outburst. "Can you drop your professional demeanor for just one minute and tell me something I really need to know?"

Un-fucking-ruffled, she reached for a notepad. "I recommend medications only when they seem likely to advance a client's recovery — when talk therapy is not sufficient."

On the note she handed me was scribbled a name. *Debbie Clarke.* "As I remarked earlier, high divorce rates are among the symptoms of police trauma syndrome. Ex-wives often exhibit 'loose lips' syndrome. Perhaps this particular ex-wife can be found in the phone book. If not, perhaps someone in the force who's sympathetic to your cause can help you contact her." She glanced at her watch. "I'm sorry, Jane, but I have a client waiting."

I regretted most of the incivility it took to reach her disclosure. "Thank you very much." I crumpled up the note and tossed it back to her. "I've already lost what you gave me. And I apologize for my ... hostility."

"Under extreme pressure we all resort to whatever means we have at hand. Your apology is accepted. And I wish you extreme good luck in your search."

Smiling tightly, she rose and offered a parting handshake. My damp palm met her dry one.

I was about to open the door from her office when she observed, "I would have been sorely tempted to leave Laura's client file open on my desk throughout this interview. But the police removed it from the office in the course of their internal investigation into the circumstances surrounding Detective Sergeant Tom Clarke's suicide. It has never been returned."

A guy who looked cute enough to be a firefighter was

pacing the waiting room. I ventured a final glance at the fish-tank.

Ma Krib was engaged in another fierce attack on the red-nosed guys.

CHAPTER 24

OBLIVIOUS TO THE FACT THAT SHE IS ONE, Etta only wishes she'd been born in a theme park. Following her successful "Man in Black" night, she scheduled a Western film festival to run the course of the summer — ten weekly "Horse Opera Nites" on which she'd screen genre classics.

Sweet Dreams got decked out in appropriate style. Sawdust was scattered on the floor, the ceiling shot with fake bullet holes. The knotty-pine walls were plastered with fabulous stills and authentic framed gems from Etta's vintage poster collection: *The Great Train Robbery* — SENSATIONAL AND STARTLING "HOLD UP" OF THE "GOLD EXPRESS" BY FAMOUS WESTERN OUTLAWS. My favorite, from *Stagecoach:* "a powerful story of 9 strange people." They shared space with repro tin signs in period wood typeface crafted by one of her regulars: "Gentlemen will please refrain from Smoking, Spitting and Profane Language during the Performance."

Etta hosted opening Nite, "Birth of the Oaters," which featured *The Great Train Robbery, The Covered Wagon* and *The Iron Horse.* She bounded onto the stage decked out in Annie Oakley drag, her buckskin shirt sagging with enough medals to suggest that she'd served heroically on every front since the Battle of the Boyne.

My mother, a Ph.D. manqué, delivered a pithy eulogy to the early days of Western cinema, tracing its roots back to colonial folk music, the works of James Fenimore Cooper, Francis Parkman, Mark Twain and Brett Harte. She documented its first stirrings, its flowering and its heyday. That it might have suffered any decline in quality or popularity she failed to note — although *Blazing Saddles* was declared the Antichrist and spaghetti Westerns were excommunicated. Her audience, which included a lot of folks whose closest brush with culture was E. coli, sat enraptured.

She concluded by gesturing to one of the tin signs. "Gentlemen — smoking's allowed, confine your spitting to the urinals, and profane language is welcome. You gals can do whatever the hell you want! The menu's baked beans and beer. Beans are on the house."

By way of signaling the projectionist, she drew her cap gun and pretended to shoot the ash from a regular's cigarette, then fired it into the ceiling.

Slumped alone at the table the farthest from the stage, I could have pretended she didn't belong to me, but why bother? By now, everybody knows me. Since I got whacked by my first hormone cascade, Etta has devoted herself to scripting a mental movie that begins with how she found me nestled under a cabbage leaf. Since the moment I realized that Etta bore no intentional resemblance to other kids' mothers, I've incubated a fantasy that Diana Ross abandoned me five minutes after birth. For mother and daughter, the time had finally arrived to admit that we were yoked, surely as a Conestoga wagon to its cayuses, through desert and dry gulch.

The joint was packed, Etta's usual posse of scruffy regulars augmented by a few university types. Etta figured they were film buffs. I assumed they were sociologists. A great evening was had by all. I suggested only one revision to the format — that she scratch the baked beans from the menu. By Nite's end, Sweet Dreams was redolent of the farting-around-the-campfire scene from the Antichrist.

I dutifully attended the second Horse Opera Nite, themed "A Squaw's Love" and devoted to depictions of Native Americans in silent Westerns. Surprisingly, Silver had agreed to take to the stage costumed as Mona Darkfeather, aboriginal starlet of the silver screen. Etta swore to me that Silver had been delighted to accept her invitation to host.

And so it appeared. While country music fans often tilt to the right of the ideological spectrum, political correctness has penetrated even the shadowy corners of Sweet Dreams. Silver must have figured this gave her a mandate to insult her mostly white audience. She startled everyone by pointing out that most of the early Westerns that centered on Indians were idyllic love stories — *Grey Cloud's Devotion, Silver Wing's Dream, Little Dove's Romance*. The stereotype was a positive one: the Indian was a figure of integrity, stoicism and reliability.

"Think about it," she challenged, "if this representation wasn't true to life, would white capitalists have used the Indian as an advertising trademark on fruit, tobacco and other merchandise?" I wanted to stick up my hand and confront her with Aunt Jemima of pancake-box fame, but only Silver could convert the cigar-store Indian into a heroic icon.

Contrarian that she is, she then introduced her picks — two early D. W. Griffith films, *The Indian Runner's Romance* and *The Redman's View* — surprisingly sympathetic portrayals of Indians from the director who soon thereafter graced the world with his ode to the Ku Klux Klan, *Birth of a Nation*.

"Fast-forward to today," she concluded. "The silent Indian is silent no longer. Fact is, he's kicking up a storm. And the once-silent squaw may be getting it on with another squaw."

The silence that followed her exit from the stage was profound.

The third Nite came to be mine through blackmail. During the festival's early planning stage, I'd wandered into Sweet Dreams just to check up on the old cowgirl. I found her seated at the bar, nursing one of her shocking-pink Shirley Temple cocktail horrors. Her color-coordinated acrylic fingernails were impatiently tapping a mock-up of the program. She handed it over to me (not for my approval, as it turned out).

My eyes froze when they hit "The Serial Queens: Heroines of the Silent Western" — *a screening hosted by Jane Yeats.* Etta's brief bio of her only child ran thus: "I can't think of no woman more fit to introduce fans to this bunkhouse of wonderful cinematic tomboys than my own daughter, Jane Yeats, who sits astride her Harley proud as Dale Evans atop Buttermilk" (at least she hadn't written "Roy").

Our ensuing Gunfight at the Sweet Dreams Corral lasted only five minutes before I conceded defeat. In no uncertain terms, I told Etta that she was presumptuous and domineering. No way would I host that event. Just as I was concluding that she had run out of blackmail threats ("I'll tell the world you cancelled 'cause you were too drunk, in labor or in jail"), she hit on the only one that had real teeth. "I'll tell them you're in rehab."

"Etta, that hit so far below the belt, my toenails are turning black and blue."

"Well, you have quit smokin' and drinkin' ..."

"That's true, but it's still no reason to broadcast the tragedy. It's not like I've become a born-again temperance queen."

"Most women would be proud."

"I'm not most women."

A rare flicker of sorrow transversed her pancaked brow. "Yeah, that's why I dream about havin' found you in a cabbage patch."

"And how do you suppose I feel about having you for a mother?"

She stubbed out her Cameo. "Proud. Damn proud."

As I reluctantly boned up on my topic under Etta's tutelage, I found myself quite enthralled by it all. After screening dozens of serial-queen melodramas, I settled on three starring heroines so tough they made Bette Davis look like Goldilocks: *The Perils of Pauline,* of course, and two lesser-known gems, *Ruth of the Rockies* and Mack Sennett's *Mickey* (whose queen cross-dresses as a jockey to win a race and her man). My heroines got in fistfights, fired pistols, leaped from speeding locomotives, jumped off two-story buildings and rescued distraught men tied to the railroad tracks. It was the stuff of my dreams.

I dressed as the deservedly forgotten actress Edith Storey. Actually, I looked more like a demented Girl Guide. Among other things, my introduction tackled such thorny academic issues as the role played by the Women's Christian Temperance Union crusade in driving men to the frontier. "Can it be an accident that the characteristic indoor setting for Westerns is the saloon?" I thundered.

Among the audience, it had become a cult salute to the Nite's host to fire off their cap guns as she left the stage. My head swelled a bit as the fusillade ensued.

I made my way straight to the bar for a Coke. Kenny the bartender was gaping at me.

"Be honest, Kenny, is it my hooters or the holster?"

I laughed as his eyes popped.

"Mother of God, is that blood? Jane, I ain't jokin'. Look at your arm."

Sure enough, my denim sleeve was rapidly taking on a deeper hue. I got Kenny to it cut open.

"Fuck, man, somebody shot me."

As my lights went out, I heard Kenny screaming for Etta.

CHAPTER 25

ALTHOUGH I FELT MORE LIKE WALKING the short distance, I returned home from emergency at Toronto Western Hospital in a taxi. The nurse had advised me to take it easy for a few days, and I intended to be fully compliant for the next several hours. The same nurse also told me that the person who'd given me first aid immediately after the shooting knew what he was doing. I assumed she was referring to a paramedic — until Etta informed me that a handsome man had rushed to my rescue after I fell into an unseemly swoon. He stopped the bleeding and called 911.

The bullet had been removed from my arm and the incision stitched up by a young doctor who, in a previous life, had probably worked on the Bayeux tapestry. His needlepoint was that good. Not to mention the fact that he was sweet enough not to comment on my cowgirl attire, although he couldn't resist asking about my reattached fingers on the other arm. Hey, these days even cowgirls get shot up. Dale Evans be damned: now we do more than make coffee for Roy and warble "Happy Trails to You."

I was pissed off to the max. The wound would heal, leaving me with yet another scar to add to my growing collection. No way had the shooter mistaken a genuine 9 mm handgun for a copy. No way had a stray bullet made its searing way into my arm. Some SOB had sent me a sharp "back off" warning. Not sharp enough to kill me: maybe that was an insult to how much of a threat I wasn't at this stage in my investigation.

As I stepped out of the taxi in front of my hamster cage I took considerable comfort in knowing that the dumb-ass shooter was a better marksman than a profiler. He hadn't done sufficient research into the personality of his target.

Lots of things scare me: Max getting sick; cars backfiring within close range (I always assume the exhaust pipe set its sights on my ass); my furnace failing on the coldest day of the year and when the service calls are backed up for three days; rapists; dinner parties; pedophiles; priests; Etta when she's on a rampage; psychopaths. A few things immobilize me: cancer, the very thought of losing Etta ... But thanks to my departed father's devotion to bullying, mocking, baiting and beating me when I was a mouthy kid, attempts to intimidate me have the opposite effect. I morph into the granddaughter of Buffy the Vampire Slayer and Xena, Warrior Princess. And thanks to my dates with the gym, now I was fit enough to execute all my revenge fantasies.

Before I'd unlocked my purple front door I was scheming payback time. Longing, white-knuckled longing, for a beer. Forget the Smithwick's, Guinness, Murphy's, Harp, Boddingtons, Kilkenny, Newcastle Brown — even a can of domestic would suffice. I settled instead for pouring a pint of cranberry juice spiked with soda water (which momentarily gave the illusion of a thin head) into my favorite, forsaken mug. As I paced the first floor my little gray cells got to work. Max picked up the marching beat and paced alongside me.

Some prick wanted me to look no further into the circumstances surrounding Pete's murder. That had to be someone with a lot to lose if I persisted. I couldn't hope to flush out the shooter, but at least I would let him know that I had no intention of ceasing and desisting. Short of renting every billboard in the city, I could think of no better way of broadcasting that intention than to write an article detailing my investigation to date. Revealing nothing truly pertinent to where I was headed next, but alluding to the likelihood of a successful outcome. As to style, I'd choose "personal confession" — a tearjerker mode — over my trademark hard-hitting, true-crime voice.

Just as I was about to begin scribbling out my venom, someone knocked.

Nothing like a cute guy at your door bearing flowers to perk up a girl's dull day. Cute enough to tuck in my jeans pocket for future reference. Problem was, I knew who he was.

He smiled at me in megawatts. "Hi, I'm Hunter."

"Me Jane, " I replied, wanting to flush him out. Couldn't have him thinking that anyone with only one name who isn't Prince or Madonna gets recognized in a flash.

"I'm sorry. Detective Sergeant Joe Hunter. Homicide. Was at the bar when you got shot. Just wanted to check in. Make sure you're okay."

Just how old was this dude? He was talking e-mail speak, like a kid raised on message boards and chat rooms.

Of course I was harboring a hidden agenda: I wanted to turn the tables and interrogate Hunter. This was the investigator who had obtained Short Willie's confession to the five murders. And etiquette, always my prime mentor, dictated that I should thank him profusely for having taken charge after the bullet entered my arm.

"Please come in," I invited, accepting the fleurs.

I tore off the paper to expose a bouquet that looked to me like $75. "They are gorgeous. Thank you so much — especially because, from what my mother tells me, I am the one who should be making this gift." Lord, how I do carry on when I'm lusting for information.

"The pleasure is all mine, Jane. I'm just relieved to see you looking so well." He seated himself on the sofa.

Hunter's reference to my appearance made me suspect that he, too, was lusting for something. I was looking rather like a mature Anne of Green Gables whose fetching wardrobe had gone south. Lean frame, chestnut hair — forget the pigtails — and freckled skin. Albeit a few decades down a road a tad more dodgy than any that intrepid young lass checked out. And shabby, shabby threads.

He, by contrast, looked as if he'd just emerged from a makeover detailed by a gay fashion stylist. Mid-thirties, tall and broad-shouldered, cheekbones as sculpted as his muscles, strong face with a neatly cleft chin, teeth by Crest Whitestrips, short black hair gently gelled into subtle spikes, clothes by Gap without the gaps. All in all, gay chic for sure; even the few indications of sartorial carelessness seem contrived. No evident traces of overindulgence in booze, drugs or nicotine. Coolly assertive, secure in his look. Eye candy for women who like that sort of image.

What I wanted to learn from Dapper Dude, since he was here, is what on God's sweet earth persuaded him to accept Short Willie's alleged confession. That pockmarked, more-holes-than-a-Toronto-street piece of shit failed to convince Jonathan Rosenberg, B.B. Claiborne, me and at least one good crime reporter that Willie had done the deeds. Hunter's career had benefited grandly from his having extracted that confession — from a slimebucket who'd pretend in front of a credulous audience to have created the world in seven days. The police brass had been overly eager to hang the murders on anyone with a record for flashing the family jewels on a subway car.

I turned my attention to piercing his facade, while he turned his to discreetly shooing Max from investigating his crease-free pant legs. Bless my beast.

"Given your intimate connection to the case — not to

mention your reputation as a crack private investigator, you must know that I was involved in the investigation leading up to William Shortt's arrest and conviction."

Hah! "Push" must have come to "shove" for him, too. No more e-speak. I decided against feigning ignorance of his self-described "achievement." And I calculated the risk of pretending that I had no current interest in the reopened file on Ruth Rosenberg's murder. I chose to be honest, given the efficiency of grapevines and Hunter's record of calculating intelligence.

I feigned approval. "Yes, for sure, I do know. But first, may I offer you a beverage? I'm sorry, but I have nothing alcoholic. A wonderful selection of juices, though." *Lord, what brought me to this sorry pass?*

"Orange juice would be great, thanks. No problem about the booze-free thing. I don't drink."

As he recounted his version of the shoot-up at Sweet Dreams that creased my arm, I so hung on his every word that one might have thought I was having the secret of eternal life revealed before me. And I expressed my gratitude for his part in my deliverance with praise worthy of an Academy Award presenter.

"Was it difficult, getting Shortt to confess?"

He shook his head. "That perv was so hot to brag about his crimes it was easier than trapping a mouse. You should have heard him. It was all I could do to shut him up so I'd get a decent night's sleep — but I kept thinking that if I let him go on and on, he might toss in some more incriminating details."

I nailed him with fierce eyes. "And given that you had nothing else to tie the murders to him, you must been hungry for an airtight confession — I mean, one packed with details only the real killer could have known."

For the first time, his body language spoke "uneasy." He flicked his left index finger against his nose and shuffled his butt on the sofa as if a spider had invaded his boxers.

"Well … yeah … of course." Hunter paused to slurp his orange juice. "But, I mean, if you had read the transcript, you'd know for sure we got the right guy."

No point in telling him I had studied the transcript with the attention of a Torah scholar and come away feeling that it was about as reliable as the document offered as "Hitler's diary" by an ambitious forger.

I smiled, lizard-like. "Surely you don't mean 'the right guy' for Ruth Rosenberg's murder."

Again the imaginary spider traversed his testicles. "Well, maybe even for hers. That DNA test from the new autopsy means squat. So what if it didn't match up with Shortt's? Maybe she got laid by another guy."

Probably in anticipation of my next question, he added, "And so what if it didn't match up to her boyfriend's? Thanks to the feminists, these days chicks get it on as much as guys do."

"I thought I read something in the paper about Shortt's claim to have strangled Rosenberg in the way he said he did being kind of hinky?" No point in alerting him to my ability to scan autopsy results with the same finesse normal women do recipes.

Hard upon swigging his last gulp of calcium-fortified Tropicana, he said, "The Centre for Forensic Sciences? Don't get me started. If my pet hamster died under mysterious circumstances, I wouldn't take it there. Do you realize how many cases we've lost, or didn't even push to trial, because of their screwups?"

I'm not in the habit of replying to rhetorical questions. My pregnant pause gave Hunter time to squirm anew. Perhaps he'd reminded himself of how I earn a living. Whatever else you can say about my methods, my books tend not to be driven by undermining the forensics folks, even taking into account their rare missteps. If a canary croaked in the jaws of a neighborhood cat, I'd not be the first person the owner would consult re cause of death.

"Let's just leave it at this: I was there, I was the man he confessed to. Years in the force have taught me how to read a suspect. Trust me, we nailed the right guy for those murders."

"And that's including the murder of Peter Findley?"

His eyes welled with something resembling compassion. "Yes, Jane, including your partner."

My expression befitted that of the Blessed Virgin being greeted by the Holy Dove. "Thank God — and you, of course. I couldn't sleep at night if I thought Pete's killer was somewhere out there enjoying what passes for an ordinary life."

As he rose to his feet, doubtless by then regretting the fleurs, I zinged my final question in his direction. "About Shortt's confession — I know investigators make a practice of holding back some vital details of the crime scene, something about the MO or, say, a signature. You know, the kind of details known only to the police and to the killer. In the course of confessing, did Shortt divulge any such particulars?"

"Oh yes, of course. That's how we confirmed him as the murderer."

Once again, I pretended to accept his statement. Obviously the man was such a careerist that he wouldn't shy away from a little mendacity when it promised to enhance his solve rate.

"I really hope my work on the case contributed something to easing your grief."

Max growled hard on his departing heels.

Hunter's work contributed to compounding the complexity of my project.

CHAPTER 26

I PLUNKED DOWN ON THE SOFA, feet up on the coffee table, iBook on lap, and tapped out the article. I always avoid letting subjectivity slip into my prose, guided by Norman Mailer's contrary example. And having made a lifestyle out of keeping myself to myself, I soon found that writing this close-to-the-heart stuff was way harder than I anticipated. So I pulled out of the hat a trick little kids resort to when they're repeatedly sexually abused: I sealed off my real self in a hideout somewhere very safe (imagine Kansas, Dorothy), while my professional-writer self sailed off on a dangerous flying carpet, back to the night I learned of Pete's murder.

I wrote for hours from a survivor's viewpoint, a kind of victim-impact testimonial. And I concluded it with my personal recipe for transforming oneself from victim to activist. This recipe was not for every palate: it included difficult ingredients like when the person you love is murdered and his killer goes free, try to find him; and when you are shot as a direct consequence of that effort, get over it and on with your investigation.

I did allow myself a brief paragraph of autobiographical indulgence, speculating that *perhaps* it was my interest in the alleged suicide of a drug squad officer that had earned me a bullet in the arm.

Five thousand words later I gave Max a snack and flopped exhausted onto my bed, boots on, still dressed, leaving my article unread and unrevised. Enough already.

Cradling my hurt arm on a pillow, I slept for a record eight hours, much of it hagridden by nightmares. At eight the next morning I woke up startled to find myself feeling sane — well, less fraught. Maybe all those self-help boffins are bang on the money about the healing powers of "talking about it." God help me: should this grow into a habit, I'll be capable of emptying entire crowded rooms five seconds after opening my mouth.

As Max raced through the park chasing seagulls, real and imaginary, I pulled a final draft of the article together in my head. Two hours after we returned home, I had a solid polished copy in order. Fifteen minutes later I had secured a swift agreement from my old editor at the *Toronto Post* to read it. Within an hour of receiving it via e-mail, she accepted it for publication the following day.

My article appeared on the first page of the "Metro" section of the morning paper, headlined (not by me) "Angry crime writer seeks revenge." I would have preferred more subtlety. Sam phoned me minutes later to tell me that a big buzz was already growing around my revelations — in some interesting places, like the Toronto Police Services.

Actions have consequences. No-brainer that may be, but it's a lesson I've been fated to absorb in retrospect.

To date, the profile of me as generated by my neighbors must include decrepit dresser, chick who kicks, Harley ho, booze hound, owner of cur with kindred spirit. And that's the short-list. This morning it plunged a major notch at the precise moment five police cruisers pulled into every available parking space close to my home.

Shortly after 8:00 a.m. Max howled up a storm as the front door suffered under a thunderous pounding that alerted me to my castle being under siege. I opened it wide enough to take in

a small SWAT squad apparently led by the officer who presented me with a search warrant and read me my rights as I scanned
it.

WARRANT TO SEARCH
Canada,
Province of Ontario.

To the peace officers in the said territorial division:
Whereas it appears on the oath of [left blank], of
Toronto Police Services that there are reasonable
grounds for believing that research materials
(including but not limited to hard copy and electronic files) breaching the privacy of an ongoing
police investigation are in the possession of Jane
Yeats at 6 Shannon Street, Toronto, hereinafter
called the premises;

This is, therefore, to authorize and require you
between the hours of 6:00 a.m. and 9:00 p.m. to
enter into the said premises and to search for the
said things and to bring them before me or some
other justice.

Dated this 16th day of August 2002, at Toronto.

Below the signature of the justice of the peace came the fine
print that bellowed out the motive behind this raid. As a
stalling tactic, I took my sweet time reading every single word:

Operation of computer system and copying equipment

(2.1) A person authorized under this section to
search a computer system in a building or place for
data may

(a) use or cause to be used any computer system at

the building or place to search any data contained in or available to the computer system;

(b) reproduce or cause to be reproduced any data in the form of a printout or other intelligible output;

(c) seize the printout or other output for examination or copying; and

(d) use or cause to be used any copying equipment at the place to make copies of the data.

Duty of person in possession or control

(2.2) Every person who is in possession or control of any building or place in respect of which a search is carried out under this section shall, on presentation of the warrant, permit the person carrying out the search

(a) to use or cause to be used any computer system at the building or place in order to search any data contained in or available to the computer system for data that the person is authorized by this section to search for;

(b) to obtain a hard copy of the data and to seize it; and

(c) to use or cause to be used any copying equipment at the place to make copies of the data.

Now I was seeing through a glass much less darkly. This was payback time for my article. Their justification for getting it issued was pure bullshit.

So much for my rights. Had I any apparent choice, I would have dispatched those cowboys back where they came from, along with the cruisers they rode in on.

Once I admitted them, my sanctuary became a war zone. Faster than a Grey Cup football team, they fanned out and into their best game strategy. One officer began shooting photographs of each room. Something told me his results weren't destined for the cover of *Gracious Living* magazine. Him I trailed with my digital camera, shooting him as he shot every room from every conceivable angle.

His justification for his activity did nothing to allay my anger. "We do this before every search begins and after it ends to ensure that no complaints laid by the occupant about damage to the dwelling or its contents can be substantiated."

"Ah, so you're from Molly Maid. Stupid me for thinking you came on behalf of Attila the Hun." I snapped a candid shot of him failing to respond to my repartee.

Detective Mallory, the lead plunderer, had assigned a young officer to keep me in his line of vision at all times. Would this include trips to the can? Max hadn't stopped barking. I could tell he was one flea removed from sinking his fangs into the next blue leg that ventured within a foot of his face. When I heard another jerk suggest that they "remove the mongrel," I phoned Silver to ask her to pick up Max ASAP.

I've never been a woman who stands mute witness to her own undoing. Yet the sight of my home, the only refuge I've known since Pete's death, being systematically desecrated was making me crazy. Difficult to plan your next move when a home invasion is in full swing. Books yanked off the shelves, shaken and tossed on the floor. Drawer and cupboard contents ransacked. Sofa stripped of cushions, beds of linen. Photos and posters removed from their frames, backings torn off. Fridge and stove disassembled. Whatever the hell they thought they might find — or, in lieu of discovery, might plant — I knew I had to collect my wits PDQ.

I phoned Sam, asked him to phone the editor of the *Post* to get their best lawyer over here. Maybe only my space was being violated; I needed to know if I had any remaining rights. Surely I must. This is Canada. We take collective pride in peacekeeping. We did not join the war on Iraq. This is not a police state. We believe in freedom of expression, backed up by our Charter of Rights and Freedoms. Yeah.

Only one person in the house looked as if he was registering higher on the anxiety scale than me and Max — that would be the guy who'd been charged with questioning me. My refusal to answer even one of his queries was sending him ballistic. No way was I prepared to volunteer anything without a lawyer's counsel. While he tailed me like an orphaned chick, I continued to follow the marauders with my digital camera. *Just keep your body in motion*, I told my harried brain, *until help arrives.*

Max stopped yodeling when the front door burst open. Filling close to every inch of the door frame was Silver, near six feet high and half as wide, full Mohawk warrior attitude plugging whatever space remained.

She paused only to offer Max a consoling pat and to whisper something in his ear. Instantly he calmed down and stuck to her right leg as she went straight for the nearest cop, who was still browsing and defiling my living-room bookshelves with the intensity of a Ph.D. researcher. I noticed that he'd begun constructing a column of reference books from my crime shelves. When he hit the bedroom, a sister column of erotica would match it in height.

Planting her considerable presence only inches from his back, Silver bellowed, "Who the fuck's leading this rape?"

He jumped to his feet, turned and took in his interrogator. Looking seriously intimidated, he stuttered, "Detective Sergeant Mallory, ma'am. He's in the basement."

Silver whacked him on the shoulder. "Man's gonna be in way deeper than the basement when I'm done."

Buddy momentarily rallied his diminished powers. "You're not about to threaten a senior police officer are you, lady?"

"No, sweet pea," she thundered. "Not just me — me and

the entire Mohawk Nation. And not *just* a senior police officer — your entire crew will be beadwork before we're done with you sorry lot of palefaced pricks."

My house is leakier than my journalistic sources. Heat zooms out. Sound travels. Mallory appeared to relieve his beleaguered junior. "Lady, this is a secured area."

Seemed likely he had more territory to piss out, but Silver cut him off at the pass. "No one ever mistook me for a lady. Maybe because I'm a raging dyke warrior who successfully prosecuted two RCMP officers for transgressions against my people at Kanesatake."

Surely she hadn't intentionally added "lawyer" to her résumé. Guess she figured "artist" mightn't have much currency in the present company.

Her eyes narrowed to black slits. "Secured area, my fat ass — this is the home of a prominent Canadian writer who, and probably this is no coincidence, has a professional hard-on for nailing crooked cops. Maybe you don't want to upset either one of us any further."

It was Mallory's turn to rally diminished powers. "Perhaps you could press your Pause button and tell me why you are here — before, that is, exiting the scene without any further ado."

Silver stepped closer to bring her formidable index finger into biting range of his teeth. "I speak three languages, asshole, and I've never been scared off by any 'ados' in any of them. I am here to liberate the dog, which action I'll execute without any fucking interference from you and your partners in crime. Any more lip and I'll accuse you of racial profiling."

Mallory looked as if his head hadn't hit a pillow for a week. "Just take the dog."

My friend, Max still clinging to her side, paused before exiting. "One more thing, Mad Mallory. You make just one false baby step in this whole raid — and that includes causing Ms.

Yeats here any more grief, and I'll take way more than the dog. You'll lose your badge faster than you lost your integrity."

My dog took advantage of the pregnant pause to position his flank next to Mallory's leg and deposit a wee stream of territorial warning. Only then did he and Silver make their exit, backs straight, heads high, proud and undiminished.

CHAPTER 27

NEXT TO MAKE A SCHEDULED APPEARANCE were Sam Brewer and the *Post*'s top legal counsel, Robert Golden. My journalist buddy, shabby but comfortable in his usual rags, didn't even register on the *GQ* scale. Golden, resplendent in name and Hugo Boss, scored a ten.

While I filled Sam in on the manic proceedings, Golden interrogated my interrogator. Assured that I'd been read my rights, he proceeded to Detective Sergeant Mallory. Their swift exchange of knowing glances assured me that this was not their first meeting. I knew Golden to be on the cops' Top Ten List of "hated = to be feared" defense lawyers.

Golden might have been performing one of his notorious courtroom gigs. First he slowly cast his eyes from Mallory's sparsely occupied scalp to his scruffy department-issue boots. His sartorial self winced out loud. Score one for alpha male. Next he glanced at the search warrant as if he'd been handed a dog turd. Contempt garnishing every syllable, he stared at Mallory. "The reasonable grounds for believing that Jane Yeats is in possession of leaked documents concerning the ongoing investigation into allegations surrounding the drug squad, while not stated here, doubtless are based on the perilously thin ice of her having published an article in yesterday's *Toronto Post*." His stare intensified. "I have read that article, several times. Even a literary critic couldn't deduce any such nuance or implication."

"If a judge hadn't agreed that we had reasonable grounds, the warrant would not have been issued." Having taken refuge behind some big black robes, Mallory looked more confident.

"You don't want to get me started on judges who'd happily sign off on a warrant to strip-search the Virgin Mary for evidence of contraceptives. Thirty years' experience tells me that this particular judge would conduct the search himself. But — for the moment — I can't get in the way of your intention. I can promise you that within hours your headquarters will be papered with so much legal bafflegab there won't be space left to hang a Post-it note."

He held up the offensive document. "Surely I am not to assume that this counterfeit authorization gives you leeway to ransack my client's house?" His tone was beyond rhetorical as his eyes scanned the deconstruction of my house.

"We wouldn't be here otherwise," Mallory asserted.

Flicking an imaginary fleck from his free arm, Golden scorned him. "This warrant, purportedly authorized by a judge, purportedly allows you to scour Jane Yeats's home for notebooks, documents, computer files, agendas and virtually any other information possibly harbored from roof to foundation. Attached to it is a special order prohibiting access to any information relating to the warrant, including the identity of the confidential informant, on the grounds that any such disclosure might compromise the nature and extent of an ongoing investigation. He paused to laser in on Mallory's unsettled face. "Am I reading this accurately so far, sir?"

Mallory executed a nervous two-step before parrying, "So far you've confirmed that you know how to read."

Golden's hitherto deceptively mellow voice rose several decibels. "Now I'm going to exhibit my capacity to read between the lines, Officer. I believe that the undisclosed purpose of this search is to seek the source of a leaked document used by my esteemed client in writing her article. Ms. Yeats alluded to pressing issues surrounding the ongoing drug squad investigation. She made brief but compelling reference to certain hitherto concealed details surrounding that investigation. In the process she must have ruffled more than a few feathers in the chief's bonnet. Not even Goldilocks could believe that the article and this warrant are unrelated."

Mallory's blusterhoard held a few reserves. "We could be seeking the source of her information in the interest of widening our investigation."

"If that were the case, you'd be directly seeking out the source. In my experience, such 'leaks' most often originate from *within* your own force. From my perspective, your real intention is to prevent her from publishing any related articles — indeed, even to discourage her from pursuing any further journalistic inquiries into the nefarious activities of your thoroughly discredited drug squad."

Mallory underscored his authority. "We are conducting this search under the lawful authority of a warrant. You are impeding our progress. So you'll excuse me while I resume my mandate."

Golden adjusted his tie. "And you, Officer, will excuse me while I caution my client and remain present at her side to invigilate any further questioning." He glanced disdainfully at my erstwhile interrogator, who'd been marking time on the sidelines studying a photo-collage of female nudes hanging on the wall. His furrowed brow hinted that maybe he was struggling to interpret the fine line that sometimes separates porn from art. Or maybe he just liked nudes.

Within a heartbeat any points Golden might have scored were erased from the game slate. A bright-eyed, bushy-tailed goon took the stairs from the second floor in a flash. He was clutching a Baggie. "Found this in the suspect's underwear drawer, sir," he reported.

"Lingerie drawer," I corrected before Mallory could respond.

We all stared at the bag currently dangling before Mallory's eagle eye. Oh shit. I recognized that particular Baggie. Déjà vu all over again.

Last year a remarkably similar item fell off the back of a truck into my hands. Shit and double shit. I was in it up to my eyeballs.

Sam excused himself while he could still do so without a police escort. I suspected that he was already mentally composing an exposé of these shenanigans.

While Mallory positively glowed vindication for his raid, the hitherto imperturbable Golden appeared only moderately disconcerted. "One has, of course, only the word of your officer that this item of alleged evidence was, in fact, actually found to be residing in my client's lingerie drawer."

He glanced my way. "Doesn't belong to me," I affirmed.

"I see no reason to alter my assessment of your proceedings. What are your immediate intentions regarding this ... um ... discovery?"

Maybe my reckoning was way off base, but Golden seemed to be baiting Mallory into arresting me. Instead Mallory turned to his junior and ordered, "Bag it."

"Bag the bag, sir?" asked Eager Beaver.

Mallory totally lost his professional demeanor and bellowed, "Just fucking bag the fucking bag!"

I took advantage of their sparring match to study the warrant more closely, specifically that section pertaining to "Operation of computer system." This gave them authority to use my precious iBook to search everything it contained and use my printer to make hard copies of whatever caught their perverse interest. My blood pressure soared.

I unstuck my lawyer from his antagonist. "Robert, I need

you to clarify a delicate point or two here. What criminal activity related to my iBook might they be searching for?"

He ticked off a list from five fingers sporting professionally manicured nails. "Software piracy, distribution of pornography, fraud, theft of computer services, income tax evasion and a whole range of regulatory offenses. And it's not just about search: it includes seizure of your entire computer or only the files relevant to their investigation. They're more inclined to take the entire computer system. The information they want may not be in identifiable files that can be opened using readily-available hardware and software. You might have complex databases or accounting programs they can't access without the associated software. You might have hidden or encrypted files on your hard drive. Perhaps you've programmed your computer to wipe out incriminating files while they are actually examining the system. Maybe that's what you should be fretting about at the moment."

"Robert, if I had the skills to run complex databases and accounting programs I wouldn't be fretting about a damn thing. I'd be basking on a beach in the Cayman Islands studying my stock portfolio."

Smiling politely, he resumed. "They can remove from this house all the tools of your nefarious trade, thereby causing you serious hardship. I can't think of a more effective method of silencing you, even if I apply to court to set aside the search warrant and direct the police to return your property. They can hold whatever they seize for up to three months while they decide whether to lay charges, and they can apply to a justice for an extension of the three-month period."

I fought off the impulse to pitch a seizure. "To go back to your list of criminal activities. I'm only guilty of two of them."

Robert studied his nails. "Please make every effort to refrain from sharing the specific details with me at the moment. You've just hinted that the police might be rewarded with evidence of ... shall we say ... in excess of one crime. So stop worrying about any crimes you've committed in addition to publishing leaked information."

I performed a lightning-fast mental inventory of my iBook's documents and an assessment of how much damage the seizure of my laptop would inflict. Squat. I stifled a giggle. This was information I didn't share with Robert.

Etta's insistence on my frequent presence at Sweet Dreams consumes so much of my time that I keep my old PowerBook in her second-floor guest room above the bar. That way I can slip upstairs and write when my services as a plumber, cleaning woman, server or bartender aren't in high demand. At home, I back up any new files I've generated onto a compact FireWire drive that passes from my hands into those of the beatific Nina next door. In exchange I fine-tune the devout widow's morning shortwave Vatican radio broadcasts and weed her rose garden and bait her mousetraps.

And I had stashed at Sweet Dreams all the documents that might, should they be discovered, get my contacts into trouble: the photocopies of the files Ernie lent me, Jonathan Rosenberg's copy of Shortt's confession and Sam's materials.

Future issues surrounding software piracy and income-tax evasion I'll worry about if and when they materialize. But at that moment I saw no reason not to feign extreme agitation at the very prospect of my iBook sprouting legs. Perhaps I could augment my income by suing the force.

A glance through my eight-by-ten-inch picture window revealed my growing publicity machine. Time to feed the beast.

Daniel thrown to the lions couldn't have wished for a better crowd. A bevy of newshounds packed my short block. Look on the bright side, Yeats. Regard this raid as yet another of life's many unsolicited learning experiences. Make hay. Exploit the media coverage. Bear down much harder on the nerve you've just exposed.

Fast-forward to likely outcomes. Worst-case scenario, I get arrested. Best case, I flush out the rodent who's behind this attempt to shut me up. Either way it goes down, more publicity for my cause.

Dutifully I reported in to my handler. "I'm crossing the street for a slice. Pizza. Domenic's. Can I get you anything? Slice, maybe a sandwich — sausage, meatball, steak, veal?" Buddy's pained look told me he'd prefer a laxative.

Robert did his best to get in the way of Motormouth Unhinged as I blabbed into every mike that passed under my nose en route to and from Domenic's.

Four hours later, Attila and company departed 6 Shannon Street. My iBook, floppy disk drive, modem, Zip disks, floppies and five boxes of binders, files, books and magazines accompanied them. Before following in their wake, Robert assured me that he'd be filing an application to terminate the order denying access to information used to obtain the warrant. He wearily suggested that I phone him before making any more statements to the press. He refused my offer of a tranquilizer.

CHAPTER 28

I TURNED ON THE RADIO. CBC's news on the half hour alerted listeners to my plight. I checked out the telly and was cheered when Citytv news announced that a report on the raid would head off the six o'clock local broadcast.

By morning my appetite for celebrity was sated. All three morning papers were chock full of coverage. No surprise. Last year the circumstances leading up to my four fingertips suddenly departing my body had captivated ghouls citywide. This time my shit had hit a much bigger fan: freedom of the press. Overnight I became poster girl for the single issue most likely to drive the latest terrorist attack off the front page.

My favorite tabloid outdid its shabby self: "Mystery raid on crime writer's house. 'This break-and-enter beyond outrage,' accuses suspect Jane Yeats." Beneath the headlines was an unflattering photo of me. Pity I'd been cropped at the waist. My jeans and boots are my best profile.

> TORONTO (CP) — The search of an award-winning writer's home by Toronto Police Services seeking evidence of an undisclosed crime "smacks of a police-state mentality," bellowed an outraged spokesperson for the Canadian Association of Journalists.
>
> "Everyone in this beleaguered nation should rush out to their nearest bookstore and pick up a

copy of *1984* by George Orwell," said the head of the Writers Union of Canada.

Their voices were joined by that of prominent civil rights lawyer and counsel for *The Toronto Post,* Robert Golden. "This kind of action would do an ayatollah proud. It has no place in Canadian democracy. It violates my client's rights under the Constitution of this country. It violates the Charter of Rights and Freedoms. Indeed, it violates us all. What transpired yesterday is only chapter 1 of this scurrilous saga."

I was just getting into the meat of it when the phone shrilled.

I recognized the click of her Bic. Could almost smell the Cameo. "You've never been photogenic, dear, but a good hairdresser could make you look like you don't sleep in a wind tunnel, eh?"

No one on the planet can exhaust my patience faster than my mother. "Etta, before you segue into the miraculous transformative powers of 'a little lipstick,' maybe you'd like to know how I am."

"That much I already know. I seen the photograph — you're a mess."

"So be grateful, Mom. It's my mess alongside your Tammy Faye Bakker impersonation that makes you look like Miss Geriatric Universe. Call us the Odd Couple."

"Trying to talk any sense into your head is like farting into a high wind."

She banged down the phone, in her demented innocence never guessing what welcome relief that action bestowed on the sole fruit of her womb.

This snippet of mother–daughter dialogue put me in mind of next of kin. How was Max? Was he in the throes of separation anxiety, not to mention post-traumatic stress disorder? When I phoned her, Silver allayed any fears I had about his well-being. I've suspected for a few weeks that he'd nominate her as surrogate mother in a flash. My dog is hypersensitive to the fact that I have not been balancing work and family life.

Silver did disconcert me, though, by strenuously suggesting that I go on-line and Google myself. She further suggested that I narrow down my search by adding the words *sucks* and *blow job*.

I ran around the corner to borrow a few minutes on a neighbor's computer, reminding myself en route to ask Robert if I could charge the police force for the rental of a laptop until such time as mine rematerialized.

My neighbor, a nice lady notwithstanding her Christian fundamentalism, obliged. Unfortunately, her blond and blue-eyed rugrat persisted in observing all my computer moves as I booted up to a Teletubbies screensaver, went online and Googled as per Silver's instructions.

Staring me in the face was the handiwork of some demented Photoshop buff who'd seamlessly pasted a nice head shot of me onto a porno picture. While I don't much fancy being seen as a woman who knows a Clydesdale more intimately than is seemly, I did appreciate the generous curves of my grafted stuntwoman's body, not to mention her astonishing agility. If ever I want to resume dating, I just might post this collage on a dating-service Web site.

From behind my back the forgotten rugrat's voice accused, "You never told me you had a pet horse." As I turned around to bluff my way out of a scene he'd never been treated to in a Bible storybook, his mother swept down liking a starving eagle on a bunny rabbit and flew him out of the room.

"That Internet is full of surprises, Amy," I babbled as I hurried my way to exit stage right. "Maybe you should put some filters in place before Andrew gets any older."

She glared. "I think my son just aged fifty years."

I resisted telling her that after a certain age, one didn't even have to think a dirty thought, let alone commit the related sin, to further besmirch one's reputation. The very act of breathing guarantees each of us a minimum of one unmerited dump of pigeon crap a day.

"Rent laptop" pole-vaulted to the top of my to-do list.

On re-entering my house, I pretended that Max was back. "Boyfriend, my sex life has been a topic of conversation among the erotically challenged since the day Etta presented me with my first box of Kotex. Is she straight? Is she gay? Maybe bisexual? Transgendered (this came hard on the heels of my first Harley)? This morning a new spark got added to that speculative fuel, sweet dog of mine. My accusers never guessed the twisted truth: like Princess Anne, the lady prefers horses."

Only God knows for sure where my sexual inclinations lead me, and she has more pressing things to attend to than the number of times I hadn't been laid in the past six years by man, woman, sheman or beast. So did I.

My attempt to discover the flat rock harboring the identity of the scumbag behind the raid was short-lived. I got stonewalled at every turn. Even Sam could milk not a drop from his extensive sources. In a desperate move I soon regretted, I cajoled Ernie Sivcoski into sharing a burger with me at the Dundalk. I pleaded my case with all the eloquence of a refugee seeking asylum. Venus, goddess of love that you are, forgive me: I even paraded the charms that once drew him to my bed.

He spoke the truth when he reminded me that the foundation stone of police culture is loyalty to one's fellow officers.

"No way would I give up a name, Jane — even if I had it. And why are you acting so shocked and appalled by this alleged 'transgression' of your rights? You can't have imagined that your goddamn book trashing us would win you any fans on the force. I can think of at least a dozen officers who'd delight in seeing you publicly humiliated, just as you did to them. And who's going to blame them? You brought down several careers, woman, two of them attached to decorated officers. So it could be that you've just been given a show of muscle flexing. Maybe one of my fraternity is getting nervous that you've set your sights on a few more badges. If that's the case, consider yourself lucky that you've escaped with only a slap on the wrist."

"And a bullet." I pointed to my bandaged arm. "Those bastards were bent cops, Ernie. They brought themselves down. We're all better off without them around to further pervert the course of justice."

"Since when did you start genuflecting before the statue of Justice?"

"From the moment I learned that Pete's killer was still out there. Thanks, in large part, to the failure of your frat boys to conduct a *proper* investigation into five seemingly related murders. Hey, I've only just begun to get religion. My love for Pete could even prompt me to hail Mary, Mother of Perpetual Help."

Ernie stood up. "Jane, hear this: you stay on this misguided vengeance trip and you'd better be hoping Mother Mary is listening."

"I never knew you were a Catholic, Ernie."

"There's a whole helluva lot you don't know about me."

I raised my good arm and made the sign of the cross. "Bless you, my son. For I know you've sinned."

He was thundering down the stairs before I could ask for the bill.

And so fled my best contact on the force, leaving in his wake the tatters of our odd friendship.

Leaving in his wake also my undiminished resolve to

check much, much deeper into what was riling him and his colleagues.

CHAPTER 29

CUSTOM-FITTED INTO ONE WALL was an enormous entertainment system, with a Sony fifty-inch plasma TV at its center. The screen was filled with life-size inmates of Jerry Springer's zoo, clamoring for raw flesh at feeding time. Ah, the miracle of satellite dishes, collapsing all time slots into a five-hundred-channel garbage pail.

"Why don't you just settle in while I get us a snack," invited Debbie Seeger, the late Detective Sergeant Tom Clarke's ex-wife.

You could fit the entire ground floor of my house into this living room, with space left over for a grand piano.

"Do you watch the soaps?" she asked.

"Not since they cancelled *Dark Shadows*."

Debbie vanished, leaving me resenting how some women give off "hot, hot, hot" signals as naturally as breathing. Me, I have to make a serious investment in hooker lingerie to achieve even a lukewarm approximation. Her stretch pants, equally tight silver top, pink eyeshadow and matching lips reminded me too much of Etta when she's dressing down.

On the TV wall, a bottle blonde bulging from a shocking lemon track suit was hollering at the audience. "And y'all won't believe what my bitch of a sister done next. After I find out she's been fucking my own husband, then my mother-in-law tells me she caught the lying bimbo giving her husband a blow job in the rec room. And the stupid cop asks me why I shot her?"

Jerry Springer should have quoted Tolstoy: "All happy families resemble one another, but each unhappy family is unhappy in its own way." Instead the jerk said with a smirk, "I'm not sure Dr. Phil would approve of your reaction."

On the marble surface of an oversize coffee table Debbie placed a silver serving tray. Sara Lee Brownies still in their foil tin and a large Diet Pepsi. She decanted the Pepsi into leaded-crystal water goblets and liberated the brownies onto Royal Doulton dessert plates.

"Martin — he's my new husband, you know —insists that I serve guests sherry and those fancy little sandwiches. When he's not home I revert to my old self. I always was more of a Big Mac–double fries kind of girl."

Well, blow me over with a feather duster. Big Mac girl certainly had landed herself a mansion in which to indulge her dietary transgressions.

She patted her jeans. "And before Martin gets home from work you can be sure I always slip into something classier."

My Top Ten memory offered up its own editorial: *Hey! Little girl / Comb your hair, fix your makeup / For wives should always be lovers too ...*

"Thanks for the snack, Debbie. It looks tasty." Already two brownies down the hatch, she was glued to the screen. "I'm sorry to be interrupting your show." Hell's bells, in reality I was doing her brain a favor.

"No problem. I tape them all." She muted the sound on the remote but left the picture flickering. Guess the lady likes crowded rooms. "I'm happy to have company. It gets lonely rattling around in this big place while Martin's off drilling teeth."

"I hope he's a dentist."

"That's so funny. I can already tell that I'm going to enjoy your visit," she said, and giggled.

Perhaps her enjoyment would head south when I told her

why I was here. Thinking it best to catch her off guard, I hadn't phoned in advance to arrange a meeting. But my unexpected appearance at her door hadn't fazed her one bit. When I introduced myself and told her I'd like to ask her a few questions about her ex-husband, she invited me in — after being reassured that I wasn't a cop.

I had been afraid she'd be unwilling to talk about Clarke. After all, the man had *chosen* to depart for Glory on the wings of a speeding bullet. "Do you mind if I ask a few questions about your former husband?"

"Ask me absolutely anything you want. But first, I'm dying to know. Why are you interested in him? He's been pushing up weeds in Mount Pleasant for six years now."

I didn't want to tell her that the unlamented Weed Pusher was the closest thing I had to a suspect in my search for Pete's killer. Surely even the most bitter of ex-wives wouldn't want to know she had been married to a murderer.

I took a deep breath. "My fiancé was murdered six years ago, not long after Tom passed on. The police never caught his killer." I fumbled around for the psychobabble beloved of talk-show hosts. "You see, I've never managed to work through my grief and move on with my life. So I finally decided that maybe I could find closure if I could at least understand why Pete died."

She set down her Pepsi to clap her hands together. "Far out."

My ears must be misinforming me. "Pardon me?"

"Oh gosh, I mean that's awesome. What you're trying to do. Sure, anything I can do to help. Just fire away." She hit on another brownie and settled back into the sofa as if I was a goddamn TV show about to entertain her with shocking true confessions.

"I understand that at the time of his death your ex-husband

had been seeing a therapist named Laura Payne. Ms. Payne was with my fiancé the night they were both murdered. I believe that she was the killer's target and that Pete just happened to be at her apartment. It's entirely possible that she was killed by one of her clients — obviously not your husband, who died a few months before the murders ... "

"Whoa, just hang on a minute here. I'm already confused. Why would you be interested in asking about Tom, then? I mean, if he couldn't be a suspect?"

"From what I understand, Laura was very upset about something Tom told her during one of their sessions. I was hoping you might have some idea of what that was."

She studied her fingernails, lacquered even more brilliantly than Etta's. "Well, we were already divorced when he started seeing that therapist. Maybe if he'd been willing to see one before our marriage fell into the dumpster I never would have left the poor bugger. But he kept coming back to see me, especially when he was drunk." She paused to shift a brownie crumb from the corner of her mouth to her tongue. "Which was frequently."

"How did you feel about those visits?"

"Oh, I always let him in. He had a lot on his mind and he needed someone to talk to who wasn't on the force. Figured listening to him rant on was the least I could do. You see, he never even challenged anything I asked for in the divorce. It was like he felt so guilty about screwing up our marriage that he reckoned he couldn't pay me enough in damages. Funny thing, there wasn't once after each visit that I didn't find some gift he left for me. A nice piece of jewelry, some expensive perfume, that kind of thing. And it wasn't like he thought he could get me back. He knew I'd bailed permanently." Debbie rose from her seat. "Excuse me for a minute, honey, but I have to pee."

She returned from relieving herself clutching a huge bag of

ketchup potato chips and resumed her narrative without prompting. "I don't know if you've heard about what it's like being married to a cop, but I can tell you it's no walk in the park. The way I see it, cops should have to be celibate, not just priests. By the time we were through, Tom managed to rack up a perfect score on your 'Why Cops' Marriages Fuck Up' list.

"It's not that he was unfaithful. I don't think he had the time or the energy left over for messing around. And he didn't beat on me, like some cops do — or at least, not till the end, when the pressure was really getting to him. He wouldn't tell me what was going on, just went into his tough-cop act. 'Image armor,' the shrinks call it. When he did talk to me, he ordered me around like he was confronting a criminal. After eight hours of being a cop, he couldn't switch roles," she said, pausing to glance at the television.

"He was so angry all the time that he used to sit in front of the TV and shout at the screen when I wasn't around to pick on. Then one night he came home late, drunk as a skunk, complained that his dinner was cold and slapped me across the face. The next week it was a punch. The morning after he punched me I stood in front of the mirror staring at the bruise on my face and I added up all the reasons our marriage was the pits. I started talking to myself, saying 'I'm mad as hell and I'm not going to take it any more.' Then I told him. When I said it was all over and he had to go, he already knew why. Didn't even try to talk me out of it. I think that's what hurt me the most. Just left the next day with his tail between his legs."

I cast my trout fly, hoping to get a strike. "Given that he finally started pouring out his heart when he was drunk, you must have known what was troubling him so much near the end of his life."

"You're damn tootin' I did. Same reason he broke down and went to that therapist in the first place. You're a crime writer, you must follow the news. Remember when the RCMP was investigating the drug squad and all those rumors were flying around about who was going to get busted next? For fraud, theft, assault, dealing, you name it? Tom hadn't been arrested yet, but he could see the writing on the wall plain as the nose on your face. He knew what was coming. Told me he'd started having panic attacks."

I took a big swig of my Pepsi, pretending it was a Newcastle Brown. "You mean, Tom was a bent cop?"

She chortled. "Honey, you think we bought a house like this on nothing but a dentist's income?"

And here I thought you could buy a house bigger than the Royal York on a dentist's income. "What are you saying?"

"I can trust you, right? What I'm going to tell you won't go no further than these walls, eh?"

"I swear on Pete's grave. And that's sacred ground. My only interest is in knowing why Pete had to die. Anyway, Tom's dead. Nothing you tell me can do him any harm."

"No," she agreed. "But it could … um … eat a hole in my lifestyle. A prosecutor could claim that some of what I'm living off of is the avails of crime. It might even be true. But I don't have one single pang of guilt about it. I earned it just by putting up with him all those years. Guess you could call it the Police Widows' Compensation Fund."

"Please go on."

"You ever wonder why so many cops want to get onto the drug squad when it's such a shitty, dangerous job? I mean, it's not like it puts you in touch with the kind of people you'd introduce to your grandmother. But hey, if you're one of the dirty ones, getting that particular promotion is like waking up in a bank vault. Of course I knew Tom was bent — he even admitted it to me in the end, when the RCMP started closing in on him."

But Laura had told her father and Hazel Duncan that her

client presented a clear danger to himself and to others. Perhaps she felt guilty because she hadn't done anything to prevent his suicide. But where did "a clear danger to others" fit in?

"Debbie, did you ever feel that Tom was a dangerous man?"

Her laugh was bitter. "Only to himself and to drug dealers — and them he considered the scum of the earth."

"Then you're telling me that he killed himself because he couldn't face the music?"

Her voice grew shrill for the first time in our conversation. *"Killed himself?* Who the fuck said Tom killed himself? Anyone else with all those pressures on him maybe, but Tom was a bloody Catholic. That's why he felt so much guilt about everything. It might sound funny to you, me saying that, given all the sins he did commit, but Tom *never* would have killed himself. Not that he went to Mass much after we got married, me being United Church and all, but he actually believed all their horseshit. Suicide would have been a mortal sin. Screwing up drug dealers was peanuts in comparison." She shook her head. "Go figure."

I'd sure as hell hit a nerve. Debbie jumped up to fetch a black book from a shelf on the entertainment centre. "Look, this is Tom's Catechism. I keep it to read whenever I get to worrying that maybe he did kill himself — and that maybe it was me leaving him that pushed him over the edge." She opened it and pointed to the relevant section as she handed it to me. "Look, he even highlighted this part."

The stark text needed no fluorescent yellow to accent its already harsh and unequivocal statements:

> Suicide
> 2280 Everyone is responsible for his life before God who has given it to him. It is God who remains the sovereign Master of life. We are obliged to accept life gratefully and preserve it for

his honor and the salvation of our souls. We are stewards, not owners, of the life God has entrusted to us. It is not ours to dispose of.

2281 Suicide contradicts the natural inclination of the human being to preserve and perpetuate his life. It is gravely contrary to the just love of self. It likewise offends love of neighbor because it unjustly breaks the ties of solidarity with family, nation, and other human societies to which we continue to have obligations. Suicide is contrary to love for the living God.

2282 If suicide is committed with the intention of setting an example, especially to the young, it also takes on the gravity of scandal. Voluntary cooperation in suicide is contrary to the moral law.

Grave psychological disturbances, anguish, or grave fear of hardship, suffering, or torture can diminish the responsibility of the one committing suicide.

2283 We should not despair of the eternal salvation of persons who have taken their own lives. By ways known to him alone, God can provide the opportunity for salutary repentance. The Church prays for persons who have taken their own lives.

All this was too familiar to me — as if I needed any reminders about why I used to pitch panic attacks at Mass.

But I wasn't convinced. Debbie had a vested interest in believing that Clarke's death was accidental: that interpretation was a big sop to her conscience. Who knows, maybe the poor bastard took comfort in knowing that he was about to act from diminished responsibility and that the Church was praying for him. I had to press the point.

"I'm sorry," I said. "That was the cynical crime writer in me speaking. I jumped to the conclusion that his death was a suicide because the reason police departments all over the continent give for cop suicides is 'died while cleaning his gun, which accidentally discharged.' Covers their butt, preserves the officer's reputation, spares the family any more pain and ensures that the widow and kids get his pension."

She shook her head vigorously. "No, no, it wasn't like that. It really was an accident. Joe Hunter — Tom's ex-partner — found him. Hunter went over to his apartment one day when they'd planned to go out to have a few beers and get caught up. When Hunter got there, the front door was unlocked. He found Tom slumped over the kitchen table with all his gun-cleaning gear in front of him."

"I met Hunter. A real lifetime cop. Wouldn't he, maybe, cover up the real cause of death? Loyalty to your partner is the First Commandment in the police Bible."

"No way. Joe Hunter is a totally straight arrow, one of the few guys associated with the drug squad who wasn't sweating buckets over the investigation. In fact, Hunter had asked for a transfer to Homicide before the shit even began to hit the fan. He told Tom he didn't want his reputation *sullied* — he actually used that word — by association."

"Given how you've just described Hunter, Tom must have felt incredibly guilty about being part of the rot that was eating away at the drug squad."

"You'd think so. I figure that added to Tom's depression. Imagine what it must have been like for him, working every day beside Jesus."

Good on you, Nancy Drew. You've just suffered the ingestion of two brownies and sixteen ounces of Diet Pepsi without getting any wiser about Laura's dilemma than you were yesterday.

Debbie interrupted my self-flagellation. "It did strike me as odd, though. When we were together, I never once knew Tom to clean his gun at home. Never even knew there was a cleaning kit in the house."

Maybe I was a baby step closer.

I indulged her summary musings as she munched on a scarlet potato chip. "I was really lucky to find Martin, you know. It's not like I was exactly looking for another husband. Not after Tom, no-sir-ee. Martin was filling one of my cavities when our eyes locked the way they do and you both know instantly that the next time you get so close together it will be naked. I always tease him that he traded in one cavity for another."

She stopped foraging in the Hostess bag. "Not too romantic, eh? But he's so good to me you'd think I was a princess."

"Romance is overrated, Debbie. You've found the real prize, a man who treats you well."

She gave me a big hug at the door. "Jane, I'm really sorry you lost your man."

In the months following Pete's death, I cried a river. Then one morning I awoke to discover that I'd lost the capacity to cry. Were it still intact, I'd have cried at that moment.

CHAPTER 30

"YOU KNOW, SAM, THERE'S NO ONE I'm more comfortable talking to about my —"

He laughed. "Let's not waste any more time while you flail around for euphemisms. Can't we just agree to call it your 'work'?"

"'Work' will do. But my comfort zone with you extends well beyond that. Where we were both at emotionally a few years ago cemented our friendship."

That would be when he lost his wife, Dawn, to cancer, and I lost Pete.

"Yeah, you could put it that way. Since then we've been more than just colleagues, for sure. You, and having Louise in my life, got me through a lot. I still worry about you, though," he appended.

When I said nothing, he began fidgeting with his napkin.

We'd come to Fast Eddy's for lunch. The ambiance was standard-issue chain pub — repro decor, thriving plastic plants, the menu modest and reliable, a dozen good labels on tap, the service prompt and attitude-free. And I had a soft spot for the owner, who'd sent me a complimentary feast while I was in hospital last year for fingertip reassignment.

Lunch was my invite: besides the consolation Sam's company always provides, I needed him as a sounding board. He almost always sees something I've missed. I wanted to talk through the trail I'd followed from the Laura Payne–Tom Clarke connection *maybe* to the next stage. I thought Sam might

have an idea or two about whether Clarke had committed suicide – and, *if* he had, why. The links were tenuous, but fine
spider threads can lead you to complex webs.

I recommended the burger and fries. Sam asked if I minded him ordering a pint.

"Sam, you could set up a brewery in my house and I
wouldn't be tempted."

"You're that committed."

"I'm that obsessed. And today I need you to give me the
straight poop on where you think this obsession is leading me.
Right now I feel like I'm tilting at windmills because they're
the only targets I can sight. I don't really have any facts. I feel
like I'm itching to scratch a phantom flea bite."

Sam swallowed a hefty swig of his Steam Whistle. His evident enjoyment left me white-knuckled with longing.

He didn't notice. He said reflectively, "You know, my best
stories always began with some small detail that kept nagging
at me until I scratched away at it."

Sam is one of the best investigative journalists in the country. His research often outshines the work of detectives investigating the very cases he writes up. And his memory is legendary, especially among journalists who now rely on Google to
do their remembering.

I nodded my recognition of the syndrome.

"Funny thing, that," he went on, "how a loose thread that
no one else noticed, or noticed but deemed insignificant, can
flood your vision. I guess we all take in different details. Last
week Louise dragged me off to the Art Gallery of Ontario.
While she was rhapsodizing about some beautiful little ivories,
all I could notice was the flimsy lock on their case. Where she
sees art, I see theft."

"Could be worse, Sam. Where other people see life, I see
death."

His eyes nailed down mine. "And the prospect of you getting past that morbidity, lady, is the only reason I'm encouraging you to get on with your ... work."

"Okay, then. Listen up. I need to hear your take on police suicides. What I'm particularly itching to scratch around is the death of Detective Sergeant Tom Clarke."

"I remember the guy — profiled him in an article I wrote on cop suicides. The publication of that one sure didn't win me any fans on the force."

"So it was definitely suicide?"

Sam swallowed a mouthful of fries too quickly. After navigating them past his esophagus, he said, "I don't know that for certain, but look, here's my take on cop suicides in a nutshell. On every tour of duty cops face more horrors than most of us confront in a lifetime. Being shot at, viewing murder scenes and violent accidents, assaults, rapes, child abuse ... However high the stats are on their suicides, it always amazes me that far more of them don't kill themselves — especially given that the rest of us actually have to plan the means. A cop has immediate access to a weapon."

"Aren't there usually several factors at play in a suicide — like marital and financial problems?" I paused. "And maybe some work-related issues — such as you are a bent cop whose activities beyond the law are currently the subject of an internal investigation?"

"Now that's a deft segue back to Tom Clarke," said Sam. "So explain your interest in the deceased. If you're suspecting that the coroner's finding the cause of his death to have been an 'accident' was a kindly — not to mention convenient — conclusion, I'd have to say you're probably correct. The evidence for a 'gun-cleaning accident' was laid out like a diorama. There were enough exculpatory circumstances surrounding his death to satisfy even the Pope."

I lifted the lid of my burger and poured in some HP Sauce. "Yesterday I met with Clarke's ex-wife, Debbie. She's absolutely sure that he didn't kill himself. She showed me his own personal highlighted copy of the Catechism — evidence as rock solid as Moses' tablet, in her view. I don't think it's just a matter of believing what she wants to believe. She even admitted to her own self-interest. She told me she would have backed up the coroner's finding, no matter what she thought: she's still living off the avails of Clarke's crimes. Plus she still feels guilty that *if* he did eat his gun, she wasn't there for him. How honest is that?"

Sam's response typified why he is so fine a reporter. "Honesty doesn't necessarily add up to the full truth about anything." He set down his fork. "Jane, when I wrote that article on officer suicides, my primary motive was not to raise public awareness of the subject. I placed Tom Clarke's story at the heart of it by way of tossing a grenade at the internal investigation unit: a few of us still don't buy their bullshit, however elegantly they've garnished it."

"So you only *implied* in your inimitable crafty style that Clarke killed himself."

We polished off our burgers and fries. Sam had set aside the raw onions, maybe in deference to Louise's nostrils. The server removed our empty plates and Sam returned to his beer.

"I was careful to cite his death only as an example of the pressures cops work under. No judgments were made, no conclusions drawn. That was as much as I could hope to get past the scrutiny of the *Post*'s lawyer — you remember the guy: reads birthday cards from his aunt for libelous comments."

The pub's *Big Chill* CD had hit "I Heard It Through the Grapevine." As our server set down our coffee cups, I asked, "Sam, were you privy to anything leading you to suspect that Clarke offed himself?"

He chuckled. "Like you, when I'm caught between a rock and a hard place I fall back on my guts. Enough already with the cleaning-his-gun crap, with the too-good-a-Catholic crap. Not only was that sorry bastard confronting the ruin of his career — which was all he had left — he was probably off to the slammer in the bargain."

"How does that distinguish him from his fellow bad apples on the drug squad? None of them took the down escalator."

Sam emptied his coffee cup and returned it to its saucer with a clatter. "None of them had Joe Hunter for a partner."

Sam rarely indulges in expressions of anger. What was behind his outburst? When he seemed disinclined to elaborate, I baited him.

"And you think Hunter had some kind of influence over Clarke — or what? I should tell you Hunter just made two unexpected contributions to my life. He rushed to my aid when I got shot at Sweet Dreams, then showed up at my house the next day with a bouquet. He was acting all concerned, but I didn't entirely buy it. Whatever his role in the drama, he's a player, Sam, he's a player. Debbie Seeger told me it was Hunter who discovered Clarke's body — and confirmed his death as accidental. She added that a straighter arrow never graced the drug squad. You think she's wrong about him?"

"I just don't like the guy. Self-promoting, self-righteous ... Hunter spent ten years on that squad and shot out the far end as Teflon boy. Not one bit of shit stuck to him. While most of his colleagues were drowning in shit, not a clump clung to him."

"So that's what you meant about him being a bad partner? He was so righteous that he abandoned his own partner and fled to Homicide to maintain his image? Debbie said something about that too."

"That's partly what I meant. But mostly, I don't buy into

Hunter's squeaky-clean reputation. I already knew about him well before Clarke's death. He remained the squad's golden boy right through the days when his colleagues, good or bad, were getting tarnished beyond anything the chief could do to restore their luster. I don't know how he did it. Shit, *I* even wrote a laudatory article about him. It was after he shot a drug dealer and the rest of the media reacted like a lynch mob because the dealer was Black. One hack even cited Hunter's shoot as an example of racial profiling at its extreme. I rose to his defense because of the principle, *not* the man. "

"Was that partly why he made the jump to Homicide?"

"I doubt it. As well as wanting to remove himself from a squad gone wrong, I'm sure he wanted fresh territory to conquer. And he's gone on to do just that. He's closed more cases than you can shake a service revolver at."

"Sam, there's something about Hunter that nags at me. Clarke was Joe Hunter's ex-partner. Hunter heard Short Willie's confession. Hunter was on the scene of the Laura and Pete murders. And you, my friend, followed it all. Is there something I'm missing here?"

Sam said, "No, probably not. The guy was his partner, after all. Seems natural that they'd still hang out together. And Hunter would have been called to Laura's apartment because he was working the serial killer case."

"So why am I witnessing this rare spectacle: Sam Brewer rampant in the kind of attitude way more typical of his friend Jane Yeats?"

Among the men of my acquaintance only Sam retains a talent for blushing. "Because I'm ashamed of myself. I hate the arrogant bastard. Must be something about virginity that gets up my nose — that's all there is to my loathing for the man."

He blushed a deeper hue when I teased, "Then I can trust that you've always been a foot soldier in the war on virginity."

"Nah. Forget what I said about Hunter. It was totally unprofessional and unfounded. And so what if he covered up his ex-partner's suicide? He was just following one of the unspoken rules. At the end of the day, what does it matter? There were only two possibilities: accident or suicide. In such cases, the coroner has other options: natural causes and homicide. But not in this one."

Then it would follow that Laura Payne was so conflicted about Clarke's disclosure because the man had been a clear danger only to himself. She was contemplating breaking client privilege because she felt she should report his suicidal frame of mind to the force. And he had died while she dithered.

"Thanks so much for the conversation, Sam. One last question: have you heard anything about the status of the Ruth Rosenberg inquiry? I wouldn't be asking you if I thought Ernie might oblige, but lately he's been in no mood to help me into anything but an early grave."

"I'm surprised Sivcoski thinks you need any help. Don't take his attitude too personally, though. The blue brotherhood is far stronger than friendships outside the force. And nope, nothing to update you on the Rosenberg. The cops are keeping a very tight lid on that one."

"Yeah. Guess they don't want to screw it up the way they did first time around."

As we left the restaurant and were preparing to go our separate ways, Sam paused and said, "Jane, wait a minute. I'm busy for the next few days with some home reno stuff Louise is keen on. But I'll make time to hit on a source or two around Hunter's recent doings. I don't think that your contacting him directly is a good idea. Once he realizes what you're up to, he'll move mountains within the force to obstruct your investigation."

"Sam, I will heed your advice. Call me paranoid, but I'm guessing he might have been behind the raid on my house.

More obstructions I don't need."

The music gods were presiding over us. James Taylor's "You've Got a Friend" began playing. I pointed in the direction of the speakers. "Call it our song, buddy."

"Works for me, girl. Keep in touch. In the meantime, take care — special care. You've already taken a bullet and been subjected to that full-dress raid."

"I love you, Sam Brewer."

"Tell me something I don't know, Jane Yeats." Gruffly delivered, of course.

We parted at the corner of College and Shannon.

Lord, do not let me act in any way that disappoints Sam — short of executing Pete's killer.

CHAPTER 31

THREE OF SAM'S SENTENCES, although almost parenthetical to our conversation, echoed in my ears: *I wrote a laudatory article about him after he shot a drug dealer and the rest of the media reacted like a lynch mob because the dealer was Black. One hack even cited Hunter's shoot as an example of racial profiling at its extreme. I rose to his defense because of the principle, not the man.*

My research into that event in Hunter's career led me straight to my next visit.

From behind the door of number 301 a rough-around-the-edges female voice answered my knock with a slurred, "Yeah? Whaddyawant?"

I had just climbed the stairs to the third floor of a vintage thirties yellow-brick apartment building constructed around the time Billie Holiday recorded "Strange Fruit." Vintage, but in such disrepair as to rule it out as a collectible.

It had taken Maeve almost half an hour to deliver me to this Scarborough address. The vast bedroom community of 600,000, a 'burb in the outsprawl of the city, recently suffered a rash of violent gun crime, most of it connected to the drug trade. The place was making me nervous, even though it was broad daylight — not that I could tell if the sun was shining. The hallway, from which led four apartments, was unlit.

"I'm looking for Hope Askew."

"You a cop?" Her voice as raspy as Marianne Faithfull's.

She must have heard my ironic laugh through the cheap

wood. "No, I'm a woman whose boyfriend got screwed over."

Magic "Open, Sesame" words. Facing me was a haggard woman, late twenties and headed for an early grave. Defeated clothes hung from her wasted frame. Faded sweatshirt frayed around the neck and cuffs, torn blue jeans big enough to be a man's discards. Bare feet with dirty toenails. Running her hand through lank hair in a pathetic effort to tidy it up, probably a gesture from an earlier life when quick fixes worked, she looked at me with eyes whose liveliness had long deserted them. Perhaps no parents should send a child out into the world named Hope: it's just asking for trouble.

She sucked hard on her cigarette, then gestured me inside. I followed her along a narrow dark hall to the living room overlooking the street. At least, that was my assumption: the curtains were drawn nearly shut and the sliver of glass they revealed too grimy to see through. The naked light bulb on the ceiling had burned out. Perhaps she preferred to live in the dark. Certainly what could be seen of the room screamed for concealment. A makeshift dining-room table was piled with Chinese and pizza takeout boxes, their remaining contents in various stages of decomposition. Empty beer cans outnumbered the pop cans strewing the table and the floor around it. In one corner a dead rubber plant slumped over its container.

She lit a du Maurier from the end of the spent one she then stubbed into an overflowing ashtray. I was grateful for the smoke, not because I yearned for a secondhand toke but because it helped mask the pervasive stench of neglect. That she would apologize for the smoke was as unlikely as that she'd ask me to excuse the mess. My guess was that this young woman was way past being sorry for any of her sins of omission.

A laugh that sounded like a crone's cackle issued from her chapped lips. "You said your boyfriend got screwed over. Mine got shot."

"So did mine, Hope. And I know that Luther was killed. I'm very sorry for your loss."

"Yeah, well, he's been dead for seven years, and you're the only person who ever told me that. How come you know his name?"

"I think that whoever killed my boyfriend — his name was Pete — might have been connected to Tom Clarke, the cop who was on the scene when Luther was shot." I was careful not to say *Tom Clarke, the cop Luther was fixing to shoot when he got shot.* "I'm trying to find out everything I can about Clarke because I really need to know why Pete is dead."

"And you think that's going to make you feel any better?" Funny, there was no disbelief in her tone of inquiry.

"Yes, I do. I'm one of those people, maybe like you — the closer I come to understanding something, the more I can accept it."

"I get you. I used to be like that."

Sadly I wondered what else she once was.

"I mean, I even tried to find out what *really* happened when Luther got shot. Everything the cops told me was a pack of bloody lies. If you don't trust me on that, you could ask any of his friends. The ones who are still alive, anyways."

I'd get more from her if she felt trusted. Though her testimony would be instantly dismissed as unreliable in any cop shop or courtroom, I was inclined to believe her. "I do trust that you're giving me an honest account of your beliefs. Please know that, and keep giving me as much information as you can. Maybe after this conversation I'll be a step closer to proving your beliefs."

At the edge of my vision a small animal skittered into the room and along the baseboard. *Please let it not be a rat.*

With a few softly whispered urgings, Hope coaxed the creature over to the sofa. She bent down to pick up a scrawny gray kitten and cooed into its ear. "This is all the family I have left. Found her in the laneway behind this dump a couple of days ago. Her name's Rita." I hoped she was feeding the poor thing, which didn't look big or bold enough to be a mouser.

Keeping this conversation on track was going to take some work. "Hope, you did something I admire. After the cops dismissed your concerns around the shooting, you went to the media and told them that you knew the cops were lying."

"Oh yeah. Even before they finished their investigation, I figured for sure they'd come out looking like Mr. Clean. Cops murder somebody, other cops investigate the shoot. In the end, the shoot always turns out to have been a righteous act. What kind of asshole would expect any different result? Cops are like doctors and lawyers and priests. Whenever one of their own does something gross, all their buddies fall into this mutual-protection racket."

She had a good point, one that many critics of internal investigations have voiced until we're all hoarse. Her words were simply a cruder rendering of that lingering injustice around accountability and scrutiny. But her boyfriend had been no Mr. Clean either.

"Hope, could you tell me about Luther — what kind of guy he was? It might help me a lot."

She paused to light another cigarette, set Rita into the corner of the sofa and crossed over to a small cupboard leaning away from the wall on three legs. From the top drawer she extracted a photograph in a Wal-Mart black plastic frame. Reseating herself on the stained sofa, she stared at the image for a minute before turning it around in my direction.

Looking back at me was a very handsome young Black man, his long arms encircling a small boy on his lap. Both were laughing into the camera.

"That's Luther. I took this a few weeks before he got shot."

Suddenly she stood up and darted over to the garbage-heaped table. She kicked one leg as though it was a dog who'd bitten her. A large roach fell to the floor.

She spun around. "And that, that beautiful little boy is our son. Martin."

From what I'd seen of the small apartment there was no trace of a child. No jacket hanging from the hall coat hooks, no little shoes or boots beneath. No toys scattered about. No video game console plugged into the TV.

She tugged a strand of hair away from her face. "If you're wondering where the kid is, Children's Aid took him from me a couple of years ago. Much as I hate those motherfucking social workers, you can't really blame them. After Luther got killed and after I couldn't get any satisfaction around why he got killed, I started drinking. Then I got into crack when the booze didn't kill the pain. And it's not like I'm ever going to get clean and sober, not even to get Martin back."

Her utterly defeatist self-assessment was delivered defiantly, as though she had every right to destroy her own mind and body. Maybe she was right; after all, I'd taken a similar, if less drastic, route myself — and for the same reason. Maybe I was wrong in thinking that she should have tried harder because she was a mother. Single parenting, probably with no family support and insufficient money, must have added intolerable stress to the load she was already carrying.

Maybe if I returned her attention to the photograph she'd get back on track. "They are a good-looking father and son, Hope. And they look so happy."

"Yeah, they were, the three of us were. Most people assume when your boyfriend's a drug dealer, then everything else about his life and yours must be shitty and you must be bad parents. It just wasn't true about us. Luther was a good man and he made me and Martin laugh so hard. He'd be playing his Bob Marley and air-guitaring and dancing us around like every single day was one big carnival."

"Um ... how did you feel about his selling drugs?" I asked.

She shrugged. "Hey, why would I have a problem with that? Luther was a smart man, but he screwed up his education the first time he got busted. He started out stealing cars, but the last time he got released he said he was getting into drug dealing. Way bigger profits and less risk, the way he saw it. So him dealing was okay with me. He brought home a lot of money, and the way I figure it, and I am some kind of an authority, is that ... us junkies are going to get our fix anyways, doesn't matter who's doing the selling."

She resumed patting the kitten, who'd returned to her lap. I was surprised to hear the little beast purring. Didn't look like it had the energy. No way was I going to challenge her rationalization for supporting Luther's dealing, although I passionately disagreed with her. Her shopworn excuse reminded me of the Nuremberg defense: I was only taking orders, or, if I didn't do it someone else would have. Ours is the great age of demolished responsibility. Cover your butt, point the finger elsewhere, devil made you do it. Look closely enough into any transgressor's past and you'll be able to prove him or her a victim of somebody else's transgressions in a never-ending chain that reaches back to Eve sinking her teeth into the irresistible apple. Ouroboros, the snake that swallows its own tail in an eternity of evasion. Nobody is accountable. The triumph of liberalism gone rotten.

"So bring me up to speed here, Hope. Luther's a good man, but he's a drug dealer. Cops hunt down dealers. Somebody gets shot. Could be a cop, could be a dealer. It's an old story. What's different in Luther's script?"

With the hand that wasn't stroking Rita, Hope lit another cigarette. First I noticed that both hands were shaking badly, then that her body was picking up the manic beat.

"Hey, I mean ... I'm starting to jones here. I'm going to need to fix up soon — real soon, you know what I mean?"

Her eyes, across the tinge of apology, told me what she meant. God forgive me, I reached into my jeans pocket for my wallet. Extracted a fifty, placed it on the gray-specked surface of the coffee table, beside the ashtray, as if I was laying down a napkin.

Her hand darted out so fast to retrieve it that Rita was alarmed and fled back to her sofa corner. Hope tucked the bill into the waistband of her sweatpants, making me think she hadn't bothered to put on a bra. I could guess why she wanted the money out of sight, given there was no chance it was going to disappear in her own apartment. She felt shame. Shame not for her habit but for hitting me up for money.

She relieved my embarrassment. "Thanks. And you didn't need to do that, eh? I would have kept telling you stuff anyways. It's been a long time since I was sitting across from anybody who took me serious and showed some respect. But thanks anyways."

She smiled sweetly and my heart cracked.

Well done, Yeats. You've just crossed another of your moral lines, and this time it wasn't even necessary to advance your mission. What else are you capable of doing? By the time you're done, will anything be left to separate you from the bastards you revile?

Hey, my inner thug answers, *those bastards do far worse things than fix up a junkie.*

CHAPTER 32

"YOU ASKED ME WHAT WAS DIFFERENT about Luther getting shot up. Here it is, and you can laugh as hard as you want, but I swear it's the whole truth, nothing but. My man never carried a gun. He never owned a gun. He was so into Rasta stuff he outdid Bob Marley. I mean, if Luther wrote the song, it would have gone, 'I didn't shoot the sheriff and I didn't shoot no deputy.' He hated guns ever since the day he watched his father shoot his mother."

I badly needed to introduce a reality check. "But, Hope, how long is a dealer going to last in this city when word gets out that he doesn't carry?"

She ticked off her response on trembling fingers. "One, the man was such a huge motherfucker — we're talking 240 pounds on an empty stomach and buck naked. That was enough to make anybody who might have been thinking of screwing him over start to thinking twice. Two, the man was fit as an Olympic athlete and way meaner when he was pissed off. He had no problem scaring people shitless when he needed to. Three, he boasted a whole lot about some son of a bitch who'd fucked him over on a deal, so he shot him. That was a total lie. But the cops never solved the murder and Luther was happy to take credit for it on the street."

I ransacked my memory for recent research. "The way Clarke and Hunter told the story, they chase Luther down an alley behind a club, corner him, he draws on Clarke, and Hunter blows him away. Not only have they got two officers' testimony, they've got the crime-scene guys photographing Luther with the gun in his hand."

Hope's laugh was caustic enough to etch a diamond. "You never heard of a plant? Not to mention that the weapon they stuck in Luther's dead hand was a crappy Saturday-night special? Luther had class. If he ever had took to packing serious heat, trust me, it would have been a gun with a whole lot more class than that piece of shit they claimed he was carrying. So what do *you* think really happened?"

She was looking straight into my eyes, challenging me for some answer, any answer that made sense of the event that had plummeted her into her present sorry condition.

I spoke honestly. "You've got me thinking that the truth about Luther's death disappeared down the same black hole as the truth about what really happened to my boyfriend."

But I had a problem: while Hope's words rang true to me, I still had no way of verifying them — beyond my gut instinct. If Luther had drawn a gun on Clarke, who could reasonably expect two cops threatened with imminent death not to shoot? But where did the Saturday-night special fit in? She'd put me on to something very problematic about the shoot, but I urgently needed some kind of evidence, any small detail that I could follow up on. I felt so close to finding out something about Pete's death that if this turned out to be another blind alley, I'd be a complete mess.

Trying to control my voice so desperation wouldn't turn my words into a plea, I said, "I totally believe you on this. And I'm hearing you. But I need something to go on. Can you think of *anything* that might help me prove that your story is the true one?"

Hope shook her head. "All I've got is what people told me after the shoot. Luther kept a nice stash of money hidden in the place we were living then. So nice a stash I wouldn't have to be living in this dump if I hadn't blown it on booze and dope. I grabbed a wad of that money and took it to the funeral home. Wound up giving him the kind of send-off he deserved, him having been so good to me and Martin. Little as he was, I wanted Martin to remember his dad as a man who was a somebody. Somebody to reckon with and somebody who was loved back as much as he gave."

She looked at their photograph. "Close to everybody Luther ever knew showed up at the funeral home or came to the funeral. And the ones real close to him were mega-angry. They all told me the same thing: your man got murdered, is all. His best friend, guy he'd known since grade school, swore to me he was going to get the fucker who shot Luther, but I figured that was just his grief and a mickey of rum talking."

She checked out a spot on Rita's belly that the kitten had been worrying. "Must have been just that. Nothing but hot air and booze. Because that prick Hunter who assassinated my man is still alive."

"But is Luther's friend still alive?"

Her fingers pinched on Rita's belly. "Shit, if I wasn't shaking so bad I would have caught that flea. This cat needs a flea collar. This cat needs real food. This cat needs a visit to the vet."

Again I reached into my wallet for another fifty. "Okay, Hope, Rita's got her flea collar. Rita's got her Meow Mix. Rita's got her trip to the vet. That makes me the needy one here: is Luther's friend still alive, and if he is where can I find him?"

Her eyes wandered from the second banknote to my left wrist. "What time is it?"

This was not feeling like value for my money. "It's almost noon."

She scooped up the fifty. "Then if you sit tight, you'll find Luther's friend right here in about ten minutes. He's my dealer, eh? Dealing is what C. J. does, like it's his business. But a couple of times when I was dead broke and too wrecked to turn a trick, he fixed me up anyways. Like he was doing it for Luther. Taking care of me."

God forbid Silver should take such care of me. Friendship speaks many languages, though.

Twenty minutes later the apartment door sounded the same hollow notes it had echoed to my knocking. I overheard fragments of a pressured exchange.

"Gal, yuh noh dead yet?"

"Cut the patois ... got company ... want you to come in ... meet a woman."

"Ain't here to see no bitch 'cept you, girl."

" ... Luther, how he got shot ..."

Reluctantly trailing behind Hope, reluctant but alert enough to pull his gun, a guy in a black hoodie, black jeans, black Nikes entered the living room.

Our introduction was nothing a girl might find in an etiquette manual. I stood up and met his "fuck you, bitch" stare with my best Clint Eastwood glaring-into-the-desert stare.

"I've got only one interest in talking to you," I said. "Nothing to do with your line of work. Everything to do with how Luther went down. So get that gun out of my face or I'll pull mine."

C. J. placed his gun on the table and pulled the hood back from his head, liberating a cascade of dreads. Good sign. He was relaxing.

"So talk, bitch."

Under any other circumstances, the *bitch* word would have earned its speaker a swift kick in the balls. In one very terse paragraph I brought him up to speed, ending with "So tell me why you know Hope's got it right about Luther being assassinated."

He flicked away my stare and took to staring down his expensive sneakers. "Hope, here, would have told you Luther never carried no weapon. Never. Gospel truth."

He remained standing beside the sofa, leaning over twice to stroke Rita. Gentle gestures from a hard man. "Problem is, ain't nothing about that shoot could ever stand up in any court. No witness, nothing. Just what anybody who don't carry a badge and who happens to meet them while they doin' their particular line of work knows about the drug squad — knows about them two mothafuckers in particular."

He glanced from the kitten's head to me. I nodded. *Yes, I'm with you.*

"Yo. Mothafucka number one, that being Clarke. He was on your case, you could count on being beat up, robbed, whatever. But if you happened to be rich that particular day, you could buy him off. That mostly worked for us: like hos, you give the cop free blow, you don't get busted. That is not cool, but it's part of doing bizness. You think I'm lying, you ain't been watching TV. All that shit what went around, now it's coming back around— to the fucking drug squad."

"I'm with you, C. J. So tell me about his partner."

C. J. glanced over at Hope, who had absented herself from the conversation to snort up his latest consignment. While she blissed out and the trembling subsided, C. J. picked up his narrative.

"Yo. Mothafucka number two. That being Hunter. The man is not bent — at least not bent like the rest of his crew. The man is a freak. None of us never seen Hunter steal from a dealer. Not kicking ass, not robbing us, not dealing what he stole like his badass buddies. That kinda shit we all learn to live with, like I said."

"A good friend of mine hates him, too."

"Hunter, he is evil. He scared the shit outta even the

hardest bro. Man's got eyes that cut holes. A sadistic freak who gets his rocks off by putting people in fear of their death. That mothafucka reminds me of this preacher at the church my mom dragged me and my sister off to when we was too little to refuse. One of them low-rent born-again churches with a high-voiced preacher that ripped off all the old women with his bullshit. Thing about Hunter always put me in mind of this preacher — eyes that went all weird when he got hisself worked up about sin, 'specially s-e-x-u-a-l sinning. That preacher man started working up a lather so bad even a kid could tell — like chapter and verse in the Bible was his pornography. Push his holy nose into shit and he jerked off on the smell."

C. J. could have been a preacher man, of sorts. "And maybe Hunter jerked off on shooting a dealer who wasn't armed?"

He grinned through really white teeth. "Girl, you got it."

"Help me here. I got it, but what I still don't have is any clue how to *prove* that what went down in that alley was an assassination."

"Girl, that part's real easy to get: you know that when a Black dealer or druggie gets wasted, cops call it 'urban renewal'? What you don't got is why some other bent *officer of the law* got wasted." His smooth voice managed to ice the words *officer of the law* with pigeon dung.

"Which particular officer of the law got wasted?" I asked, lacing my question with the same garnish.

"Dude was a prison guard. Got to know him when I done hard time. Name of Jerry Stone."

Jerry Stone, Jerry Stone, Jerry Stone ... my brain came up with a match. "Guard at Millhaven. Fatally stabbed during a riot."

"Bumfucker. Pervert. Enough to make him dead. But rumor is, maybe he got too friendly with Hunter."

"I'm not making the connection, C. J. Fill in the blanks."

"Us boyz in the trade know 'bout Stone because it was him we could sell to. We provide him wit quality blow, he pays good, never any problems. Then he feeds our shit into the system, keeps all the junkies on the inside happy, turns a serious profit, earns a lot of favors."

I was sinking up to my neck in perplexity. "Where does Hunter fit into this ugly picture?"

"He fits front and center. Like, you don't think a narc with his rep didn't know what was going down with Stone?"

"But why didn't he bust Stone, especially with his hate-on for dealers? Stone must have looked to Hunter like the worst of the worst — a guy on the side of law and order who'd crossed over?"

I knew from C. J.'s eyes that he'd exhausted his hoard of goodies on Hunter. All he said was, "We all need an insurance policy."

"C. J., I'm feeling there's nowhere else you can take me on this connection. Am I right?"

He laughed. "You're right and I'm hoping you're righteous." He pulled up his hood. "Girl, you nail that mothafucker Hunter, we'll party."

"C. J., I nail the mothafucker, you come to my wake."

"Whatever, I'll be there."

My unreluctant informant gave a parting farewell pat on the head to Rita and Hope, both blissed out beyond awareness.

At the door he turned to say, "I had a serious crush on this lady way before Luther even set eyes on her. You should have seen her back then."

How very much more I should have seen back then.

CHAPTER 33

AS THE WISE RABBI SAYS, "Well, on the one hand ... "

I'd heard plenty from the one hand, the weak hand in any poker game, the discredited hand, the hand of the ostensible cheaters: Luther Banton's girlfriend and his best friend. Their story was detailed and very interesting, but my source was dubious because both of them were deeply involved in drugs and both had a special interest in wiping Banton's slate clean.

Now I intended to hear from the other hand, the ostensibly clean hand, the one dedicated to protecting our human rights by ensuring that cops who violate those rights remain accountable. That would be the Special Investigations Unit, created twelve years ago and charged with investigating incidents of death and serious injury involving cops.

As I see it, public accountability mechanisms with real teeth are our only hope of guaranteeing that rogue cops get nailed. When such mechanisms fail, or are subverted, people lose confidence in the police. When they fail, they are worse than no protection, because self-interested cops more inclined to break than enforce the law — like certain members of the drug squad — can use them to act criminally with far more impunity than the rest of us. They are charged with the awesome power of using lethal force. If they use such force to save lives, their own or others, that's cool. If they use such force for any other reason, that's murder.

Given the track record of the SIU, even if it's murder, it's apparently not murder. Some 513 probes after the provincial Tory government hired a new director of the police watchdog — and beefed up his tool kit to the tune of a $5-million budget, 72 investigators, their own personal forensics labs and computer-equipped vans — charges have been laid in less than 3 percent of cases. The likelihood of my waking up a millionaire tomorrow morning is far greater than the likelihood of any of those charges eventuating in guilty findings and sentencing.

The SIU is a controversial, thoroughly discredited unit, one that I've had the pleasure of kvetching about in several articles. In fact, every year since its establishment, I've made a point of writing one piece updating its dismal lack of progress for newspaper readers who actually give a shit. You could say nipping at the sorry ass of the SIU has become a minor hobby of mine.

My choice of hobbyhorse did not endear me to the man who'd agreed to meet with me this morning. The director of the SIU, Ernest Sparkle, former military man who brought to his appointment a reputation for being low profile, methodical as a library cataloguer, by the book. Whatever bounty the Tories gave him and whatever he brought to the task, his performance had been dismal. That's not true. Two sides to every story. From a police perspective, his performance couldn't be surpassed. The civilian take was less charitable.

How does a woman dress for such a meeting? I dismissed battle fatigues. Sparkle might not share my delight in quoting his background. Impatiently I grabbed the usual shit-kicking suspects in my wardrobe. The black boots, black jeans, Harley T-shirt (their butchness gently subverted by black lacy bra and panties). I was in no mood to dress in any fashion but one that signaled my intention to get down to serious business. Cops do not intimidate me. I've had enough experience of them to have acquired a lot of practice in dealing with any stone walls or menaces they put in my path. Whatever nervousness I might have felt about meeting the head honcho himself had been quickly overwhelmed by my "attitude" about the tax-voracious chunk of window dressing he presided over.

I screeched Maeve to a gravel-spewing halt outside a building in an industrial park off Highway 427 in Mississauga. Cunningly located to keep itself out of the face of cops who feared it; perhaps they didn't study its findings too closely. Not much to fear there. Place looked like a discreet Home Depot.

Subtracting the hair cropped too short on a bullet-shaped skull, a mustache trimmed closer than Errol Flynn's, a suit and shirt so wrinkle-free they betrayed no evidence of human occupancy and shoes so highly polished they reflected his own manly chin right back into his bland face, Ernest Sparkle didn't look one bit like an ex-military man. Right. Certainly the handshake he gave me was no firmer than I'd expect from General Patton. For all the boot-polishing echoes of his past, there was still something about a man in a uniform out of a uniform that I found distinctly unattractive.

He'd accepted my request for an interview knowing that I was a true-crime writer, and surely aware that my take on suspected and alleged police transgressions was less than generous. Still, I was surprised to see how well he'd armored himself. Against one wall of the boardroom into which he'd led me was a battery of stuff worthy of Steve Jobs about to unveil Apple's latest gift to the tech world. I pretended not to notice.

Unroll the blarney, Yeats. "As I told you on the phone, Mr. Sparkle, I'm here to ask you for some background on an article I'm preparing for the *Post*. You were probably relieved to hear that I'm not writing another piece highlighting some of the ... ah ... weaker aspects of your unit. As I told you, my interest is very specific: I'm here to ask about your decision in the case involving Luther Banton, the young Black man shot by Detective Sergeant Hunter six years ago."

The police chief claims his men are color-blind, even after a superb series of investigative articles on racial profiling in the *Post* proved otherwise. Sparkle undoubtedly makes the same claim. So "Black" would piss him off. "Black" might alert him to my suspicion of a shooting maybe gone wrong because the suspect had more melatonin than Sparkle, who looked as if he bathed in Javex.

From the inside pocket of his jacket he pulled an elegant silver cigarette case. Wow, I hadn't seen one of those in years. Sparkle must have been a tad anxious: lighting up signals there's at least one thing over which you have no control. His cigarette took quick life from a matching silver lighter. No Zippo, that baby.

"The very fact of your interest in anything even vaguely approaching my jurisdiction does nothing to relieve me. I'm painfully familiar with your bibliography."

"Yeah, well, we all get some bad press now and then." I slumped down into the chair, crossed my legs at the ankles and examined my boots.

Something about Sparkle's constipated smile told me he did not appreciate my sense of humor. He spoke through lips pursed tighter than Max's when I try to feed him a worm pill. "The Banton investigation concluded five years ago. It was a textbook case of a justified shooting on the part of a police officer. What could possibly be attracting your attention?"

Almost imperceptibly, he winced when a flurry of his cigarette ash failed to meet the ashtray. A tidy freak.

I gave him my best my-heart-is-an-open-book smile. "The decision you reached is attracting my attention."

Another flutter of cigarette ash onto the mahogany table. "Textbook case. Textbook finding. As I recall —" he actually paused strategically, as though he were scouring long-ago contents of his memory hoard, as though he hadn't briefed himself prior to my arrival "— I ruled that Hunter was legally justified in shooting Banton. I found that Banton, who was fleeing police down an alley, drew his gun on Clarke, thereby posing a very real threat to the officer. In fact, I later commended Hunter for saving his partner's life."

He drew a single sheet of paper from the folder resting just out of reach of his ashtray misses. Because he had agreed to see me only on condition that I tell him the subject of my interest, he had had time to prepare.

Before accepting it, I commented, "In the vast majority of SIU investigations — about 97 percent of them — evidence of criminal activity is not found and no charges are laid."

"Precisely what you'd expect with Toronto Police Services, arguably the best force in the country." This time his ash hit the target. He passed me the sheet of paper. "Please take a minute to refresh your memory. That press release is part of the SIU's mandate to communicate information about our investigations to the public."

Insufferable, presumptuous prick. I speed-read the contents printed beneath the SIU's logo:

NEWS RELEASE • COMMUNIQUÉ
IMMEDIATE RELEASE
SIU Updates Investigation into Fatal Shooting in Toronto
TORONTO (September 30, 1995) — The Special Investigations Unit (SIU) has assigned seven investigators, including two forensic identification technicians, to investigate a fatal shooting that occurred at approximately 1:12 a.m. on August 1, 1995.

The SIU was notified that Toronto Police Service (TPS) officers were pursuing a man who was reportedly implicated in suspicious activity in the downtown area. In an alley located behind the Blue Note Club the pursued suspect drew a gun on one of the officers, resulting in his being shot by the second officer. The 27-year-old suspect was rushed to Toronto General Hospital, where he was declared dead on arrival.

The deceased has been identified as Luther Banton. A postmortem is scheduled today.

The SIU has now designated one subject officer and one witness officer from the TPS. The investigation is continuing and the SIU is appealing for anyone who witnessed this incident to contact the Unit at 416-641-1879 or 1-800-787-8529.

I nodded. "Yes, of course. I remember reading this at the time it was issued. Might you, just by chance, have a copy of the press release you provided at the conclusion of the investigation? To refresh my memory."

At approximately 1:12 a.m. on August 1, 1995, two Toronto Police Service (TPS) officers approached a man attempting to conclude a drug deal in a downtown nightclub. The man fled into a laneway at the rear of the club. When the officers ordered him to stop, he drew a gun on them. He was ordered to drop his weapon, which he refused to do. Instead, he continued to move his weapon about, pointing it in the direction of one of the police officers. The subject officer drew his revolver to stop the man from shooting his partner. The man refused a second order to drop his weapon and continued to point his weapon at the witness officer. The subject officer fired a single shot, fatally striking the man in the torso.

The SIU dispatched five investigators, two forensic identification technicians, one investigative supervisor and the SIU communications manager to the scene of the incident. During the three-week probe, investigators interviewed 11 police officers, including the subject officer, and 31 civilian witnesses and reviewed numerous TPS documents and communication tapes. The Director found that it was entirely reasonable that the officer involved believed it was necessary to shoot the deceased in order to protect his partner, himself and others in the vicinity from either death or grievous bodily harm. Therefore, the officer was legally justified in his use of lethal force, under the provisions of section 25 of the Criminal Code of Canada.

I looked across at Sparkle. "Your reports are as tidy as your wardrobe. Personally speaking, I'm a big fan of the loose thread, the dangling question that dogs even the tidiest of reports. I'm a big fan of lifting up the carpet to see what got swept underneath. Especially when there are no witnesses to an event — except those whose testimony may be tainted by self-interest."

My instructor was rapidly losing patience. He strode over to two evidence boards propped against the wall, displaying numerous color photos of the night in question. The boards I'd been ignoring, just to heighten the aggravation factor. Now, as I studied them, Sparkle extracted from his file several detailed diagrams of the incident scene.

The color photos were items I hoped Banton's loved ones had been spared. A young man, his life drained into a pool of blood that extended from his torn chest to form a startlingly large puddle beside his body. That wasted body in a tight fetal curl. I have seen many such photos. They never fail to horrify me.

Hiding both my horror and the rising nausea it induced, I studied the diagrams Sparkle had handed me. I'd seen many such diagrams, too. In cases involving a shooting, there are always symbols showing where bullet casings were found. These diagrams were different. No casings. That's common in professional hits. But this was a cop shoot. Had the casings been removed from the scene, I'd have been very interested in the explanation. Probably they were lurking out of sight. I've only just learned to shoot a gun. My expertise does not extend to the finer points of bullet trajectories. These diagrams I had no intention of handing back to Sparkle. They might come in handy.

Not wanting to send up a red flag on the site of my interest, I tossed out what had to be a throwaway question. "It would have been helpful, would it not, had there been a witness to this shooting?"

He barked a nasty laugh intended to make me feel like a total stupid. "When drugs and drug dealers are involved in a critical incident, it's highly unusual for any witnesses to step forward and assist us in our investigation. You must be familiar with the classic situation. Man gets shot in a club. He's surrounded by two hundred people. Nobody saw anything. Some witnesses are afraid that anything they tell us will be used to incriminate them, even though we give them the Witness Confidentiality Assurance that any information they provide will be held in confidence."

Right. I've always assumed that Little Red Riding Hood received a similar assurance from the wolf.

Sparkle was on a roll. "Most of them are more afraid that anyone they might incriminate will retaliate." He shrugged. "Even if a witness steps forward, we always ask ourselves how much credibility he's likely to get — given where he was, given the company he keeps. In any case," he concluded, "one is always more inclined to accept the testimony of the witness officer."

"Why?" Call me stupider.

If ever I was going to push Sparkle to lose his cool, this was the moment.

"I wouldn't be holding the position I do if I wasn't respectful of the law — and the officers who daily risk their lives enforcing it."

Shades of Nelson Eddie and Jeanette McDonald, *Sergeant Preston of the Yukon*. There's always something touching about naïveté — from the mouths of toddlers, that is. Never from the mouths of adults with eyes wide open to the brutal realities of law enforcement. I decided to let his credo pass without challenge.

"The weapon Banton drew on Clarke. I'm assuming that your forensic ident techies secured it as evidence?"

"Your assumption would be correct." His voice quavered a bit.

"And that the subsequent forensic examination confirmed the victim's fingerprints, expected placement of bullet casings, etc.?"

His confidence seemed to rise a notch. "That assumption would be correct."

I jumped to my feet. "But none of those findings would be worth a sewer rat's sorry ass if the gun didn't belong to the alleged potential shooter. Right?"

"Correct again. However, had there been any such indication, charges most certainly would have been laid against the offending officer."

Time to bully him with a real fact. "Your unit is unique in Canada. Every other police oversight agency gets its direction for an investigation from the public, in the form of public complaints. Yours alone has this unhappy difference: Ontario cops themselves are responsible for reporting any incident that may warrant investigation by the SIU."

"True enough, but we have a built-in safeguard against situations in which that difference might be perceived as having been abused. Any member of the public is free to step forward and advise the unit of situations he or she believes may require investigation. That includes coroners, members of the media, medical professionals and lawyers."

"Does that safeguard extend to members of the victim's family?"

"Of course."

"And so far as you are aware, no one stepped forward from Banton's family or circle of acquaintances to cast any doubt on the official version of the incident?"

"No ..." He paused. "There was a disturbed young woman who showed up at the police station making wild accusations. We interviewed her, but she was obviously a drug addict and barely coherent. We established that she was not present at the scene, warned her against making false statements and let her go. An attention seeker, but she had no reliable information."

Sparkle was on shaky ground but appeared blandly confident. Something was dreadfully wrong about all of this.

In the dim hope that his goodie bag held one more nugget, I asked to see his report to the attorney general.

He snapped shut the cigarette case. "I'm somewhat startled by your ignorance of the fact that director's reports are not made public when no charges are laid, Ms. Yeats."

"Ah, so that particular recommendation from the Adams Report into your shenanigans hasn't yet been implemented."

That really got up his hair-trimmed nostrils. Sparkle handed me yet another sheet of bum wipe. "Here is a summary of information concerning the case, which we released to the public."

I wanted to scream, *I'm not the fucking public. I am an investigator, a self-appointed overseer acting on behalf of the public in this particular case because you, the government-appointed watchdog, have lost your balls.* Why bother? A man knows when he's been castrated.

As Sparkle rose and turned to escort me to the door, I slipped the drawings into my jeans pocket.

"A pleasure to meet you, Ms. Yeats."

This time I returned his handshake with equivalent force. His mustache twitched.

"The pleasure was all mine. I've never met a PR machine with a pulse."

CHAPTER 34

A WOMAN LIVING ALONE, a woman never given to homemaking in the first place, always recognizes the first sign of an appalling mental-health day: she housecleans.

And while I housecleaned, I reviewed my progress to date. I'd talked with Debbie Seeger, Tom Clarke's ex-wife. And I'd talked with Hope Askew, Luther Banton's girlfriend. And I'd talked with C. J., Hope's dealer, also Banton's best friend. And I'd talked with Dickless Tracy, a.k.a. Ernest Sparkle, who'd brought down the SIU report on Banton's shooting.

What did my expenditure of time, fuel for Maeve and possibly some risk to my longevity add up to? Let me count the gains. One, Banton's death *might* be an officer-involved shooting gone sour. Two, Clarke, the officer Banton *maybe* had pointed a gun at, was a dirty cop. Three, his hot-dog partner Hunter, the officer who killed Banton, *ostensibly* took that action to save Clarke's life. Four, Hunter was *probably* a mean SOB (even gentle Sam hated him). Five — and most intriguing — C. J. told me that Hunter had an *alleged* connection with the late Jerry Stone, prison guard. And Jerry Stone *might* have given the order for Short Willie to be killed, which meant ...

Meant what, exactly? That any conclusions to be drawn from them were tentative only, studded with enough contingencies to satisfy a weather forecaster. So what if Clarke shot himself accidentally or on purpose? So what if Hunter had no justification for shooting Banton? That wouldn't make him unique in Toronto cop history. And so what if Hunter did cultivate a relationship with Jerry Stone? Prison guards are useful sources of inside information to drug and homicide cops who cultivate them in the course of bringing down some more bad guys.

What the hell did any of this have to do with Pete's death? How was it even tangentially related?

My failure to answer any of these migraine-inducing questions pitched me into this bad mental-health day.

Shortly after moving into my hamster cage, I had torn off the kitchen cupboard doors, the ones above the counter. That exposed all my glass and crockery, which I'd arranged somewhat artistically, forgetting they would also be exposed to free-flying kitchen and nicotine grease, which in turn acted as an efficient trap for particulate matter. I was nearing the end of washing every last piece of tainted kitchenware when the phone rang. Only because I craved a break did I answer it.

"Jane, I'm so pleased you're home."

I didn't recognize the voice; that usually means I've never heard it transmitted via Ma Bell.

"I'm sorry, but who is this?" I emptied my voice of hostility. Marketing researchers rarely have the audacity to use one's first name.

"Goodness, don't be sorry. I should have identified myself straightaway. It's Rodney Payne, Laura's dad."

How sad that seven years after his daughter's death he's still identifying himself by his paternity. Sad, but in no way surprising. I'm still Pete's lover.

I'd not recognized his voice because it sounded much perkier than I remembered.

Professor Payne quickly summarized his reason for calling. After meeting me for lunch at the Faculty Club, he had returned home with new hope that Laura's killer would be discovered.

That hope gave him the courage to do something he'd previously avoided: he examined those contents of her apartment that had come into his possession after her passing and that he'd kept. Paper stuff, mostly: books, magazines, correspondence, etc.

"I came across something I know will interest you. It's a kind of work diary, Jane. Perhaps specific to one of Laura's clients: Detective Sergeant Tom Clarke. Her notes clearly establish that she intended to write an article on ethical issues arising from confidentiality provoked by her interaction with a client. I'm not at all sure that Clarke is the client, but there is much in her notes to indicate that he's the one she had in mind."

I could see my pulse thumping from inside my wrist. "Rodney, I so want to see the diary — if you're willing."

"I feel very guilty about the condition under which I'm willing to allow you access. Are you available to come to my place for dinner tonight?" His voice quavered around the invitation.

"I'm so totally, unabashedly available it would make a hooker blush. What time should I present my hungry mind at your door?"

He chuckled. "I've got a three o'clock lecture. Would six be good for you? I'd like a free hour to cook before you arrive."

We agreed to meet on his clock, and he gave me directions to his home.

Be still, my heart. Twice in the past, an investigation I was mired in got advanced more by serendipity than by wearing down Maeve's rubber treads. Maybe I was about to luck out.

At six on the nose, I stepped onto the porch of a lovely Victorian brick row house in the Annex. Not the kind of row house Max and I inhabit in Little Italy, built by a slum Irish landlord with whatever fell off the back of a cart, but the kind that gets called a "mews house" in London. Taking in its picture-perfect exterior and glorious rose garden, I reminded myself that lust is a deadly sin.

The door chime sounded melodiously. Armed with a good bottle of white wine and a huge bouquet of wildflowers, an impulse purchase, I felt like a suitor of the other gender.

Professor Payne's radiant expression on receiving my gifts erased my embarrassment. He led me into a graciously appointed living room. Brown leather sofa and armchair, worn Persian carpet, a Tiffany ceiling fixture, walls painted a delicate sea green and decorated with framed botanical woodcuts, two dark oak sectional bookcases — an art deco coffee table situated between them sounding the only off-period note.

He was dressed more casually for this meeting. Aran sweater and worn chocolate cords, leather loafers. "I can't thank you enough for these beautiful blooms, which I'm about to put in my favorite vase. May I get you a beverage while I'm at it?"

"A glass of juice would be lovely. Tap water, should you be short on juice." A beer, two fingers of single malt — God help me, even a tot of sherry would do the trick. But no, I'd taken the pledge.

He returned with a tall frosted glass of orange and cranberry juice, my selection at the Faculty Club. Nothing wrong with his memory. As he set it down on the coffee table, he remarked, "This table was Laura's. Not really my taste, but ..."

"I'm familiar with the syndrome. A truly dreadful Grateful Dead poster Pete bought at a garage sale hangs in my living room."

Sipping from a glass of amber sherry, he said, "Jane, I'm going to be very naughty and ask if we can devote ourselves exclusively to enjoying each other's company until we've finished dinner."

I nodded. "Sounds lovely to me. Today I'm very tired of

business." We clicked glasses and plunged into one of the best conversations I'd enjoyed in years. Unlikely as it seemed, Rodney and I shared enough interests to animate the dialogue: Baroque music (he let me choose from an impressive CD collection), gardening (his established, mine aspiring) and, most surprisingly, left-wing politics (he was an old friend of a renowned socialist colleague at the university).

Seated at a pine country table set against a wall in the kitchen, we ate the dinner he'd prepared. Vichyssoise, maple-mustard-crusted salmon fillets, sprouts and new potatoes from his back garden, Dufflet's pastries with ice cream.

What a charming and accomplished man. Pity Etta's not available. Dumb thought. Etta is suspicious of any food that's more haute cuisine than Buffalo suicide wings — and anyone who prepares it. Nor has she ever been found out dating a respectable man, let alone one who's not at least a decade younger than she is.

When we returned to the living room, coffee cups in hand, Rodney went straight to one of his sectional bookcases. He handed me a hardcover notebook the size of a thin novel.

"You can well imagine how very foolish I'm feeling for not having examined Laura's things after they came into my possession. Hazel Duncan took away all her clothes for me. I decided to keep her books. I've always found the books a person keeps such a good map of her mind."

I shuddered to think what peculiar mental cartography he might spin from my books, almost all of them devoted to crime, with a special interest in violent death.

"Laura's books and professional journals reflected my daughter quite accurately. Most had to do with psychology. There was a nice selection of contemporary fiction, including novels by Australian, Japanese, Czech, Irish and Caribbean authors — places she visited on her holidays. She also loved murder mysteries, especially police procedurals. And she'd kept all the books her mother and I gave her when she was a girl. That touched me. But after shelving them upstairs in her old bedroom, I never really gave them another glance. It just comforted me to know her books were there."

He smiled at me. "Then I met Jane Yeats. After returning home from our lunch, I wondered if there might be anything I could do to advance your investigation into her death and Peter's."

He looked so much perkier. How I hoped I wouldn't disappoint him.

"Yesterday it occurred to me that I should look more closely at her books and journals. Keeping in mind her concern about that problem client, I paid particular attention to anything on the subject of patient privilege and confidentiality in counseling. I came upon a number of articles in journals and others that she'd downloaded from the Web. It was obvious from her annotations and highlighting that she'd studied them with considerable care. I assumed from these that she had simply been clarifying her position vis-à-vis anything her problem patient, seemingly Tom Clarke, might have confided."

He paused to sip his coffee. "Forgive the digression, Jane, but I'm a bit suspicious about some aspects of trauma counseling. It's become an industry, one that often delivers dubious benefits *and* occasional harm. And it saddens me that vulnerable people no longer have the community resources they once took for granted. Tribal and familial bonds have been weakened in our culture, so distressed people now often have no alternative but to turn to hired professionals. However, no one ever came to any harm from seeing Laura. Of that I have no doubt. Many, I'm sure, she helped. Even before she took her professional training, all the right instincts were in place. Laura was compassionate and pragmatic — a great help to me after my wife's death."

"Pete had good taste in friends, Rodney. Obviously your Laura was no exception. I wish I'd met her. Pete had mentioned her name as an old friend, but we always seemed to be too busy to do much socializing."

"I'm sure you would eventually have met, had this bloody awful thing not happened." He collected himself. "As I studied the articles she'd marked up, a pattern began to emerge. I got a distinct sense that she was researching an article she intended to write. You see, she'd marked a good number of sentences with an asterisk and the phrase 'see my notes.' I then removed every book from the shelves and shook it out, thinking that perhaps she'd filed her notes in the manner I do. I found nothing. But one book caught my attention."

He gestured to the hardcover resting beside me on the sofa. Eager as I'd been to devour its contents the instant he'd handed it to me, I held back until he finished talking. "May I?" I asked.

"Of course. I'm sorry my preamble took so long. Elderly professors have a way of diverging from the topic."

The spine was cobalt blue imitation leather and stamped in silver "Book Notes," the boards covered in lighter blue marbled papers. The endpapers reproduced an eighteenth-century engraving of a large library, the bewigged scholars all male. The copyright page indicated that it had been a book club offering. The journal pages were organized alphabetically, each section opening with a collage based on a letter of the alphabet, each in a different typeface, and an allusion to a literary reference starting with that letter. The letter *S*, for example, featured a typeface called Snell Roundhand placed at the centre of a witty collage titled *Gertrude Stein*. From the tip of each of three roses twining from the letter sprouted the head of Gertrude Stein. Witty. Five blank pages for note taking followed each letter.

I quickly leafed through it. Laura had made entries on roughly one-quarter of the pages from *A* through *H*, apparently paying no attention to the particular letter under which she wrote. The first page contained only one line, inscribed in a tidy hand: "This article is for my father, who taught me how to reason with passion and to struggle toward a higher moral ground."

I read her words aloud. "That's a beautiful tribute, Rodney."

Tears welled up in his eyes. "You can imagine how much her dedication means to me."

Her neat handwriting made my speed-reading a quick task. The bulk of her notes summarized in point form the articles she considered germane to her inquiry. They were followed by a series of notes that interrogated their conclusions, based on the particular ethical dilemma she intended to present as a case study. Of particular interest to her were two articles dealing with then-recent court decisions upholding the right of psychotherapists and social workers to maintain the confidence of their clients.

She noted that one ruling upheld the necessity of breaking confidentiality in certain prescribed situations, such as clear danger to self or others. A police officer who shot and killed a man had participated in counseling sessions with his organization's employee assistance program. His therapist was a licensed clinical psychologist. When the family of the deceased sued the officer and the city, the officer refused to answer the lawyer's questions about his counseling sessions, claiming privilege. The therapist herself refused to turn over her notes and testified only about the timing, duration and number of their sessions. The court granted her privilege.

Laura seemed interested in the ruling upholding the necessity of breaking confidentiality in other circumstances.

Immediately following this note, she wrote, "When an officer is suicidal, therapists contracted by the TPS employee assistance program are required to report immediately to the force, whose policy it is to remove the officer's weapon and provide medical intervention immediately."

The three pages following this entry concluded Laura's notes. They differed from the preceding pages. Her handwriting deteriorated, as though she'd quickly scribbled them down, and the letters *J*, *L* and *M* took the place of proper names. Why not *C*, *H* and *B* — for Clarke, Hunter and Banton? *Because life is not about easy solutions, Yeats.*

Those three pressured pages added up to a brutal, frag-mented and enigmatic narrative. About one cop shooting a sus-pect who never drew a weapon. About his partner, witnessing this unjustifiable shooting, then proceeding to help the offend-ing cop plant a wiped gun in the young Black man's dead hand and reposition the body. Laura's final sentence read, *"What do I do with this knowledge, told me in therapy by M?"*

Crestfallen, I looked across at Rodney. "The details in these final pages could well correspond to an officer-involved shoot-ing by Tom Clarke's partner. But Laura encoded the names of the participants. The letters *J*, *L* and *M* suggest either that her problem client was an officer other than Clarke — or that she deliberately concealed the identities of the participants."

"Jane, I am handsomely paid by the university to twitter on about dead philosophers. It would seem that your particular expertise is called for here," Rodney said, throwing up his hands.

"I know how much this notebook means to you. If I promise to guard it with my life, will you let me borrow it for a few days? I want to go over it with a fine-tooth comb."

"Of course, my dear. We'll turn you into a scholar yet."

I laughed. "I'm even willing to risk that eventuality, should it lead me to an answer."

He set his reading glasses on the coffee table. "Alas, most of the best scholarship simply opens up more lines of inquiry.

Cases are never really closed, because conclusions are suspect."

"Murder is the ultimate conclusion. Laura's notebook may help me narrow down my suspicions around why she and Pete aren't with us tonight."

CHAPTER 35

SOBRIETY HAS ITS BENEFITS. I returned home from Rodney's with energy to burn. I took Max for a brisk run around the park, which looked deserted. But with all those trees dense with July foliage, one could never be sure that some freak wasn't lurking about. A young woman had been sexually assaulted at the Queen Street end of the park late one night about three weeks ago. That didn't deter me from coming here or from enjoying its calm, the humidity having dropped to almost bearable. If ever I let fear of what sometimes goes down in my neighborhood restrict my movements, I might as well add agoraphobia to my list of neuroses. Not to mention that Max would rip the throat from anyone dumb enough to attack me ... if my Significant Other pulled himself from squirrel chasing in time to do the savage deed.

Once back at my hamster cage, I fiercely resolved to break Laura's code before I slept, having concluded en route from the park that her assigning letters in place of names — letters that did not represent the names of the three men involved in the shooting — in all likelihood was provoked by her commitment to maintaining confidentiality. Perhaps also in the interest of protecting herself, should the notebook fall into other hands. After her death, the SIU had seized everything from her office that might be relevant to their investigation into Tom Clarke's demise. But this notebook she'd taken special care to carry home with her every day after work. If she had left any clues to why Clarke killed himself or — *dared I suggest?* — was killed, they'd be here.

My examination of the notebook at Rodney's home had been cursory. After quickly leafing through the pages, I had settled on those bearing Laura's notes, the ones from *A* through *H*. Coffee mug in hand, I curled up on my sofa and began to examine each page, from first to last, for any evidence of Laura's passage. Max positioned himself as close to me as he could manage, short of leaping up on the sofa, and languished into a profound snore.

I found three further traces of her annotations. A tiny asterisk beside the letters *J*, *L* and *M* caught my attention. I could make nothing of *J*, typeface Jenson, collage "Jack and the Beanstalk." Move on to *L*. I stared at the elegant typeface in which it had been executed, then flipped over the page recording its name and history. Bingo! Designed by Panache Graphics, Copyright FontHaus. Name? Luther Fraktur. Name of man shot by Hunter? Banton, *Luther.*

Maybe I shouldn't have been surprised by how easy it was to crack this part of the code. Laura could have intended her encoding to be not impenetrable to the diligent eye. Maybe her concern over the knowledge she bore was strong enough to make her fear for her life; in which case, she surely would have wanted to point an incriminating finger from her grave.

My celebration of my semi-cleverness turned out to be premature. I could make nothing of *M*, typeface Minion, collage "Moll Flanders." Flipping back and forth between *J* and *M*, I racked my brain for associations between the names of the typefaces, the titles of the books ... nothing. Put my brain in freefall. Jack and the Beanstalk: fairy tale, author unknown ... Moll Flanders: eighteenth-century novel, author Daniel Defoe, Moll my favorite female character in the Beginnings of the English Novel course I'd studied in third year. I stared at the collage. Moll entertaining a gentleman friend. Moll a prostitute, a whore ...

Then it struck me. Why was I racking the limited contents of my pea brain when I could put the world's most capacious memory to work on the problem? I raced upstairs for my rented iBook. A bare-naked search for "Moll Flanders" yielded 39,800 hits. Even the most generous prediction of my life expectancy wouldn't get me through a fraction of them. Okay. Refine your search. Use your brain. Google needs your little gray cells.

What was I looking for? Two names, anything to connect those two letters with them or something associated with them. Beside "the exact phrase" I entered "Jack and the Beanstalk." Beside "at least one of the words," "Tom Clarke Joe Hunter." The search results were skinnier: only 23,100 hits.

Time to go lean and mean. "Jack and the Beanstalk" plus "Clarke" for "all of the words": 907 results. Try substituting "Hunter" for "Clarke": 4,660 hits.

Enough already. I added to the last search a few names associated with Luther Banton's shooting, including "Hope": 1,630 hits. I glanced at the ones at the top. First two were dead-enders, a university project to put on-line an authoritative text of the fairy tale and another educational project, three versions of the classic tale.

The third hit grabbed my attention, doubtless because I've been a crime-fiction addict since Nancy Drew was in diapers.

> Ed McBain
> ... 1981) Beauty and the Beast (1982) **Jack and the Beanstalk** (1984) Snow ... The Cross-Eyed Bear (1996) The Last Best **Hope** (1998) ... EVAN **HUNTER** NOVELS: The Evil Sleep! ... www.edmcbain.com/books/allwork.asp - 17k - Cached - Similar pages

I teleported to the site. McBain, he of 87th Precinct fame, was an old favorite of mine. In 1984 he'd published the fourth novel in his Matthew Hope series, *Jack and the Beanstalk*. Good on you, McBain, born Salvatore A. Lombino, a.k.a. Curt Cannon, Hunt Collins, Ezra Hannon, Matthew Hope ... SHITE! Also a.k.a. Evan Hunter. HUNTER. HUNTER. HUNTER.

God bless Google. I was on a roll. I checked out the list of titles under each pseud. Hell's bells: God bless Mary, Mother of Perpetual Help, and prompt me ever to hail her most powerful name. Writing as Evan Hunter, in 1996 Salvatore A. Lombino published a novel called *Privileged Conversation.*

The keyboard sounded a hollow plunk as I punched around for Amazon.com and checked out the reviews for the promising-sounding title.

Just as I finish downloading the reviews, Max stumbled to shaky legs and pawed my leg. He was telling me to go to bed. He hates sleeping with the lights on. I glanced at the clock: 2:30 a.m.

"Max, can I just read this — if I promise to take my iBook up to bed and do it there?" He thumped his tail in the affirmative.

Before turning out the bed lamp, I read through computer-wasted eyes:

> *Privileged Conversation*
> by Evan Hunter
> Editorial Reviews
> From *Publishers Weekly*
> The blurred border between fantasy and obsession is explored in this latest from Hunter ... When happily married psychiatrist David Chapman rescues dancer Kate Duggan during a robbery in

Central Park, the chance encounter inspires a sexual fantasy that has disturbing echoes in the revelations of some of his more troubled patients. It's only after David sees Kate dancing the part of Victoria in a performance of *Cats* that the fantasy is realized. During the course of a summer affair that becomes obsessive, the psychiatrist alternates weekends with his wife and family on Martha's Vineyard with wild evenings in the city with a woman he knows little about ...

Copyright 1995 Reed Business Information, Inc.

Yegawds, Laura can't have been sleeping with Tom Clarke.

My brain had short-circuited. Information overload.

Slow down, Yeats, you haven't nailed down the entire puzzle.

J = Hunter. L = Banton. That left M.

The final sentence of Laura's rough narrative came back to me: *"What do I do with this knowledge, told me in therapy by M?"*

Bingo! M = Clarke.

And so, to sleep ...

CHAPTER 36

FRUSTRATION AGES A BODY. This morning I am feeling old. I found a white hair. It was not growing on my head. Maybe it was just a trick the light was playing over my newly showered body. More likely it had sprouted when my brain hit the wall last night.

Although I now had Laura's notebook disclosures to bolster the notion that Hunter shot an unarmed man, I could see no point in throwing any more time into attempting to verify the unverifiable. Both witnesses were dead. The SIU had accepted the officers' accounts of what went down. Hunter was not about to change his story — and self-incriminate — in exchange for me treating him to a pint.

I decided to work from the hypothesis that Hunter made a bad shoot. Apparently he had done so on the assumption that Clarke would cover for him. *But why did he shoot Banton?* Before and subsequent to that event his record was unblemished. Exemplary.

The official version didn't wash: Hunter wasn't defending anyone. He did not fire his gun to protect his partner or himself. Nor were there any people in the vicinity who might have been endangered. He can't have been afraid: the suspect was unarmed, and Hunter was an experienced officer who could easily have taken him down without violence, even without Clarke's help. Had the motive been robbery, well, Clarke had ripped off many dealers and roughed up some of them in the process. But he'd never had to kill one to steal his drugs. That fact would have been well known to Hunter.

Hunter must have known his partner was bent. Knowledge is power. During their partnership and after, when Clarke was subject to investigation, Hunter maintained his silence. Every officer on the drug squad was under the spotlight, including Hunter. Even when he went so far as to request a transfer to Homicide to keep even a hint of corruption from soiling his reputation, he refused to rat out his partner. Hunter seemed to be holding all the cards.

But had he assassinated Banton, Clarke was the sole witness. Knowledge is power. Now the scales were balanced. Should either man talk, he would ruin the other's career and maybe see him sent to prison. Both would go down in the process. *That night in the alley, why did Hunter risk what he most valued?*

I had no clue. Given what appeared to be a motiveless crime, I was in the dark about what to do next. Knowledge gets buried in silence. As do people who threaten to break the silence and reveal some dark secret they've been harboring. As do people who can no longer bear their own guilty secrets. Tom Clarke fell into both categories: he had broken the silence around his own criminality when he confessed to Laura in a therapy session and he had killed himself. *Or had he?*

As in Luther Banton's case, the official version of his demise differs from what those close to him believe to have happened. Debbie, Clarke's ex-wife, is convinced that his deep religious convictions erased the suicide option as a quick route out of an intolerably pressured life. Banton, who enjoyed a rich personal life, was not carrying a weapon and, in any case, was unlikely to have jeopardized that life just to escape another prison sentence.

This line of reasoning led nowhere. Even if had Clarke been killed by a hand not his own, I saw no way of corroborating any suspicion of homicide. Motives abounded when it came down to who might have been inclined to send him south on the express train. All those dealers he'd beaten, ripped off and arrested. One could even imagine a group of them banding together and electing one among them to get him out of the way. I rejected that scenario, partly because I couldn't go anywhere with it.

My awareness of two links persisted in nagging me. Clarke knew too much. He passed the baton on to Laura. Both were dead, linked by shared knowledge of police misconduct. That did not mean their deaths were anything but a coincidence. I could think of only one person who might know what Laura had planned to confide in Pete. Laura's colleague — Hazel Duncan.

Perhaps Hazel Duncan was initially disinclined to accept my dinner invitation because I'd shown up at her office unannounced at the end of her working day. Perhaps because I was dressed like an extra in a biker flick and she thought I might hit on her. Perhaps because she caught me feeding her fish. I was only trying to distract Ma Krib from bullying the cute little red-nosed guys. But when I mentioned that I'd come from a meeting with Laura's dad, with her late colleague's notebook in hand, her interest perked up. That proved to be the carrot.

Elated, I offered to pick up the dinner tab; she even got to choose the restaurant. To the shock of my bank book, she led me to an upscale Mexican restaurant close to her office. Last month, the *Globe and Mail's* restaurant critic had given El Gastrónomo Revolucionario the thumbs-up — and suggested a dinner-for-two cost that would have kept a Mexican family in tamales for a decade. That put me in a ratty mood. When people invite me out for dinner, I try to select a joint accessible even to folks skirting the poverty line.

Ensconced in a plush banquette facing me, Duncan did look pleased with her choice of venue. She ordered a margarita. How

I'd love a cold glass of Corona with a lime slice. Having eye-balled the list of nonalcoholic drinks, and thinking how much more potable *refrescos* made them sound, I settled for a *horchata* on the rocks.

Her margarita arrived topped with a freaking chrysanthe-mum. My melon-seed drink was unadorned. Before sipping, she flicked her tongue around the rim like an anteater in search of a snack. She had to know she was tormenting a recent convert to sobriety.

Next she made a pretense of studying the menu before asking sweetly, "What, precisely, is it you do?"

Bitch. I hate that question when, as it now seemed to be, it's asked with the presumption that what you do establishes your sta-tus, defines you as a somebody to be reckoned with — or not.

Looking intently at a decent Diego Rivera knockoff mural on the wall beyond her head, I stated, "I've never done anything precisely, apart from constructing a sentence. I'm a writer."

She blanched, then stared at my defective fingers, and then turned a whiter shade of pale. Bit unprofessional in a profes-sional devoted to raising self-esteem like a phoenix from the ashes of damaged lives.

"Oh my goodness, you're *that* Jane Yeats." Had she not known that prior to our first meeting?

I shrugged. "I guess. There's only one of me in the Toronto phone book."

She adjusted her expression into a semblance of something more professional. Affirmative. Uplifting. Positively motiva-tional. "Don't be so modest. You've written a number of very highly regarded books. I've even read one of them — *Benign Neglect,* I think it was called."

"*Malign Neglect,*" I corrected.

"Whatever. I found it very useful."

Useful? How to get your fingers chopped off in ten easy

chapters? Twelve Steps to Insobriety? God forbid my books should be fodder for shrinks. As is my wont when in the presence of wannabe mind readers, I marked a moment of silence while I continued to inspect the wall.

Score one for Yeats the Inscrutable. Duncan glanced nervously over her shoulder. "What intrigues you about that mural?"

Sure, lady, throw me a Rorschach and think I won't know. "How very difficult it must be for an artist living in a climate as chilly as ours to imitate an artist as hot as Rivera. Does she or he have a lover as fascinating as Frida Kahlo? Could a nouveau Kahlo survive bourgeois Toronto?"

Duncan extracted her napkin from the brilliantly colored papier mâché ring and fiddled with it, worrying away at the creases. "Ah, what an interesting mind you have. I wish I could say the same for most of my clients."

She was looking at two Kahlo posters. Surprisingly, neither was a tortured self-portrait. I knew them both. *Still Life with Prickly Pears*, in which the poor fruits look like the contents of an autopsy bowl. *Weeping Coconuts*, in which one coconut is shedding milky tears.

"A rather dangerous feminist icon, don't you think?"

I nodded. "She should have been drowned at birth, along with Dorothy Parker, Stevie Smith, Sylvia Plath, Gwendolyn MacEwen and a host of other unhappy women artists."

Chill, Yeats, chill. Do not let your inborn hostility to shrinks make this specimen clam up. But my aggravation was more layered than that: Duncan seemed ill at ease with herself, as though some irritant had permanently lodged inside her — and that discomfort infected her communication with me. I observed another moment of silence, this one in memory of Diego and Frida.

"Do you have a work in progress?"

Soon that napkin would be worn thinner than Archie Bunker's undershirt. If I told her that my current work in progress was about locating Pete's killer and blowing away the SOB from brain to bowels, she might get the right idea. Get alarmed, even.

"No, the royalties from my last book have given me the luxury of taking a break."

She saluted my words with a tip of her margarita glass.

I clicked hers with my elegant flute of lemonade.

"How lovely. I envy you. Do you travel?"

"No further than I must, which rarely takes me beyond the GTA."

"So your interest in Laura's death doesn't stem from ... um ... any research you might be doing?"

How many times did she need me to hit the same nail on the head? "Why don't we order?" I was hungry enough to eat the fucking chrysanthemum.

I declined her suggestion that we share an appetizer, mahi-mahi ceviche with jalapeños and coconut. Did the woman feel no conflict between nurturing fish in her office and eating them raw a mere two blocks from her aquarium? Had Frida not alerted her to the sorrows of coconuts?

"You mentioned that Professor Payne lent you Laura's work diary. I knew that she kept one, but I always wondered why she bothered, what with all her computer records — which she faithfully backed up every twenty minutes."

If ever I could pry from her tightly clenched ethics what it was that Laura told her, the contents of that diary were my only bargaining chip. I wasn't about to give them up so easily. "Even the faithful can end up with their computer and all its artifacts seized by the police."

"Oh, I very much doubt that's why she kept the notebook — I mean, for any devious purpose. Laura had nothing to hide, apart, of course, from her patient records. Those she guarded with her life. Like me, she was deeply committed to observing client confidentiality."

Duncan made this remark in a tone reminiscent of a Catholic schoolgirl awaiting praise from a priest for her correct response to a Catechism question.

Carefully did I measure the tone of my response. "Confidentiality is not always a sacred trust. It can have its down side. No one, ever — not priest, lawyer, doctor, shrink, whoever — should harbor information that might result in harm to another person. From my perspective, that is simply a given."

Duncan's smile betrayed a hint of condescension. "With respect, Jane, yours is a very simplistic take on the subject."

Funny, I couldn't detect the respect.

She wiped a dribble of lime juice from her chin. "It's clear from your writing that you are a feminist. So, for a moment, look at this issue of privilege through that particular lens. As the law currently functions, women who have been sexually violated have to give up the privacy of their doctor-patient relationship, if they want to bring their attacker to justice. How weird is that? The alleged rapist started the chain of events, yet the law says the victim has to expose her entire private life to the public to prove her innocence. That's the price a rape victim pays for seeking justice."

I swallowed a heavenly chunk of beef short rib in molé as she tackled her equally aromatic rack of lamb. "No question about your example," I said. "It sucks. But this is different. Let's reverse the lens this time around. The client in this hypothetical case is a police officer. He confides in his therapist that he has committed crimes *and* that he has witnessed a serious crime being committed by his partner. That client has come under investigation by the SIU. Are there any limits on confidentiality in such a situation?"

"Oh yes!" she exclaimed. "For example, if someone tells me that he has committed a crime and the court finds out, my files can be subpoenaed and I must appear in court."

"What course do you follow should his crime *not* be discovered?' That one might stick in her craw.

"If his crime involves child assault, I am legally obliged to notify CAS. If a client tells me that he plans to kill his wife's lover, I must take steps to prevent that crime from happening. In such a case, I would break my client's confidentiality." She signaled our server to "refresh" her drink.

Thirsty as her action made me, I was beginning to see a huge advantage in sobriety. My tongue stayed precisely where I intended it to, while my boozy companion's seemed about to boogie beyond its owner's wisest practice.

"Have you ever broken client confidentiality?"

"Yes. I've reported two clients to CAS. Both were subsequently found guilty of child abuse — thanks, in large part, to my handing over my client file and testifying in court."

She put her lips to the glass with the pleasure of a bee sipping nectar after a drought. Tossed me a seductive smile. "But I've never enjoyed the frisson of a client confessing to his desire to ... um ... eliminate someone. That's a scene from *The Sopranos,* not real life. I'm not saying, of course, that many people don't fantasize killing someone. Even I have to confess to having enjoyed some pretty wicked thoughts about my exboyfriend."

Get fucking real, I fumed. Six people were murdered in Toronto the Good this past weekend, two last night in four separate incidents. In far less time than it takes to shoot an episode of *The Sopranos.* Most people who kill don't waste any time fantasizing the event. They plan it. When time doesn't permit, they just fucking do it. As I would if I knew who killed Pete.

Shoot the bastard, run him over with a car, strangle him.

I decided to cut to the chase. "Laura found herself in exactly the situation I just described as 'hypothetical.' She was very troubled by Detective Sergeant Tom Clarke's disclosures. Did she tell you anything about how she intended to act on that information?"

"My understanding was that the possibility that Tom Clarke might take his own life was her only concern. Laura was reluctant to jeopardize his career by notifying his supervisor unless she became more convinced about that possibility."

I looked her directly in the eyes. "Funny, isn't it, that she failed to tell you that her overriding concern was that his partner shot a man in cold blood?"

Never have I posed a question that elicited such a dramatic response. My dinner companion's face turned crimson, her eyes bulged and she clutched her throat as if to strangle herself. "Nuts," she gasped. "I have an allergy."

As I leaped up, our server rushed over to the table. "I think she's about to go into anaphylactic shock," I told him. "Please call 911 for an ambulance."

Before he could rush for the phone, Duncan revived sufficiently to remove an EpiPen from her bag. She plunged it into her thigh, right through her skirt. She soon relaxed enough to ask our alarmed server to call for a taxi.

"I'm sorry, Jane. I should know have known better than to come here. Mexican chefs are nuts about nuts. But I'll be fine. My allergy is inconvenient, but it's not life-threatening."

The upside of the episode was that the restaurant owner refused my attempt to pay our bill. I saw my companion right to the door of her condo. Clearly she would live to raise another client's self-esteem.

I returned home with the distinct sense that what triggered the allergy drama was my reference to Joe Hunter.

I fell asleep regretting that I will probably die without ever knowing the alluring zing on my tongue of *espuma de chocolate de metate,* the dessert I was obliged to forgo.

CHAPTER 37

AT FIVE THE NEXT MORNING I was wakened by what I mistook for my first night sweat. Must have been the discovery of that white pubic hair that brought it on. My locks clung to my head, my oversize T-shirt to my body. Straightaway I brought my laptop to bed and checked out the humidex on-line. This sweat turned out not to be early-onset menopause. This was the sauna Toronto summers have become.

And I had indigestion. Not from last night's spicy food. My stomach is more inclined to belch at bland. My brain was dyspeptic. Much about my truncated meal with Hazel Duncan was acting up. But the most indigestible thing about her behavior was the way she changed when she heard that I had Laura's work diary in my possession. Until that point she had been professionally evasive, throwing up client privilege as a smoke screen every time I asked a question. But once she heard about the diary, her whole demeanor became "friendly." She wanted to know what I knew, and it showed. Why was she so concerned?

Had she chosen a particularly convenient moment to pitch an allergic reaction? It seemed to me she'd pulled a drama queen right after my mention of Hunter. I went back on-line and quickly researched anaphylactic shock.

> The resultant, and usually very swift, effects are muscle contractions and swelling, often closing the throat, making it difficult to breathe, and a sudden

decline in blood pressure, which leads to fainting or unconsciousness. The most visible signs are often swelling and rashes on the skin, or on the lips and tongue if it is a food allergy. True anaphylactic shock requires immediate treatment with adrenaline injection. However, such is the speed with which anaphylactic shock takes hold that even immediate treatment with adrenaline is not guaranteed to save the victim's life. So any person who shows signs and symptoms of anaphylaxis will require treatment in a hospital's emergency department where the condition can be closely monitored and lifesaving treatment can be given.

No sensible sufferer, especially a health-care professional, would take a rain check on that race to the hospital. And the few symptoms Duncan manifested could easily have been faked. I saw no swelling or rash, she showed no sign of being about to faint. Indeed, she spoke an entire paragraph in the midst of reacting. Ergo, my amateur diagnosis: she was merely auditioning for the part.

Anyone who'd put that much effort into evasion would stick to the first principles of her profession like scrambled eggs to an iron fry pan. I dismissed any thought of phoning to see if she was still breathing. Already Duncan had wasted too much of my time.

My mention of Hunter ... Hunter having made a bad shoot: that's what triggered her.

Three hours later I phoned Sam.

"Girl, you're starting work early these days. What can I do for you?"

His voice was excessively cheery. I assumed he'd just been laid.

I quickly recapped last night's dinner. "It seems that Hunter figures in the puzzle, Sam. I've pretty much exhausted my sources on him. What I'm left with is the probability that he shot Banton for no reason that I can fathom. Last time we spoke, you mentioned that you might check out a source or two on Hunter. Can you help me out here, buddy?"

He chuckled. "Your timing is good. I was going to phone you later this morning. You and I were both wondering why Hunter would have made that shoot — assuming Banton wasn't armed. I haven't checked out my sources yet. What I decided to do first was dig into my archives, poke into Hunter's record on the drug squad prior to Banton. I came up with an item that just might give our golden boy a motive to gun down the first dealer he encountered in a situation singularly lacking any witness but his partner."

I could hear him slurping his coffee. "Sounds like manna to me, Sam. Feed me, feed me."

"Maybe I shouldn't have said 'motive.' What I mean is, what might have 'triggered' him to shoot Banton, no pun intended."

Sam's nugget weighed in as pure gold. Hunter and Clarke were doing a routine surveillance on the home of a suspected dealer. Drew Knox was lowlife with a record you could shake a shillelagh at (six arrests and four convictions). His neighbors had phoned in a number of complaints about peculiar comings and goings throughout the day and night by folks who clearly didn't work on Bay Street. The lady next door reported that she suspected him of beating his wife. A guy across the street groused about Knox's mean-tempered pit bull nipping at the heels of local kids, etc. All in all, a nasty piece of work any drug squad officer would itch to bust, especially because Knox seemed to be dealing at a fairly high level.

Anyway, the night of their stakeout, Hunter and Clarke

noted a rush of activity for a couple of hours, roughly between eight and eleven. Then things got quiet. Maybe Knox was catching the news before retiring, maybe he shut down shop at eleven. Just as Hunter and Clarke were about to call it quits for the night, they heard gunshots coming from inside the house. *Bam!* Short pause. *Bam!* Longer pause. *Bam!* They rushed the house, kicked in the front door, adrenaline pumping, weapons drawn.

In the living room they come upon a scene to make Quentin Tarantino's teeth ache. Knox's wife with her face and chest exploded, bleeding into the sofa. Knox, staining the carpet, his brain matter blasted onto the walls. Hunter confirmed the obvious: they were both dead. It appeared that Knox shot his wife, then bull's-eyed his own skull. Clarke phoned it in. While he checked out the first floor of the house, Hunter went down into the basement, where a naked light was burning. At first glance, the basement looked innocent. Usual detritus. A tap was dripping over the laundry tubs. One tub looked about to overflow. In the dim light Hunter looked closer. Reached down to pull out the plug. His hand encountered what was really plugging the drain: the body of a baby. The water was red. The infant's throat had been cut so deeply that his head was almost free-floating. Hunter freaked. Lifted the tiny boy from the water, his head supported, held him in one arm, started blowing into his mouth. Put him on the floor. Gently applied CPR.

When the homicide cops and crime-scene folks arrived, he was still working at reviving a child who was so clearly dead — to anyone in his right mind. He was crying, cradling a baby whose head threatened to fall off when Hunter stopped supporting it.

At the end of Sam's recital, I was close to tears. "Sam, if I'd experienced what Hunter did, I'd be hell-bent on shooting the first person I encountered in the line of duty who abused aspirin, let alone dealt the big shit."

"And wouldn't we all? From what the cops eventually pieced together, Knox caught his wife shooting up heroin after the last of his customers left that night. She'd sworn up and down that she'd kissed it good-bye forever, according to her brother. Ironic as it sounds, Knox apparently figured that any mother who used was worse than no mother at all, that any baby with a junkie for a mother was better off dead. He went ballistic, grabbed the baby from its crib, slaughtered him with a kitchen knife in the laundry tub, probably in front of the mother, dragged her up into the living room, shot her, then himself. I guess nobody knows better than a dealer the devastation his own wares inflict."

"Right," I said faintly. "When did this happen?"

"Just ten days before the Banton shoot."

"My God. So maybe the next atrocious act played out this way, Sam: ten days later, Hunter comes across Banton dealing. Chases him into the alley. Executes him. Wrong target, of course: Knox is already dead. Banton shares the same scummy occupation, though. In the state of mind Hunter must still have been in, he probably thought, It's just another dead parasite."

"There's a helluva good chance Hunter was still out of his mind when he shot Banton. In a total hate rage. Ready to wreak vengeance on anyone plying the same toxins. Maybe especially another dealer with a vulnerable wife and child."

"Makes twisted sense to me, Sam."

"Jane, where do you think this information is leading, though? I have no clue."

"Nor do I. But for sure it's going to keep me on Hunter's tail."

Sam coughed. "So what's next ... what I really mean to ask is, are you far enough ahead in your planning to think of something I might do to help? I'm hating retirement, Jane. Rescue me."

"Don't give me any crap about retirement. You write books. If you're retired, then I'm unemployed."

"Yeah, but surfing the Web for research materials, then punching a keyboard for four or five hours just doesn't cut it with me. I miss working the crime beat. It got me out of the office every day, put me in contact with interesting people. I got to drink beer and eat junk food. Honest to God, it's gotten so bad I'm beginning to draw vicarious breath from your edgy existence."

"Living at least one remove from my reality will extend your life, Sam."

He ignored my remark. "If your right brain isn't telling your left — or me — where the hell you're headed with this Hunter stuff, I've got an idea. Sounds like you'd be pissing up a rope trying to wring anything more from Hazel Duncan, Drama Queen. So let's try a totally different tack. Go back to the beginning of your nightmare: Short Willie. Why would he have confessed to killing Laura and Pete?"

"Why would he have confessed to killing the other three women?"

"Listen up, Super Sleuth. Yesterday I phoned Ernie."

I interrupted. "Sivcoski? Did the bastard pass on his regards? He hasn't done squat for me since the cops raided my house. He owed me that much. I want my iBook back. I want all its lovely devices and peripherals back. I want my books and files back. I want my dignity back!"

"You're right to be bitter. Over the years you've done at least as much for Ernie as he's ever done in return."

Yeah, I thought, and that includes in bed.

Sam was in his persuasive mode. "I'm not making any excuses for Ernie, but think about where he must be at right now. Major nonstop heat coming down from the chief to close the books on those five murders ever since word got out that

Short Willie intended to retract his confession. Then the Rosenberg autopsy established as fact that he hadn't murdered at least one of the victims."

"Pass me the crying towel."

"Ernie's the lead on the Rosenberg case, right? When I phoned him to ask a few indirect questions about Hunter — he of the immaculate closure rate — Ernie didn't have much to say, except the usual laudatory crap. He did admit that Hunter might be a bit on the overly ambitious side, but that's probably professional jealousy speaking. Hunter is rising through the ranks so fast he'll leave Ernie choking on his gunpowder. When I wished him luck on the Rosenberg case, he told me that they were about to make an arrest — and reminded me that 'luck' played no part in the investigation. Ever the eager boy reporter, I asked him how many murder charges they'd be laying."

"Belt it out, Sam."

"He told me *three.* Then our conversation got a bit cat and mouse. He refused to tell me which three, so I named Ruth Rosenberg, Linda Bailey and Sandra Priest. 'You'd win the Early Bird Prize for that guess, Brewer' — that's what he said, Jane."

I gasped. "Then I have been on the right track all along. Somebody else killed Laura and Pete. Hang on a sec, Sam." I set the phone down and walked into the backyard. Let out three victory whoops.

"My friend, I love you," I then squealed. "Now my head's clear. Here's what we have to do."

Saying "we" was a huge step for me. It signified my willingness to relinquish sole ownership of my mission. But the invitation it extended was disingenuous. If Sam had even a vague sense that I intended to kill anyone, he'd consent to assist me only straight into a padded cell. That was a lie of omission I intended to maintain.

"Are we partners?" I asked.

"What's new?" was his laconic reply.

My heart was racing as fast as my mind. "Okay. Here's what I propose. You look into where Hunter was the night Pete and Laura were killed — and I mean including *before* he showed up on the crime scene. Find out anything you can about the role he played both on the scene and during the investigation right up until Short Willie confessed."

Sam readily consented. "Works for me. You know I followed those murders very closely. Especially after Pete's death," he added softly.

"Thanks. Here's the fish I've got to fry while you're busy at that. Remember Jerry Stone — the prison guard, head of the union, who got killed in the riot not long after Willie flew back to his maker on the wings of a coal black dove? Shortly after I started sniffing under flat rocks, an ex-con known as Ferret entered the picture. He told me that Stone set up the jailhouse hit on Willie. Last week, when I was interviewing Banton's buddy and colleague in dealing, known to me only as C. J., he claimed that Hunter was supplying drugs to Stone. Stone, in turn, was selling them to the inmates. When C. J. told me that, I more or less wrote it off as sour grapes. He's still so pissed at Hunter for killing Banton that he'd nominate him as the guy who shot the Pope back when disco music was still in vogue."

"But now you're beginning to think there might be some substance to his allegation?"

"It's an angle that screams to be checked out. May lead to a dead end, but I'll poke around and see if I can shore up Ferret's claim. And see what the grapevine's got to offer on the subject of who wanted Short Willie silenced before he could begin flapping his gums."

"Jane, this could be totally out in left field, but maybe the guy Ernie is planning to arrest arranged to have the hit put on Willie. Maybe Willie was about to name him as the real killer."

I agreed. "That's a possibility. But whoever he is, they're not charging him with Laura and Pete's murder. The bastard who killed them will still be in the clear."

"Yeah. So now you're wanting to connect the dots from Short Willie to Jerry Stone to Hunter ..."

" ... and looping back from there to Clarke and Laura and Pete."

I could hear his desk reverberate to the thumping of his fist. "Let's go for it, lady. And be sure to take that cell phone you hate with you — everywhere you go, even to the toilet." His voice dropped into that surly-sounding tone I know means affection. "Watch your back, Jane."

CHAPTER 38

"FUCK, MAN — I MEAN, WOMAN ... hooters like yours, who could forget?"

It was Ferret speaking. Such a fetching way of assuring me that he remembered who I was.

I'd phoned him on his cell and caught him at work.

"Ferret, can we talk for a few minutes?"

"Hey, hey, hey ... tell me you've turned yourself back into a normal straight woman. You straightening out. That would be a win-win situation for me, eh? Narrows down the competition from you for the broads and maybe I get to take you up to heaven with me. If you get what I mean."

"I hate to disappoint, Ferret, but my doctor tells me I'm growing some kind of nasty fungus on my private parts that's way more likely to take your dick to someplace far hotter than heaven. Otherwise you'd be my man. For sure."

"Damn straight? Swear on your grandmother's grave?"

My grandmother had been deeply committed to mendacity. "Damn straight, Ferret. And I swear on that sweet lady's grave." Granny's grave marker was nontraditional: "She pissed off the whole world. One person at a time."

"All right! Call me back when you're cured, eh?"

"I'll do that, man, but in the meantime I really do need to talk to you."

"Hey, we could go for a few beers at that new country place in the east end. Maybe next week. Your fungus would be dead by then, right?"

"Right, but I've totally got to talk to you no later than an hour ago."

"Okay, okay. I'm hearing you. Must be about that mother-fucker Jerry Stone."

"You hit the nail on the head. It is about that particular motherfucker. Ferret, I'm just an inch away from outing him for the hit on Short Willie."

"So why would I give a flying fuck? I mean, Stone's dead."

"Yeah, but what I'm planning to do will bring down some bad cops, maybe even a few more guards," I enticed.

"Sounds like you've got a plan I'd like to buy into. Not to mention that seeing you again wouldn't hurt me none. If you promise to wear a tight sweater, you can come and meet me right here at work. I'll take my break when you show up."

An hour later I revved up Maeve. And I was wearing a sweater borrowed from a neighbor's child. Size: constricted. Call me a slut.

Ferret's current job had him working for a roofer. Today's work site was in the west end, a fifteen-minute ride from my place.

My would-be informant and his co-worker were laying asphalt on the flat roof of an old four-story apartment building. When I dismounted Maeve, Ferret shouted down to me that I should climb up the ladder.

I don't like heights. In my lexicon "heights" are anything higher than an NBA hoopster's best leap. I swallowed my phobia and scaled up an unsecured ladder to meet my number-one fan.

"Good work," he greeted me. "Lotsa broads are scared of heights, eh?"

His right ear was still missing.

Ever the gentleman, ever the secretive little weasel, he escorted me over to the far end of the roof. Where his partner couldn't hear us. From where I could look over his shoulder four stories down — and hurl. From where he could push me over with a tap to my shoulder.

As he cracked open his break snack, a can of Blue, his eyes worked the sweater. "Man, the sight of you almost makes this fucking job worthwhile. It's 110 de-fucking-grees out here in the sun, you know. And that ain't counting in the humi-fucking-dex. The minute I get paid for this job I'm telling the boss to shove it. This honest-job bullshit is not for me. No way a guy with my talents was born to be getting goddamn barbe-cued up here on a day like this."

"Look at it this way, Ferret: the air conditioning can't be up to much in jail."

"You're right. And my girlfriend cooks better. But that ain't saying much."

"Hey, I really appreciate you agreeing to see me this morn-ing." The heat and humidity up there were so intense that I was sweating enough to give my sweater that winning wet T-shirt cling. Ferret's eyes hadn't yet risen to meet my face. "And I real-ize that your break must be a short one. So I'll get right to the point. Last time we met —"

"— best night of my life. Fucking Man in Black Johnny Cash tribute at your mom's bar. Awesome."

"Glad you enjoyed. That night you told me that Jerry Stone arranged the hit on Short Willie. And that a cop who supplied Stone with drugs to deal to inmates persuaded him to have Willie offed. Now, I'm thinking that Stone's original supplier might have been a cop named Clarke. Am I right?"

When Ferret nodded, two rivulets of sweat drained down to his weak and narrow chin to exit the cleft. "Asshole's name was Tom Clarke. Used to steal from the dealers he was supposed to be busting, eh? Then he'd, like, recycle the shit he already stole by selling it to other dealers — like Jerry Stone."

"Right. Now fast-forward five years. Somebody on the outside wanted Willie dead. So he'd just have to lean on Stone to get the job done — but he'd need to have some serious leverage to persuade Stone. If that someone happened to be Stone's new supplier ..."

"Yeah, yeah," agreed Ferret, nodding his weasel head. "All he's gotta do is tell Stone that his supply will dry up faster than Krazy Glue if Willie is still breathing twenty-four hours later. So that means Stone's gonna get the job done damn fast, right? If he don't and then he's got no shit to deal on the inside, he's dead. He is so totally fucking dead. And he's getting dead the slow and painful way. So Willie gets himself shanked in the cafeteria."

"After Clarke killed himself, who took his place as Stone's supplier?"

"Killed himself? No way that sonuvabitch ate his gun. No way Clarke done it accidental. He got hit, eh? And Stone would have had a brand-new source overnight once Clarke was croaked. Like the guard who took over Stone's job — he knew who to go to."

"But do you know who was supplying Stone at the time of Willie's death?" My informant had a talent for creatively filling in the blanks when facts failed him.

Ferret slurped down the last of his Blue, extinguished his cigarette butt in the can and tossed it over the edge of the roof. "Coulda bin the dead cop's partner. That bastard's name is Hunter. He knew what his buddy Clarke was up to all along. And how he done it all. Only makes sense, right? But it wasn't him. Hunter didn't fuck around with stealing and dealing. Anyways, I heard he got transferred to Homicide."

"Ferret, your brain is turning over as smooth as a

well-tuned Harley. So give me one more goodie while you're on this roll. Could Hunter have set up the hit on Willie by going some other route?"

"Could Johnny Cash sing?"

I slipped in a final question. "Do you have any clue why Hunter might have wanted Willie dead?"

"Nope. He was one of the Homicide guys who brought Willie down, eh. Why bump off a lifer you got convicted?"

In spite of his BO, I moved closer to slap my favorite roofer on the arm. "You are a genius anyway. Thank you so much."

"Babe, I am a fucking horny genius." He scratched his nuts. How could I object to a schoolyard gesture that traces back to Michael Jackson and found fresh life in Eminem's crotch?

"But it's too hot up here to be even thinking about getting laid, so I'll let you leave without hitting on you. Hee-hee. Be sure to phone me when that fungus is history, eh?"

Merrily I waved him good-bye. "You'll be the first to know."

As I headed back to the ladder, I heard my suitor enthuse to the other asphalt guy, "Has she got a pair — or what?"

I managed to descend to ground without tossing my cook-ies. Barely.

En route home, my cell phone, which I had craftily mounted on the right handlebar, began to vibrate against the chrome. I pulled over.

"Where the hell are you? I can hear traffic."

"That's because I'm in the middle of it, Sam. What's the scoop?"

"Something urgent has come up. So wherever the hell you are, race on over to my place and I'll fill you in."

CHAPTER 39

SHADES OF BEING A TEENAGE DAUGHTER who's blown her curfew. Sam was standing on his porch, arms crossed, when I pulled Maeve into the driveway of his down-at-the-heels bungalow.

He didn't even give me time to pull off my helmet before his mouth started flapping. This was not typical of the man. He was in an agitated state.

"Christ, cost of that bike you should have been here an hour ago," he fumed.

"Harley Davidson doesn't make magic carpets, Sam." I glanced at my Swatch. "Twenty minutes since you phoned me. We must be in different time zones."

"You've got that right. I'm living in the countdown to an execution." He gestured me inside.

When they had married, Sam's second wife, Louise, had moved into his place. Since then she had tried to focus his energy on renovating the house. His wardrobe remained unimproved. Today he looked like an aging baseball fan who'd been obliged to hop a fence in order to get into the ballpark.

"Sit, but don't expect any offers of food or drink."

My stomach was howling for attention. And ever since I went on the wagon my abandoned inner inebriate has been screaming for relief. "Swallow an anti-anxiety pill, man. What could be so urgent?"

He paced around the Sally Ann sofa on which I'd plunked my bones. In monologue mode, he was. "After the last time we talked, I'm thinking. In the course of duty, Hunter came upon those three bodies, one of them a baby. Ten days later he makes the Banton shoot. According to cop protocol, just *one* of those critical events would have had his superiors shipping him off for counseling. Probably after the first event he would have been manifesting all kinds of symptoms typical of post-traumatic stress. Like increased aggression — what we figured probably provoked him to execute Banton for no apparent cause. So which therapist might he have been referred to?"

Sam interrupted his pacing in front of me and tapped his brow. "How clever am I? This clever: knowing that the force makes a ton of referrals to Hazel Duncan's Trauma Management Group, I figure that they'd be likely to send Hunter to the same lot of therapists as they did Clarke — given their connection as partners who shared in both events. So I phone her office. Not in the person of Sam Brewer, veteran reporter, but as Walter Keddy, police accountant with the Employee Assistance Program's billing department."

Time to stroke the ego. "Brilliant, my colleague, brilliant."

"And a good thing that I faked my identity. Office receptionist hands me over to Duncan, who turns all officious on me. I tell her that we're just going over the year-end records and I've discovered a 'maybe' anomaly in our invoices. Could she please confirm the number of appointments she's had with Hunter, and the start and end dates of the therapy —"

"And?" He was driving me nuts with anticipation.

Sweet Sam actually danced a wee jig on his worn area rug. "And what she tells me boils down to this: within a week of the Banton shoot Hunter had his first appointment with the lady *and she is still seeing him.* Fucking Tony Soprano, is it not?"

"So Hazel Duncan gets to play Jennifer Melfi, Tony's shrink. No wonder she pitched an allergy attack in the restaurant when I really pushed her about Hunter. As his therapist, she may be in even greater danger than Laura was."

"Yes. And we know what happened to Laura."

"And to Pete, who needed therapy as much as the Pope needs another rosary." There, I'd done it again: silenced a marathon monologue artist. "Sorry, Sam, I'm guessing you already knew that."

"Don't apologize, lady." He patted my shoulder. "After Dawn died, I found myself inserting her name into conversations with the paper boy about the weather. I think it's just another way of coping — throwing up a verbal red flag to warn folks that you're not yet ready to deal with the world, and maybe reminding them that you've lost a dear one who can't be replaced, kind of pointing to the grave marker they can't see and you can't not see."

"I guess we're exacting tribute, Sam."

"Whatever, life does go on. But it's never the same, even when you luck out on a new partner."

His words confirmed my deepest fear: *never again will things be the same.*

"Here's the good news, Jane. Time diminishes."

This consolation didn't take root in my soul, as I'm sure my grief coach could plainly see on my face.

He wasn't about to give up. "Don't be discouraged. I'm about to get to my next stroke of genius — the reason I had to get you over here. We've both agreed that Hunter seems to be some kind of a magnet, attracting most of the dirt that clings to six homicides — in spite of his Teflon rep. But we need more incriminating detail on the man, the kind of stuff we're only going to get by pressing hard on a cop who knows how Hunter operates, preferably a cop who would love to see him brought down."

Sam tapped his brow again. "Then it hits me: *Deep Throat, my own personal Deep Throat.* Guy named Gary Nolan. He's been on the drug squad since Janis Joplin discovered Southern Comfort."

"Why would he rat out Hunter?"

"Nolan is what you might call disaffected. For a very long time, he's been nursing a grudge against the force in general, and Hunter in particular. He's the 'trusted source' I quoted at least a dozen times in various articles I wrote on corruption in the drug squad. After the last one he told me never to call him again, because he was through talking, and planning on taking early retirement. So I took him off my list of contacts. But I phoned him right after I talked to Duncan and asked him if we could do it one more time. He agreed to meet us here" — Sam consulted the clock on the mantelpiece — "in ten minutes. On condition, of course, that every single word he speaks is off the record."

"Yeah, yeah. Who's writing up any of this? I'm looking for ammunition, not copy."

"Let me do the questioning, Jane, at least until we can tell if he's warming up to you. He's a bit of a curmudgeon, and he doesn't like women."

"Those two qualities alone probably got him hired in the first place."

It was Nolan's day off. Bald, red of face and nose, unshaven, paunch to rival Homer Simpson's, he looked as though he had dressed for an undercover operation in a men's hostel. Sam seated him in an armchair facing the sofa we occupied and placed a cold beer in his hand. Only then did he get around to introducing us.

Nolan's bleary eyes scanned my body as if he had X-ray vision. "So this is the famous Jane Yeats. Every guy on the force, from the chief down to the latest recruit, knows your name. The smartass broad who wrote two books dishing the dirt on Toronto's finest."

I squirmed in silence.

He laughed. "Guess you can't be all bad."

I smiled demurely, not wanting to dampen his nascent affection.

"Your boyfriend got killed, didn't he?"

"That would be why I'm here."

Sam coughed nervously and volleyed the ball to his end of the court. "So, Gary, how are the plans? Still thinking about retiring soon?"

Nolan knocked back the remainder of his beer and crushed the can. I scurried off to the fridge for a refill while Sam lubricated him with feigned interest in his future. I was betting that Nolan would slurp back a minimum of four cans of ale during his visit. Guy had all the signs of being a lush, I thought. Virtuously.

"I'll be gone by the end of this summer. My brother, Chuck, and his wife live outside of Sault Ste. Marie. A couple of months ago, an old fishing lodge up there came on the market. We put in an offer. If the mortgage gets approved, it's ours and I'm out of this city faster than you can say 'Take this job and shove it.' Soon as we've renovated the place, we'll be open for business."

"Sounds like a great plan, Gary. Good luck with it," said Sam.

"Thanks. I haven't been this excited about anything for years." He sucked back half of his second beer. "Sam, you said on the phone you wanted to talk about Hunter. I won't ask why if you promise that this meeting never happened, should anybody ask."

I spoke up. "Gary, we promise never to name you, in word or print — especially because I've got this feeling that anyone who mouths off about Hunter and his shenanigans maybe should make sure he has his funeral arrangements in order first."

"Already I can tell you've been doing some deep digging into the man. So what do you need to know?"

Sam went for it. "Anything you can tell us that *isn't* on his glowing record of accomplishment. Starting with his performance on the drug squad."

"Just remember that every word you are about to hear comes from the mouth of a very pissed-off cop. It's because of guys like him that I got passed over for promotion again and again. So you're not listening to someone who's making any effort to be objective."

He slurped more beer. "In fact, I'm glad you contacted me, Sam. Crapping on him will lighten my load. I'm still loyal enough to the force, though, that I wouldn't have volunteered to crap on Hunter."

I nodded. "That inclines me to trust you."

"From his first day on the squad, you could tell that any rank Hunter held was just another rung in the ladder. He was climbing upstairs in a hurry. So ambitious you could smell it. Way more interested in advancing himself than being part of a team. That should be the kiss of death to any cop's career," commented Nolan, reaching into the pocket of his flannel shirt for a five-pack of cheap cigars.

"Hunter is a hard-core fitness freak. Apparently he just missed making the Olympic diving team some years back. So he's a real competitor. But police work isn't about being an athlete, like some kind of star quarterback — you know, catching a high one and racing for the touchdown, shoving everyone, including your own teammates, out of the way as you streak for the end zone. Risking everything to gain a few yards. The guy plays to win for himself only, and fuck anybody who gets in his way.

"None of us could figure how Clarke could stomach him for a partner — that is, until word got around that Clarke was one of the rottenest apples in the barrel. And that Hunter had been covering for all the shit he did. Stealing, dealing, assaults ... all the crap we, the good guys, are hired to bust the bad guys for."

Before Nolan could crush his can I fetched him another. This gave me a brief respite from the stench of cigarillo smoke.

"Cops cover each other's butt every day, Gary. But usually for small shit. What was in it for Hunter to keep his mouth shut around major offenses that could have landed Clarke in the slammer?" I asked.

"I figure it this way. Maybe all along Hunter had some big scam of his own going down that nobody but Clarke knew about. But I don't think so. Before Hunter shot that kid in the alley, he was so strung out that word got out the brass figured he was on the verge of a psychotic breakdown. You see, after he found those three bodies he just continued to show up for work every day and carry on like he hadn't been a witness to the aftermath of the Texas Chainsaw Massacre. He agreed to see a counselor but acted like it was just for form's sake. He presents himself like the Man of Steel — as if to say, 'I'm so cool and in control that fucking nothing fazes me.' We all know different, eh? The kind of scene he walked in on messes with your head big-time. A few days later, he shoots Banton, a suspect who probably wasn't even carrying a weapon. This time it's Clarke's turn to return all the favors."

Sam stirred on the sofa. Maybe, like mine, his butt was centered on a wayward spring lurking beneath a frayed sofa cushion. "So your thinking is that Hunter protected Clarke as insurance for some rainy day — such as when he needed his partner to back up whatever bullshit he claimed went down the night of that bad shoot?"

"Uh-huh." Nolan's laugh was as bitter as boiled coffee. "When I joined the force a rogue cop could get away with murder, literally. Then the public, egged on by journalists like you guys, started asking questions about how almost every cop under investigation by the SIU got found innocent. Now we can't even take a piss without worrying about being charged for indecent. Media has our nuts under the microscope. That kind of scrutiny has to have bent cops shopping for insurance."

I ventured another question. "So Clarke backs up Hunter's account of the Banton shoot. And almost before you can say, 'Bang! Bang!' Clarke blows his brains out. The RCMP don't even get to lean on him for his drug transgressions. Are we looking at a coincidence here?"

As Nolan gestured in my direction with his cigar, a large ash fell to the carpet. It nicely blended in. "You maybe see coincidence, I maybe see the beginning of a pattern. Hunter setting up Clarke's suicide to look like an accident can't have been that tricky to pull off. After all, it had the result everybody on the force and Clarke's family wanted to see.

"But a lot of the guys liked Clarke, bent as he was, so we're getting together over beers after his funeral and saying to ourselves, 'Maybe it's not an accident either.' One guy gets so drunk he comes right out with it: 'Could be Hunter shot him.' There's this big silence. I buy the guys another round. Then we start speculating about why Hunter might have shot Clarke.

"What we come up with is based on how squirrelly Clarke had been since the RCMP investigation was drawing its bead on him. Tom was a bit of a joke, you know, him being more Catholic than the Pope. So we're thinking maybe he was ready to blow the whistle on himself — *and on Hunter.*"

This time Sam made the beer run.

"And shortly thereafter Hunter requests — and gets — a transfer to Homicide," I said.

Nolan nodded. "You know, when I was a kid, my mother told me that virtue got rewarded. Right, maybe in heaven, but not on this earth. There's our boy, maybe two murders behind him and still rising up the ladder. Now, the rest of what I have to tell you comes straight from the mouth of my best friend,

Barry Brompton. We were rookies together. So Barry's been in Homicide for about eight years when Hunter comes on the squad. In no time at all, the SOB manufactures a way to make himself a sensational splash. He pushes himself into working on the serial killer investigation" — Nolan glanced my way — "that would be the one that eventually included your friend Pete as a victim."

Sam squeezed my hand, bless him.

"Next thing you know, Hunter suggests to the lead investigator that he be allowed to conduct an interview with William Shortt. Now, keep in mind that Shortt has been wrongly eliminated as a suspect at the time. Hunter claims that he's familiarized himself with the serial rape files and wants to re-interview everybody, including Shortt. He says he's just acting on a vague hunch. Wouldn't be the first time a serial rapist graduated into being a serial killer, he says. He cites the case of Paul Bernardo who, at the time, was very fresh in our memory. Always will be."

"Between us, Jane and I could come up with several more examples of rapists who escalated," Sam commented.

"Right. Anyway, he's granted those interviews, so he pulls in Shortt and talks to him. About a month later, after Laura Payne and your Peter have been killed, he presses for a second interview with Shortt —"

"That first interview Hunter had with Shortt — it wasn't audio- or videotaped, was it?" I could not recall having seen any record of it in the murder files.

"No — and that's highly irregular. We've learned to cover our asses by making sure we catch it all on tape. But Hunter insisted that he needed to gain Shortt's confidence. It's not like the lead was going to refuse any of his investigators a reasonable request at a time when pressure from every possible source was coming down on the force, right? In any case, him not playing by the rules and that being overlooked is almost routine —

thanks to his solve rate. Like they say on TV cop shows, the man turns red to black."

Nolan exhaled deeply as he relaxed back into his chair. "And the rest is history. During the second interview, which was audiotaped, Shortt spilled his guts. In one fell swoop, twelve rapes and five murders are solved, all thanks to the deductive derring-do of Hunter the Magnificent."

"Fast-forward to six years later, Gary, and Hunter's brilliance is looking more than a bit frayed around the edges. It turns out that Shortt copped to at least three murders he didn't commit." I watched Nolan's face closely.

He lit another cigarillo and puffed a rank cloud at the ceiling. "And before you know it — *poof!* — two more astonishing coincidences crop up: Shortt and Jerry Stone get couriered back to their Maker courtesy of two random acts of prison violence. Shortt because he was about to bring Hunter's rep down a major notch by shouting to the world that he had made a false confession, and Stone — if my favorite jailhouse rat tells it true — because he set up the hit on Shortt."

My pulse was racing faster than a prize greyhound's as he streaks toward the finish line. "Surely to God a man as ambitious as Hunter wouldn't cross so far over the line?"

Nolan leaned forward. "Think hard about this, Jane Yeats. Maybe his ambition is so controlling it drove him to do anything it took to keep his job. The man *is* his job. Without it, he wouldn't exist."

I nodded in agreement. "And add to all the other incriminating crap we've talked about the fact that he sometimes crops up in critical places at critical times — like Clarke's place just after he allegedly shoots himself, like my mother's bar when I get shot."

Nolan gave me a deadeye stare. "This is not adding up to a pretty picture."

I averted my eyes. Nolan was bang on the money. The picture was about to get even uglier. I was gearing up for Hunter's final curtain.

Sam must have noticed me getting steamed. He was looking at me in an uncharacteristically solicitous way. "Slow down, Jane."

As if pacing myself was in my control. "Gary, does this scenario work for you? Hunter, first on the scene, before the bloody scene has even unfolded, killed his partner. Being first on the scene means you get to stage a death however you want. Hunter, probably having memorized every detail in the serial killer files, kills Laura and Pete. I am over the top with this?"

Nolan shook his head. "Maybe not, but answer me this: in both situations we've got means and opportunity for him to kill and to cover up. But what in hell is his motive for murdering Laura and Pete?"

"Laura was Clarke's therapist, Gary. He's confessed to her both his own crimes *and* Hunter's bad shoot. Hunter knows, or suspects this. So she has to be silenced. Pete gets killed because he happened to show up at Laura's when Hunter was already in her apartment. Pete becomes collateral damage."

Sam and Nolan exclaimed in unison, "Fuck!"

The two men got so heavily engaged in discussing the finer points of how Hunter might have pulled off all of this that they didn't seem to notice my silence. I retreated into an atavistic space, the dark heart from which vengeance springs, after reason has fled.

At that moment I could see clearly the entire tragic mess — from the Banton shoot right through to Jerry Stone's demise. A chain had been forged as strong as a shot of the truth served up neat, each of its six links a murder, together forming a noose clamping ever tighter around a single throat.

The hours Hunter had left to live amounted to just so many grains of sand funneling through an hourglass.

CHAPTER 40

BEFORE EMBARKING ON A PERILOUS JOURNEY, most of us might be tempted to draw up a mental shortlist of people for whom we want to leave a final message — in the event that we do not return. I concluded that such acts are reserved for the pure of heart, for those who go into battle armed with a clear conscience and worthy intentions. All those Christian soldiers, crusaders marching onward. Like Clarke, like Hunter. Onward into battle against the villains.

My motives were honest.

I did drop off Max at Silver's, my own personal doggie day-care, knowing my friend would adopt him should I not be around to dish up the burgers and love. I told Silver only that I had to make a brief but important trip. She gave me a queer look.

I had told Sam the same thing as I left his house during Gary Nolan's visit. He looked surprised when I made my hasty exit but seemed reassured when I explained my need to be alone. I promised him that we'd meet first thing in the morning to plot a revised agenda.

Back at 6 Shannon Street, I was confronted with a difficult wardrobe decision. All my dithering about my capacity to kill the perp had ended. So I asked myself, *How does an executioner dress for the occasion? Is the basic black hood still in vogue?* Canadians haven't exercised the death penalty since way back in 1962. So I settled on my basic black Harley gear, sans hood. Simple outfit for a simple operation. First I would torture a confession from Hunter, there being no hard evidence against him. Then I would kill him, with not an iota of remorse.

As I polished my SIG Sauer into gleaming, I mused on how Hunter had been the one missing piece required to fill in the jigsaw puzzle of a particular landscape littered with six seemingly unconnected murders. He was the key piece, the one that put a name and a design to who killed Luther Banton, Tom Clarke, Laura Payne and Pete — and maybe indirectly William Shortt and Jerry Stone. Five of them stemming from the first, Banton, a young man in the business of doing what the ghetto schooled him into. And he died because Hunter had a homicidal hate-on for drug dealers. A crazy hate-on engendered by the shock of discovering an infant slaughtered by his dealer father. Being in no mood to entertain ethical shades of gray, I did not pursue the compassionate interpretations of the case.

Even in the midst of my own murderous rage, I remained sane enough to recognize that I was functioning on automatic pilot, my every move dictated by this thirst for revenge. Perhaps it was my one remaining shred of civility that drove me to walk around the corner to St. Francis of Assisi.

As I entered the church, dusk was falling as gently as fairy dust over the street. I moved slowly to the front pew, pulled down a kneeler worn to polished concavity by thousands before me and I prayed.

Unholy words. *Guide me through to the end of this mission, my resolve undiminished, my trigger finger sure as the certainty that what I am about to do is but the logical inevitability of that bastard having killed my love. Then do what you will with my soul. For soon, I lay me down to sleep.*

Father Gregory appeared out of nowhere, looking like a stand-in for kindly Friar Tuck. "Jane, what brings you here tonight? May I help?"

Rising quickly to my feet, I blurted out, "Forgive me, Father, for I am about to sin." I turned my back on the dear man and exited his sanctuary.

Five minutes later I kicked Maeve into roaring life, regretting only that I'd never thought to write this beautiful beast into my will. Another ten minutes and I was parking her outside a fifty-five-storey lakefront condo, the penthouse of which Hunter called home.

I entered a cavernous lobby boasting more marble than a mausoleum. Tucked against the right wall was an old dude in a silly uniform. He scanned my clothes with a rheumy eye and raised a skeptical eyebrow.

"Do you have an appointment, madam?"

I flashed my TPS badge, a recent eBay purchase. "Detective Sergeant Martha Rayburn. Beam me up to the penthouse. If you notify the occupant that I'm on my way, you'll find yourself handcuffed and under arrest within two minutes. My partner's watching."

It was reassuring to hear myself sounding more like Dirty Harry than Clint Eastwood.

The poor bugger's brow instantly popped sweat beads, and his right forehead vein began to thrum a visible tattoo. "No problem, Detective. I'm a law-abiding citizen."

"Yeah, aren't we all? That's what keeps officers like me employed."

With me in his hasty wake, he scurried over to a concealed elevator door just off a short corridor. When he pushed a plastic card into a slot, the doors silently slid open.

I ascended to the clouds without having to eyeball the flashing red button that normally indicates how far I've passed beyond the height guaranteed to trigger my phobia. This elevator had no button, I guess because it went from the ground floor straight to the moon. My ears began doing odd things just as the doors opened along greased channels. I stepped out, anticipating meeting another door, on which I planned to rap with my gun, fully expecting Hunter to greet me with his own drawn weapon.

The doors opened directly into Hunter's suite. Yegawds. My grip on the gun tightened.

An unarmed man with a facial expression befitting the most gracious of dinner-party hosts turned from his contemplation of the sunset and greeted me. Even though the penthouse felt like a comfortable sixty-eight degrees, he was wearing only a tight pair of bike shorts. Two full-length mirrors suggested their purpose was to gratify his narcissism. Or maybe I caught him in the midst of getting dressed.

"Jane Yeats. I've been expecting you." He gave no indication of discomfort at being clad so revealingly.

"Said the spider to the fly."

"I won't suggest that you put that lovely gun away. It becomes you so."

With my gun pointing precisely midway between his nipples, I stepped farther into the huge room. The south wall was a single curving span of glass affording a panoramic view of Lake Ontario. Almost breathtaking enough to make me momentarily forget why I was here. *Almost.*

"So, Hunter, I'm impressed. A room with a view."

"May I offer you a drink?"

I caught my voice just short of it issuing in a scream. "*No,* you may fucking *not* offer me a drink. This is *not* a social call, so what you had better do in a nanosecond is sit your ass down on that sofa and keep your oily mouth shut until I tell you to speak. And work very hard at *not* twitching one of your toned muscles."

However much my bravado seemed to amuse the man, it

did have the intended effect of immobilizing him physically and vocally.

My gun, now fixed on his nuts, had the effect of deflating his penis. I took advantage of his silence to absorb my surroundings. This vast room was Spartan, not an item in it without a function. No artwork, no plants, no knickknacks, nothing merely decorative — except for a tall pewter vase resting on a glass-and-steel coffee table. In it rested a handblown glass calla lily, which I interpreted as an exercise in funeral-home irony. Nothing organic, nothing living. The walls, ceiling and floor covering were an identical shade of off-white. Everything else was silver or gray. Homage to our high-tech age. Plasma TV and Bose sound system, titanium PowerBook with matching speakers, camcorder and digital camera, microphone.

"Let me guess what you're thinking: this place needs a woman's touch."

I shot out the calla lily. As Hunter's startled ass gravitated back onto the leather sofa cushion, I hissed in a tone as cold as the decor, "Make no mistake: I am in no mood for frivolity. Speak only when I give you permission."

By way of punctuation, I shot out the coffee table. Fine slivers of glass settled on Hunter's bare feet, yet he twitched not a muscle.

"Here's the deal. First, walk very slowly over to your sound equipment and press Record. Then demonstrate to me that my interrogation of you is being recorded for posterity. You know the drill: state your name, the date and time, location. You can leave out the bit about your confession being freely offered because I'm prepared to torture every last word out of you. Then scurry back to your seat."

That mission accomplished, he reseated himself and watched me through dark eyes grown wide with caution.

"I'm going to give you six names, in chronological order of

death dates. When I recite a name, you tell me *why* you killed that person or had him or her killed. Be concise. This exam is less than thirty minutes long and it's not multiple choice. So you don't get to boast or thrill to reliving your crimes. Anything else I want you to tell me, I'll let you know. And if you're wondering why you should tell me anything, just contemplate the fate of that poor calla lily. Now nod if you understand me!"

I felt good as he nodded. Power over a bad guy is not corrupting; it's a stoner. Maybe he was dumb enough to think that by talking he was buying time — time to figure out how to add my name to his kill list.

He was dead wrong about having any significant stretch of time left to purchase. I needed his confession to justify his execution.

My trigger finger was twitching.

CHAPTER 41

"BANTON, LUTHER."

He paused only briefly. "I shot Luther Banton because I was tired of men like him littering the streets. I can still see him begging for his life as I pointed the gun at him. When I found out later that he had a girlfriend and a kid, all I thought was, Rats breed, too."

"We have a criminal justice system to deal with the Luther Bantons. Your fatigue over its shortcomings does not justify his murder. It is entirely unreasonable that you believed it was necessary to shoot the deceased in order to protect your partner or yourself from either death or grievous bodily harm. Banton posed no such threat.

"Clarke, Tom."

"Clarke had 'confessed' our mutual sins to Laura Payne. Of course, even if he hadn't, I would have been forced to kill him anyway. I could tell that as the narcs got closer and closer to nailing him to the wall for all his drug-related offenses, he was stretched so tight that he was ready to snap. I figured that they'd play on his weakness and offer him a deal in exchange for ratting out his fellow officers, me included. So he had to go.

"It could have ended there and I would never again have had to be concerned about my career. The good old SIU had vindicated me for shooting Banton and the only other person who knew otherwise was dead."

I tightened my grip on my gun, which was aimed right at

his empty heart. "In betraying you, Tom Clarke honored his conscience. He was a dirty cop, but even his elastic ethics could-n't stretch to accommodate being an accomplice to murder. This partner thing with cops, Hunter, I always took it to be as seri-ous a relationship as a nun becoming a bride of Christ. Did you feel no compunction when you shoved his gun into his mouth?"

"I felt nothing. He could have been my mother and I would have felt nothing. No guilt. No remorse. My feelings shut down the night I found a murdered baby in a laundry tub."

"I call that twisted logic: in response to a violent act, you become what you most despise."

I raised the barrel of the gun to a point dead center between his eyebrows.

"Payne, Laura."

"Tom was sent to her for therapy. He was so spineless, such a pitiful Christian that the terrible burden of guilt he was car-rying as a result of his own transgressions prompted him to blurt it all out to Payne. That obliged me to silence her, too."

"And then and there your little spree might have ended. But no, six years later it picks up again." I'd hit very thin ice at this stage in my interrogation. I needed to move cautiously now as I intimated that I had rock-solid knowledge of events that I really only pieced together from hearsay and speculation.

"Shortt, William."

His initial look of surprise quickly morphed into some-thing resembling admiration.

"Your explanation of the 'why' of his murder needn't be so brief. I think we've moved into a short story, yeah?"

I wiggled the SIG Sauer.

"When I realized that Payne also had to be out of the pic-ture, it was a whole new deal. Her murder would be connected to Clarke's, Clarke was my ex-partner … etc. You know the old line: once is chance, twice is coincidence, three times is a pattern. So I had to get someone else to kill Payne — or take the fall for killing her. But I'm getting ahead of myself here.

"When William Shortt fell into my lap I knew I had a guardian angel. I'd just transferred to Homicide, was hell-bent on impressing my new bosses. That was the summer when the entire city was screaming for an arrest in the serial homicides. Three young women already dead, same MO, and obviously more to follow if the bugger wasn't caught first. If I could be the shiny new homicide boy who brought him down, then overnight my profile would shoot so high that I'd be in line for the next promotion. By chance, one night I was listening to a radio documentary on serial killers that mentioned how many of them stepped up from serial raping.

"It wasn't much of a leap to figure that maybe the guy responsible for the dozen unsolved and linked rapes might have graduated to killing his victims. So I stayed awake for nights studying the files on our prime suspects. I pulled some of them in for questioning. Finally I homed in on William Shortt. For a number of reasons, I really liked this guy to have done them. Here's where my guardian angel made her entrance. The poor bastard was ripe for the plucking. Turns out he never expected to be 'unacknowledged,' as he put it, after so many rapes. Shortt was like Mark Chapman, the pathetic loser who killed John Lennon. Total write-off who figured his only route to fame was to commit something so over the top and newsworthy that he'd become an instant celebrity.

"So we cut a deal during my private interview with him. The next time I interview him, he will confess to four murders — one of which hadn't even taken place yet. I feed him information about his three alleged victims and the MO from the serial killer files. In the meantime, I will murder Laura. Of course, I don't tell Shortt that. The MO is perfect for my purposes: the killer leaves no DNA, no significant trace evidence at

all, there are no witnesses. My part of the bargain is this. After
murdering Laura, I interview Shortt a second time. He confess-
es to the rapes *and* all five murders — the fifth having been
unplanned, of course. Two birds with one stone: Shortt's a hero
in his own mind and I'm a hero in the eyes of an entire city."

Hunter sat back to bask in his own cleverness.

"Don't stop there, Killer Man. Spell it all out: why does
Short Willie wind up in the prison cafeteria with a knife in his
back instead of a hamburger on his tray?"

"Six years have passed. Short Willie is an aging has-been. A
younger generation of rapists and killers have scooped all the
headlines. He figures he's got one good card up his sleeve to play
in order to regain his old notoriety. All he has to do is confess
that his original confession was false. I get it from a bent guard,
who heard it on the prison grapevine, that Willie's called his
lawyer to set up a press conference. Then I 'persuade' the guard
to set up an inside hit on Willie. The end result is that the mag-
got gets terminated — just as he would have in any country
sane enough not to have abolished capital punishment."

"Stone, Jerry."

Hunter awarded himself the luxury of a tight smile. "Good
guess: he was the bent guard I got to put out the inside contract
on Short Willie. But 'bad guess' if you think I had Stone killed.
His timely demise in that riot wasn't random. The man was
hated by dozens of inmates for his sexual proclivities — proclivities that he forced on some of the men. I had nothing to do
with him being so conveniently silenced. That was the hand of
God moving through my guardian angel."

"End of story, is it, Hunter? And a happy ending, too."

At that moment his demeanor changed. He straightened
his spine against the soft leather cushion and studied me from
head to toe in a slow scan. *Was he preparing to make a move?*
Perhaps calculating whether or not I had the resolve to transport him

straight into the arms of his guardian angel?

I did have the resolve. I held the gun steady. I looked forward to pulling the trigger.

He shook his head. "No, the ending is tonight. When you showed up, I actually felt relieved. You see, I shot Luther Banton in a reflex action. I was out of my mind with pain from having found that little child. By executing Banton, I started something that became self-perpetuating."

"Violence is like that."

His mouth twisted. "I grew up wanting to be a good guy. Not just a good cop, a Super Cop. And what I set out to fight against turned me into something I loathe."

"Yeah, loss of self-esteem is never a good thing. You must have learned that from your own personal therapist."

He stiffened. "Leave Hazel Duncan out of this discussion."

"You are *not* the one giving orders here, Hunter. You are my robot."

It was then that I was struck by the full force of what he had been calculating during his earlier moment of silence. For the first time, Hunter spoke without permission. Role reversal.

"We must be using different calculators, Jane Yeats. Your list of names is not complete. Given that your memory has curiously failed you, let me supply the missing one: Findley, Peter."

So this clever bastard's strategy was psychological. He had pressed the right button.

"Shut the fuck up this instant or you are a dead man."

"I've been a dead man walking since the moment I squeezed the trigger on Banton. So before you complete the act that finally gets me buried, let me tell you why — and how — your lover died."

Strange necessity compelled me to listen.

"I never targeted him. He was collateral damage, as our American military friends like to put it. Just as I was dispensing with Laura, your friend burst through the door like freaking RoboCop. I couldn't just shoot him with my service revolver. After all, I had a script, an MO to follow. His murder and Laura's had to look like the work of the same serial killer. That's the bad news. The good news is that your sweetheart lived just long enough to leave you a message. 'Find a way,' he burbled, 'to tell Jane Yeats — '"

It was my intention to shoot him stone cold dead before he could utter another syllable. I knew he was about to put indescribably cruel words in Pete's mouth. I fired.

So badly was I shaking that the bullet succeeded only in grazing his left arm.

The blast restored my moral compass. Its needle had been veering wildly during the entire duration of my hunt for Pete's killer. I paused.

Hunter sprang from the sofa. "Put down that silly gun. It was never intended for the likes of you."

He strode with an athlete's grace through the open balcony doors. Mesmerized, I watched him step onto a patio chair, then onto the balcony rail. His toes secured his balance, his arms slowly extended back into flight formation, his knees were bent and perfectly aligned. Iconic, like an Olympic high diver immortalized by Leni Riefenstahl, he pushed off and upward into the sky in a balletic swan dive. Majestic as an osprey.

Not before shouting " — to tell Jane Yeats I love her."

Ladies and gentlemen, Elvis has left the building.

CHAPTER 42

FOR A BRIEF INTERVAL, time stood still. Perhaps ten or fifteen minutes passed as I slumped on the floor of Hunter's balcony, my brain locked on that Riefenstahl moment, my body paralyzed. After his spectacular leap I had slipped into a damn good imitation of catatonia.

I don't know who phoned 911 to report Hunter's splat. It certainly wasn't me. How they put a name to his remains I can't imagine. By the time two homicide cops entered the suite, I had come back inside, where I sat glued to the armchair. The problem was, I couldn't think of what to do next — not having thought that there would be any "next" in my life. Not one I would witness.

I expected to receive rough treatment from the officers. After all, Hunter was one of their own and a celebrated one at that. Their assumption would be that I had pushed, or otherwise persuaded, their colleague from his balcony, having led him there at the point of my gun. Which gun I readily handed over.

Fatigue, born of shock and years of repressed grief, drove me to maintain complete silence in the face of their initial questions. No, I did not want to have a lawyer present. I wearily pointed to the bit of high tech still recording the suite's every sound.

I was transported to the station in handcuffs. By the time their questioning began, it was clear that my interrogators had listened to the tape. Their attitude was close to apologetic for any inconvenience caused by detaining me. Right. They must have been grateful that Hunter had nosedived into concrete, thereby sparing them the ignominy of a highly publicized trial. Their PR guys were already busy trying to figure out how to put an even vaguely positive spin on Hunter's exit (stage south).

Three hours later they offered me a ride home. I accepted a ride back to the condo parking lot where I'd left Maeve.

Hunter had come to ground on the far side of the building. I did not check out whatever activity still might be transpiring on that unhallowed spot.

Max was barking a separation-anxiety message from the backyard as I wearily inserted my key in the door. Silver must have snuck him back home to greet me just after I phoned her from the station on my release. With my beloved beast splayed contentedly on the floor in front of me, I collapsed onto the sofa and into the deepest, most nightmare-free sleep I've known in years.

The "thunk" against my door of the morning newspaper wakened me. Before making coffee, even, I removed the elastic band and unscrolled the thick roll. Front-page headline: "Homicide officer plunges to his death."

The ex-reporter in me did not envy the staffers given the assignment. "At this early stage of our investigation, we can provide few details of the tragic circumstances surrounding Detective Hunter's demise," the chief was quoted as saying. All the salient details were already known to the force, of course. Who could blame Underhill for taking a time out to pretty up the public story of their star homicide cop himself turned murderous?

And never send to know for whom the bell tolls. This particular bell implicated the force at its highest levels — *and* the organization that invigilates the force when it goes wrong. Its tolling would not be quickly silenced. Already the chief had to be worrying about my next book. And with very good reason. Certainly my subject had found me.

But I planned to consider none of that until my spirit had healed. A few weeks back on Manitoulin should see me beginning the slow work of restoring myself to a less demon-haunted life. I would pack no books, no research materials, no iBook. With no TV, no phone, no Internet connection, I could immerse myself in wildflowers, loons, sun and moon over rippling water … and assure Shirley Scarecrow that finally I had defeated the Windigo.

Oh yeah. I had just begun to believe in the efficacy of this plan when the phone rang.

"So you quit drinking and smoking only to find better ways to kill yourself."

"Good morning, Mom."

"Don't 'Good morning' me. In fact, don't 'Mom' me. God forbid we hadda been born Protestant, I could have raised even you in Belfast and you'd have been safer."

"Hail, Etta, full of piss 'n' vinegar. Disown your own daughter and not even the Lord will be with you."

Silence. Uh-oh. Then the click of her Bic as another Cameo flamed into toxicity. Worse still, the sound of my mother crying.

"Etta, please don't cry. I mean, can't you just shout it out — *Jane, I'm glad you're alive?*"

She blew her nose, right into the receiver. "I admit to that and I'll be setting myself up for going through this kinda horror all over again next time you go shoving your nose into trouble."

"Mom, there was no way on God's green earth my nose wasn't going to lead me to Pete's killer."

"I know that, girl, and I guess I'm mighty proud of you."

"Thanks, Mom. This morning I feel better than I've felt

since the last time I saw Pete."

"Yeah, and that's the best news I've heard since then, too. But do me a favor, eh? Promise to stay out of trouble for at least a year. Whenever I get to worrying about you, my sex life falls apart."

"I promise."

"Jane, I'm glad you're alive."

My turn to cry.

I took only two calls after that. One from Silver, who found different words to voice essentially the same message. I took advantage of her gratitude for my survival to ask her to help set up my return visit to Manitoulin. She happily agreed to babysit Max during my absence. And I thanked her for keeping me and my mutt alive.

"No problem, white woman. Just keep the two of you healthy."

The second call was from Sam, who was exceedingly crabby about my having hared off in pursuit of Hunter without notifying him. When I informed him that I set off after Hunter armed and with every intention of killing the man, he revised his reason for being crabby. When I suggested that he write the in-depth stories surrounding Hunter's suicide, he cheered up considerably.

The remaining phone calls, and there were many, I let pile up on the answering machine. The media would have to do without my "input." In my own eyes, I knew that I couldn't be made into any sane person's idea of a hero. A clutch of reporters and camera folk did show up at the house. To them I opened the door only once, having instructed Max (on pain of prolonged hamburger deprivation should he not comply) not to bite anyone but to snarl and snap as though that were his passionate intention. He obeyed so convincingly that I thought I might have to call a lawyer.

Over the next few days I took time to decompress and to make simple preparations for my journey. The evening prior to my departure, I treated Professor Payne to dinner at Giancarlo's. For once, for this special occasion, I dressed like a totally respectable woman, fooling even myself. Ours was a quiet celebration, full of reminiscences, regrets and reconciliation. His gratitude for my role in hunting down Hunter was undeserved. Mine had been the most selfish of undertakings. That I had been a player in his newfound peace gratified me enormously. We parted, both truly committed to maintaining our friendship.

My mellow mood proved very short-lived. As I hit the sidewalk in front of my house, my ears pricked to a frightening small sound issuing from within. A low moan, surely born of pain. It was Max.

Fumbling with my key, I muttered: *Please God, let my dog be okay. Hell, I've only been happy for a few days.*

The front door banged against the interior wall as I rushed into the entrance. Max was lying bleeding onto the kitchen tiles, looking damn close to dead. As I bent over him, his eyes fluttered open and fixed not on my frightened face but somewhere beyond my shoulder.

Just as I heard what his acute ears had picked up — a flurry of swift movement behind me — my lights went out.

CHAPTER 43

"DON'T DIE ON ME YET, BITCH."

I had died and gone to hell. I was on the floor next to Max, and leaning over me was Hazel Duncan. Sweating, breathing hard, perky hairdo collapsed, no makeup, clad in workout gear, the lady was in a total state of disarray. Her disorientation seemed far worse even than mine. Poster girl for a psychotic break.

My head throbbed, presumably from the blow delivered courtesy of the large wrench lying beyond my reach — not that its placement mattered, my grasp having been rendered utterly ineffective. My hands and feet were tightly bound with enough duct tape to gift wrap City Hall. I turned my blood-wet face from her lunatic visage to look at my dog. Max's chest was scarcely moving, his eyes fixed shut.

"Max," I whispered, "Max, hang in there, boy. I'm here."

Her laugh rang shriller than fingernails clawing a chalkboard. "Jane Yeats, you are a total joke. There you lie, utterly useless and mere minutes from your own death, and you're talking to a frigging dog. Guess that's what happens when you don't have a man to worry about."

Rage overrode any momentary consideration I might have given to talking this woman down.

"I don't have a man to worry about because your client killed him. You know that. Probably you've known that since Joe Hunter murdered Pete."

"My dear, I have known that for all your lonely, sex-deprived years. *Not only that, but you might even say it was my idea.*"

How could I think clearly with Max bleeding out beside me? If my scraggly beast and I were to enjoy another run through the park, I had to somehow defuse this lunatic long enough to break free and get Max to a vet. So keep her talking. Doubtless she had a nasty confession she was eager for me to hear. Lunatics can't keep quiet: that's what finally ensnares them. *I hope.*

As I began to speak, the salt tang of blood quickened my tongue. "Was that why you recited 'client privilege' like it was your own personal rosary whenever you were asked about Hunter?"

She kicked me in the side. "No, you stupid bitch. I didn't even answer your questions — because I fell in love with the man the moment he first walked into my office. Get real. Obviously a therapist who sleeps with a client who murders people is not going to give a deluded broad who thinks she's Nancy Drew any help with her amateur investigation. I thought I could get you off the scent by sending you to Tom Clarke's moronic ex. But you wouldn't leave it alone."

While my stunned brain was struggling to process her words, I was investing all my physical resources into fighting to stretch the duct tape. The damn stuff had no give. Oh Max, were you conscious, I bet you'd cleverly gnaw it away for me. Just like Bullet used to do in all those Roy Rogers TV shows.

Funny world: that night I lay on the floor of my own dear house, bound but not gagged (as Hunter, for all practical purposes, had been within Hazel Duncan's pernicious web), captive to a crazy woman — yet I did not feel powerless. I was sane and sober. She was drunk with madness, focused on more than killing me. First she felt compelled to justify the ways of her insanity to me. That's what I had on my side. Time — and Max's dumb, loving trust. I struggled to subdue my rage, to prevent it from dominating me as Hazel's rage was controlling her — making her waste time and thereby risk her own vile bones.

"So you knew from the get-go that Hunter killed Luther Banton *and* his own partner."

"Of course I did. Hunter was a basket case when he was sent to me. The poor fool had such a sweet heart, such a longing to see justice done, that he spilled out those petty transgressions during our very first session. Banton was a dealer in banned and lethal pharmaceuticals. Clarke was a dirty cop and a wuss to boot. From the very moment Hunter shared his problems with me, I became his mentor and his ... well, coach would be the appropriate word. You see, his conviction failed him. He needed me to encourage him to take the next step — and to help cover his tracks at every stage."

I used my tongue to shift blood to the corner of my mouth. "If half of what you say is true, you've got to be stark raving mad."

"*Half* of what I say?" she shrieked. "My credits don't stop there. I not only encouraged Hunter to kill Laura who, by the way, was an officious little bitch I never could abide, but I provided him with the details he needed to catch her at home — alone, I thought. Sad for you that your Braveheart boyfriend showed up to complicate the plan."

Her crazy eyes roamed the room. *Searching for a weapon?*

"And, to add to my credits, I played a strong supporting role in William Shortt's death by persuading Jerry Stone to set him up. You see, Jerry's poor battered wife was also one of our clients. Seems the man's sexual frustrations drove him to beat her. That gave me bargaining power."

"You are demented."

"I don't think so. Who's the crazy one here? You are my captive."

"And you remind me of that goddamn predatory fish you keep in your office."

"Yes, like my Krib I get to control the male." She smirked. "Pity, isn't it? My kind of personal autonomy gives feminism a bad name."

"No," I snarled. "It merely underscores the reputation psychopaths already have. This isn't about gender. You don't have one."

"Perhaps it's about romantic obsession."

"Nothing more romantic than a candlelit dinner over a table concealing a heap of corpses."

"When I do therapy, I consider it a successful outcome if a client can learn to live more or less happily with what he's done."

"Pity Adolf Hitler croaked before you could work your magic. Therapist, heal thyself. You are one sick Lady Macbeth. A twisted and demented case. One hundred percent certifiable."

"Hah! You're no one to talk about mental health. A solitary, depressive drunk except for that scruffy mongrel. Is it dead yet? Not quite? No, Jane you have no family to speak of, unless one counts the wizened cowgirl you call a mother. No real friends, unless one counts an obese lesbian Indian. And a career that scarcely merits the name. You're a pathetic, self-destructive alcoholic who for six years has used booze to buffer her pain because she still can't get past step one in the grieving process."

The kitchen floor was pressed against my face but I managed to say defiantly, "I try very hard not to hurt anyone but myself."

"My goodness, your self-esteem is low. Give yourself far more credit than that. You've tried very hard to hurt one person who, with your defective moral compass, you decided had hurt others. An unsympathetic soul would say that you have a messianic complex."

"Not me. Nope. The Messiah of the Year award goes to the love of your life, Hunter, who's now being sliced and diced on a stainless steel morgue table. The crime-scene team transported him there after soaking up his remains with a large blotter. It was not a pretty picture, Hazel, I promise you that. Your buff beautiful boy looked like something the pizza delivery guy dropped from a great height. Gave a whole new meaning to the term *flat-liner*."

I mistakenly thought my words would trigger her rage. Wrong. She just drifted into another zone.

Her new tone of voice befitted an actress charged with the task of narrating a romance novel. "You pushed my lover over his own balcony. That's why I came here to kill you and your flea-bitten canine friend. Before I'm caught I should have time to kill your mother and your fat girlfriend, too."

She flashed a smile sweeter than any angel could deliver. "Wish me luck, Crazy Jane."

Stepping over me, then Max, she pulled out my cutlery drawer and extracted a Chinese meat cleaver I picked up on Spadina years ago for five dollars. Pity I'd not taken the trouble to sharpen it recently.

"I'm not going to hack you to bits like some over-the-top butcher. No — I'm going to delicately and slowly torture you, as agonizingly as you must have tortured Hunter into confessing."

Damn. There was rust on the cleaver. Scared as I was, I remained lucid enough to realize that this was no time to be worrying about lockjaw.

"Me? Torture Hunter? The man's tongue could scarcely keep pace with his urge to confess. Unlike you, his conscience was still intact — not that you could relate to that disability."

Time to remind myself: there was nothing I could have

done to save Pete. That I would have risked my life to do so is merely a given. The horrible sense of impotence that afflicted me afterward had never really left me. Finally, I could sadly acknowledge that it had quietly polluted all my relationships. And yet, at that moment, my heart no longer raged. I was at peace with myself, as Duncan could never be. Curiously, that put me in control, shackled as I was. The spectacle of her unhinged rage calmed me.

"So what are you waiting for, Ms. Freud? Still in need of a bit more analysis?"

That bit of smart-ass clinched it. As she raised the cleaver, Duncan's eyeballs looked like iron filings in search of a magnet.

Suddenly the scene cued to *CRASH. Sound of breaking glass. Thud of concrete block on wood.* Followed by my Indian love goddess, Silver Maracle, heaving her big bones through the window and into my dining room.

The sound effects startled my captor into going after Silver as she unfolded to her magnificent six feet high and rising.

Duncan wildly swung the cleaver, which Silver neatly dodged.

On the downstroke, Silver disarmed her. And on the upstroke knocked her flat. "Dumb-ass broad thinking she could cut me. Before I got my first period, I'd won more fights than that cow has painted toenails."

Duncan was stone-cold unconscious. Silver stepped over her folded form and placed the cleaver in the oven. "First I'm checking out Max. He's in way more trouble than you are."

My attacker now looked diminutive, drained of the destructive energy that just seconds earlier magnified her presence and her power. Hazel Duncan had been prepared to kill me to avenge her lover's death. Jane Yeats had set out to kill Duncan's lover for the same reason. What fine line separated us? Damned if I could tell.

Five minutes later Silver had Max restored to feeble consciousness and the emergency vet summoned, me free of bondage and Duncan sporting the duct-tape look.

"Next time you ask me to pick up your dog, let me know if you have any company."